Sweet Fifteen

Diane Gonzales Bertrand

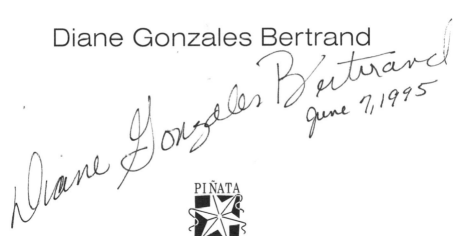

Diane Gonzales Bertrand
june 7, 1995

PIÑATA

BOOKS

Arte Público Press
Houston, Texas
1995

This volume is made possible through grants from the National Endowment for the Arts (a federal agency), the Lila Wallace-Reader's Digest Fund, and the Andrew W. Mellon Foundation.

Piñata Books
A Division of Arte Público Press
University of Houston
Houston, Texas 77204-2090

Piñata Books are full of surprises!

Cover design by Gladys Ramírez

Bertrand, Diane Gonzales.
    Sweet fifteen / by Diane Gonzales Bertrand.
        p.   cm.
    Summary: When seamstress Rita Navarro makes a quinceañera dress for fourteen-year-old Stefanie, she finds herself becoming involved with the girl's family and attracted to the girl's uncle.
    ISBN 1-55885-122-4 (cloth) — ISBN 1-55885-133-X (pbk.)
    [1. Mexican Americans—Fiction. 2. Quinceañera (Social custom)—Fiction. 3. Family life—Fiction. 4. Friendship—Fiction.]
    I. Title.
PZ.B46357Sw   1995
[Fic]—dc20   94-32656
                                                    CIP

The paper used in this publication meets the requirements of the American National Standard for Permanence of Paper for Printed Library Materials Z39.48-1984. ∞

*For
Suzanne,
Micole,
and
Gabriela—
and their
great-
grandmothers*

Sweet Fifteen

Diane Gonzales Bertrand

Chapter One

Rita Navarro carefully zipped together each side of the back seam on the lovely *quinceañera* gown. She straightened the thin pads over the teenager's narrow shoulders. Taking a proud look into the mirror, Rita admired the simple sweetheart bodice, layered with a delicate film of candlelight lace dotted with tiny pearls. The long white silk skirt, appliqued with a border of silk roses, was perfectly suited for a pretty girl like Stefanie Bonilla.

"What do you think?" she asked her young client as she stepped around to view the dress from the front.

Stefanie stood before a tall framed mirror. She spread her hand against the lace bodice covering her rib cage. "It's hard to breathe. And the dress is very itchy." She turned in profile to the mirror. "I don't like the waist on this. I look fat."

Rita's dark brown eyes widened with surprise. "Stefanie—you look fine."

"I look stupid. This whole *quince* stuff is old-fashioned and just plain embarrassing. Why do I have to do this?" Stefanie folded her arms across her chest and fixed her face into a pout.

Rita was speechless. Stefanie had been to several fittings for this dress. She had never expressed such feelings before. Why now?

Slowly, Rita lowered herself on one knee. Her fingers smoothed the hemline. Her great-grandmother's fine stitching was barely visible around the wide, hooped skirt. "I remember getting nervous before my *quince,* too. But once everything starts, and you're alone, up on the altar, it makes you feel so special, so beautiful—well, just wait! You're going to have so much fun." She glanced up, only to see Stefanie's lip trembling.

The girl stared into the mirror. A single tear rolled down her cheek. "I don't want to do this, Rita. I never wanted to do this."

Rita stood up, moving to take one of Stefanie's slender, cold hands between her own. She squeezed gently, staring down at the teen with the dark curly hair. The pained expression in Stefanie's hazel eyes struck a familiar chord in Rita.

She had always called it the look of a twisted heart, as if someone was wringing out a wet dishtowel inside her chest. Stefanie's moist eyes, the way she chewed on her lip. Rita remembered; the girl's sorrow was a ghost of her own.

"Stefanie, is it just the *quinceañera*? Or is something else bothering you?"

The teen's eyes grew round, looking almost surprised by the question. She opened her mouth as if to say something, but clamped it shut when they heard the loud jingle-jangle of the Christmas wreath bells on the shop door.

Stefanie gasped, then began wiping her face. "It must be Mom. She can't see me crying, Rita. What'll I do?"

"There's a box of Kleenex in the dressing room. I'll keep your mother in the other room a few extra moments, okay?" Rita's hands rested on Stefanie's arms for a moment, a silent reassurance that she understood the girl's feelings more than Stefanie knew.

Walking away from the mirror in the corner of the narrow side room Rita used for fitting dresses, she moved towards the central part of her dress shop where customers entered.

She shivered. Had the heater stopped working again?

Rita stopped to pick up the wedding skirt that had slid off her sewing machine table onto the floor. She folded it over the machine, then did a quick check on the carpeting around the plants in the corner to be certain none of the pots were leaking again. Only then did she put on her owner's smile, ready to greet a store customer.

She just wasn't expecting it to be Stefanie's uncle, Brian Esparza. He stood by the crowded glass counter, surveying the cluttered table, half-completed Christmas decorating, and swatches of cloth and ribbons littering the carpet. Her embarrassment at the unkempt condition of the shop froze a false smile upon Rita's lips.

"Hello, Brian."

His gaze came to meet hers. He wore glasses this afternoon, wire-rimmed frames which magnified his narrow brown eyes. He smoothed back his wavy brown hair from his forehead before he greeted her with a quiet, "Hello, Rita. It's nice to see you again."

Rita regretted she wore only faded jeans and a black turtleneck sweater under a red smock with big pockets. Her comfortable, practical clothes seemed so tacky next to Brian's expensive overcoat that had been left unbuttoned over his tailored suit. His professional appearance alone made her feel more self-conscious about everything around her.

"I—we—were expecting Iris about now. Stefanie got a ride after school from a friend, and her mother was supposed to meet us here."

Brian adjusted his tie as he cleared his throat. "Something came up at the last minute. Iris asked me to pick up Stefanie and make the final payment on her dress."

"Uncle Brian? What are you doing here?" Stefanie walked into the room, fistfuls of white skirt bunched into each hand. "Where's Mom?"

Brian turned to his niece and gave her a smile. "Hi, Stef. Your mom and I decided that I could pick you up this afternoon, okay?"

Stefanie's face tightened into an ugly frown. "Mom promised to pick me up today. She spent the morning at the cemetery, didn't she? She always falls apart when she goes there."

He shook his head, reaching his hand towards the teen. "Your mother was just a little tired this afternoon from all her packing."

"She promised me she'd be here today." Stefanie pushed his hand away. "You didn't have to come for me."

He breathed back a sigh before his hand dropped to his side. "I needed to pay Rita, Stef. I told your mother that I would pick you up and save her the trip. It would have been silly for both of us to come over here this afternoon, don't you think?"

"What I think doesn't seem to matter, does it?" Stefanie replied, biting on her lip as it started to tremble again.

Brian turned to look at Rita, who stood watching the family drama, hoping to become invisible. The problems brewing within Brian and Stefanie's family weren't her business. Why did she feel a need to get involved? Didn't she have enough troubles already?

As the tears filled Stefanie's eyes again, Rita knew she couldn't remain uninvolved. She had seen that look too often, staring from her own mirror.

With a slight hesitation, Rita touched the girl's hand.

"Why don't you go change, Stefanie? Your mother can see the dress at home. Do you want me to help you?" Rita asked.

"No." The dark hair shook around Stefanie's shoulders as she left.

Rita sighed, then looked at Brian. They weren't exactly strangers, but a few awkward sentences exchanged at a funeral hardly made them friends.

Brian coughed something out of his throat, then he pulled out his checkbook.

"What's the final payment on the dress, Rita? I lost the receipt Iris gave me. I'm sorry."

Rita suppressed a sigh. She had hoped he might ask about Stefanie's troubles, not move on to their business.

He stepped back to the counter, then pushed aside the stack of fabric samples, clusters of wax orange blossoms, and a small tiara so he would have a place to write.

"I'll get a copy of the bill from the files." Rita spoke quietly, moving behind the counter. She knelt down to rummage through the wooden file box which she kept below the display case, two clear shelves crammed tight with various gifts and accessories.

When Rita glanced up, she saw Brian staring at her. Quickly, she looked down, shuffling through the invoices, which were out of alphabetical order. Stefanie's uncle probably thought Rita was an incompetent business woman, but she told herself that she was just an overworked one. Only today, with an attractive man like Brian Esparza in her shop, she wished she could be cool and confident, able to speak easily to him. Her only consolation was a guess that Brian was a bit on the shy side. Was that why a handsome man with a successful job was still unmarried?

For Rita, staying single was a choice she made early in her life. She didn't want to be like her three older sisters, married with two or three children before they were twenty. She wanted something different; she had discovered the ways and means of doing this by using her sewing machine. Although she had been sewing since she was ten, it took years of dressmaking and the financial support of her great-grandmother to open a dress shop a few days after her twenty-fifth birthday.

Even as Rita finally found Stefanie's bill in the file box, her irritation didn't end. Her former partner's bold printing on the invoice increased Rita's impatient anger.

Last month, Beatrice eloped with her serviceman boyfriend, moving with him to his new assignment in Alaska. Then Rita discovered Beatrice had made a sizeable withdrawal from their commercial account. "It's just my share," Bea had written in a note by the check stub. "The shop's all yours now."

Bea's impulsive actions had left Rita wary of future business partners. She thought she would prefer the feeling of total control, except that the responsibilities of a business owner dragged Rita down like a long skirt made of iron.

"Is something wrong?" Brian's question brought Rita back to the present moment.

"No. Here it is." She stood up and placed Stefanie's bill on the counter. "The final payment is three-hundred fifty dollars, Brian."

He sighed, then started writing the check. "All part of being the *padrino*, I guess. I bought her baptism and communion dresses, too."

Rita paused, then chose her words carefully. "Being a *padrino* is more than a custom of buying a baptismal gown or a prayer book, Brian. It's a responsibility to watch over the godchild, too."

Brian looked up, his face reflecting the same surprise his niece did when Rita asked Stefanie about her problems.

"I—I just think that Stefanie's going through a bad time right now. As her godfather, you might be able to help, that's all." Rita had gathered the strands of wax blossoms together and found herself twisting them in her hands as she talked.

He tapped his pen on the counter twice before he replied. "Rita, I was barely fourteen when Iris chose me to be Stefanie's godfather. Since then I've been doing whatever's expected. I'll even buy an expensive *quinceañera* dress to make my godchild happy."

"But she's not happy, Brian. Right now, Stefanie's miserable."

"Why do you say that?"

"Something is troubling her. I can tell."

Brian finished writing the check, then tore it from the checkbook. He held it towards her. "I'll tell Iris to talk to her."

Rita frowned. The last time Iris was in the shop, the woman seemed more concerned about the dress than the girl wearing it. "Maybe Iris can't help her daughter right now."

"Of course she can. Iris is a wonderful mother." His eyes darkened with an intense stare before he placed the check on the counter between them.

"I'm sure Iris is a fine mother, Brian. But Iris is still trying to adjust to the tragedy herself. In the meantime, there's Stefanie. She's still a young girl who needs her father. And her mother, too."

"It's been hard on all of us since Estevan died." Brian picked up his checkbook, then slipped it into his suit pocket. "But I'm doing everything I can to take his place."

The wax flowers dropped to the counter. Rita felt overwhelmed by the emotions that Stefanie's situation had brought to the surface.

"Brian, you can't take Estevan's place. You need to help your sister and Stefanie learn to adjust to life without him."

His raised eyebrows suddenly shot downwards. "It's just your opinion, Rita. Not that I asked for it. But thank you, all the same."

Rita blushed hot under his stare. "I'm sorry, Brian—"

"Many of our friends and relatives think it's bad taste to have a celebration so soon after Estevan's death." His voice was polite, but she felt the chilly tone clinging to his words. "But I know my brother-in-law wanted a *quinceañera* for his daughter since the day she was born. When he died, I knew my responsibilities as Stefanie's *padrino*. I'm paying for Stefanie's dress, even the cake and *mariachis*. Iris and I are going to give Stefanie the best *quinceañera* we can."

"I think a *quinceañera* for Stefanie will be a good thing," Rita replied, hoping he wouldn't resent her comments. "But right now, Brian, I really think Stefanie could use your friendship. She needs to talk to someone she can trust. Someone who loves her."

With a slight bending of his head, he looked into her eyes. He seemed to be studying her, probably questioning her intentions. Luckily he spoke before the silence between them grew thick and hard.

"Rita, I'm not very good with teenagers. Besides, if there is a problem, well—I'm certain that Stefanie needs a woman to talk to." Suddenly, he removed his glasses to stare at her. "Perhaps you should talk to Stefanie, Rita. Our great-grandmothers are close friends. We could start up our own friendship as well."

Abruptly, the shop door opened, wreath bells jangling.

Rita's landlord, Mr. Arredondo, swaggered inside, slamming the door behind him. His eyes swept over the place before he grunted a "Hello" in Rita's direction.

She had to postpone an answer to Brian's comment in order to concentrate on the stocky, puffy-faced man. Swallowing the sour taste in her mouth, she raised her chin to deal with him for the first time since Beatrice left town. "Good afternoon, Mr. Arredondo. What a surprise to see you."

He smiled at her, but she sensed nothing friendly about it. "I was in the neighborhood, and since it was the fifteenth—I thought I'd save you a trip to my office."

"How kind of you, Mr. Arredondo." Rita quickly picked up Brian's check from the counter and put it into one of her pockets. "I've been so busy lately. I'm glad I won't have to close early to run across town."

Mr. Arredondo moved over to a rack of colorful cotton dresses imported from Mexico. "So business is going well, eh?" He examined the dresses, scraping the hangers across the metal bar. "And Beatrice?"

"Beatrice lives in Alaska with her new husband. They're very happy."

He grunted, then turned to look at Rita. His sharp black stare moved to Brian, who stood silently by the counter. "And will you be the next one to run out on the lease agreement with your boyfriend over there?"

Rita stiffened with anger. "First of all, Mr. Arredondo, this is not my boyfriend. This is Brian Esparza. I'm finishing a sewing job for his niece's *quinceañera*. And secondly, no one ran out on the lease agreement. I'm still in this building. I'm also prepared to pay you this month's rent. And next month's when it's due."

"The lease is up in three months. Do you plan to stay? I can get somebody else in this place, you know. It's a great location."

Rita gave him a cool stare. The shop was across the street from a cemetery. Months ago it made better sense to take the place because Bea did floral arrangements. Now the view out the front window just depressed Rita. She wanted another location for her shop, but had no time to look. And right now she didn't have the money to give two months' rent as deposit on a new place.

Mr. Arredondo grunted again. "Don't forget. I expect thirty-days notice if you plan to move out."

"I understood the terms of our lease when I signed it, Mr. Arredondo." Wanting to get rid of the man, Rita took the business checkbook out of the drawer under the cash register. Pushing aside a magazine, strips of lace, and scraps of material to lay the binder with the business checks on the counter, she wished everything appeared more organized. The front room was crowded with Christmas decorations, the last of Beatrice's silk flower arrangements, and two racks of ready-made and custom-made dresses which Rita sold. She needed more space to display everything.

"Mr. Arredondo, a few months ago you agreed to have a workman come into the shop and build us some shelves," she said, signing the check. She looked up to see the man shaking his head.

"It'd be stupid to put up shelves now. What if you decide to go like your partner did? I could have a new tenant who doesn't want the shelves. We'll talk shelves in three months." He extended his hand for Rita's check.

She wished she was handing him a rattlesnake. "I'll let you know what I decide after the New Year."

He studied the check a long moment, as if he wanted to be sure it wasn't counterfeit. "In March, the rent will go up one-hundred dollars."

"What?" Rita slammed the checkbook closed.

"My taxes went up. So it's a hundred more a month. You sign a new lease March fifteenth. I'll come by for your decision after the holidays," Mr. Arredondo said, and shoved Rita's check into the pocket of his blue nylon jacket. "*Feliz Navidad*, Rita."

She hated wishing this Scrooge a Merry Christmas, but she nodded politely. "*Feliz Navidad*. Good-bye."

When Mr. Arredondo opened the door, the cold air that came in was a welcome change for Rita who suddenly felt that the shop was was suffocating, crowding around her. When Bea left, Rita had been inspired by the challenge to keep the business going. Lately, she could hardly remember her big dreams. The reality of taxes, greedy landlords, and high rent deposits slowly squeezed the joy out of owning her own shop.

"You handled your landlord very well, Rita." Brian's voice was filled with admiration.

She looked at him, realizing that she needed someone to talk to as much as Stefanie did. She wished she had someone with whom she could discuss her business concerns. Although she was very close to her great-grandmother, she couldn't lay her business problems on the old woman's shoulders. Abuelita had done too much already.

"I left the dress in the back room." Stefanie said as she reappeared. Her nose was red, her eyelashes still damp.

Rita felt as lonely as Stefanie looked. She had really wanted to help the girl more, but Rita had her share of problems, too.

"Don't you want to take your dress home, Stefanie?" she asked.

The girl looked from Rita to Brian, then back again to Rita. "Can Mom and I get it after Christmas?"

"Of course—"

"Hey, Stef. Let's pick up a pizza on the way home so your mom won't have to cook. What do you say?"

"Sure. Fine." Stefanie shrugged herself into her leather jacket.

Rita wanted to shake her head at both of them. According to Iris, Brian was very talented at solving problems within the most sophisticated computer systems. Why couldn't he show a little of that same creative determination in dealing with his niece?

"Rita, you can talk to Iris tomorrow about what we discussed," Brian said, buttoning up his overcoat. "You ladies can decide what to do." He put his arm around Stefanie's shoulder. "Let's go, Stef. Good-bye, Rita."

The bells jingled again, and the two of them left.

Rita returned to the dressing room to hang up Stefanie's gown. As she handled the lace dress, she recalled that the celebration of her *quinceañera* was the best day of her teenage years. Like Stefanie, she did not have a father who walked beside the mother when they presented their daughter inside the church. But someone else had given Rita an inner strength and self-confidence she would need as a young woman to face life's challenges.

How different my life would be, Rita mused, if I didn't have Abuelita.

❤ ❤ ❤ ❤ ❤

"Abuelita, Stefanie Bonilla's dress fit her perfectly."
Rita set the plate of steamed vegetables between them
on the small table in the kitchen of her great-grandmother's house. She served each of them a portion of
vegetables and a spoonful of rice from the small platter
to her left. "I wanted to do a good job since they're Josie
Esparza's relatives. Now the only problem is Stefanie
herself. She seemed so unhappy today. I wanted to talk
to her, but her uncle came into the shop. I tried to
explain to him that something's bothering her, but—
well, I don't think he understands her. And her mother?
Well, Iris reminds me a lot of the way Momma used to
be."

"Do you talk just to hear yourself? Or can I talk,
too?" Isabel Navarro folded her long hands upon the
table, tilting her head to one side. Under the bright
kitchen lights, her gray braided hair was like a crown of
silver surrounding her wide, round features.

As usual, her great-grandmother's question and
expression made Rita stop and smile. "I'm sorry. I'm a
little lonely since Bea left. I'm just glad to have someone
to talk with."

"I don't mind talking about Josie's great-grandchildren. Rita? You must help them with their sadness."

"Me? I'm a dressmaker, not a family counselor."

Abuelita raised her gaze to catch Rita's. "You can
help more than you think. Your papa died when you
were thirteen."

That old ache tightened inside Rita's chest. She
tried to ignore it. "Why me? Why not her own family?"

"Maybe her family can't see the problems. We do."

Abuelita's words brought Brian Esparza to mind.
He wanted to take his brother-in-law's place for Iris and
Stefanie because he thought it was the best way to help
them.

Rita knew firsthand those painful feelings of insecurity because her father had died. And she'd never for-

get her mother's terrible mood swings as she tried to adjust to life without him.

"Maybe I can relate to Stefanie's problems, but—oh, Abuelita! I really don't have time to get involved right now." She shook her head, then picked up her fork to start eating, only to put it down again. "You know, I think I like sewing for strangers more. You don't get involved in their personal problems. They just want a dress."

"Just a dress? Then why don't they go to the store like everybody else? Women who come to dressmakers have a certain idea up here," she said, tapping her forehead. "And they need it to fit in here." She pressed her heart. "They want a dress special only for them. To know what they want, you listen, no? Then you start the cutting and sewing. And while you fit here, measure there, the woman talks more. Soon, you're friends. Strangers? I never sewed for strangers."

"I guess it'll take me a while to get established with my own customers, strangers that I can call friends. Many of the people I sew for, knew you. They don't really know me," Rita said.

"But you're a Navarro. We make the most beautiful dresses in San Antonio. Josie Esparza remembered, no? My _comadre_ has been in Del Rio many years. But she told Iris to call you. She knew my great-granddaughter would make a dress perfect for her Stefanie's _quinceañera._"

Rita had been grateful for the recommendation last summer. However, all the joyous preparations halted abruptly with the news of Estevan Bonilla's fatal car accident in July. Then, two months after the accident, the tearful widow and her quiet teenage daughter finally re-appeared in the shop and said the _quinceañera_ would still proceed as planned. However, the event now seemed driven by duty and obligation rather than a desire to celebrate a birthday and rejoice with hope and optimism in Stefanie's new role as a young woman.

"Rita, the dress is finished. But the girl needs more from you. Can't you help her, only a little? Josie is my *comadre*. I'm godmother for two of her children." Abuelita's words only re-emphasized the bonds between the two families. "For us, being *comadres* is stronger than being sisters."

Rita gave her great-grandmother a long look, as if to say, do you realize what you're asking of me?

Abuelita reached over and patted Rita's cheek. "Just remember what I always tell you. Take each problem one at a time."

Her great-grandmother had more faith and trust in Rita than she had in herself. Wrapping her fingers around Abuelita's wrist, she could feel the hard work leathered into the old woman's skin.

"I owe you so much, Abuelita." Rita's voice shook with unspoken fears. Would she ever be able to repay her great-grandmother's loan that enabled her to open her shop? And what could Rita do or say that could really help Josie's great-grandchildren?

"I'm grateful you came to live with me when your mother moved away. The two of us, we do okay, no?"

"We're doing just fine, Abuelita," Rita answered automatically.

The old woman squeezed Rita's hand. "And tomorrow we'll see Josie and her family at the anniversary party. Who would have guessed my godson Charlie, that skinny goat, could stay married fifty years?"

Rita managed a smile. She was glad to take Abuelita to see Josie and her family under happier circumstances than their last reunion at Estevan Bonilla's funeral. However, Rita had a nervous twinge at the thought of seeing Stefanie, Iris, and Brian again.

She felt as if she stood before a great length of beautiful fabric with no pattern or picture to follow. All she had were her instincts to guide her scissors, needle, and thread.

Chapter Two

Firmly taking a hold of Abuelita's elbow, Rita helped her out of the car and up the steps of the two-story brick home of Charlie and Carmen Esparza. The winds blew strong and cold tonight, and Rita had to be extra careful not to get in the way of Abuelita's wooden cane. They walked onto the tiled porch, then Rita pushed the doorbell, hoping for a quick rescue from the cold front that had blown in so suddenly.

The door opened only seconds later. Within the wedge of heat and light, Rita saw that Brian had opened his grandparents' door and smiled when he saw them.

"Hello. Come inside." Brian stepped back, opening the door wider.

"Hello, Brian," Rita said, her voice raspy from the cold. She steered Abuelita inside the foyer of the house. "Could you help my great-grandmother, please? I want to move my car out of the driveway."

"You take care of your great-grandmother, Rita. I'll move your car."

She stammered a protest. "Oh, no. Really. That's not necessary. Besides, it's cold outside. You don't even have your coat on."

"I don't need my coat," he said, seeming to ignore the fact that he pressed his shoulder against the door so the wind didn't catch it. "Where are your keys?"

"In the ignition, but—"

Abuelita silenced Rita by squeezing her arm.

"Thank you for your kindness," Abuelita said to Brian. He nodded and then went out the front door, closing it behind him. Turning, she gave Rita a disapproving stare. "Rita, let him do for us. It's a nice thing. Just say thank you."

Rita's face heated with embarrassment. Of course Abuelita was right. She felt foolish, but tried not to think about it as she helped her great-grandmother out of her coat.

"Isabel! We're so happy you could come!" A short woman in a green dress came forward to greet them. She hugged Abuelita, then turned to Rita. "I don't know if you remember me. I'm Carmen."

"Yes, we met—" She stopped before she almost said, "at Estevan's funeral." She stepped closer to press her cheek against Carmen's "It's nice to see you again. And congratulations on your golden anniversary."

"Thank you. Actually, I deserve a gold medal for living with Charlie for fifty years," Carmen said, her brown eyes crinkling with humor. "But I'll take a cruise to the Virgin Islands instead." She extended her arms for their coats as Rita unbuttoned hers. "Let me have your things. You both go into the living room. Mamá Josie is thrilled you and Isabel could come tonight."

Rita made a quick look in the mirror on the wall, smoothing back her short hair. She was relieved she didn't look as wind-blown as she felt.

From the paneled entry, Rita and Abuelita moved into an open area furnished with two comfortable brown sofas, assorted cushioned chairs, and wooden tables. Quickly, Rita surveyed the room, looking for Iris or Stefanie, but she didn't see them anywhere in the living room or in the adjoining dining room.

Rita walked a slow pace with Abuelita, who stopped to greet other members of the Esparza family and introduce her great-granddaughter. Several of them said, "So you're the dressmaker," and Rita would nod and smile. Eventually they made their way to the slender old woman with shoulder-length gray hair. She sat catty-cornered to the brick fireplace. Steady flames leapt from the pile of logs inside.

The two women embraced each other, then Abuelita sat down in the wooden chair next to her friend Josie. "You picked the best seat in the house, *comadre*."

"I can keep warm here. And with a night like tonight, I know everyone will come to me sooner or later. See? Here comes my great-grandson now."

Rita turned where Josie pointed and saw Brian coming in the direction of the fireplace. His cheeks and nose still wore the red sting of the Texas winds.

"It's colder than it was an hour ago." He spoke to all of them, then turned to Rita. "When you're ready to go, tell me. I'll bring your car around."

She shook her head. "Thanks, but that won't be— oh!" She felt the tip of Abuelita's cane poke her ankle. "Thank you. That's nice of you, Brian."

He extended her black purse. "I found this in the front seat. I thought you might want it."

"Thanks." As she took it from him, their hands touched. She felt a spark of electricity scramble up her hand.

"Isabel, have you met my great-grandson Brian? He makes computers," Josie told her old friend.

Brian chuckled, raising the palms of his hands against the warmth of the fire. "Mamá Josie, I don't make computers. I—" he gave Rita a little wink. "I just fix them."

"A mechanic? That's good." Abuelita nodded her approval. "Mechanics make good money, too."

Rita chanced to smile at Brian. When he grinned, she felt an intimate warmth, as if they shared a private joke.

"Do you remember that mechanic on Culebra who wanted to marry Eva?" Josie said suddenly.

"He was a welder, no?" Abuelita answered.

"No, he was the mechanic. The welder was after your Consuelo."

"Let them reminisce." Brian leaned over, his voice close to her ear. "Would you like a glass of wine?"

She enjoyed the scent of his cologne when he moved closer. She glanced down at Abuelita, who was still discussing the welder and the mechanic, then looked back at Brian's face. Did she like him more with or without his glasses? Tonight he had left them behind. She liked the way she could study his brown gaze and tried to read his thoughts.

"Rita?"

Realizing she was staring at him, she felt as if she had stepped too close to the fireplace. "I'm sorry. What did you ask?"

"Would you like some wine?"

"Yes, thank you." She put her purse down by Abuelita's chair and heard her great-grandmother say to Josie, "Does your great-grandson, the mechanic, have a girl friend?"

Rita wanted to hear the answer, but Brian placed his hand under her elbow. She had no choice but to move towards the dining room.

At that moment, Iris burst through the swinging door at the other end of the dining room. She shook an empty crystal goblet in the air. "Old witch! What does she know about what I need?"

Dressed in an off-the-shoulder red dress, Iris had the stature of a model: slender and stylish. Tonight her hazel eyes looked dark. Strands of auburn hair had come loose from a red and green hair-tie.

"Why did you ever convince me to come, Brian? Aunt Bertha says a widow must never wear red. Who gave her the rule book? And Mom always feels she has to make excuses for me. Why doesn't everybody just get off my back?"

"Keep your voice down, Iris," Brian said, putting his arm around his sister's waist. "Just calm down. Now, where's Stefanie?"

Iris pressed the goblet against her forehead, closing her eyes. "Hiding in the kitchen. Brian, can you pour me some wine?"

"Wouldn't you prefer something to eat, Iris?" he asked.

"You, too?" Sighing loudly, she opened her eyes to give Brian a look of ice. "You sound like Mom, who probably isn't speaking to me since I told Aunt Bertha to butt out of my life." Then she noticed Rita. One of her eyebrows raised. "Was Stefanie supposed to have another fitting for her dress tonight?"

Rita just ignored Iris's question. "Your grandparents invited my great-grandmother and me to their anniversary party. I had hoped though, that we might discuss something important later."

"Didn't Brian pay you?" She glared at her brother. "I thought you were going to pay her today."

"I paid Rita yesterday. Iris—"

"I want a glass of wine." Iris pushed her brother aside, and moved towards the silver ice bucket, bottles of wine, and liquor.

Again, the door to the kitchen swung open. A pair of women came out. One of them Rita recognized as Brian's mother. And the other woman in the blue dress was the infamous Aunt Bertha. Abuelita had introduced Rita to them earlier.

However, it was through the swinging of the door that Rita caught sight of Stefanie, sitting alone at the kitchen table eating a generous square of chocolate cake. Leaving Brian and the others to deal with Iris, Rita quietly moved towards the kitchen where Stefanie had been left behind. The teenager glanced up when Rita entered the room, then speared her fork into another chunk of cake and stuffed it into her mouth.

Letting the door swing closed behind her, Rita gave the girl a slight smile. "Hi, Stefanie. I just came in to get a glass of water. Where does your great-grandmother keep her glasses? Do you know?"

When the girl didn't reply, Rita thought she was being mean. Then Rita saw Stefanie struggling to chew and swallow so she could speak.

"Left side," she finally said, pointing to the kitchen cabinets. "Middle shelf."

"Thanks." Rita went through the motions of getting a glass tumbler and filling it with tap water just to waste time. She really didn't know where to begin a conversation with Stefanie. She just felt the girl shouldn't be alone.

"Did you tell my mother the dress is finished? I can have such a happy little *quinceañera* now," Stefanie smugly said.

Rita slowly turned from the sink. She wasn't sure how to respond to Stefanie's sarcastic tone. "I can talk with your mother another time."

"You'd better hurry. She's leaving tomorrow." Stefanie leaned her cheek against her left hand, her elbow resting on the kitchen table. She continued to eat, but in smaller bites.

"Leaving?" Rita came to sit at the table across from Stefanie. Her heart tightened with compassion when she saw again that pained expression in Stefanie's eyes. "Where's your mother going?"

"She decided to go see her friend Linda in New Mexico. Just like that, she's going. And not a care about me, of course. She didn't even tell me she was planning this trip."

"Perhaps it would help her to visit a good friend for a while." Rita thought some distance from well-meaning family and a house full of memories might help Iris regain control. Although she didn't know Iris too well, she understood that the tragedy of losing a spouse set everything way off balance. "I know you will miss your mother, but sometimes a person just needs to leave town in order to appreciate what she has at home."

The girl smashed her fork against a white flower decorating the chocolate icing. "I just don't want to spend my Christmas holidays in Del Rio with Granny and Gramps. It's so boring there."

Rita tried to be patient with Stefanie's selfishness. "Your mother shouldn't have to worry about you while she's gone. That's why she wants you with your grandparents."

"If Grandma and Grandpa Esparza weren't going to the Virgin Islands, I could stay here."

"Stefanie, do you really want your great-grandparents to cancel their trip just so they can stay here and care for you?" Rita asked.

"I just want to stay in San Antonio," Stefanie replied. Then her voice lowered. "But no one wants me around. Not Aunt Bertha, not Aunt Terrie, nobody. Everyone says I should just go to Del Rio until Mom comes back. Even Uncle Brian doesn't want me around."

Rita's eyebrows raised. "Why can't you stay in town with your Uncle Brian?"

"He works. He doesn't want me to be alone during the day." Stefanie sighed. "How stupid. I'm alone every day. Mom hides in her bedroom. Or she sits in the cemetery, crying for hours."

And leaves Stefanie feeling unwanted, Rita thought. She knew exactly how lonely and sad it felt.

Drumming her fingers upon the table top, Rita thought back to her own experiences when her father died and her mother was so unhappy. Abuelita started inviting young Rita to her house and getting her involved in simple sewing tasks for Abuelita's customers. Rita earned extra money, but more importantly, she gained a sense of confidence in her own talents and skills. And she learned how to make positive choices for her own benefit.

There was no doubt Rita needed extra help during the holidays at the shop. Perhaps there was a way to help Stefanie and help herself at the same time. When she looked at the teenager though, licking the last of the chocolate frosting from the fork, Rita knew she might have a bigger challenge than Abuelita ever did. They weren't related, and Stefanie probably had never done much work. If Rita wanted to help Stefanie, she needed the support of someone in Stefanie's family.

Suddenly, the kitchen door swung open. Looking up, Rita saw the concerned face of Stefanie's godfather.

"Just wondering where you went," Brian said, closing the door behind him.

"You were busy with Iris," Rita answered. She saw the lines of worry etched in his forehead. "Is she all right?"

He glanced at Stefanie, who had raised her eyes for his answer. Walking to where his niece sat, he paused, gently stroking her hair. "Iris is just tired. Perhaps I should take Iris and Stefanie home."

"I'm tired, too." Stefanie slid her chair back with a loud scraping noise. "I'm tired of Mom ruining all my fun." She stood up and glared at her uncle. "And I'm tired of you treating me like a little kid."

She turned away, pushing Brian aside just as Iris had only minutes ago. The evidence of his sister's and niece's rejection was a badge of pain Brian wore solemnly. He stared after his niece, watching the door swing.

Rita couldn't just sit there and not offer some words of encouragement. "Stefanie's not really mad at you, Brian. She just doesn't want to go to Del Rio while her mother's away."

"Stefanie's right though. I do treat her like a child." He glanced in Rita's direction. "You were right, too."

"Me?" Rita rose from her chair.

"Stefanie needs someone to talk to. Iris does, too. I hope visiting Linda will help her get over this awful mood she's in."

"But what about Stefanie? Who's going to help her?"

Brian turned to face Rita directly. "I tried last night. Stefanie won't talk to me. She either ignores me or runs off mad."

Her instincts told her that Brian needed help as well. She was no expert, but she could offer her opinion.

"I think she just told you why she won't talk to you. Did you listen? I mean, really listen, to what she said?"

"She said I treat her like a kid." Brian sighed. "But she is."

"She's a young woman, Brian. What good is the *quinceañera* if you never let Stefanie grow up?"

Slowly his gaze moved over her face. "When I was in your store yesterday, I asked you to talk to her." He stepped closer to Rita. "Will you help me to help Stefanie? I think she needs you."

The best incentive to get involved with Stefanie stood right before her. Rita smiled, wondering why she didn't think of it sooner.

"I might be able to help you, Brian. And I have a certain idea in mind already. Stefanie told me that she doesn't want to go to Del Rio. She said she'd stay with you, but you're worried about her being alone in the house while you work. What if she could work with me in the shop during the day, then spend the evenings with you?"

"You'd hire Stefanie to work in your shop?" he asked. "But she doesn't have any experience in dress-making."

"I need a helper to straighten out the place. She can answer the telephone, and I could teach her to use the cash register. It's a simple machine."

"But she's never taken on the responsibilities of a job before."

"Don't you think she can do it?"

Brian's eyebrows furrowed. "Of course she can do it."

"I could really use some help during the Christmas holidays, Brian. And if Stefanie wants to stay in town, she needs to keep busy while you're at work. It seems like a logical solution for everyone," Rita answered.

The frown on his brow slowly relaxed. His lips parted with a smile, revealing a row of very straight teeth.

"I think you have a good idea," he said. "You're a very smart woman, Rita. In many ways."

She savored the compliment, but as her eyes met his, she knew there would be more to this arrangement than he might realize. "Just remember that she's only working for me, but she's living with you. You must try to talk to her while you've got this time together. She needs a best friend as much as Iris does."

His smile took on a more intimate quality before his fingers touched her arm. "Perhaps I'll have you come to supper this week. So you can show all of us how to be friends."

His touch quickened her heartbeat, while his words only heightened Rita's awareness of her attraction to him. Standing so close to him, feeling his eyes upon her, left her scrambling for words. Then she felt as if a wad of cotton had lodged itself into her throat. She managed to croak, "Shall we talk to Stefanie now?"

Nodding slowly, he expressed a whistle of a sigh. "I guess so. Shall we go find her?"

"Uh—why don't you bring Iris and Stefanie in here?" Rita suggested, her mind finally coming back under her control. "The less family that gets involved in this discussion, the better. Don't you agree?"

"Yes." He nodded again. "Stay here. I'll be back."

As Rita watched him go through the kitchen door, she worried about Iris's emotional outbursts, Stefanie's bratty moods, and Brian's tendency to overprotect them both. She had to keep reminding herself of Abuelita's advice to deal with one problem at a time.

❤ ❤ ❤ ❤ ❤

"You want to put Stefanie to work while I'm gone? What could you be thinking?" Iris paced the kitchen floor, her hands fluttering like leaves caught by a whirlwind. "She can't even thread a needle. You two want to put her in a dress shop? Just send her to Del Rio with Mom."

"But I don't want to go to Del Rio," Stefanie said with a whine in her voice that sounded like a spoiled brat. "I want to stay with Uncle Brian." She leaned against the refrigerator, unconsciously opening and shutting the door. "I can take care of myself during the day. I sure don't need Rita for a baby-sitter. Or Uncle Brian either."

"I don't plan to be a baby-sitter." Brian spoke from the other side of the room. Standing closest to the kitchen door, Rita wondered if he was there to block their escape. His face showed a calm determination she had not seen before. "If you want to stay in town, Stefanie, you'll have to agree to this arrangement. Besides, your grandparents already have their hands full caring for Mamá Josie."

"It's not like Stefanie's a baby, Brian," Iris answered. She stopped long enough to give her brother one of her icy looks. "She'd be in the house and no one would even notice."

That's the whole problem, Rita thought. She moved towards the teenager, fixing a friendly smile on her face. "I think Stefanie might enjoy working with my customers. I have a lot of interesting people who come in everyday. She can help me with sales, organizing the shelves, things like that."

Stefanie rolled her eyes to the ceiling. "Who wants to work during Christmas vacation?"

"I know a dozen young people who would jump at the chance to earn extra money for Christmas." The nonchalance in Rita's voice pleased her. She wasn't going to beg the girl, after all. That's probably what Stefanie wanted. "I just thought I'd offer the job to you first." Rita shrugged. "I'm sure once I put a 'Help Wanted' sign in the window, I'll have a dozen good workers to chose from. Just enjoy your Christmas break in Del Rio, Stefanie. I hear it's a very exciting town."

The teenager stared at Rita. She merely raised her eyebrow to emphasize the decision was Stefanie's. What

would the girl do with this chance to be treated differently?

"Mom, I want to stay." Stefanie turned to look at
her mother. "I guess I can help Rita out. And Uncle
Brian lives in that big house all by himself. I can keep
him company. I want to stay in town, okay?"

"No, it's not okay," Iris said, her voice tight with
emotion. She had stopped beside the table to point a
shaking finger at Stefanie. "I want you with Mom and
Dad. They know how to take care of you."

"I can take care of myself." Stefanie's eyes reflected
an icy glare that she had inherited from her mother.
"You haven't done much for me since Daddy died. All
you do is sit and cry all day. Now you're off on a vacation
all by yourself. You're getting what you want. I'm going
to do what I want."

Iris's eyes widened, her face paled. She clutched at
the nearest chair, whispering her daughter's name and
a few garbled words about taking care "of her baby girl."

Brian walked to his sister, putting his arm around
her shoulders, supporting her, just as Rita saw him do
during the funeral services six months ago. "Iris, I'll
take very good care of Stefanie. The most important
thing right now is for you to take care of yourself. Trust
me. Stefanie will be fine."

He spoke with strength and patience. Iris's head
dropped to his shoulder as she leaned against him.

"What are all of you doing in here?" A loud voice
crash-landed into the middle of the room. Aunt Bertha
had pushed the kitchen door open and stood there staring at all of them. "Is something wrong?"

Since Rita had made the decision to get involved,
she decided to help Brian, Iris, and Stefanie deal with
this nuisance, too. "Hello! Remember me? I'm Rita
Navarro, Isabel's great-granddaughter. You're Bertha?
I've heard so many things about you." With a sudden
smile, Rita walked forward. The woman's mouth
dropped open, but she took Rita's outstretched hand.

"We were just talking about preparing a toast for Charlie and Carmen. Do you know where we could find some champagne? The only thing we can't decide is who should make the toast. Whom do you suggest, Bertha?"

"Well, I don't know. Perhaps Nato Ruffo. He was their best man. I guess I can go ask him."

"Great idea. Why don't you do that, Aunt Bertha?" Brian's voice carried a new energy. He had sat Iris in a chair while Rita had distracted Aunt Bertha and moved towards the refrigerator. "Stefanie, did you see any champagne in the refrigerator? Why don't you look?"

"I thought you were taking Mom and me home," Stefanie said, crossing her arms over her chest.

"You can't leave before we toast the guests of honor," Rita proclaimed. "That would be bad manners."

"Rita's right." Brian's tone was firm. "We came to celebrate Grandpa and Grandma's happiness, and that's what we're going to do. Iris, go find Grandma and ask her what glasses we should use. Aunt Bertha, find Nato and ask him if he'll do the toast." He opened the refrigerator. "Ah-hah. Here it is, Stefanie." He handed one green bottle topped with gold foil to his niece, then took two more bottles from the refrigerator. "Iris, go ask about the glasses, please."

Iris stood up, straightened her red dress around her shoulders, then walked out. Aunt Bertha followed her.

As they left, Rita sighed. "Thank goodness there was champagne in there."

"Thank goodness you thought of the toast." Brian smiled, then looked at Stefanie. "And Rita thought of a way to keep you in San Antonio, too. She's pretty smart, isn't she, Stef?"

The teenager shrugged. "She kept Aunt Bertha out of our business. That's good." She walked towards Rita, then pushed the champagne bottle into Rita's hands. "I just hope Mom doesn't get drunk off this stuff because of your brilliant idea." She tossed her long hair over her shoulders and walked out.

"I'm sorry she was rude," Brian told Rita, moving to where she stood watching the swinging door. "Are you sure you still want to hire her?"

She had wondered the very same thing. If Stefanie used that tone with Rita's customers, they'd never return. Despite any reservations that she had though, there was little she could do now. "Well, if I hire her, I can also fire her."

Her honesty took him one step backwards. That frosty look appeared for the first time in his eyes. "You say you want to help Stefanie. Now you say you'll fire her. I don't get it."

"Stefanie doesn't get it either, Brian. She acts like she's doing both of us a great favor by staying in town. I don't intend to treat her like a piece of expensive silk. We gave her a choice, and now she has to make the best of it. We all do."

His answer was silence. She was reminded that human relationships could be trickier than matching tiny plaid lines.

"We can all learn to adjust to something new, right?" Rita added.

"Adjust seems to be one of your favorite words," he said. "Some problems can't be solved no matter how much adjustment you make."

"Let's just take it one problem at a time," Rita told Brian, almost smiling at the sound of Abuelita's advice coming from her lips. "Leave Stefanie at the shop on your way to work Monday. I promise not to fire her before noon, okay?"

She wanted to make him smile, but she saw no amusement in his brown stare. Deciding to leave the situation as it was, Rita walked towards the living room. Under the circumstances, moving forward seemed the best direction to take.

Chapter Three

Rita locked the shop door behind her. She liked to arrive before eight on Monday mornings to take care of the bookkeeping. After plugging in the coffee pot, she gathered the checkbook and her cardboard file box of invoices and bills and moved to a small table behind the counter to go over store business.

As she entered figures in both the expenses and income columns, she wondered again if hiring extra help was smart. But to have someone keep the shop orderly and help customers would give her more time to finish the wedding gown for Councilman Guerra's daughter. If she completed the dress by January, the final payment could be a good start towards the amount she needed as a deposit for a new place of business. A store where iron burglar bars didn't cover the windows. A place with enough floor space so she could set up figures wearing dresses she sewed. A store that sold the most beautiful dresses in San Antonio.

Rita sighed. She could spend hours fashioning her dreams, but the reality was that she sat in a crowded, cold shop trying to decide how to squeeze a helper's salary out of this month's profits. And what a helper she had picked!

"You did a good thing," Abuelita had told Rita as they drove home from the anniversary party.

Still Rita had doubted the wisdom of getting involved. After their private discussion in the kitchen, Brian seemed to avoid her the rest of the evening. He had left early to take Iris and Stefanie home with only a polite good-bye directed more at Abuelita and Mamá Josie than Rita.

"I hope this all works out, Abuelita."

"The girl only needs someone to teach her about herself."

"Like you did for me?"

"You did for yourself, Rita. You were just a seed. You needed time to grow."

If Rita was only a seed, then Abuelita was sunlight, water, and rich soil. The decision to hire Stefanie, to become her friend, was sown in her desires to repay Abuelita for all those years of unconditional faith and love. Abuelita thought of the Esparza family as her own. Here was a chance to help one of them. If Rita could just become a friend to the teenager, perhaps Stefanie would realize she wasn't alone to face the problems which troubled her. Besides, Rita was looking forward to company in the shop again.

A loud knock on the shop door startled Rita. She looked behind her, never expecting to see Stefanie and Brian peering through the shop window.

She moved quickly to let them inside. "I guess I should have asked you what time you report to work, Brian," Rita said. "I assumed you were a nine-to-fiver."

Stefanie stepped into the shop first. "We've been up since five-thirty. Seems like I ate breakfast hours ago."

Brian closed the shop door behind them. "Neither one of us got much sleep last night. And I thought if Stefanie was here early, you could explain her duties to her before your customers arrived."

His eyes darted from Rita to Stefanie, then back again. She saw the look of a man who was having second thoughts about a difficult decision.

Rita smiled and put her hand on his arm. "You had a good idea, Brian. Mondays always seem to be more hectic than other days. Would you like a cup of coffee?"

"No, but thank you." He gave her a slight smile.

She turned to look at her new employee. The girl was dressed in a striped short dress and navy stockings. Her high-heeled leather boots looked stylish and expensive. Stefanie looked ready to attend a dance, not assist Rita, who had a variety of jobs for her helper this morning. "Stefanie, on the other side of the bathroom is a small storeroom. Hang your jacket and purse in there. Then I'll put you to work while I finish the books."

Silently, the girl left the room.

"I wonder if we're doing the right thing for Stefanie," Brian said in a quiet voice. "She's hardly said a word to me since her mother left. She stayed in front of the television, then went to bed. She didn't want to go to Del Rio, but I don't think she really wanted to stay with me either. And I feel like I'm taking advantage of you by leaving her here during the day while I work."

"I asked Stefanie to work for me, Brian. She could have said no," Rita said, then moved towards the coffee pot behind the counter. "If none of this works out, she can always take a bus to Del Rio and stay with your parents until Iris comes back. That's her choice, too." She poured herself a cup of coffee, then turned to look at Brian.

One corner of his mouth had lifted into a smile. "I like your confidence, Rita. Makes me wish I could send Stefanie to my job, and I could stay here and learn from you."

Rita's fingers tightened around the coffee mug. Heat seemed to spread from her hands over to her face, down her neck, to her toes. She lowered her eyes, taking a sip from the coffee, trying to find a way to reply to such an enticing statement.

"So? What do I do now?" Stefanie walked into the room, looking around the shop. She was frowning, looking resigned to her fate rather than anticipating something new and different to do with her time.

Rita regretted that Stefanie's first task was menial, but it was one that had to be done before the shop

opened for business. Especially today, with four customers coming in for dress fittings. "Get the vacuum
from the storeroom and go over the side room there.
Then vacuum your way in here. Be careful moving the
potted plants in the corner. It'll be a real mess if one
gets overturned. Then you can start cleaning the glass.
Windows, display case, you know."

Stefanie merely stared at Rita. "You want me to
vacuum and move plants? Clean windows? You never
told me that. You said I could help customers."

"There's a lot to be done before the shop opens. I
need to finish the books and set out dresses for today's
fittings. I'm hoping you work quickly, so I have time to
show you how this register works. Then you can wait on
customers while I'm fitting dresses."

Stefanie looked at her uncle as if to ask him, must I
stay? In turn, Brian looked at Rita. Did he think she
should be less businesslike with the girl? But Rita knew
she couldn't treat Stefanie any different than a stranger
she might have hired.

Before Brian put on his protector's shield for Stefanie's sake, Rita said, "I guess you need to get to work,
too, Brian. Can you pick Stefanie up about five?"

He opened his mouth as if to say something, then
thought better of it. He reached out to pat Stefanie's
arm. "I'll be back about five, Stef. Do you need any
money for lunch?"

"Mom gave me plenty of money," Stefanie said.
Then she groaned, turned away from both of them, and
stomped her way towards the storeroom.

"Did I say something wrong?" Brian frowned, looking at Rita.

"Who knows? You go on to work and I'll take care of
her." Only Rita didn't feel quite as confident as she
sounded. What if the girl didn't want a friend? Would
she even follow orders as an employee?

Then she glanced at Brian. He gave her that same
look of admiration when she had stood up to Mr.

Arredondo. A boost of determination recharged her spirit.

"Don't worry about us, Brian. But if you like, you can call me at lunch and see if the store's still standing." Rita grinned, hoping to hide her anxieties from him.

A touch of a smile relaxed his frown. He reached into the pocket of his suit coat and withdrew a leather wallet. From there, he pulled out a white card and handed it to her. "Here's my card. I'll be in the office most of the day. If not, the secretary always knows where to reach me."

Rita took his business card, studying the raised black printing. She possessed a connection to Brian she didn't have before. The thought made her feel like a school girl getting a note from a boy she liked. How silly, she thought. But how very nice, too.

The whirring of the vacuum cleaner brought her back to business.

She put the card on the counter and gave Brian a cheerful smile. "I guess I'll see you again about five."

"Yes—well—" He turned towards the door, walked a few steps, then stopped. "Uh—Rita?" His hand straightened the evergreen garland alongside the shop window. "I thought Stefanie and I would go to a movie tonight. Would you like to join us?" He cleared his throat, then finally looked at her.

She wanted to say yes. But she knew she needed to survive this first day with Stefanie before she joined the girl and her uncle on an outing. "Can I let you know later?"

He released a great sigh, as if he had been holding his breath. Then he gave her a nod. "I'll see you about five. Good-bye, Rita."

The jingling of the wreath bells followed Brian out the door of the shop. She looked forward to his return.

❤ ❤ ❤ ❤ ❤

"Your machine looks easy." Stefanie punched up a mock sale on the electronic register then canceled it with a series of beeps. "My friend Angie works in her aunt's flower shop. She said that if the register comes up short, she has to pay it back herself." She eyed Rita suspiciously. "Is that your rule, too?"

"Only when it's short a hundred dollars." Rita laughed when Stefanie's mouth dropped open. "I'm just kidding! Just be careful. Don't only rely on the machine. Count the change to yourself and count it out loud to the customer."

"What if I make a mistake?"

"Just apologize. Everyone makes mistakes." Rita moved away from the counter to unlock the front door. "Now, while I'm sewing over there, I'd like you to start working on the display case here. It looks so crowded."

Stefanie bent down to peer inside the glass case. She moved around a few items then sighed. "Why do you sell all this junk?"

"I try to make things convenient for my customers, Stefanie. I make a lot of first-communion dresses. Often a *madrina* wants to buy the child a prayer book or rosary as a gift. Those gold lockets could be given as bridesmaids' gifts or to teenagers celebrating their *quinceañera*. The lace collars can add a new look to last year's dress."

Rita sat down behind the sewing machine in the corner of the front room. She used to sew in another room, but moved her machine after Beatrice left. Now, she liked working in the main room where she could wait on customers yet continue to sew if they were merely browsing. The only drawback was that she had to toss loose threads and tiny scraps into a trashcan, not on the floor like she usually did.

She began to pin together a white satin sleeve for Alyssa Guerra's wedding gown. "We might be able to store some of the extras under the counter. Then it won't look so junky."

"This whole place looks junky," Stefanie replied.

The blunt statement upset Rita, even though she knew the teenager was right. But unless Rita wanted to work in the shop twenty-four hours a day, she had to keep her insecurities under control and just do the best she could. She took a calming breath then said, "Stefanie, if the place looks junky, it's because I need an assistant. That's why I asked you to help me in the shop."

"Well, tell me what to do and I'll do it."

Rita tried to diffuse the anger she heard in Stefanie's voice. "You already know what do, Stefanie. Try to make this place look less junky. Don't you think you can do that?"

The girl's eyes narrowed. "Do you really care what I think?"

Rita's answer was delayed by the ring of the black telephone on the wall behind Stefanie. The bells on the door wreath jingled seconds later as Mrs. Díaz arrived for the Christmas dress Rita had altered.

"Stefanie, I have to trust you to do what needs to be done. Use your best judgment. You can organize things as well as I can. Good morning, Mrs. Díaz. I have your dress ready. Stefanie, please answer the phone."

"But what do I say?"

"Say, 'Hello, this is Rita's Dress Shop. Can I help you?' and then go from there." Rita stood up, putting the wedding gown aside. She smiled at Mrs. Díaz, then led the way towards the side room.

While Mrs. Díaz tried on the dress in the privacy of the dressing room, Rita took a quick peek back into the main area of the store.

Stefanie had pulled a lace collar out of the display case and laid it on the counter. She smoothed out a wrinkle then set it aside. She paused for a moment, rubbing her chin as she stared into the case, then reached for the tangled pile of ribbons and boxes and began to sort them.

The morning seemed to pass quickly as Rita fitted a wedding gown and three bridesmaids dresses while Stefanie straightened up the counter area, answered the telephone, and rung up a Mexican dress Mrs. Díaz had purchased.

Near noon, two customers came in at the same time. Stefanie gave one woman the wrong red blouse. Luckily, Stefanie realized the mistake before the woman had driven away and was able to exchange packages with her. The other customer teased Stefanie about joining the school track team after she ran to the car and back. Rita could tell Stefanie felt very embarrassed.

"I've mixed up orders, too, Stefanie," Rita remarked when they were alone in the shop. "Only I did it with two wedding gowns. This woman about a size eighteen went home with a size five dress. I drove all the way to her home in Helotes to exchange the dresses. At least you caught your mistake here."

The telephone rang again before Stefanie could reply.

"I feel silly having to interrupt you every time a lady wants to know if her dress is finished. Could you make a list so I wouldn't have to bother you so much?" Stefanie said after she hung up the telephone.

Rita turned the finished sleeve right side out and started pinning it into the arm hole. "I don't feel bothered. Actually, it's easier to tell you whether a dress is finished than it is to leave my sewing and answer the telephone."

"But how do you remember everyone's name and what you made for them?" Stefanie walked around the counter towards Rita. "How do you remember if it's the dress that still needs hemming or a blouse that needs a collar? Can you even remember if the customer has paid or not?"

"When it comes to money, I don't trust my memory." Rita grinned. "I have invoices that I file and use. But it's easy to keep clothes straight." Her fingers continued working silver pins into the satin material as she talked. "When I take someone's idea and turn it into a special dress, piece by piece, I spend a lot of time thinking about the person. By the time the dress is ready for a fitting, I've visualized so often how the woman will look, she's like an old friend." She paused then and looked at Stefanie. "My great-grandmother reminded me only a few days ago that a dressmaker never sews for strangers. Suddenly, I understand what she meant."

It was the first time all morning they had time for conversation, or for Rita to remember why she wanted Stefanie to work in the shop. She gave the girl a gentle smile. "When I began working on your *quinceañera* dress, too, I kept picturing you in my mind. I thought about how our great-grandmothers were close friends, *comadres* even, and that four generations later we were all getting to know one another as friends, too."

Stefanie reached down to pick up a sliver of white material that Rita had trimmed from the sleeve seam, then tossed it into the small silver can under the oak sewing machine cabinet. She offered Rita a brief smile before she moved towards the back of the store to straighten up the dresses on the rack.

Sensing the teenager wasn't ready to talk, Rita returned to her sewing. She had learned lessons of patience from Abuelita, too.

For the rest of the afternoon, Stefanie managed to keep busy and avoid any conversation except to ask where things belonged or mention she was hungry and would walk to the hamburger place on the corner to buy her lunch.

By late afternoon, the teenager had done an efficient job straightening up the store. Piles were fewer, the glass case under the counter neatly displayed the variety of accessories that Rita sold, and Stefanie moved the silk flower arrangements so they didn't look like an obstacle course the customers had to dodge in order to see the dresses.

Because Rita didn't have to stop to answer the telephone or take the time to straighten the shop herself, she made considerable progress on the Guerra wedding gown. As she shook the dress out, then hung it on the brass rack behind her, she took great pride in the day's accomplishments.

"You're a natural organizer," Rita told Stefanie, who stood in the side room restacking bolts of fabric on the shelves.

"My friends call me Miss Neatly. I just like to be able to find something when I want it. Now if someone calls and wants to know if we sell tiaras or white rosary beads, I can see them with no problem." She patted the top bolt of white slipper satin. "I've never seen so many shades of white material. I used to think white was white. Not anymore."

"You have a keen eye. Others could look at that stack and not see how this fabric has a subtle pattern, or this one has a hint of pink. My ex-partner used to say, 'Just make it white. What's the difference?' but to me, it makes a big difference," Rita said.

"Tell my mother that."

Stefanie shivered slightly then wrapped her arms around herself. She turned away from Rita, walking towards the chrome dress rack.

Among the half-dozen dresses hanging, there was Stefanie's own *quinceañera* gown. She fingered its sweetheart neckline then slid her hand down one lace sleeve.

"Is something on your mind, Stefanie?"

She stared at Rita a long time, as if she was deciding whether to trust her. Finally she spoke. "My mother thinks Uncle Brian should take my father's place in church. For the *quinceañera*, you know? I'm sure she wants him to greet people as if he was my father, too."

Rita put her hand on the girl's shoulder. "He's your godfather, Stefanie. I know he loves you very much."

"But he's not my father. My father's dead." Her eyes darkened with anger. "And isn't it the father who's supposed to present his daughter? Isn't that the whole point of this stupid *quince* idea?"

"Stefanie, I understand what you're feeling. My father wasn't alive for my *quinceañera* either," Rita said, only to see the teen's eyes glisten with a fine sheen of tears.

"I know it's traditional for the father to present his daughter to his friends, but this custom started during the days when young Mexican women were sheltered, kept away from outsiders until they were of marrying age. Nowadays, fourteen-year old girls have more maturity and freedom than our great-grandmothers ever did. Now you can celebrate your *quinceañera* as your day to tell everyone you're ready to take the next step in becoming an adult. This is the time to discover for yourself what you really want to make of your life."

"But no one cares about what I want." She still sounded like a petulant child, not a reasonable young woman.

"If you want people to listen to you, Stefanie, then you have to listen to them. Learn to compromise. But first, you have to be willing to talk. Why not begin with your Uncle Brian?"

Stefanie sighed. "It's very hard to talk to him. He's like a stranger to me. When I was little, he was away at college. Then he traveled a lot for his job. He's been around more since Daddy died, but—well—he's weird, Rita."

"What do you mean, he's weird?"

"He never has any fun. He goes to work, then comes home to this big house that looks like no one lives there. When he's at our house, he watches news shows on public television. The only people who could make him laugh were Mom and Dad, and well—now, no one wants to laugh anymore."

"Well, maybe this week while your mother's gone, you could make sure he has a little fun," Rita said. "He told me he wanted to take you to the movies tonight. Choose a crazy movie. One that will make both of you laugh."

Taking Rita's hand in hers, Stefanie gave Rita a shy smile. It resembled Brian's expression this morning when he invited Rita to the movies. "Could you come with us tonight? Maybe you need to laugh, too."

Rita nodded. Everyone deserved to laugh after a hard day's work.

❤ ❤ ❤ ❤ ❤

"I cannot believe that you took me to see a movie where the best acting was done by a corpse," Brian said as the three of them walked up the carpeted aisle and out of the dimly lit theater.

Stefanie giggled as she buttoned her jacket. "My favorite part was when they lost the body in the subway. The old lady never noticed. She just kept talking and talking and talking. Kind of like Aunt Bertha."

"I knew she reminded me of someone we knew." Brian chuckled happily, putting one arm around Stefanie's shoulder and the other around Rita's. "All right, ladies. What shall we do next? Ice cream?" He smiled down at Rita.

"Sounds delicious," she said, enjoying the relaxed happy expression on Brian's face. Throughout the evening, spending time with Brian and Stefanie, she realized it was her job to agree with whomever made a suggestion first. Stefanie wanted Rita's support when she suggested they go see this odd-ball comedy. Brian turned to Rita for approval when he suggested they have dessert afterwards. This role amused Rita all evening.

They left the theater through a metal exit door and found themselves near the food court of the mall. This area was crowded with Christmas shoppers carrying bags or wrapped boxes. Echoes of excited voices and crying children mixed in with the Christmas carols from a choir of teenagers standing on a stage near the white stone fountain in the middle of the court.

"Look! There's Angie and Micole." Stefanie pointed in the distance. "I have to talk to them. I'll meet you by the ice-cream place later." She moved away from Brian and Rita and walked towards a group of girls who were sitting at one of many round tables watching the choir.

"I'm happy to see Stefanie enjoying herself," Brian said, pausing to let a woman pushing a double stroller pass by first. "She seems more relaxed today than she was yesterday. I guess it's because she's been with you. Usually, all I get from her is the silent treatment."

"That's because she feels like you're a stranger," Rita told him. Then she gave a gentle chuckle because Stefanie's other description of Brian had been humorous, too. "She also thinks you're weird."

"I see. And do you think I'm weird?" His voice carried a hint of concern. His eyes darkened with the seriousness of his question.

Had she hurt Brian's feelings? She never expected him to take it personally, just dismiss it as something typical for a teenager to say.

"I don't think you're weird, Brian." She placed her hand on the lapel of his brown suede jacket. "I just think Stefanie needs to get to know you better." She also wanted to tell him that he was the nicest man she had met in a long time. He had beautiful eyes, a smile that made her heart flutter, and a wonderful laugh she wanted to hear more often. But she was afraid to say more until she understood Brian better herself.

His hand rested gently over hers. "Stefanie and I are lucky to have you as our friend."

She managed a smile, but she had wanted to hear more personal words between the two of them. How could she let him know that she wanted more than friendship between them?

Something green above Brian's head caught her attention. She looked up to see a crystal sphere decorated with sprigs of mistletoe a few feet above them.

Brian tilted his head back so he could see what she saw. She heard a gurgling noise in his throat before he lowered his gaze to meet hers.

"We're standing under mistletoe." Her voice was teasing.

His hand tightened around hers. "I heard that kissing under the mistletoe can bring good luck."

As he moved his face closer, a wave of excitement rippled down her. His lips covered hers in a velvet-soft kiss, complete with pleasant lingering effects.

"I feel lucky already," she whispered.

And when he smiled, she knew the mistletoe had done its job well. The rest of the relationship was in their hands now.

Chapter Four

Stefanie stood on a short stool, stringing up tiny blinking lights within the evergreen garlands that outlined the front window of the shop. "That was the ugliest dress I ever saw. Uh—sorry, Rita. The dress wasn't so bad, but that woman looked terrible in it."

Pushing her hand through her black hair, Rita expressed the long sigh she held inside her since Erica Gato, one of Bea's former customers, had left the store. "I knew when Erica first showed me a picture, the outfit wasn't right for her. She looked like a red penguin to me."

Stefanie giggled. "A red penguin. That's a good one." She climbed down from the stool then gestured toward the window. "Well, what do you think?"

Walking around the counter, Rita moved to stand beside Stefanie. She put her hand on the girl's shoulder. "It looks very merry. You had a good idea to put lights up around the window."

"At least you have a wreath and a few lights to show it's Christmas. It's weird to stay in a house with no Christmas decorations." She uttered a short sigh.

Rita signed too. "You need to be patient with your mother, Stefanie. Maybe when she comes home, you can decorate for Christmas."

"No, we have a tree and stuff. Gramps and I set it up last weekend when they came in for the anniversary party. I was talking about Uncle Brian, Rita." She rolled her eyes, sighing again. "I feel like I'm living in a hotel while Mom's gone. He even has white towels. I've never known anyone who had white towels in their bathroom."

"Well, if all his linens are the same color, it will make washing easier." She felt a need to defend Brian, especially after last night's conversation. He had looked so hurt when she said Stefanie called him weird. "Maybe he doesn't decorate because he's not home much. Didn't you tell me that he travels a lot in his job?"

"Well, yeah, I suppose. But he could at least put up a tree."

"So why don't you volunteer to decorate Uncle Brian's house a little? I'm sure he wouldn't mind." She winked at her young helper. "Even hotels decorate for Christmas."

"Wouldn't it be fun if we convinced him to buy a tree this year?" The eagerness in Stefanie's eyes gave Rita a warm feeling.

"I should make a list of all the things he should buy," Stefanie said as she started to walk away. Then she turned, looking over her shoulder at Rita. "I'll make sure he buys plenty of mistletoe, too." Her eyebrows raised twice before she wandered towards the counter, giggling.

Rita didn't know what to say. Stefanie hadn't given any indication last night or this morning that she saw Brian kiss Rita. She tried to keep her voice free from the embarrassment she felt. "Perhaps you should just ask Brian to buy a tree and a few lights."

"I've never seen Uncle Brian with a girl friend before. It seems funny that it would be you." Stefanie grabbed a pencil from a box by the cash register, then tore a sheet from the pad nearby.

"We're just friends, Stefanie. Our families have known each other a long time." Her stomach tensed nervously as she spoke about Brian. Looking for something to do, Rita saw the stool and returned it to its place by the sewing machine.

"I saw him kiss you. But it's okay, Rita. If you like Uncle Brian, I mean." The tone in her voice changed.

"Okay, a tree. Lights. Ornaments. Tinsel. What else? I wonder if he wants a manger scene."

As Rita glanced at Stefanie writing on the paper, she felt a slight sense of relief to have Stefanie's approval of her "friendship" with Brian, kiss and all.

He arrived near five to pick up Stefanie. Rita looked up from her sewing when he came into the store, and he greeted Rita with a smile that added a warm luster to his brown eyes.

"What do you think of the store?" Stefanie asked him as soon as her uncle stepped inside. "Do you like my decorations?"

Brian turned to his niece then looked from the counter to the window and finally back at Rita. "Everything looks very nice."

"Oh, Uncle Brian! You didn't even notice the lights." Stefanie scowled at him, placing her hands on her hips. "I put tiny lights around the window. Didn't you see any difference at all?"

"Sorry, Stef." Brian moved a quarter turn to examine the window again. "It looks very pretty. Actually, I noticed them as soon as I drove up."

"Yeah, right."

"No, really. It gives the store a nice Christmas feeling. Maybe we should string some up around the windows at my house this week," Brian said. He walked closer to the counter where Stefanie had been organizing cards of buttons into the separate compartments of a wide tin box. It was a job Rita had been meaning to do since she found the long, flat container at a neighbor's yard sale, but had never made the time.

"I haven't made any plans for tonight," he said. "Perhaps we could buy a tree and do some decorating. I want Santa Claus to come to my house, too, you know."

He gave his niece an easy smile, but as the girl's eyes narrowed, Rita could tell Stefanie wasn't charmed by the mention of Santa Claus. She rose from the sewing machine, putting the wedding dress aside for today.

"Decorating a tree tonight could be fun," Rita said. "Stefanie even made a list of things you might need. What did you do with that list, Stefanie?"

Slowly, the girl's frown relaxed. "I have it in my pocket," she said.

"Stefanie was very thorough, Brian. I think she even has a manger scene on the list. Do you own any statues for a nativity?" Rita asked.

Tilting his head slightly, he gave Rita a thoughtful stare. Then his eyebrows raised. "Yes, I do. I have the nativity set that belonged to Mamá Josie. It's been packed away for years."

She regarded him with an affectionate smile, knowing how much she treasured things Abuelita gave her. "Then it's time to unpack Mamá Josie's set, Brian. Use it in your home. Isn't that what she wanted when she gave it to you?"

"Yes," he said. Their eyes met and she felt such a desire to touch him, it made her hands tremble.

"Rita, why don't you come over to Uncle Brian's house and help us?" Stefanie's enthusiastic voice broke their visual link. "Wouldn't you like that, Uncle Brian?"

She regarded Stefanie's question carefully. Did she really want Rita's help, or was Stefanie pushing Brian and Rita together on purpose?

"That's a wonderful idea," Brian said. "Why don't you spend the evening with us, Rita? We can buy a tree and decorate my house."

Another evening with Brian and Stefanie was a delicious offer, but Rita felt a little guilty leaving Abuelita alone tonight. She gave Brian an apologetic look. "It would be fun, but I really should spend the evening with my great-grandmother. She'll be leaving tomorrow for Brownsville to spend Christmas with her daughter and—"

"Bring her, too. Really, Rita. Both of you can come to my house tonight. There's a great Mexican restaurant nearby. We can order food to go, have a nice supper, then decorate a Christmas tree." His eyes and smile radiated a party spirit. "It would be wonderful if you and your great-grandmother could come over. She could tell us all how our families came to be friends."

How could she refuse? Abuelita didn't go out often, and Rita knew her great-grandmother enjoyed visiting friends and talking about old times most of all. Besides, after all Stefanie told her, Rita was very curious about the place where Brian lived. "I'll have to check with Abuelita, but I'm sure we could come for supper and help you decorate your house, Brian. Thank you for inviting us."

❤ ❤ ❤ ❤ ❤

Brian's house lived up to its street name, Cityview. Even from the driveway there was a picturesque view of San Antonio's skyline.

As soon as Rita entered the one-level ranch-style house, she felt that Stefanie's description of "a house where nobody lived" was very appropriate. All the rooms were furnished with comfortable, well-matched furniture, probably arranged under an interior designer's trained eye. But there were no personal items in any of the rooms Rita saw. No family pictures, no magazines tossed carelessly on end tables. Not even a house plant to hint anything about the owner.

The entry closet where Brian hung their coats was relatively empty, with only his gray overcoat and Stefanie's leather jacket inside.

"For a man who lives alone, you keep a clean house," Abuelita commented as Brian led the way towards the dining room. "My nephew Carlos lives alone. I'd never eat in his house."

Rita felt her face turn the shade of her rose-red sweater. Why couldn't Abuelita just admire the view from the windows?

Stefanie was fixing place settings around the table in the center of the room. Six mahogany chairs with green-striped seat covers surrounded the table. It was covered by a white linen tablecloth.

"Hi," she said, smiling when she saw everyone.

"Stefanie, I don't think you've ever been introduced to my great-grandmother. This is Isabel Navarro. Abuelita, this is Stefanie Bonilla," Rita said, putting her arm around Abuelita's shoulder.

"Thank you for helping Rita." Abuelita smiled at Stefanie. "She says you do good work."

"Thanks." She shrugged away the praise. "The job's not too hard." She looked at Brian then. "We're ready to eat now."

Conversation around the table was relaxed and friendly, with Rita and Stefanie doing most of the talking. Brian seemed content to listen, and Abuelita added stories here and there, mostly anecdotes from the past when she made dresses full-time or recalled something that happened in the neighborhood when Josie Esparza and her family lived on Ruiz street.

After supper, Brian insisted Rita, Abuelita, and Stefanie begin decorating the Christmas tree in the den while he loaded the dishwasher and cleaned up. Rita offered to help him twice, but Abuelita finally pulled her close and whispered, "Be glad he doesn't want you as his maid. We would treat our guests the same way, no?"

The den was off the kitchen, a room shaped like a diamond, with two long windows reaching a point then slanting inwards towards a rock fireplace on one side. An elaborate stereo system ran along the other wall, complete with a television set, a video player, and a small cabinet underneath to store tapes.

Brian had set the tall Douglas fir tree where the windows met, and it filled the room with a pleasant pine scent. Abuelita sat on the sofa putting tiny hooks on the new ornaments which Rita unpacked from their boxes. Stefanie concentrated on the lights, laying strands over the branches until she reached the bottom.

Rita and Stefanie were both hanging ornaments when Brian came into the den. He was carrying two long blanket boxes, which he set down on the floor near the sofa. He smiled at Abuelita.

These might look familiar to you," he said as he lifted the lid from one gray cardboard box. The contents were covered by wads of yellowed papers which Brian tossed aside.

He seemed oblivious to the mess he made as he unwrapped various painted statues and began to set them on the coffee table. Both Rita and Stefanie stopped working in order to help him unpack the rest of the nativity set.

Abuelita reached out to hold the statue of Joseph, a plaster figure about six inches high. Its face was authentically painted with rich flesh tones and a golden brown beard. His bluish-gray gown was draped with a green mantle; he carried a brown walking staff in one hand.

"From Josie's home, no?" she said as her shaky fingers tightened around the statue. "Josie put them under the tree every year. She always loved Christmas."

"Uncle Brian, these are so lifelike," Stefanie said as she unwrapped a white sheep and set it beside the statue of the black-haired shepherd holding a lamb in his arms. "Mom's set is a gold ceramic. It's pretty, but I like these better."

"I don't remember who bought these," Abuelita said more to herself than to anyone listening. "Was it Mary or Charlie? Maybe Gilbert."

Rita unwrapped a bulky wad of white tissue to find a statue of one of the kings, dressed in scarlet robes and carrying a gold chalice. As she placed it on the coffee table, she looked at Brian. "Even if you don't put up a tree, you should always put this set out. It's beautiful."

"I feel like I've found a buried treasure." His gaze reflected a variety of emotions. "When my parents moved Mamá Josie to live with them years ago, these were packed away and forgotten. Mamá Josie gave them to me when I bought the house two years ago, but I never thought to use them." He gave Rita a grateful smile then reached over to run his hand down Stefanie's dark hair. "We always spend Christmas together, but not here. I guess I never saw a reason to decorate when I'd be the only one to see it."

Stefanie turned to look at him. "But Uncle Brian, you have to make this place feel like someone lives here. If not, it all seems so lonely."

Rita glanced from Stefanie to Brian, pleased that the girl offered her criticism with a gentle tone, but wondering how her words would make Brian feel.

He rested his hand on Stefanie's shoulder. "There's a great difference between living alone and feeling lonely, Stefanie. I guess I've lived alone for so long, I never gave it much thought. But I suppose, to you, it must seem very lonely. Your house was always filled with people, and your mother decorated for every birthday and holiday. Frankly, I thought the groundhog statue on the porch was going a little overboard."

"I used to get embarrassed whenever friends came over and saw that silly thing." Her thoughts shaped a smile upon her lips. "And those turkey throw-pillows she uses in November are kind of dumb, too. But I'm used to it after all these years." She turned then and stared at Brian, her eyes revealing something sad and serious. "She forgot all about the Thanksgiving pillows until I reminded her. And it was Gramps and I who put up the tree this year. Everything's changed so much."

Rita held her breath, waiting for Brian to reply.

"Don't worry, Stef." Brian brushed the hair from her shoulder. "I'm going to do everything I can to help you and your mother. I want things to be like they used to be as much as you do."

Stefanie's eyes widened then narrowed in an expression Rita likened to lightning. The girl just scratched her shoulder where he had touched her, then rose from the floor to return to hanging tree ornaments.

There was a tense silence in the room. Rita reached for another statue to unwrap. She glanced at Brian, who wore a confused look on his face as he moved the statue of Mary beside the one of Joseph that Abuelita had set back on the table.

"Keep your hand out, Brian. No matter how many times she pushes it away." Abuelita's quiet voice held the confidence of age and experience. "She may hold it, may not. But she knows it's there."

Her great-grandmother's words were good advice, but Rita still felt disappointed by Brian's response. She finished unwrapping the last statue, the third king, dressed in a black cloak and dark green turban. Then she started gathering the various papers back into the box closest to her. Brian followed her example and started cleaning up the rest of the mess.

"Would either of you like some coffee?" Brian suggested, dusting his hands against his jeans after he replaced the lids on the boxes.

"Thank you," Abuelita said, nodding. "I would like coffee. Let Rita help you get everybody something to drink."

Her great-grandmother's suggestion took Rita by surprise, especially after she practically scolded Rita for wanting to help Brian with the dishes. At least this time Rita knew he'd accept her assistance. She knew he had too much respect for Abuelita to go against her wishes.

"Stefanie, do you want something to drink?" Rita asked.

"No, thanks." She stood back from the tree, studying her work, her hands sticking in the rear pockets of her blue jeans. "I think we need some tinsel now," she said as if she was alone. "And a few more ornaments on the left there."

Brian reached down to help Rita from the floor. She enjoyed the feel of his arm around her as she stood up, and offered him a smile of thanks.

The two of them returned to the kitchen.

"Well, I have a couple of flavors of decaf coffee."

"Whatever is easiest, Brian. Where can I find coffee cups?"

"The cabinet to the right of the stove."

She brought three cups and saucers down as Brian put coffee in a filter, filled a pot with water, and turned on an automatic brewer on the counter behind her. She turned around as Brian did.

Shyness seemed to envelop both of them as they stood staring at each other. Rita felt so awkward and nervous that she wanted to run out of the kitchen. She couldn't; her feet seemed glued to the floor. Glancing around, she said the first words that came to mind.

"That's a nice coffee pot." A hot blush streaked across her face.

He cleared his throat and glanced down at the floor. "It was a birthday gift from Iris."

"Oh. Has Iris called lately? How's she doing?"

Brian crossed his arms across his chest, relaxing his body against the counter behind him. "Stefanie calls her every night. I haven't spoken to her yet. But Stefanie tells me she's enjoying her visit with Linda and seeing New Mexico. I'm glad."

"I'm sure you are. But just the same, I bet you and Stefanie miss Iris a lot." Rita started to feel more relaxed about their freedom to talk alone. "Do you know when she's coming home?"

"Friday night. We'll drive down to Del Rio Saturday morning to spend Christmas with my parents and Mamá Josie. Usually, they came here and we all celebrated with Iris, Estevan, and Stefanie, but—well, my mother wanted something different this year. Iris, too, I think." His stare seemed to look past her, as if he was trying to discern something in the distance. "It seems so strange not to be celebrating Christmas in Iris's house. I wonder if it wouldn't help Iris more to do things like she always did before Estevan died."

"But even if you spend Christmas at Iris's house, things would be different. Nothing will ever be the same again, Brian."

Rita's memories of Christmases with her father, then without him, settled upon her like a thin shawl that couldn't keep the chill away. "When my father died, my mother insisted that nothing would change at Christmas. She still made tamales, we still had family come over and eat with us, and we opened gifts after midnight Mass, just like we had all our lives. But there was still this empty spot where my father used to stand, and fewer presents under the tree." Her throat tightened; her words escaped with a tremble. "No matter where you are, the memories exist. Only in time, they stop hurting so much."

With one step he touched her, his hands slipping up her arms, then pulling her close to him. Her head fit perfectly in the hollow between his shoulder and neck as her hands slid around him. His embrace was a welcome fire after a cold, lonely walk.

"I'm sorry about your father, Rita. But now I understand why you relate to Stefanie so well." He sighed. "Sometimes, I feel like I'm the only one who's stumbling in the dark trying to find the light switch."

She raised her head to look at him. "Stefanie and Iris are stumbling, too, Brian. But all of you have to move forward towards the light, no matter how painful it is. You can't just sit in the dark wishing things were the way they used to be."

His eyebrows lifted slightly. "I only wanted to make Stefanie feel better."

"It's not about feeling better, Brian. It's about being a friend and listening. Trying to let her know that you share her sad feelings. It's okay if you don't have an answer. She'll find her own answers. So will Iris."

"I hope so." He let her go and walked towards a drawer on the other side of the stove. He pulled it out and took three spoons from the white plastic tray which organized his silverware and cutlery. "I just want Iris and Stefanie to be happy. I spend my days solving computer problems, yet I can't seem to get a handle on their problems."

"Brian, maybe there isn't a true solution, just a matter of living with something different. Sometimes, don't computers need new programs?"

He closed the drawer then looked at her. "Yes, but with computers I usually know what to do. In this case, I feel very unqualified."

Rita took a step towards him. "You are very qualified to handle this, Brian. You love Iris and Stefanie. They are your family. What else do you need?"

He stepped closer, took her hands. His fingers wrapped through hers. "It seems that I need you, Rita. To help me find the way to that light switch I'm looking for."

His lips met hers in a kiss which inspired a new intimacy between them. He circled her body with his arms and continued kissing her.

I need you, Rita, swirled through her thoughts. Every time he said it, she felt her own insecurities fading away. No one ever made her feel so self-assured, and within that confidence she made a silent promise to be the person he needed, always friends at heart.

"I changed my mind. I think I want a—whoa! Sorry!" Stefanie's entrance into the kitchen was a surprise for everyone.

Rita abruptly broke off the kiss, expecting Brian to pull away and let her go. Instead, he kept his arm around her waist as they turned to face Stefanie, who stood at the doorway grinning.

"You didn't even wait until I put up the mistletoe! I was going to surprise you later." She put her hand over her mouth as she giggled.

"I don't think we need mistletoe, do we, Rita?" Although Brian's voice sounded nonchalant, she could see the dark blush across his face. She just smiled, amused at getting caught by Stefanie and by Brian's attempts to act like he had everything under control.

"I just came in to get a soda." Stefanie laughed her way to the refrigerator, took a can from the side rack on the door, then shut it. "And to tell you that the tree is finished."

"Let's see it," Brian said. He winked at Rita before he took her hand as they followed Stefanie back to the den.

The green tree was decorated with strands of tinsel, red, blue, and green ornaments, dozens of white blinking lights, and topped by a lighted star made of gold foil. The nativity scene was arranged upon a plain white tree skirt.

"It's beautiful, Stefanie," Brian told her.

"I think so, too." She stood by the fireplace, smiling at her creation. "It's just as pretty as the one in our living room. And I did that one, too."

He gently squeezed Rita's hand. "I think you have a talent for decorating, Stefanie. Maybe you need to think about interior design as a career."

"Can you specialize in Christmas decorations? That's all I can do, Uncle Brian."

"You don't know yet what you can or can't do. You've just gotten started." He gave his niece a smile. "Perhaps I need to send you through the rest of the house and see where else you can add a little Christmas cheer."

Stefanie shook her head. "No, this is enough. Just a pretty tree and Mamá Josie's manager scene. Now, it looks like a home."

"You must take a picture for Josie." Abuelita had been sitting quietly on the sofa. "She would like that."

"I have an even better idea," Brian said in an eager voice. "I'll get my camera and take a picture of her *comadre* by my Christmas tree. She would like that, too."

"And a picture of you and Rita together." Stefanie put her soda can on the coffee table. "I'll take that one!"

Rita and Brian exchanged a grin before Brian left the room to get his camera. When he returned, they took several pictures, including one Rita snapped of Brian and Stefanie by the tree. Then they enjoyed coffee and Abuelita's humorous stories about her favorite godson Charlie, Brian's grandfather.

After they had left Brian's house, Rita still felt the blessings of old memories and new friendships, and the promise of romantic love. During the drive home, she was warmed by her thoughts and feelings.

"Always when I visit Teresa, I worry about you, Rita," Abuelita said as they left Inspiration Hills and drove west towards their house. "But now you have Josie's family to watch over you while I'm gone."

Rita's thoughts turned away from tonight's memories and towards the upcoming holidays. Suddenly, it seemed like the car heater had stopped working. A cold chill shivered down her back.

Abuelita was preparing to leave town for two weeks. And Brian said he was taking Stefanie and Iris to Del Rio for Christmas. That left Rita to spend another holiday with her older sister Anna, her husband, Frank, and their four kids. This Christmas, Rita would not only miss Abuelita, but also would miss Brian. She fought hard not to give into her lonely feelings and managed a smile for her great-grandmother's peace of mind. "Don't worry about me. You just have a good Christmas with Tía."

"When I talk to *Comadre* Josie on Christmas, I'll tell her how happy I am our great-grandchildren are becoming such good friends."

Rita nodded, but she was thinking of Josie's family on a more personal level. She had grown accustomed to Stefanie's presence in the dress shop and to spending her evenings in Brian's company. When Iris returned from New Mexico, there would be no need for Stefanie to work with Rita, or for Brian to come by the shop on a daily basis. Where would Rita fit into their lives then?

As a seamstress, Rita knew that changes always seemed more complicated when she had no pattern, just a picture to follow. Right now, Rita's relationship with Brian and Stefanie suited all of them. Would Iris feel comfortable with Rita's new designs, or would Iris want to go back to the same old style of living? She could only hope that Iris was ready for something new, something different, too.

Chapter Five

The dress shop door slammed loudly, the wreath bells clanging in protest of the rough treatment.

The noise startled Rita so much she spilled hot coffee over her hand. Jumping up from the table behind the counter with a loud *"Ay yi yi,"* she spun around to see what caused the commotion.

She barely caught sight of Stefanie storming through the shop, making a direct line for the storeroom.

Rita raised her burned hand to her mouth and blew on the painful sting spreading over the back of her hand. She patted the reddened skin, wincing.

Abruptly, the shop door opened again, the bells hitting each other like rocks breaking glass. But this time Brian stood in the doorway, his hand still on the knob, looking around as if he had misplaced something and was angry because he couldn't find it.

"Is something wrong?" Rita asked, knowing it was a stupid question, but asking it nonetheless.

"Good morning, Rita." Brian frowned in Rita's direction then stepped inside the door and closed it behind him with a firm slam.

She paused before answering, regretting she ever put up the wreath with ten silver bells on the shop door. "Hello, Brian." Glancing down, she slowly clenched her fist, relaxed it, and winced each time. "When Stefanie came in, I spilled coffee on myself." She looked at Brian. "What's going on between you two?"

He sighed, shoving his hands deep into the pockets of his overcoat. "We've been arguing since breakfast.

First, she wanted to wear jeans and a sweater to work. I tried to tell her how inappropriate that would be, and suddenly it was war. She finally changed, but she's just furious with me. Can you believe it?"

"I don't enforce a dress code in my place of business," she said, irritated by her stinging hand and his snobby tone. "Do you think I should?"

Folding her arms across her chest, Rita gave him a hard stare. She was wearing new black jeans and her white sweater decorated with a green satin Christmas tree. Before she left for Brownsville this morning, Abuelita had told Rita how attractive she looked, even teasing her about wearing clothes that showed off her curves in order to catch Brian's attention. Evidently, Brian didn't approve of what she wore in the store.

"It's hard to wear a dress if I'm going to be crawling around a hemline trying to get it pinned up correctly," she told him.

Brian slipped his finger under his maroon tie and collar button of his white shirt. He tugged them away from his neck. "I'm sorry. I guess that didn't come out right. The argument wasn't really about Stefanie's clothes. She told me she was going skating right after work with her friend Angie."

Rita frowned at him. "Well, it would save time if Stefanie didn't have to change. I can't believe you made such an issue of her clothes, Brian."

"No, you don't understand." He stepped closer and she sensed his frustration growing. "She just told me she was going skating. She didn't ask permission, she just said 'I'm going skating after work.' What she was wearing to work this morning got tangled up in the whole argument."

"I told you that I have Mom's permission. I asked her last night on the phone." Stefanie entered the room again, her voice raised in the same frustrated anger Brian expressed. Dressed in a red dress, she was looking very pretty, despite the pinched look on her face. "She said I could go, Uncle Brian."

"She's in New Mexico, Stefanie. I'm the one who's responsible for you. I thought we all agreed that if you stayed with me, you had to follow my rules." Brian turned to face his niece.

"I'm not breaking any of your rules. I just want to go skating with my friends. Why can't I do that?" Stefanie looked at Rita.

Brian turned to look at Rita, too. "Angie's brother was going to pick up Stefanie here then get the other girls. I'm supposed to trust my niece to a teenage driver I never met?"

Feeling a slight throbbing in her hand, Rita looked down to see a thin blister starting to form on her thumb. "Why don't you just drive her there yourself, Brian? Stefanie, just tell your friends you'll meet them at the skating rink about six. Now, I need to run some cold water over my hand. Excuse me."

She walked out of the room and headed for the tiny bathroom in the rear of the store. She was holding her stinging hand under the running faucet when she sensed someone come up behind her.

"Are you all right?" Brian's voice was quiet, concerned.

"Well, considering I burned my hand this morning, got insulted about what I wear to work, and had to settle a ridiculous argument between two stubborn people, I guess I'm doing just fine." She regretted the tone in her voice, but she felt justified in unleashing some of her discomfort on the man who caused most of it.

He stepped around her, sliding his hand down her arm, until his fingers reached the spot where the cold water trickled on her hand. Ever so gently, he raised her hand up, looking over her shoulder as he examined it.

"Does it hurt much?"

"No—I'm—it's okay," she stammered.

"I'm sorry," he whispered. "This was all my fault." He kissed the sore spot ever so gently. "Will you forgive me?"

"Of course," she said, gulping down the words.

Brian pulled back to stare at her. Slowly, one eyebrow raised. "How do you feel about a trip to a skating rink tonight?"

"Stefanie doesn't really need a chaperone tonight, does she?" she asked, wanting him to give the teenager a little more freedom. Stefanie needed some time with friends her own age, and she and Brian needed time alone. She wasn't going to give in to her feelings for Brian until she had a more definite idea of where this relationship was taking them.

"I'll drop Stefanie off, then come pick you up. We'll go from there." When she nodded, he smiled. "And wear this sweater. I think it looks great on you."

"I thought so too until you made your comments a while ago."

"I'm sorry. I guess I said a lot of dumb things this morning. To you and to Stefanie. Are you sure you want to go out with someone like me?"

She heard the telephone ring in the front of the store.

Rita reached up and planted a kiss on his lips. "Go to work, Brian." She was glad when he laughed then moved out of the bathroom. She reached down, turned off the faucet, and went back into the store.

"Bye, Stef. See you this afternoon," Brian said as he passed his niece at the counter. She just waved to him since she was speaking on the telephone.

"That was Mrs. Díaz. She said she wants us to hold on to that turquoise dress with silver buttons. She'll be in tomorrow to buy it," Stefanie said, hanging up the telephone.

"Well, that's good news." Rita looked over at the wall where she and Stefanie had pinned up the colorful dress from Puebla only a few days ago. "I guess you better pick out a different one to put up here."

"Rita, I'm sorry Uncle Brian and I pulled you into our fight," Stefanie said, moving around the counter. "Is your hand okay?"

"I'll survive." She turned to look at Stefanie. "It all sounded like a pretty silly argument. Did you mother know that Angie's brother was doing the driving?"

"Well, not exactly. But, well—Angie and I thought it would be a good time for me to talk to him about—" She paused, and her hazel eyes searched Rita's face as if she was trying to find an answer there. Finally, she sighed. "I wanted to ask him if he would be my honor escort. For the *quinceañera*, you know?"

Rita placed her hand on Stefanie's arm. "Yes, I know. And I think your Uncle Brian would have understood, too, if you had told him the truth."

"If I called him at work and asked again, do you think he might change his mind?"

"Probably not. He has a good point, Stefanie. He doesn't know the boy, and you're still a little young to be alone with someone who's old enough to drive. How old is Angie's brother anyway?"

"Seventeen, but he's only a freshman."

She didn't want to ask why. Instead, she smiled at Stefanie. "I convinced your uncle to drop you off at the rink, and we'll come back for you later. That should give you plenty of time to ask Angie's brother to be your escort. I hope he says yes."

"Thanks, Rita. You're the best!" Stefanie said, then moved away to take down Mrs. Díaz's dress from the wall display.

❤ ❤ ❤ ❤ ❤

"Did Stefanie ever tell you why it was so important that she go skating with Angie and her brother tonight?" Rita asked Brian later than evening.

They sat inside an informal restaurant not far from the skating rink. It was a large place, with booths along the windows and dozens of chrome tables that took the customers back in time to the 1950's. Decorated with nostalgia bits on the walls and ceiling, there was also the shell of a red convertible which housed the salad bar and condiments for hamburgers, the main item on the menu.

"Stefanie wanted to ask Angie's brother if he would be her honor escort for the *quinceañera*. She thought if they were alone in the car a while, she could ask him. I guess she didn't want anyone around in case he turned her down."

"Why would he do that?" Brian's eyes shone with a defensive anger. "Stefanie's a great girl. She's pretty and smart. Any guy should feel privileged to stand with her at the party. If he says no, she's better off without him."

"And if he says no, what then? She might need your moral support, Brian."

He looked down at the table a moment then raised his gaze. "So, who escorted you when you celebrated your *quinceañera*?"

Laughter sugar-coated her memories of being fifteen, skinny and clumsy, and painfully shy around boys her age. "My cousin Roger," she told him. "Mom paid for his tuxedo, and I saw Uncle Gilbert slip him a twenty-dollar bill when the party was over. So much for my coming of age." She grinned at Brian. "What were you like at fifteen?"

His brown eyes rolled to the ceiling. "I try to block out those adolescent years as much as possible." He chuckled nonetheless. "People who are kind would call me a bookworm, but I'm sure others called me the class nerd. You know, serious, glasses, always reading. I spent more time in the computer lab or working on physics projects than playing sports or thinking about girls."

"And now?" she inquired, raising her eyebrows.

"Things aren't too different, except I like the way I am now. Well, for the most part. I like my job and I have hobbies I enjoy. And, then there's you." He rewarded her with a slow smile that made her feel very comfortable about the way things were progressing between them. "What about yourself? Here you are, a talented dress-maker, owner of a business. Did you picture your life turning out this way when you were fifteen?"

Brian reached across the table and took her hand in his. She shrugged her shoulders together as she tried to respond honestly to his questions. "I know I've always wanted to make my living as a seamstress. Sewing relaxes me, and I enjoy the creative part of my job. But I'm not very comfortable in the role of a business owner. Actually, since Bea left I've had to accept how very little I know about running a business."

"You know how to handle pushy landlords pretty well," Brian said, a slight chuckle lightening his words.

"I learned how to deal with bullies at school, that's all."

"So? What are your plans? Are you going to move your store?"

Rita's response was a look right into Brian's eyes, searching for the confidant she had desired the past few weeks. The pressure of his hand upon her own gave her a sense of security, a bridge of trust between them.

"What I want and what I can do seem like two different things right now," she told Brian. "I don't like the location of the shop and I definitely don't trust Mr. Arredondo. But most places demand two months' rent as deposit. And I'm not sure I can raise an extra thousand or two in the next two months."

"So, talk to a bank about a loan," he suggested.

"We tried that when we opened the shop, but we had no collateral. So Abuelita loaned us the money to start the shop. We were doing well in repaying her, too, but—well, when Bea eloped last month, she took most of the cash with her."

"Rita, have you talked to a lawyer? What about your partnership agreement?" His fingers tightened around her hand. "She can't just take off with the business' money that way."

Lowering her gaze, she tried to keep the burning sensation in her eyes from dissolving into tears. "There were no partnership papers. The only thing I ever signed was a lease with Mr. Arredondo. Our loan agreement with Abuelita was sealed with just a hug and a prayer. And I haven't told my great-grandmother that Bea took the money. She hasn't even mentioned that I didn't pay her this month. What can I say? I'm a great seamstress, but a lousy businesswoman." Her emotions crackled into her words then, and she pulled her hand from Brian's, using her fingers to conceal her trembling lips.

"Oh, Rita." He leaned over the table, his hand resting on her upper arm, rubbing it as he spoke. "What happened to you happens to a lot of business owners. Big corporations have employees, even CEOs, who rip off the company. And I'm sure they steal a lot more money than your partner did."

Nodding, struggling not to cry, she tried to take solace from his words. Yet she still felt responsible for not taking better steps to protect Abuelita's investment. Her heart twisted inside her, a bitter pain she could hardly stand.

"Rita, everything is not as bleak as it seems. It's not like you're ready to file bankruptcy papers, or your great-grandmother's going to get evicted from her house. You just need to establish some goals now. You must determine the next step carefully. It's your business. What do you want to do with it?"

His calm confidence pulled her away from hysteria and set her thoughts back on rational decisions she had to make if she wanted to salvage her business and repay Abuelita.

She took a cleansing breath then clasped her hands together on the table. "I'm just not sure where to start, Brian. Everything seems tangled up with something else. I need to work harder, so I can finish dresses, get paid, and save the money for a deposit. But there are only so many hours in a day. And if I sewed during all of them, when would I find time to look for a new location? And how do I keep up with extra or new customers who come into the store if I'm so busy sewing? And what if I manage to earn the rent money? I'll need more to decorate." She finally looked at Brian and shook her head over the obstacles that seemed to be in her way no matter where she turned. "I think just putting all my thoughts into words makes me feel more frustrated. I feel like I'm sewing with a machine that has no needle and thread."

He chuckled softly. She was surprised when she found herself smiling, too, in spite of everything she had just said.

"Actually, having Stefanie in the shop has been wonderful. Last week, I hardly wanted to go to work because the shop looked so 'junky,' as Stefanie put it. But she's cleaned up and moved things around so well. I feel proud of the place again. But I also look forward to work because I know that she'll be there. I hate being there with no one to talk to." Impulsively, she extended her hand and caressed Brian's cheek. "And I like having this chance to talk to somebody about my worries. Thank you for listening."

He turned his face into her hand, kissing her palm. "My pleasure."

Rita couldn't remember when she enjoyed herself more. They talked more about business, but moved into other topics of conversation. She and Brian discovered they shared a passion for old movies, especially Marx Brothers and John Wayne westerns, yet they both liked reading mysteries and watching Star Trek shows on television. They laughed over the list of song titles in the small jukebox on the table, and teased each other with crazy bits of trivia they knew about famous people.

After sharing one thick chocolate shake with two straws, they walked hand in hand outside the restaurant into a clear romantic night. The cold weather was a good reason to walk close beside each other and take the time for a warm hug once they were seated inside Brian's car.

They returned to the skating rink a little after nine.

Brian had just opened Rita's door and was helping her out of the car when they heard Stefanie's voice.

"Don't bother to get out, Rita. I'm ready to leave. Let's go." Stefanie appeared like a spirit from the cold night. She stood at the tail end of Brian's car, her face easily readable under the parking-lot lights.

Rita turned to look at Brian, willing him to say something to his niece. This time, she wasn't going to play go-between.

He frowned slightly, but adjusted his position towards Stefanie. "We don't have to leave right away. Don't you—"

"Everyone left. An hour ago. Can we go home now?" Her clipped tones and icy glare made her feelings very apparent. "This was a stupid idea."

"What was stupid? Brian asked her. "Going skating tonight, or asking Angie's brother to be your escort?"

The girl took one step back. Her eyes moved from Brian to Rita. "You told him? Now I really fell stupid!"

"Don't be angry with Rita. I'm glad she told me. But I wish you had trusted me enough to tell me about Angie's brother this morning." Brian moved towards Stefanie. "I know what it feels like to ask someone out. To feel scared they might not want to be with you as much as you want to be with them. To feel stupid because you took the chance and instead they just stomped on your heart and probably walked away laughing."

Stefanie turned and banged her fist on the truck of Brian's car. "He's a jerk! A great big jerk! And I hate him!"

Brian got to her as she began sobbing. He pulled her into his arms and hugged her tightly as she cried.

Rita watched them. She sympathized with Stefanie's tears, wishing there was a way to fast-forward through teenage heartaches and get right to wisdom and maturity. But there was no escaping the pangs of disappointment, especially in matters of the heart.

"Can we go home, please?" Stefanie pushed herself away and wiped her cheeks with her fingers. Her head was down, waves of dark hair hiding her face from them. "I just want to get out of here."

"Sure, Stefanie, let's go home." Brian turned back to the car and gave Rita a slight shrug.

When Stefanie passed her to get into the car, Rita gave the girl's arm a gentle squeeze. "I know it really hurts, Stefanie. I'm sorry Angie's brother turned you down."

Stefanie only nodded her head and got into the car.

The drive to Rita's home was empty of conversation. Everyone seemed to dwell within their own thoughts or listen to the soft rock music playing on the radio.

"Should I try to talk with her again?" Brian asked when they walked alone up the sidewalk towards Abuelita's house.

"What do you think?"

"Well, I think she's embarrassed, and talking about it would only make her feel worse."

"Then you have your answer, Brian. You let her know you understand her feelings. That may be enough, and if it's not, she'll let you know." Rita took her key from her purse as they reached the cement porch. She turned back towards Brian after she opened the front door. "You were a good listener when I needed one. Stefanie may not want to talk tonight, but she may need you later. Just do for her what you did for me. Be her friend."

Brian leaned close, then kissed her lips. "I can do that. For both of you."

A cozy warmth wrapped itself around her. A few days ago, none of them were friends. Now all of them had a chance to find missing pieces, to fill the blanks and the empty spaces.

She reached up to give him one more kiss. "I'll see you in the morning. Thanks for everything."

He smiled, whispered, "Good night," then turned back to the car where Stefanie sat waiting for him.

Rita stepped inside and closed and locked the front door. She moved to the living room window and watched Brian's car until he drove off. She knew the next few days would be difficult for Brian, Stefanie, and Iris. And that night before she went to sleep, she said a prayer for each of them.

Chapter Six

"Rita? Where are you?" Stefanie's voice echoed in the empty store.

"In the bathroom. The roof's leaking." Rita continued wiping the sponge mop over the vinyl floor around the toilet. A cold drop hit her scalp, and she glared at the ceiling.

When she awoke this Friday morning and heard the rain coming down, her first thoughts were worries over the leaky roof above the store's bathroom. She often left a bucket on top of the toilet just in case, but yesterday had been clear weather and she didn't see a need for the precaution. The past thirty minutes, mopping up the water, she promised herself to leave a bucket every night, no matter how much the sun was shining.

"Yuck! What a mess." Stefanie was standing near the bathroom door.

Rita squeezed the wet mop into a metal bucket. "You'd better pray the rain stops, or you'll have to balance the bucket in your lap when you use the toilet."

"Good morning, Rita. Can I be of some help?"

Despite her foul mood, Rita managed a little smile for Brian, who had come up behind Stefanie. As usual, he was meticulously dressed, today in a charcoal-gray suit with a colorful tie. She didn't think he should walk into his office splattered with mop water.

"Thanks, Brian, but I'll do it," Rita said, then noticed Stefanie was dressed in black pants and purple sweater. "Stefanie, you look nice today. That corner where you set all the plants leaks sometimes. You'd better move them back in front of the counter."

"It's too bad no one will buy them and just get them out of here," Stefanie replied, turning to leave. "I'm tired of moving them."

"I'll help you, Stefanie," Brian offered, and followed his niece into the other room.

Rita dumped the water into the toilet, flushed it, then closed the lid and set the bucket back on top, only to feel another wet plop on her head. She set her mind to call Mr. Arredondo again and complain about the leak. And if he didn't send a roofer, Rita would just hire one herself.

By the time she washed her hands, unrolled her pants legs, straightened her green sweater, and returned to the main part of the store, Brian and Stefanie had put the silk flower arrangements and the last four live plants around the counter. Rita didn't like their placement, but she didn't want anything ruined by a leak. If anyone did buy those flowers, she'd make a nice profit.

"I guess I'll be going now." Brian reached for a khaki-colored raincoat he had tossed over the counter and put it on.

"Thanks for your help," Rita and Stefanie said at the same time, then harmonized again with laughter.

Brian grinned then walked over to Rita and surprised her with swift kiss on the lips. "I pick up Iris about seven, but I thought I might drop by your place later. Would nine o'clock be too late for a visitor?"

She wondered what had happened to that shy man who could barely ask her out to the movies on Monday. Now he was kissing her good-bye before he left for work and asking if he could "drop by later."

"Nine o'clock would be fine, Brian," she said, pleased with the new dimensions in their relationship. "And drive carefully. The streets are slick."

He nodded, then turned to leave. "Bye, Stef. See you about five."

"Are you excited about your mother coming home?" Rita asked Stefanie once Brian had left the store.

The teenager was winding a yard of red ribbon back onto its spool. Rita had tossed it on the counter last night when one of Abuelita's friends came in just before closing, looking for new ribbons to decorate last year's Christmas wreaths.

It took two winds around the spool before Stefanie responded to Rita's question. "I've missed Mom. I'm glad she'll be home tonight. But I just don't know what to expect now." Suddenly, she looked up, hugging the spool of ribbon against her chest. "Rita, do you think I could keep working here?"

"Keep working here?" Rita's eyes widened with surprise.

Stefanie nodded. "For the rest of my holidays. I like it here."

"Well, I—I really don't know. I hadn't planned—"

"I know, I know. You were just doing this as a favor for Uncle Brian," Stefanie replied. She bent down to put the ribbon away in the box Rita kept under the counter. "There's no real reason I should keep working here."

Rita didn't want Stefanie to feel like a material scrap, tossed aside once a job was finished. The girl had been a capable assistant and good company the past few days. "Your Uncle Brian really didn't have anything to do with your working in the store. That was my decision, Stefanie. And you've done a wonderful job. Thank you very much." Rita patted her shoulder. "I'd like you to keep working here, but your mother might have other plans."

"Nothing but planning this stupid *quince* party. She told me last night on the phone that she wanted me to decide what kind of bouquet I wanted to hold." Stefanie groaned as her eyes filled with that same sad expression Rita saw last week. "I just don't want to do this. Now, more than ever."

"It means a lot to your mother, and to your Uncle Brian, that you celebrate your *quinceañera*. Trust me. It will be one of the most memorable days of your life."

"Oh, it's already memorable. I've asked two different boys to be my escort, and both said no. I told you last week that this *quince* is a stupid tradition. Why can't my mother just give me a gold watch for my fifteenth birthday? Why do I have to parade around in a fancy white dress, say prayers in church, then go to a party where the only men who will dance with me are relatives?"

"Stefanie, the quince celebration is not about a dress or the party. It's not about dancing with an escort. A *quinceañera* is just for you. It's one day in your life when you'll be the focus of everyone's love and best wishes. With all that positive encouragement, you'll feel like you're ready to take on anything life tosses your way. Just wait." Rita smiled, knowing how much she valued her own memories. "You know, a woman can have more than one wedding, but there will be only one time in your life for a *quinceañera*. Enjoy it."

Stefanie sighed loudly. "But I want a special escort, Rita. It will be so embarrassing if I have to be escorted by a cousin, or the son of one of my mother's friends. I'd like someone that I want to be with."

She remembered saying the same thing to her mother over ten years ago. Her mother had been very unsympathetic and insisted cousin Roger was "good enough."

Inspired by the recent developments in her relationship with Brian, and her growing affection for him, Rita offered optimism to his niece. "The celebration's still six weeks away. Someone special might come along when you least expect it."

"Yeah, like someone will come into the store today and buy all these flowers," Stefanie said, her voice thick with sarcasm.

So when a young woman entered the shop just before lunch and asked about buying the flowers, both Rita and Stefanie could hardly keep from laughing.

"Which arrangement do you like?" Rita asked the customer, an attractive black-haired woman who looked to be about Rita's age. Underneath her stylish raincoat, she wore a green dress and a red silk scarf decorated with Christmas symbols.

"Why, I like all the flowers. And the plants, too. They're for sale, right?" she asked, looking from Rita to Stefanie.

"Sure! I'll even help you carry them to your car." Stefanie responded with such enthusiastic spirit that Rita chuckled.

"Oh! But this isn't just a flower shop. Look at the beautiful dresses!" The woman positioned her black purse strap over her shoulder and made her way to the circular silver rack where Rita kept the dozen evening dresses she had sewn and others Beatrice had ordered from a catalog.

"If she buys a dress, do you think she'll still buy those flowers?" Stefanie spoke out of the corner of her mouth.

"Let's not be greedy. A sale is a sale," Rita whispered.

The customer was very complimentary when she discovered Rita had made most of the dresses on the rack, and insisted on taking time to try on two she liked, "Even though I promised my boss I'd only take thirty minutes for lunch today."

She decided on a silk blue dress with some of Abuelita's delicate embroidery decorating the scalloped edges around the neckline. And to Stefanie's obvious pleasure, the lady still wanted to buy all the plants and silk flower arrangements. "Only, I'm going to pay cash for the flowers and write you a check for the dress. Can I have two different receipts, please?"

When Stefanie mumbled, "You can have as many receipts as you want," Rita smiled.

Luckily, the drizzle subsided long enough for the flowers, plants, and the dress, in a plastic bag, to be loaded into the woman's olive-green car.

"That was a tight fit, but we got everything in," Stefanie said as she closed the door to the shop. "Now we can walk around in here!"

Rita smiled, continuing her work at the cash register. She removed the large bills the woman had given her and placed them in a special zippered bag she kept hidden under the ribbon box. It had been weeks since she had to worry about having too much cash in the register, but she enjoyed the satisfied feeling of making such a profitable sale, especially on such a dreary day. Best of all, she had sold the last of Beatrice's flowers. Now the place looked only like a dress shop.

"You know, Rita, now that we have the floor space, why don't we get that mannequin out of the storeroom and let me dress her up."

The girl's enthusiasm made Rita laugh. "Stefanie, it's not a mannequin. It's just a sewing figure. It doesn't even have a head or legs."

"I'll think of something. You'll see. It'll look great," Stefanie said, heading for the storeroom without a glance in Rita's direction.

❤ ❤ ❤ ❤ ❤

"Wow. Where did this lovely creature come?" Brian said as he came into the shop that evening and saw the figure in the red evening dress, a sequined, long sleeved creation which represented Bea's attention-grabbing taste in clothes.

"This is Stefanie's idea," Rita said, basting the taffeta slip together for Alyssa's wedding gown. "Now I just need a place to match my elegant mannequin. Think I should open a new shop in Alamo Heights?"

"I think the west side of San Antonio needs their own elegant shops. We'll just have to find you a place that doesn't leak," Brian answered.

Rita smiled to herself at Brian's use of the collective "we." Stefanie had used the same word today. Often. It was if they all had an investment in Rita's work, Rita's success, and especially Rita's happiness. She was glad to know they cared about her, and began to stop feeling as if she might be abandoned once Iris returned and the holidays were over.

"Oh, Uncle Brian, we've had the best day!" Stefanie came in from the side dressing room which she had been straightening up after four consecutive dress fittings. "We sold all the flowers and plants to one lady, who even bought a dress. Later, I put a peach-colored dress on Rita's sewing figure, and when Mrs. Guerra saw it—you know, the councilman's wife?—she decided she like it. And now, Rita's going to alter it for a special event she's attending. What do you think of my lady's dress now?"

"She looks beautiful, even if she doesn't have a head," Brian answered, and everyone laughed.

While Stefanie went off to get her coat, Brian knelt down on one knee by the spot where Rita sat sewing.

"I haven't seen Stefanie so happy in a long time. Iris will be very pleased."

"I hope so." Rita didn't look up from her stitching, but Brian's low voice and his closeness to her made her fumble with the needle. She felt a tiny prick, but kept right on with her work. "Stefanie's going to ask her mother if she can keep working during the rest of the holidays."

"I know. She told me that at breakfast. Do you want her to keep working here?" His hand brushed the hair back from her face.

Another pin prick! Rita fought to keep a steadier hand, but Brian's fingers against her cheek played havoc with her nerves. "I don't mind if she wants to keep working. Stefanie's my lucky charm. I made more money today than I have all week. I can afford a helper now."

"I'm glad. I know it's important that you get some extra cash right now. Perhaps once I get back, we can start looking at some other shops to rent."

"I'd like that." She smiled, knotted the thread, and reached for the scissors. "Finished. I should have the dress ready for Abuelita's beadwork by the time she gets back. I guess I'll cut the train out tonight and start working on that tomorrow. They don't require as much concentration, and since I'll be alone in the shop, interruptions won't matter." She snipped the white thread, stuck the needle back in the stuffed red tomato pin cushion by the machine, and finally looked at Brian.

His eyes sparkled from a smile which had appeared on his lips. Her heart seemed to vibrate with the momentum of a sewing machine, only she couldn't quite get her foot off the pedal to stop it. She wanted to say something, except she forgot what she was thinking about only moments before.

"Okay! Let's go. Hey, can we get something to eat before we go to the airport? I'm starving," Stefanie said, coming into the room just as Rita thought her rush of feelings for Brian might propel her into his arms.

But Stefanie's voice sent Brian up from the floor. He turned towards his niece. "I'm hungry, too. I missed all the goodies the secretaries brought for the Christmas party this afternoon. Rita, do you want to come eat with us?"

"Thanks, but I'm going to fix something quick at home and start working on the train for this wedding gown. I'll see you later tonight, Brian." She would give Brian one last opportunity to be alone with his godchild. There would be other dinners together; she knew that now.

Rita stood up and moved to where Stefanie stood, buttoning her jacket. "Don't leave without getting your pay."

"I won't. I have special plans for this money."

Rita smiled as she walked by Stefanie and went behind the counter. She opened the register and took a white envelope from under the drawer. "I would have added a Christmas bonus, but it's company policy that you work here a year first." She winked then laughed when Stefanie grinned. "You did a great job this week. Thank you very much."

"You know, when you first came up with this idea, I didn't like it at all," Stefanie said, taking the envelope from Rita. "I thought it would be boring, or I'd feel stupid because I knew nothing about sewing and stuff. But this job—it worked out okay after all."

Rita was surprised when Stefanie walked around the counter and hugged her. "Thanks for everything, Rita. And have a wonderful Christmas."

She thought she would cry, but she just hugged the girl closer. "Thanks," she whispered. "And Merry Christmas, too." Then she pulled back so she could smile at the girl. "Give Mama Josie and your grandparents an extra Christmas hug from me, will you?"

Stefanie nodded. "I promise."

Rita walked Stefanie and Brian to the door of the shop. "Give Iris my best. I'll see you later, Brian."

He placed his hand at her waist and kissed her. "It's already getting dark. Don't stay here too late, Rita."

"I won't." She was touched by his concern for her safety. "I'm just going to hang up Alyssa's wedding dress, then I'll be out the door myself." She gave him a kiss on his lips then sent him on his way. With his warning still echoing in her thoughts, she quickly hung up the gown and emptied the register. Today's profits were valuable, instrumental to her plans. She didn't want to take any chances of some thief taking anything away. Not now, when all her best dreams seemed within her grasp.

A short while later as Rita drove home, she felt an excited optimism she hadn't felt since she first opened the shop. The only thing that tarnished the glow of her feelings was coming into an empty house and not being able to share it all with her great-grandmother. But as she looked around the small living room with its antique paisley cushioned love seat and the cheerful Christmas tree in the corner, she remembered there was someone special with whom she could share her thoughts tonight. And perhaps, he might share his own thoughts, too, maybe even a word or two about his personal feelings for her.

Brian arrived after nine, and Rita invited him into the living room so they could talk. It was very romantic, since she let only the Christmas tree lights and the two small brass lamps on both sides of the love seat illuminate the room.

"How's Iris?" Rita asked, taking her place beside him on the love seat.

"She was very quiet. I'm sure she's just tired. She said there was a long delay in El Paso." He reached his arm across the back of the seat and let it settle around Rita's shoulders. "And she told Stefanie that Linda would definitely come for the *quinceañera*. Stefanie didn't say much after that."

"Doesn't she like Linda?" Rita asked, remembering the conversation during the anniversary party.

"Linda is Stefanie's godmother, although she hasn't seen Stefanie since she was born. But they've talked on the phone and Linda's always remembered Stefanie's birthday and other special occasions. Actually, I thought Stefanie would be glad to hear the news. But it didn't seem that way in the car."

"Brian, has Stefanie talked to you much about the *quinceañera*?" She rested her arm on top of his and let her hand slide back and forth along his shoulder. His black sweatshirt, with the Spurs basketball team logo embroidered in silver, was cottony soft under her fingers.

"This week we talked a lot about her work in the shop." Brian's lips lifted into a smile. "And you. We talked a lot about you, Rita."

A wisp of fire seemed to appear just below the surface of her face. "You two talked about me?"

"Oh, yes. You're our favorite topic. And one we never disagree about. Stefanie thinks you're great. I think so, too." His hand curved around her shoulder, pressing her body in his direction.

She responded by circling her arms around him and lifting her face to kiss him. It was his gentleness, his willingness to take things between them slowly, that she treasured as a precious jewel.

When he released her from his kiss, her head dropped to his shoulder, and he held her, resting his cheek against her head.

"I've never asked you, Rita, but is there someone else in your life? Do I have any competition?"

"There hasn't been anyone for a long time," she answered, her voice almost drowsy from the warmth she was feeling. "And the one that was, decided to marry someone else. I made the baptism dress for their baby last year."

"That was nice of you."

"He thought he should get a discount. I charged him full price."

"Good for you." Brian chuckled, hugging her closer to him. After a while, he said, "Aren't you going to ask me about my personal life?"

Now it was Rita's turn to chuckle. "Stefanie said she's never seen you with a girl friend before. If you've never taken anyone to meet your family, I probably don't have to worry."

"Rita, would you like to come to Del Rio with us?"

His question was so unexpected she couldn't answer right away. She was flattered that he wanted his parents to know her better, but she would feel like an intruder, especially this first Christmas without Estevan.

"Thank you, Brian, but I just couldn't leave now. I have appointments set up with customers tomorrow and on the day after Christmas."

"But what will you do on Christmas Day? I don't want you to be alone," he answered, his voice sounding very somber.

Straightening up, Rita looked into Brian's concerned expression. "I won't be alone on Christmas, Brian. Christmas Eve I usually go to midnight Mass with my sister Debra and her boys. On Christmas Day, my sister Anna cooks lunch, and all of us get together there. She's got one of those conference telephones, so we all get to talk with Mom as if she's sitting right in the room with us. It's a lot of fun." She leaned closer and kissed him. "But I'll miss you. I know that."

"I'll miss you, too, Rita." His fingers moved through her hair. "Maybe next year you can come with me to Del Rio."

"Maybe next year, Iris will want everyone to come back to her house for Christmas again, and you'll stay in San Antonio."

His eyes met hers. "I like your optimism, Rita. It makes me feel less afraid about this Christmas." A frown appeared. "I sound like a coward."

She smoothed his forehead with her fingertips. "No, you don't. If you don't know what to expect, you just imagine the worst. It's only natural. Frankly, if I were in your shoes, I'd be afraid, too."

Brian sighed. Then he started talking about his experiences with his brother-in-law. Estevan Bonilla seemed to have been a "superman" to the Esparza family. He told Rita that the twenty-years age difference between Estevan and Iris made him seem wiser, more thoughtful towards all of them. Brian's parents treated Estevan more like a personal friend than a son-in-law, and he had treated Iris as his most precious treasure.

Stefanie was his little doll, and he had always wanted the world to adore her as he did.

Rita listened; she saw the glow of hero worship in Brian's eyes when he spoke about Estevan: loving husband, successful businessman. She understood why it meant so much to Brian that he honor his brother-in-law's wishes for Stefanie's *quinceañera*, and why he was trying so hard to fill in the gaps Estevan's sudden death had left in his family's lives.

She had no idea how long they sat on the love seat talking, sharing confidences, and asking for nothing more than understanding. But when they both grew quiet, sitting together with their arms around each other, Rita knew she was falling in love with Brian.

Later, when they stood together near the front door offering good-byes and Christmas wishes, Rita wanted to let him know how she felt.

She clung to the front of his jacket as he kissed her with a touch of urgency, as if they both needed this last kiss to sustain them during the days they would be apart.

"I'll call you when I get back into town," Brian promised.

"Have a safe trip." She gazed into his eyes and suddenly knew she had to take a chance and say, "Brian, I love you."

He kissed her lips with a gentle touch. "Your love is the best Christmas gift I've ever received. And just so you know—I love you, too."

They kissed again. Rita felt as if she had just been given the most priceless treasure in the world to cherish and protect.

And after Brian left, Rita sat in Abuelita's oak rocking chair, staring at the Christmas tree. It was decorated with blue, green, and red blinking lights, gold tinsel, and an unusual variety of both homemade and store-bought ornaments. On top of the tree was an angel with a tiny china face, brown doll's hair, two wings trimmed in gold rick-rack, and wearing a white chiffon gown.

"Abuelita, why don't you have a star on top of your tree like the stores do?" Rita had asked her great-grandmother when she was five. "Why did you make an angel for your tree?"

"Because the angels watch over those I love," Abuelita had answered.

Staring up at the angel this night, Rita noticed its wings were frayed, its hair had lost its sheen, and the gown had yellowed. But Rita's faith in the angels still burned strong and bright.

"Little angel," she murmured. "Take care of my Brian. It's the only thing I want for Christmas."

♥ ♥ ♥ ♥ ♥

Rita pressed the last wads of used wrapping paper into the trashcan in the kitchen then sighed. An empty house seemed like a luxury after the past two days in her sisters' homes. She loved her nieces and nephews, but the noisy chaos was something she was glad to leave behind. Santa Claus had given each child some kind of electronic toy with a siren or beeping sound and lots of batteries. The books she had carefully chosen were used for target practice or as shields in battle games. Her sisters agreed that the books had lots of pretty pictures, and some night soon, Rita should baby-sit and read them all to the children.

She left the kitchen, taking her cup of hot *canela* off the counter, and returned to the living room. Sitting in the rocking chair, comfortable in her new velour robe, a Christmas gift from Abuelita, and a flannel nightshirt form her sister Anna, Rita relaxed in the solitude.

What was Brian doing now, she wondered. How had he passed the day with his parents, great-grandmother, Iris and Stefanie? Had he told his family about their relationship? Had Stefanie spoken about her work at the shop?

As usual, Anna and Debra had inquired about Rita's personal life while they did dishes after lunch, but Rita felt uneasy discussing Brian with her sisters. She did tell them she had gone out with Josie Esparza's great-grandson and that his niece was working in the shop during the holidays. Immediately they demanded to know all the intimate details about this new relationship, but she sidestepped their questions by talking about the movie she had seen and the restaurant where she had eaten rather than focusing on the man who took her there.

The telephone rang, breaking into Rita's thoughts. After setting her tea cup down, she went to answer the hallway telephone.

"Hello, Rita. Merry Christmas."

"Stefanie? Hello. Merry Christmas."

"My mother said I could work the rest of the week if you needed me." The teenager's voice sounded very anxious. "We're driving back tomorrow, but I can be there for work on Wednesday morning. Is that okay?"

"Stefanie, that's fine. I'm looking forward to you coming back to work. I missed you Saturday and Monday."

"Did you really?"

"Honestly, I did. You organized the store so well, I don't know where half my things are." Rita laughed, mostly at herself.

Stefanie responded with laughter, too. "I'll help you find all your things when I get back. Uncle Brian is with me, Rita. He wants to talk to you. I'll see you Wednesday. Bye."

Before she knew it, Brian's deep voice filled the telephone lines between them. "Merry Christmas, Rita."

Her heart seemed to leap between beats. "Brian, Merry Christmas. I was just sitting here thinking about you—and your family, too. How is everything?"

"Things are sad, like I expected, but Mama Josie started telling old stories and cheered things up. She always does. A lot like your *abuelita* manages to do when she's around. Did you have a nice Christmas, Rita?"

She laughed. "It's nice to be in a quiet house. I like my role as *tía* because I can play with the children, but then I can leave when they get cranky or won't stop crying."

"I remember feeling that way when Stefanie was little. You know, I'm glad Stefanie and I wanted to call you tonight. I wanted to ask if you have any plans for New Year's Eve."

"New Year's Eve? No, why?"

"My company is hosting a party for both employees and clients, and I hoped you would come with me."

"I'd love to, Brian. Thank you for asking." She spoke calmly, but inside she whooped with excitement.

"I'll call you when I get back to town. We'll have to start making our own plans now that Stefanie's back with Iris."

"You know where to find me. Here or at the shop."

"I love you, Rita. Merry Christmas."

"Merry Christmas, Brian. I love you, too."

Chapter Seven

Rita was behind the glass counter searching through the tray of buttons for some tiny pearl ones when Stefanie arrived for work Wednesday morning. She was followed into the store by her mother. Iris Bonilla's face wore the pale color of someone who had been under a lot of emotional strain lately. Even Stefanie seemed different, much like the troubled girl who came into the store a week ago with little self-confidence and a lot of anger.

"Good morning," Rita said with a pleasant smile. "Hello, Iris. I hope you enjoyed your trip to New Mexico."

"It was very nice, thank you," Iris said as if she had given the answer many times. She turned and looked around the shop as if she had never seen it before. "Things look different around here. You've cleaned up the place, haven't you?"

"I told you, we sold all the plants and the flowers," Stefanie said, huffed out a sigh, then walked towards the back room, taking her jacket off.

"Stefanie's been a wonderful help to me," Rita said to Iris, admiring the way Iris wore a simple black sweater and skirt with a colorful woven belt that made the ensemble look so attractive. Being around Stefanie's pretty clothes, Brian's professional appearance, and Iris's smart fashions, was starting to make Rita self-conscious about her own unexciting wardrobe.

"I'm glad Stefanie didn't make trouble for you or Brian." Iris wandered over to the rack and began browsing through the evening dresses.

"Rita, what are you looking for?" Stefanie asked, returning from the back room.

"Oh, those cards with the tiny pearl buttons that I use on the baptismal gowns."

"There wasn't enough room in the tray, so I took all the white buttons and put them in a box beside the bolts of white fabric. Sorry. It made sense to me to keep all the white stuff together."

Rita patted the girl on the shoulder. "It makes sense to me, too. I need six tiny buttons. Pick out something pretty. Then, I'm going to teach you how to place and sew them on for me."

Stefanie's eyes widened. "Me? I'm going to sew on the buttons?"

"Don't you think you can?" Rita raised an eyebrow.

The girl gave a sideways glance at her mother before she nodded. "Sure I can. I'll get the buttons."

"Good." Rita smiled and watched Stefanie walk into the other room. She turned then to Iris who was still pushing hangers across the rack, but didn't seem to be looking at the dresses at all. "Iris, Brian usually picked Stefanie up about five, but you're welcome to pick her up when it's convenient for you."

"I'm sure she won't want to leave before five. She seems happier to be here with you," Iris answered, her voice so frigid Rita almost shivered. Iris abandoned the dresses and turned to stare out the store's front window.

Rita's stomach tightened like a fist as she watched the beautiful young widow staring at the cemetery. Would Iris spend the day there crying? Had nothing changed for her? Rita thought of Brian, how she loved him, and how she cared about Stefanie. She wanted to reach out to Iris, for their sakes, and bring her into their new circle of friendship. But how?

Her glance fell upon the rack of evening dresses, and she thought about the New year's Eve party. Last night her reunion with Brian had been filled with loving words and sweet kisses. He seemed so excited about taking her to the party. She realized again that she didn't know what to choose for the evening. She spent her days creating beautiful dresses for others, but never imagined herself ever wearing one.

"Iris, could I ask you something?" Rita said, trying to draw Iris's attention away from the depressing view across the street.

It seemed as if it took great effort for Iris to turn her pale face and glassy hazel eyes in Rita's direction. But she did, and slowly shifted her body around, too. "Yes?"

"Brian invited me to his company's New Year's Eve party—and well, it's a dressy occasion. Have you any suggestions on what I should wear?" Rita gave Brian's sister a helpless shrug.

Suddenly, the door to the shop opened, wreath bells jingling. Rita's first appointment had arrived, a slim black-haired woman who was one of Alyssa Guerra's bridesmaids.

"Hi. I'm Mildred Rodríguez. I'm supposed to get fitted for a bridesmaid's dress."

"Hello, Mildred. I'm Rita," she said as Stefanie returned with a card of buttons in her hand. Then, the telephone rang.

"I'll get that. Take care of your customer," Stefanie said, reaching for the phone. "Mom, why are *you* still here?"

Rita tried to nudge Stefanie in the ribs, but the girl moved out of range. Instead, she gave Iris a little smile. "I won't be long, Iris. Why don't you stay awhile so we can talk? I'd really appreciate your ideas about a dress for Brian's party."

Iris merely nodded and resumed her position staring out the window.

It was hard for Rita to concentrate during Mildred's fitting. She kept listening for some conversation from the front of the shop, but heard nothing except for the sounds of movement. Had Stefanie found something to do, or was Iris pacing the store like a caged animal?

"Ouch!" Mildred cried suddenly.

"Oh, I'm so sorry." Rita quickly pulled out the pin she had just stuck into Mildred's side.

The young woman left a short while later, and Rita stayed back in the dressing room to hang up the rose pink bridesmaid dress. When she returned to the front of the shop, she was surprised to see a different dress on the sewing figure. It, too, was one of Bea's selections, a short, black, crepe evening dress that had arrived the day after Bea eloped. C.O.D. of course.

"Didn't like the red dress, huh?" Rita teased Stefanie, who was still writing up Mildred's order in the deposit book.

"Don't you think this was my idea," the girl answered with traces of anger in her voice. "My mother changed the dress on your figure."

"I wanted to see how this dress really looks. You can't tell anything from a hanger," Iris said. She stood near the door, staring at the figure through narrowed eyes as if she was trying to make a decision about something. One delicate finger tapped her chin. "It looks big, but then you're a seamstress. Raise the hem, though. I bet you have nice legs."

Something between embarrassment and surprise stunned Rita into silence. Was Iris serious? Did she expect Rita to wear such a provocative dress? The off-the-shoulder dress draped low in the back, almost to the waistline. And the style mandated a curve-hugging fit, especially across the bodice and hips.

"You think I should wear this dress?" Rita said, rubbing her throat, which had suddenly gone dry. "My ex-partner ordered it for herself, but she left town. I just figured someone else would buy it."

"Go try it on, Rita. Let's see how it looks on you." Iris walked to the figure and ran her fingers down the side of the dress. "This material feels gorgeous." She was actually smiling.

"Rita, you'll knock Uncle Brian over if he sees you in something like that," Stefanie said, catching a bit of her mother's enthusiasm.

Rita looked from Iris to Stefanie then sighed. She took the black dress off the sewing figure and soon found herself trying on an outfit in her own dressing room.

For a long time, Rita stared into the mirror, seeing an attractive stranger; a tall slender woman with shiny black hair and large brown eyes watching herself turn from side to side in an extremely sexy black dress. No one had seen so much of her shoulders and back since she wore a bathing suit last summer.

"Iris, do you really think—"

"Rita, it'll be perfect once you fit it to your body and raise the hem. Simple black shoes with a high heel. You can get away with it because Brian's so tall." Iris walked around her as she shared her ideas. "And I have a pair of diamond earrings that you can borrow."

Stefanie let out a wolf whistle as she entered the side room. "Rita, I hardly recognize you."

"I hardly recognize myself." Rita stared into the mirror, still unsure about her own reflection, yet admiring the impression she made. She began to note the places which needed alteration for a better fit.

"And think of the advertising for your business," Iris said with a happy lilt to her voice. "If anyone asks you where you got this beautiful dress, you tell them 'Rita's Dress Shop, of course' as if there's no other place to shop in San Antonio but your store."

Rita giggled, enjoying the attention. "I guess I can do a little bragging while I'm out with your brother."

"You need to do more self-promotion," Iris said, straightening out the back of the dress. "You should always wear clothes you've sewn yourself while you are in the shop, too. Make some simple tops and pants in flashy colors to draw attention to your work. I know that employees in the department stores and nicer dress shops are always encouraged to wear clothes that are sold by the place. That's why they give employees such good discounts."

Iris's suggestions made a lot of sense. Rita realized she had taken her casual look straight from working in Abuelita's spare bedroom into the shop where new customers entered every day. What kind of professional image did she give when she always wore jeans and sweaters? Granted, she couldn't wear her wedding gowns around town, but she could wear more dresses she sewed and make a few blouses for herself that would draw attention to her talents and skills as a seamstress.

Suddenly, she wondered why Bea had always insisted that Rita sew in the back room. Was it really just the noise of the sewing machine that bothered Bea? Or did she think Rita didn't belong up front with customers? Unlike Iris, who seemed to have Rita's best interests in mind when she made suggestions, Bea often made Rita feel ignorant, even stupid. That morning Rita discovered Bea had taken the money, she had never felt worse. It wasn't until Brian told her that even important executives steal money from their businesses that she felt she wasn't the only one who had been betrayed by a so-called business partner.

"Rita, are you okay? You have a funny look on your face."

Stefanie's concerned voice pulled Rita out of her troubling thoughts. Blinking at this different impression of herself in the mirror, Rita placed a confident smile on her face.

"I'm just fine, Stefanie. Bring me the bowl of pins, will you? You and your mother can help me fit this dress. And Iris, thank you. I will borrow your diamond earrings."

Taking this dress for herself was only a start. She would make positive changes in every phase of her life until everything fit just the way she wanted. This was Rita's resolution for the new year.

❤ ❤ ❤ ❤ ❤

"Why doesn't Mom just go home?" Stefanie grumbled just loud enough for Rita to hear.

Rita stood behind the girl, fastening the hook and eye just above the zipper of Stefanie's *quinceañera* gown. "You can't blame her for wanting to see you in this dress before she takes it home."

"I feel stupid. What if a customer comes in?"

"That's what I said an hour ago when I stood in my red socks wearing a sexy black dress and both of you just laughed. Now, it's your turn."

"I was looking in your display case, but you don't sell white-lace gloves, do you, Rita?" Iris inquired, entering the side room.

"Gloves? You've got to be kidding." Stefanie's glare bounced off the mirror and went straight towards her mother. "Rita, have you ever heard anything so dumb?"

Rita pressed her hand against Stefanie's arm. "I don't carry gloves, Iris. But I really don't think Stefanie will need them. The dress is long sleeved, and she has pretty hands."

"Oh, Baby, you look so beautiful. Turn around so I can see you." Iris gently turned Stefanie by her shoulders. Then Iris stepped back, clasping her hands together at her heart. "You look like such a young lady. My baby girl is all grown up. With your hair up, and wearing the diamond tiara your father bought for your *quinceañera*, you'll look just like a princess."

Stefanie muttered something, then turned her back on her mother. "Can I change now, please?"

Just then, the shop door opened with the sound of bells and a call, "Rita, are you here?"

"Sounds like Mrs. Díaz," Rita said, and headed into the other room. She smiled at one of her best customers as well as the husky teenage boy who accompanied her. "Hello, Mrs. Díaz. Did you have a nice Christmas?"

"Yes. And I'm so sorry I haven't been here to pick up the dress I asked Stefanie to save it for me last week. Do you still have it?"

"We do, but I'm not sure where Stefanie saved it," Rita said, and turned her attention to the boy. "Is this your son?"

"Yes. This is Nicholas. Nicholas, this is Rita Navarro."

"Hello," he mumbled, his dark eyes shifting to the store carpet. He had dark brown hair like his mother and was a head taller than she was.

"Hello, Nicholas," Rita said. "It's nice to meet you." She turned then and called out, "Stefanie, where did you leave that dress we're holding for Mrs. Díaz?"

"Oh! I left it hanging in here. I'll get it," she called back before appearing in the main part of the store, like a mirage of white silk and lace, carrying the turquoise dress draped over one arm.

"Oh, my, aren't you lovely?" Mrs. Díaz exclaimed when she saw Stefanie. "This must be for your *quinceañera*. Rita, you did a beautiful job."

"Thank you," she said, turning to smile at Stefanie. But the girl was staring in wide-eyed surprise at Nicholas.

"Aren't you Nicky Díaz? Didn't we go to kindergarten together?"

The boy frowned, then his face opened with a devilish expression. "Yeah. You're Steffie Bonilla. We used to call you 'Don't-Get-Me-Dirty-Steffie.' You wore those lacy dresses to school everyday. And you're still wearing fancy dresses when I see you."

"Nicholas! Be nice. This is Stefanie's gown for her *quinceañera*. It's supposed to be fancy." Mrs. Díaz looked very embarrassed, especially when Iris entered the room just in time to hear Nicholas's comments.

"She looks like she's going to get married," the boy replied.

Mrs. Díaz aimed an apologetic look in Stefanie's and Iris's direction. "Forgive my son. We aren't a family to keep up with the old customs. There aren't any girls we know who celebrated *quinceañera*. Too much emphasis on American customs, I guess. But I'm glad to see Stefanie celebrating her fifteenth birthday in such a traditional way."

"That's a birthday dress? Gee, Mom, I only got a pair of tennis shoes for my fifteenth birthday," Nicholas said, with a little grin on his lips.

Rita liked the boy. He seemed to have more confidence than other boys his age. His teasing seemed friendly, especially when he gave Stefanie an admiring look.

"You do look very pretty in that dress, Stefanie."

"Thank you," she said, her gaze lowered by shyness. She gave Rita Mrs. Díaz's dress. "Here. I need to change now." And she turned to leave the room.

Rita quickly made introductions, surprised that the children had known one another yet the two mothers had never met. They exchanged a few polite "Do you know so-and-so's" while Rita rung up the sale. Stefanie returned to the room just as Mrs. Díaz and Nicholas were getting ready to leave.

"Mrs. Bonilla, we're having a few friends over for New Year's Eve supper. Why don't you and Stefanie join us? We usually play bunco, and we could use two more players to make a fourth table."

"Thank you—but, I'll have to let you know—" Iris said, her voice trembling with indecision. "Stefanie and I haven't been socializing much since my husband passed away."

"I understand. But you'd both be among friends. I hope you'll come by. Our number's in the book. Call me."

Nicholas gently punched Stefanie in the shoulder. "If you come, you don't have to wear a fancy dress, Steffie."

"Do you still like to eat ketchup and pickle sandwiches, Nicky?" she asked in a dry tone of voice.

"Still my favorite!" He raised his brown eyebrows rapidly up and down, and Stefanie giggled.

"If you come to our house on New Year's, I'll make a special pickle and ketchup sandwich just for you," the boy told her, then laughed.

"Come on, Nicholas. Good-bye, Rita. Mrs. Bonilla, I hope to see you and Stefanie on New Year's Eve. I know the children would enjoy getting re-acquainted." Mrs. Díaz waved and left the store, the echo of silver bells filling the place.

"Nicholas Díaz seems like a nice boy," Rita told Stefanie.

The girl stared through the glass pane of the front door after Mrs. Díaz and her son.

"He could always make me laugh," she said. "How weird to see him now. Here, of all places." She turned to look at her mother. "Do you think we could go to their house on New Year's?"

Iris's face started to whiten again. "I don't know, Baby."

"I'm not a baby. And what else'll we do on New Year's Eve if we don't go? Uncle Brian won't come over. He's going out with Rita. Are we just going to sit alone in the house? Gee, Mom. What fun!" Stefanie tossed her hands into the air then stomped towards the bathroom.

They both heard the door slam behind her.

"I—I just don't know what to say—" Iris glanced at Rita then lowered her eyes. "This is hard for me. Going places without Estevan. Enjoying things without him. I don't deserve this now." She sighed then walked towards the counter and picked up her narrow black purse. "I'll be back to pick up Stefanie at five, Rita. Good-bye."

"Iris, wait—" Rita reached out her hand towards Iris, but she had opened the door quickly and shut it firmly behind her.

The sigh Rita expressed didn't release the anguish she felt on Iris's behalf. She rubbed her forehead, but it was her heart that truly ached. She recalled feeling torn in half by guilt when she wanted to enjoy herself after her father died. It took many months, but Abuelita had helped Rita to understand that having a little fun often balanced out those inevitable sad moments.

But in this case, Rita felt she must ask Brian to speak to Iris. Stefanie had said that her mother depended on Brian, relied on his opinion. He had been the one who encouraged Iris to go to the anniversary party and to proceed with the *quince* celebration as planned. And since he already had plans for New Year's Eve, perhaps he could persuade Iris to attend Mrs. Díaz's friendly gathering. Especially if Rita let Brian know that Stefanie had just become re-acquainted with Nicky Díaz, a boy who, in her own words, "makes me laugh."

Just then, Stefanie peered out from behind the bathroom door. "Is my mother gone now?"

Rita crossed her arms and gave the teen an irritated look. "Really, Stefanie! You've been rude to your mother all morning."

"She treats me like a little kid," Stefanie said, coming towards the spot where Rita stood. "It makes me mad."

"Have you told her that? I mean, explained your feelings, not just stomped around like a spoiled child."

"How can I talk to her? She's off in her own little world. Some sad, lonely place where I don't want to live."

Rita reached out and took Stefanie's hands. "Then open the door into your world, Stefanie. Don't shut her out. Invite her in. She loves you very much."

The teen gave a little shrug, then sighed.

She gently squeezed Stefanie's hands. "Come on. Let me show you how to put the buttons on baby Vicente's baptismal gown. His *madrina* will be here this afternoon to pick it up."

Rita sent Stefanie out to buy them both hamburgers for lunch so Rita could call Brian's office. She was relieved he was there to take her call. Briefly, she explained about Mrs. Díaz's party, trying to be fair when she presented both Iris's and Stefanie's feelings about the invitation. Brian promised to talk to Iris, and, like Rita, hoped that if Stefanie and Nicholas became friends again, maybe there would be a special escort for the *quinceañera* after all.

When Iris arrived about five, she said very little to Stefanie, only that Brian was taking them out to supper. Stefanie immediately invited Rita to join them, but Rita created an excuse to give Brian his chance to speak to them alone.

"Iris is still very uncertain, but I think she'll go to the party for Stefanie's sake," Brian told Rita later that night when he telephoned. "I hadn't said anything about Angie's brother, hoping that Stefanie would confide in her mother. But she didn't, so I decided to tell Iris about it when Stefanie wasn't in the room. I hope I did the right thing."

"Just remember what it took for you and Stefanie to become friends. Iris and Stefanie just need to learn to depend on each other, not you, to solve their problems."

"Just like I depended on you to help me with Stefanie?" His voice had heavy undertones. "Is that why you wouldn't come to dinner when Stefanie asked you? So I couldn't get you to play mediator?"

"I want to get to know your sister better, Brian. And I'd like to become her friend, too. But I can't be the problem solver. She has to be the one to make decisions. She has to learn to trust her own judgment."

"Iris and Stefanie told me you're wearing a very special dress to my company party," Brian said in a sudden change of subject. "But they wouldn't tell me what it looked like."

"I don't want to spoil the surprise," Rita answered.

"Well, do I have to wait until New Year's to see you again?"

Rita giggled. "Of course not. It's just the dress that's waiting for New Year's. My regular clothes will go out with you anytime."

Brian laughed happily. "Then let's talk about tomorrow night."

❤ ❤ ❤ ❤ ❤

"I'm really sorry about the detour," Brian said the next night as they drove towards Iris's house instead of directly to the restaurant where they were supposed to have dinner. "Iris was so upset. I'm worried about her."

"Brian, you should—"

"I guess I'll call the guy back in the morning and order new invitations for the *quinceañera*." Brian sighed. "How could I have forgotten to tell the printer not to use Mr. and Mrs.?"

"Brian, Iris can call the printer herself. You don't need to do this for her," Rita said, trying to keep Brian from falling back into his role as protector.

He had just stopped his car for a red light, so he turned to look at Rita. The cold darkness in his eyes showed that he didn't like what she had said. But she didn't let the stiff lines of his body or the tightening of his fingers around the steering wheel change her opinion.

"Brian, you just can't do everything for Iris, especially when it comes to the *quince*. You should be there for support, yes. But you need to let Iris make decisions and do what needs to be done by herself. After all, you have your own life to lead. Are you going to run to her side every time she has to face something that's upsetting?"

"If I didn't know you better, I'd think you want me to just ignore Iris's feelings and focus all of my attention on you."

"Don't be ridiculous. I'm glad you love your sister. And she's lucky to have your support. But Iris has to move on. How can Stefanie learn to deal with the bad news in life if Iris doesn't show her how?"

The loud beep of a car horn behind them forced Brian's attention back to driving. The light had turned green, and he stepped on the ignition so abruptly the tires squealed.

Rita turned to look out the window into darkened streets. Was she jealous of the attention which Brian gave Iris? Perhaps it was just a fear that if Brian had to make a choice, he wouldn't choose her. She felt the clammy breath of insecurity at her back and shuddered, hoping the movement would send the ghosts packing.

"Iris and I've always been close, despite the age difference." His quiet voice drifted towards her. "Iris looks so delicate, I've always felt a need to protect her. I didn't worry so much when she was married to Estevan, but since he died, I worry about her all the time. I keep remembering the way Iris was, so popular; loved by everyone. If I have a chance to make her happy even for only a moment, I just have to take it. I hope you understand, Rita."

"I just think you should encourage Iris to call and order new invitations. She needs to take this step, no matter how small it is."

"I guess a lot will depend on Iris's mood when we get to her house," Brian replied, then followed his words with a sigh.

Rita nodded. She had seen Iris in her "mood," but she had also seen Iris act very reasonable in the shop. She couldn't believe Iris would prefer to let others take control of her life when she was so capable. Perhaps it was just easier to fulfill other's expectations than to discover your own. Especially, if no one ever let you try.

Chapter Eight

Even in the dark, Rita could sense the beauty of Iris and Stefanie's home. The house was set back from the street, at the end of a narrow driveway that wove its way through a forest of thin trees. A two-story stone building with large windows in the front, it was surrounded by a wrought-iron fence with a decorative black gate that opened into a courtyard laid with colorful Spanish tile.

When Stefanie opened the intricately carved wooden door and welcomed them inside, Rita remembered again about Stefanie's assessment of Brian's house, "a place where nobody lived." For this home was painted in warm hues; family pictures were lined up on cabinet tops, and there was a white grand piano that seemed to be the focal point of the large open living room. A collection of old silver coins lined a shadow box on one wall, and atop the gray stone fireplace were a dozen or more paper-mache clowns, brightly painted and posed in various acrobatic positions. Above the fireplace hung a large portrait of Estevan, Iris, and Stefanie, taken when Stefanie was still a young child.

Rita stared at the portrait, entranced by Estevan's dark attractive looks and intense stare. He looked like a man with confidence and charisma, a man who only wanted the best for his family and, from the looks of this house, didn't spare any expense to provide it.

"Wasn't my dad good-looking?" Stefanie walked closer to Rita, who stood near the fireplace. "I think he could have been a movie star."

"He's very handsome." Rita noticed the family re-
semblance right away. As Stefanie matured, she looked
more like her father, something Rita suspected all
along. She smiled at Stefanie, although sadness tugged
inside her. "Brian told me he was a very special man."

"He was old-fashioned about a lot of stuff, but he
spoiled me, too. I miss him a lot." Stefanie linked her
arm through Rita's. "I'm glad you're here tonight. Mom's
still unsure about going to the party at Nicky's house.
Maybe you can help Uncle Brian convince her to go."

Rita glanced over her shoulder at Brian, who had a
slightly guilty look on his face. If she hadn't seen him so
troubled by the invitation mistake, she might have suspected he intended to bring her here from the very
beginning.

"Where's your mother, Stef?" he said, rubbing his
hands together as if he was cold. "She called me earlier,
so I decided to stop by."

"She's upstairs, I guess. She's still mad because the
printers put daddy's name on the *quince* invitation."

"Brian, why don't you tell Iris that we're here," Rita
suggested in a gentle tone. "I'm sure she wants to talk to
you."

"Stefanie, did I hear Brian's car—oh! Rita. You're
here, too."

Everyone turned around as Iris entered the room.
Her hair was pulled back into a loose ponytail and she
was dressed in a blue velour top and pants. She still
managed her tasteful appearance even in casual wear.

"I had hoped you'd come by, Brian, but I never
thought you might have a date or something," Iris said,
coming to where Brian stood. She placed her hand on
his right arm and stared up at him with the eyes of a
forgotten child. "I guess I'm going to have to get used to
sharing you with another woman. I've never had to do
that before."

He placed his left hand over hers. "I just wanted to be sure you were okay, Iris. You were pretty upset about the invitations."

"It was just a shock, that's all. And it was sad, too. I just got overwhelmed by my feelings. Estevan should be here for this, you know? He planned this celebration for Stefanie since she was a baby."

"I know, Iris, I know," Brian murmured, nodding at his sister.

They both looked so disappointed that Rita feared Brian might join Iris in crying again.

"Iris, the *quince* is weeks away. There's still time to order new invitations." Rita kept her tone cheerful, optimistic. "If you call the printer in the morning, I'm sure you can get new ones long before they need to be mailed."

"Yes, Iris. Once you explain the mistake, I bet the printer will be more than happy to reprint new ones." Brian patted his sister's hand.

"Perhaps—since they have to be printed again anyway—we could add your name, Brian. You're the godfather and—"

"No way!" Stefanie didn't shout, but the large room and high ceilings made for an echoing sound that amplified her protest.

"You can't put Uncle Brian's name in place of Daddy's," Stefanie told them, her eyes gleaming with anger. "Just because he's paid for the dress and other stuff doesn't mean he can take Daddy's place. Not on the invitation, not in church. Not any place."

"Stefanie, how can you be so ungrateful?" Iris asked, clutching tighter to Brian's arm. "After all Brian has done for us since—"

"If you put Uncle Brian's name on the invitation, it will be like Daddy doesn't even count." Stefanie paused a moment, and when she began speaking, her voice carried a more reasonable tone. "Mom, I know it's hard for you—it's hard for me, too. But I would prefer if the invitation just read 'Mrs. Estevan Bonilla.' Please?"

"Stefanie's right," Brian told his sister. "My name doesn't belong on the invitation beside yours."

Rita knew how much it pained Brian to admit it. She yearned to embrace him, let him know she understood. But she stayed beside Stefanie, knowing she could comfort him later when they were alone.

"Iris, call the printer in the morning and order new invitations. I'll take care of the bill," he said, then gently pushed his sister's hand off his arm. "Now that we settled this, perhaps Rita and I will be going."

"Oh, please don't go," Stefanie begged. "Can't you stay longer?"

"Yes," Iris said. "Please stay. Let me make some coffee and we can visit."

Brian looked at Rita. Suddenly she recognized Iris's reluctance to share her brother's attention as something that she felt, too. She had spent the entire day anticipating an evening alone with Brian. He made her feel like she was the most important person in his life. When he was with his family though, she knew it wasn't true. There were others who were very important to him, long before Rita had come on the scene.

"It's up to you, Brian," she said, though the words almost choked her.

He smiled, but only for a moment in her direction. He looked at Iris. "We'll stay a while. Not long. Rita and I haven't had dinner yet."

"We haven't either," Stefanie said. "Why don't we all go out for dinner together, all of us?"

"Oh, I couldn't. I'm not dressed for a restaurant." Iris shook her head, glancing down at her outfit.

"You look fine, Mom. Doesn't she, Rita?" Stefanie grinned, and Rita felt she had no choice but to smile and agree with the girl.

"Let's get our coats then. Uncle Brian, where shall we go eat?" Stefanie said as she was leaving the room.

"We'll figure that out in the car," Brian said, then chuckled. Iris followed her daughter and he turned to follow them. Suddenly, he stopped and looked back at Rita. "I hope you don't mind, Rita."

Disappointment kept her silent. She merely shrugged, not trusting herself to say anything, or worried if she said something, it would make her sound selfish or uncaring.

Then Brian turned completely and walked to the place where she stood. He placed his hand around her waist. "Have I told you tonight that I love you?"

She shook her head, blinking back tears she didn't expect.

"Thank you for letting Iris and Stefanie join us tonight," he told her. "It means a lot to me that you've done so much for Stefanie. Maybe you can become Iris's friend, too. She needs someone like you as much as I do."

Then he lowered his lips upon hers.

She clung to him, returning his kiss with a fervent response, a passionate reminder that she could provide something that Iris and Stefanie could not. He must have gotten the message, because when the others returned, Brian was still deeply involved in his reply. If Stefanie hadn't started giggling, who knows where their kissing might have taken them?

❤ ❤ ❤ ❤ ❤

"Do you and my brother have a serious relationship?" Iris asked Rita point blank the next morning when she left Stefanie off at the shop.

They were alone in the side room where Rita had been checking on the amount of white taffeta she still had on hand before she ordered more.

Rita wasn't too surprised by Iris's tone. Hadn't her sisters wanted to know the same thing? Only Iris wasn't trying to pry into intimate details, or was she?

"Stefanie says you've been going out together since last week. I hardly think that's enough time to decide you're in love with each other."

"I always thought you were more of a romantic," Rita said, trying to decide if Iris approved of the relationship or not. Iris had never seen Rita and Brian together until last night. Did Iris feel threatened?

"I am a big romantic, Rita. I fell in love with Estevan during a summer vacation in Mexico when I was eighteen. But I loved a mature man who knew the difference between infatuation and true love."

"Don't you think Brian knows the difference?" Rita turned to face Iris, trying to keep her patience under control.

"He's never had a lot of girl friends—"

"How do you know that? Brian travels a lot. Maybe he has girl friends you've never met because they live other places. Siblings don't have to confide every detail about their personal lives to each other, do they?"

Iris's hazel eyes, looking very green this morning because she wore a pale jade-colored jacket, were large, cat-like, and just as suspicious. "I just want to know if your feelings for my brother are genuine. If you love him, it's because of him, not anything else."

Now Rita understood Iris's concerns. "If you think I love Brian because of his money or anything else, you're very wrong. We started off as friends, and the relationship grew from there. It's a good foundation for any relationship, Iris. And just so you know, yes, I'm in love with Brian, and yes, we have a serious relationship. But there are some things I won't discuss with sisters, mine or his."

Her eyebrows raised, then her stare was softened by a smile. "I didn't mean to get personal. I think people who discuss intimacy are tacky. It's none of their business anyway. I only need your assurance that my brother's feelings mean something to you. I don't want him hurt."

"Iris, I don't want to get hurt either. I don't plan to rush things, or pressure Brian in any way. I love him, yes, but I'm not planning to do anything dramatic. It's not my way."

"I guess that's why Brian likes you." She lowered her gaze then, sighing, said, "I'd better let you get back to your work. Stefanie doesn't like it when I stay around. She told me I make her nervous. It's hard to take this rejection. She used to turn to me for everything."

"She's growing up, Iris. It's nothing against you personally. You know that, right?" Rita worried about Iris. Dealing with personal grief, trying to accept her daughter's flight from childhood, and now losing her brother's undivided attention. Could she cope with all the sudden changes when they happened so close together?

"Iris, when the holidays are over, come by and visit me, will you? Since Stefanie's been working here, I've realized how much I miss having company in the shop. Will you come and talk to me?"

She shrugged. "I don't know. You're so busy."

Rita put her hand on Iris's arm. "I'm right across the street from the cemetery. Stefanie says you go there often. You'll be in the neighborhood anyway." She smiled, having finally found one positive point for the location of her shop. "Just stop in and say hello."

"I'll try." Iris's voice was almost a whisper.

"Iris, in a few days it'll be a brand new year. It can be a new start for you. Begin by taking Stefanie to the Díaz's party. There's no one friendlier than Cecilia Díaz, and Stefanie could celebrate New Year's with people her own age. If nothing else, do it for Brian. How will he have a good time New Year's Eve if he's worried about you?"

"Then you probably wouldn't have a good time either," Iris replied.

Rita gave her a shrug. "Yes, that's true, too."

"Perhaps I'll call Mrs. Díaz later. I have to go see the printer first." Iris's voice still lacked confidence, but her words were encouraging. "Good-bye, Rita."

"Good-bye, Iris."

Rather than walk Iris out, Rita chose to stay in the side room. She turned back to her fabric bolts, but she had temporarily lost interest in computing the yards of white fabric she still needed for Alyssa's flower girls. Instead, she started to second-guess the entire conversation with Iris. Had she sounded sincere about her love for Brian? Was it wrong to encourage Iris to attend a party just so Rita and Brian wouldn't worry about her? Had Rita said too much, or not enough? She felt confused, vulnerable. She wondered if love was like these bolts of white material with subtle patterns she couldn't see unless she concentrated on them carefully. She liked to think she could tell them apart with little effort, but she knew sometimes she saw nothing but a blank white sheet.

❤ ❤ ❤ ❤ ❤

"I think I'm nervous," Rita confided to Abuelita early in the evening of New Year's Eve when her great-grandmother called to wish her Happy New Year. "I'm meeting the people Brian works with. What will they think of me?"

"What do you think of yourself? That's more important."

Rita found herself smiling. "Well, I think I look terrific in this dress. And Brian's sister let me borrow such beautiful earrings. I think I'm ready for a wonderful new year to begin."

"Then enjoy yourself, Rita. Dance with your Brian, talk to his friends. They will like you. You're a good person. You deserve happiness."

"I am happy, Abuelita. I have you, and now I have Brian, too."

"It's a new year, Rita. I feel lucky for you. I'll see you Wednesday when Ramón brings me home. Good-bye."

Rita hung up the phone then returned to her bedroom to give herself a final look in the mirror. The dress fit her body well, but it wasn't so tight that it would draw unwanted attention. She had lifted the hemline, and her black leather high heels gave a slimming effect to her legs. She had her hair re-cut this afternoon, layering the top around her face with a wedge-shape in the back. With Iris's teardrop diamond earrings and a delicate gold chain, she felt like a woman with a confident sense of style. It was an image she hoped to keep as she met the people with whom Brian worked.

Brian arrived in an elegant black tuxedo to take her to the party inside a majestic three-story mansion near San Antonio College. She was introduced to many people in a short span of time. From the men she received admiring looks, but several women asked her where she bought her dress. She felt proud telling them that she was a seamstress and that she was the owner of Rita's Dress Shop. Two women asked her for her business card and Rita regretted she had none to give. The thought of business cards never occurred to her, but this evening she moved among professionals who often exchanged such cards.

When another woman asked her about the location of the dress shop, Rita gave the street address. The woman looked puzzled, so Rita simply said, "It's across the street from San Fernando."

"The cathedral?"

"No, the cemetery."

The woman's startled look left Rita embarrassed. Who would go to a dress shop near a cemetery to buy a beautiful evening dress?

She was glad Brian excused them from the circle of people and took her towards the buffet table.

"I didn't handle that right," Rita said, imagining that her face probably matched Brian's crimson bow tie.

"You just need to use different landmarks to describe your store's location. Why don't you tell people that it's not far from Our Lady of the Lake University?" Brian suggested, reaching for a small china plate.

Promising to pay attention to what she said and how others around her presented themselves, Rita expected the evening could be useful in learning to think more like a professional business owner.

The various downstairs rooms they moved through were crowded but not uncomfortable, and they both enjoyed sampling from the different buffet tables as well as talking with people Brian knew.

"Shall we go upstairs and dance?" he asked later.

Rita answered with an enthusiastic smile. Brian took her hand and they made their way up the wide red-carpeted staircase with its thick mahogany railings. The music room was very simple with high ceilings and plain beige walls. One side of the room was lined with windows shaped like steeples and there was a pair of french doors leading to an outdoor balcony. An oval wooden stage was built into another corner where two guitarists, a piano player, and a drummer were playing a romantic tune for the clusters of dancers moving over the polished wood floor.

Brian led Rita out to dance. She felt as if the champagne had gone to her head, but knew it was really just a light-headed euphoria because she was in Brian's arms, slowly moving to the music. It had been two years since Rita danced so closely with a man she cared about. She intertwined her right hand through Brian's, and felt his left arm tighten around her waist, pressing her closer to him.

One dance weaved into another; she felt as if they were the only two people in the world, dancing alone underneath a romantic star-lit sky.

Finally, she felt Brian stop moving. Lifting her head, she posed a silent question to him.

"The band's taking an intermission," he said, then touched his lips to hers.

"Brian! Are you having a good time at the party?"

Rita stepped around as Brian turned towards a muscular, bearded man in a tuxedo. His royal blue tie matched the silk gown on the attractive brunette woman with glasses who stood beside him.

"Good evening, Jorgen. I'm having a fine time, thank you. May I introduce you to Rita Navarro? Rita, this is my boss, Jorgen Hoberg, and his wife Sandy."

"It's nice to meet you," Rita said, extending her hand to both of them.

"We've been admiring you on the dance floor," Sandy said with a grin aimed at Brian. "You two make an attractive couple."

Brian's arm tightened at Rita's waist, but he said nothing.

"Ladies, we're very lucky to have someone with Brian's talents with our company. He's got one of the best computer minds in the state," Jorgen told them, thumping his hand on Brian's shoulder.

"And you're lucky to have this man on your arm, Rita," Sandy said with a smile that made her brown eyes shiny. "He's so thoughtful and generous. Did you know that he donated a variety of flower arrangements and live plants to the hospital Christmas auction?" Then she winked at Brian. "I know you thought you could remain anonymous, but I have my sources!" She looked back at Rita. "We made over a thousand dollars from those plants. Did you help him pick them out?"

"No, I didn't," Rita said quietly, although she felt like she just stomped on the brakes to avoid hitting a tree. She looked at Brian and saw a touch of apprehension in his eyes, a false smile frozen on his lips.

"Well, now I can thank you personally, Brian," Sandy told him and then looked at her husband. "I told Jorgen what you did as soon as I knew."

"It was nothing," Brian said, then shifted his weight from one foot to the other. "If you'll excuse us, I think Rita and I will get something to drink now."

"Enjoy yourselves. And happy new year," Jorgen said before he turned to greet someone else with a "Hello! Having a good time?"

"It was nice to have met you," Rita and Sandy said at the same time before each woman was led in opposite directions.

But Rita stopped as they reached a more secluded spot near the door. She turned to face Brian, her hands on his arms. A fine sheen of perspiration had appeared on his forehead, and she knew it wasn't just because of the dancing.

"Brian, last week a new customer came into the store and bought all the plants and flowers. She didn't even ask me how much they were. She paid cash for them, too. I should have suspected that something wasn't right about the whole situation." Rita's anger rose around her like hot steam, making her eyes burn as she looked at him. "That woman had your money, didn't she?"

"Rita—"

"You bought two-hundred dollars worth of flowers. Didn't you think I could sell them myself?"

"Rita, don't be angry. I love you. I just wanted to do something to help you," he said, placing his hands at her waist.

"Did you think I was just another charity you could support?" she answered, struggling not to raise her voice and cause an embarrassing scene.

"No, not at all. Rita, I would have donated something to the auction anyway. And when Stefanie complained about moving the plants and flowers around, I got the idea to buy them. But I was afraid if I did it, you wouldn't sell them to me. You'd get mad—like you are right now."

Rita lowered her gaze, shaking her head slowly.

"That's why I sent one of the secretaries to buy them. And it's not like I just bought them for nothing. You heard Sandy. The hospital made some money from them."

Rita sighed because she couldn't stay angry with him. As usual, Brian's intentions were straight from the heart.

"Rita, my love, I just can't stand by and let you spend anymore time in that cold, leaky building." He paused, and she looked up at him again. "I am even ready to invest in your business myself. I want you to have the money you need in order to find a new place for a better shop."

Eyes wide with surprise, Rita stared at Brian. "Invest in my business? Are you serious? Smart men invest in the stock market, not a dress shop."

He smiled, a soft chuckle escaping in his words. "I like my investments to be diverse."

Rita stroked Brian's cheek. She understood his motives, loved him for wanting to help her, but she knew she couldn't let him become her business partner. She never wanted to be obligated to him financially or use their relationship as a means of stability for her business. She couldn't do that. "Brian, I love you. I would appreciate any advice you want to give me about the business, but I can't take your money. It's not what I want from you. Can you understand that?"

"But, Rita—"

"Brian, if I'm ever going to get a business partner— and after my experience with Bea, I'm going to be very careful—I want it to be a person to share the day-to-day work with me. And if I can't afford to open a new shop in a better place, well, then the people I sew for will find me. No matter where I set up my sewing machine." And in that moment, she realized the distance between their experiences in the world of business.

In Brian's world, people exchanged business cards frequently, they socialized at expensive functions, traveled everywhere. Computers and other machines shared their workload. Even though she relied on a machine, much of her success as a seamstress came from her intuition and common sense. Her clients came through word-of-mouth recommendations. Her work required no travel and there were no company parties. But she was happy, proud of her work, and very positive her business would thrive without Brian's money.

She smiled at the man she loved. "Sandy is right. You're a very thoughtful, generous man. I love you, Brian."

"I love you, Rita. What I have is yours—anything, any time."

His sincere proclamation brought tears to her eyes. She kissed him because there were no words to express her feelings at that moment.

And later, when the countdown to the new year began, Brian and Rita stood with arms around each other, chanting the numbers together. They began the new year with a passionate kiss as confetti and streamers floated across the room, decorating their black clothes with shiny specks of color and ribbons of gold.

Chapter Nine

There seemed to be so much talking, so much catching up on family gossip and news about old friends, that Abuelita and Rita didn't settle down to talk about anything serious until after supper had been cooked and eaten and the dishes had been washed and put away.

Rita sensed that Abuelita had something on her mind; she assumed that the old woman wanted to talk about Brian. Even though they had always shared so many confidences, Rita wasn't certain she could put such personal feelings into words.

"I love him, Abuelita. It all happened so fast, but I know what I feel for Brian is really love," she admitted when they sat down on the old lumpy brown sofa in the small back room. The walls were filled with family photos, seven generations worth, and aside from the antique sewing machine and the sofa, the only other furniture in the room was the new television set the family bought Abuelita for her eighty-fifth birthday.

Her great-grandmother placed her hand on top of Rita's. "I can see what you feel in your eyes. This love is good for you."

"I think so." Rita smiled as her love settled into the cozy sensation she experienced whenever she talked about Brian. "Brian's love makes me feel stronger somehow. He says he needs me, Abuelita. And I need him. I never thought I'd feel like this about anyone. We still have a lot to learn about each other, but his heart's in the right place—a place where I can reach it."

"Your words make me happy, Rita. It makes things easier to say." Abuelita's fingers wrapped around Rita's hand. "I've decided to move to Brownsville and live with Teresa."

All evening Rita knew Abuelita seemed preoccupied, but she never expected this news. A heavy weight settled on her chest, making it hard to breathe, even speak.

"Move? To Brownsville?" Her voice caught between a groan and a whisper.

"Teresa has always wanted me there. I didn't want to leave my house. You came here for me. Now I must leave here for you."

Hot tears swam in Rita's eyes making Abuelita's face blurry, hard to see. "I don't understand. Why must you move away?"

"You have your own life, Rita. A good business. Now a man who loves you. You must make a home with him."

"But Brian hasn't asked me to marry him. I need my home. Here. With you. This is my home. This is your home. Don't leave." She swiped at the tear rolling down her cheek then clutched the old woman's hand even tighter. "I need you, Abuelita. Why do you have to move away?"

"You should not be burdened with an old woman. You need your freedom now. So that you can say yes to Brian when he asks."

"Abuelita, I love Brian, but we've never discussed marriage. That's a long way off." For the first time, Rita felt that her great-grandmother was from another generation. Hadn't Abuelita often told her that she only knew her first husband a week before they married, and her second husband only a month? "Abuelita, please understand. You don't have to leave. Not now."

"Rita, I didn't make this decision just today. It's been there for a while. I've seen you turn away from men at parties in order to stay by me. I've heard you say 'No thank you' when friends ask you to go out. You called me in Brownsville, talking about little Stefanie and your Brian. I felt your happiness. You can't let this chance slip away because you feel you must take care of me."

Tears melted down Rita's face as she listened to her great-grandmother admit something Rita didn't want to. There had been a dozen times she wanted to dance at a wedding reception but felt obligated to keep Abuelita company. And she had felt guilty because she left Abuelita alone in the house when she enjoyed herself at the movies with Brian and Stefanie. The last two weeks, Rita dropped her guard and allowed herself to fall in love. If she hadn't known Abuelita was off in Browns-ville, would she have enjoyed her holidays with Brian as much as she did? And tonight, he was out of town, so she had time to be with Abuelita. When he returned, would she feel torn between her duties as Abuelita's caregiver and her desires to spend every spare moment with Brian?

"Rita, I'm not moving to California. You'll visit me, no?"

She tried to push aside the shock of the news and think rationally about Abuelita's departure. "Will you sell this house?"

"I cannot sell your home, Rita."

"It won't be a home if you're not in it." Rita spoke her thoughts out loud, feeling tears flood her vision again. She turned her head, trying to regain her compo-sure as her mind filled with images of blank walls and empty rooms. Why would she want to live here with Abuelita? But where else would she go? Anna and Frank lived in her parents' old house. Debra lived in a crowded two-bedroom apartment. And Imelda was in Oklahoma near their mother.

"Rita, this is your home. Don't you see?" Leathery fingers pressed against Rita's palm. "You must find what you want for yourself. Without worry about me. Your life comes first now."

Swallowing the salty taste of loneliness, Rita tried to understand her great-grandmother's wishes and respect them. Eventually, it might make sense, but right now she felt a seam ripper tear through her heart, shredding the last threads of security she knew. Like her shop, this house would become just another building, one without a friendly face to share her day-to-day experiences.

"When will you go? What will you take with you?" She stared at their clasped hands, wishing there was a way to permanently bond them together.

"I'd like time to go through things, give them away to different children. I've called Minerva to help me. She'll come tomorrow and stay with us until I finish."

"I can help you, Abuelita."

"No, you've done enough. And Rita, anything you want, you keep. This is your home now."

Rita looked at her great-grandmother as though for the first time. Wrinkles had been carved on her skin by time and tragedy, and her angular body had shrunken into a soft, shapeless bag. But inside burned the unselfish, energetic spirit that would bring a wealth of wise words and deep love to the family in Brownsville. Abuelita was a treasure to be shared, not coveted. But right now, it was hard for Rita's head and heart to agree.

As usual for this time of night, Abuelita reached for the remote control and put on her *novelas*. Rita told her great-grandmother she was going to do some sewing in the spare room.

Only instead of picking up an unfinished bridesmaid's dress or dance costume, Rita walked to the long cedar chest where Abuelita kept piles of different fabrics she had bought through the years and began to sort through them, taking many of the colorful silks and lively prints for herself. She dug down to the bottom of the chest until she uncovered the long box with her mother's wedding gown and the baptismal dress which her father wore; both of them handmade by Abuelita. Without a second thought, Rita stacked the fabrics on top of the box and carried them all to her bedroom.

❤ ❤ ❤ ❤ ❤

Rita paused in her sewing to rub her eyes. She slept little last night, thinking about Abuelita's decision and its impact on Rita's career. She would miss Abuelita's friendship, but there was also the sewing expertise on which Rita depended. Whenever Rita was uncertain about a job, she could ask Abuelita for suggestions. And Abuelita's beautiful embroidery and stitching was something Rita never mastered. Who would she find to do the skilled beadwork on the wedding gowns and headpieces? Abuelita promised to finish Alyssa's dress before she left, but Rita couldn't accept any other elaborate wedding gowns until she found someone else to do that handwork.

She rose from the sewing machine and stretched her arms above her head. It was time for a break. She moved behind the counter to grab an orange she left by the coffee pot. She stood there peeling it as she studied the *Folklórico* sketches on the counter. She still couldn't believe her good fortune. When the director of *Folklórico del Verano* called the day after New Year's, she asked for a large deposit before she began the job. He didn't argue and had brought her a check and the sketches later that day.

Rita had just taken a wedge of orange into her mouth when the shop door opened. Her eyes widened at the sight of Iris Bonilla coming inside.

"Hi, Rita. I hope you're not too busy," she said, her voice soft and apologetic. Her eyes were rimmed in pink, her cheeks and face red, as if she had been crying in the cold outdoors for a while.

"Iris, what a nice surprise. I'm glad to have someone to talk to," Rita said, hoping that Iris would stay awhile. "I sure miss Stefanie. Did she start back to school yesterday?"

"Yes, she did." Iris glanced around uncertainly. "You don't have any customers around?"

"It's been very quiet the past two days. Sometimes, I'm tempted to just close the shop and do my sewing at home. Iris, would you like some coffee?"

She clutched her arms around her black coat. "Well, I—"

"You look cold. And the coffee's made. Take your coat off and visit awhile. Please. I'm lonely for another human voice. Help me keep my sanity, okay?"

Iris looked to the floor. "A cup of coffee sounds tempting. It's so cold outside—I was at the cemetery a long time."

Rita set down her orange, wiped her hands, then went to pour two mugs of coffee. "I'm so glad you dropped by, Iris. How was the New Year's party at the Díaz's house?"

"The Díazes are nice people. And bunco's one of those games that gets everyone involved."

Rita turned around with the coffee mugs, pleased to see that Iris had left her black coat draped over the chair by the sewing machine. "How did you do playing bunco?"

"I got the booby prize." Iris actually smiled as she took one of the coffee mugs from Rita. "I only won three games the whole night. But you would have thought I had won the championship. Everyone congratulated me, and I got a nice address book as a prize. Cecilia had everyone sign their name and address in it before I left. Then she made me promise to call everyone soon so we could get together again."

"But didn't you know some of the people already?"

"Well, yes—but they were just names to me before. You know, people who sent their kids to the same schools, or a face from Church. I'm embarrassed to admit that we always donated money instead of getting involved. Estevan was always so busy, and I seemed to be busy, too." Iris looked down into the coffee mug. "I've spent a lot of time wondering why I used to be so busy. Now I can't seem to find anything to do with my days."

"Well, the *quinceañera*'s only a month away. I would think there's still a lot to do," Rita replied.

Iris took a long drink from her coffee then set the cup on the counter. "If we had gone through with the elaborate celebration that Estevan wanted, I'd be very busy right now. Talking to the managers at the country club. Having meetings with all the girls in the honor court. I'd be teaching them dance steps and trying to find matching accessories for their dresses." Her eyebrows raised. "Gosh, Rita. Doesn't it get tedious sewing fourteen dresses that all look alike?"

"Sometimes." Rita shrugged. "Maybe that's why I've come to think that all the attention should focus on the girl herself. Why should she share her spotlight with fourteen friends? What you and Brian have planned makes the tradition just as important as the party."

"I'm not sure what I feel about any type of *quinceañera*. Some of my school friends had them, but it wasn't something I expected. I had a sweet-sixteen party instead. But Estevan was adamant that Stefanie celebrate *quinceañera*. People he worked with had them for their daughters, and we attended a dozen of them through the years." Iris sighed. "I don't know, Rita. It all seemed like a way to show off how much money you could spend. The party afterwards seemed more important, not the church ceremony."

"I've been to a lot of weddings like that," Rita told her.

"Me, too. Actually, I had one of those weddings. Now I realize that all those people eating your wedding cake probably don't care if you keep your marriage vows or if you end up in divorce court two weeks later. Those same people send expensive flowers to funerals, but never call you a week later to see if you need a shoulder to cry on. They act like you're supposed to die when your husband does. I felt more warmth and affection from the strangers at the Díaz's party than I ever got from these people Estevan called our dearest friends."

The bitter edge in Iris's voice made Rita almost choke on her coffee. Iris, with her fine features, appeared almost fragile, but this was deceiving. There was a hard edge to Iris, a quality that could help her survive; a quality Rita's mother never possessed.

"Perhaps it's time to find your own friends," Rita said slowly. She wasn't sure her opinion was welcome.

"I have Linda. She's always been my friend."

"Brian said she's coming for the *quinceañera*. I'm looking forward to meeting her."

"She's a lot like you. Independent. Able to get along with people. In love with my brother."

Rita's jaw dropped open. She hoped Iris was only teasing, but Iris looked very serious.

"I've always thought Linda and Brian would be good for each other. She'd add a little pizzazz to his life, that's for certain. But if he hasn't noticed her by now, I guess he's hopeless."

"Brian says Linda hasn't been here since Stefanie was a baby," Rita answered, trying not to let jealousy get in the way of common sense.

Iris lifted one eyebrow as she looked directly at Rita. "Brian's told you a lot, hasn't he?"

"We're friends. We talk to each other."

"Then, you're one up on me. I've tried to talk to Brian—like I'm talking to you now—and he's not eager to listen to what I have to say."

"Brian has an image of his big sister as a delicate creature. To him, you need someone to protect you. It took him awhile to realize that Stefanie wasn't just a little girl to be pampered. He had to see her as a frightened teenager, trying to become an adult. Maybe he needs to see you as simply Iris Bonilla—just as you are—not anyone's sister or wife or mother."

Iris shook her head, her hazel eyes filling with tears. "I don't even see that Iris Bonilla. She doesn't exist."

"Oh, yes she does! She's standing right here in my store. She just admitted that the people she knew as Mrs. Estevan Bonilla were not her real friends. She told me she had fun playing bunco with some people who want to be her friends. And she's made it clear how much she loves her brother—loves him enough to keep testing his girlfriend until she's convinced that my love for him is real. And I like Iris Bonilla. And if she'd just give herself a chance, I bet you'd like her, too. So would Brian."

The intensity of Iris's wet stare sent a hot flush across Rita's face. She couldn't believe her words came out with such a rush of emotion. Her fingers raked through her hair. "I get carried away sometimes. Sorry."

"Don't apologize. You're being honest." She glanced down at her watch then turned around to get her coat. "I'd better leave. I need to pick up Stefanie at school."

"Iris, if I promise to keep my opinions to myself, will you drop by again?" Rita offered her a sheepish smile.

"I don't know," Iris said as she slipped into her coat. She buttoned it up then wrapped and tied the belt. "But I'm starting to understand why Stefanie wanted to work here over the holidays."

Rita wasn't sure how to interpret that statement, but keep smiling.

"Good-bye, Rita."

"Good-bye, Iris. Please come again." And Rita meant it. She was starting to enjoy the challenge of discovering the real Iris Bonilla.

❤ ❤ ❤ ❤ ❤

Rita suspected that Abuelita invited Tía Minerva to spend the next few weeks at the house so that Rita could go out with Brian guilt-free, but the old woman swore that "it would take at least three people to go through the contents of the bedroom closet alone."

"Why are there so many boxes in the living room?" Brian asked Rita once they had closed the door of

Abuelita's house behind them and walked towards his car.

She sighed and instinctively slipped her arm around his waist. "Abuelita's decided to move to Brownsville and live with her daughter."

Brian put his arm around her shoulders, pressing her closer. "I'm sorry, Rita. This can't be easy for you."

"I'm trying to get used to the idea. I don't look forward to the first night I come home to an empty house."

"Then you're going to stay here by yourself?"

They had stopped beside his car. She turned to face him, welcoming the feel of his arms around her body. "I have no choice right now. Any place else requires a deposit and monthly rent. I can't afford that."

"Rita, I don't know if I'd like you here all by yourself. The street's lighting is not very good. And there's that lounge around the corner. A few times I've wondered if my hubcaps would still be on my car when I came out of your house."

"Every once in a while you sound like a real snob. Do you know that, Brian? The people in this neighborhood watch out for one another. We can't afford electronic burglar systems like you have, but a couple of dogs in the backyard do the job quite nicely. I can tell you the names of every person who lives within four houses of me. Can you tell me the same about your neighbors? And besides—"

"All right, Rita, you made your point."

Despite the bad street lighting, she could see the frown on his face. It's not what she wanted. She needed to see him smile and she wanted to feel anything but the lonely frustration which haunted her all week.

"Brian, I'm sorry. I didn't mean to start an argument. I've missed you so much." She lifted her face to kiss him.

He pulled her tight against him as his mouth covered hers. Rita gave herself up to the passionate kissing as her legs seemed to melt away.

She barely heard the sound of their bodies hitting the car, but the flashing parking lights and whooping siren of the car alarm was a very rude interruption of the romatic moment.

Brian groaned, released her, and immediately searched for his keys. It seemed like hours before he located the shut-off device on the key chain. Actually, it was just long enough for Tía Minerva's face to appear in the window and three porch lights around them to flip on.

"We'd better go," Rita said. "Someone may call the police." Then she broke into laughter, and Brian started laughing, too.

The humorous moment paved the way for friendlier conversation as they drove to the movie theater. Rita explained about Abuelita's decision to move, although she left out the part about Abuelita wanting Rita to make a home with Brian. And she told Brian about Iris's visit to her store, but didn't reveal anything personal about their conversation. She wanted Iris to feel their discussions would be kept private; something friends did for one another. And she did want to become a friend to Iris, not just because she loved Brian, but because Iris deserved to have someone on her side.

"Iris told me she had fun at the bunco party." Rita felt that was a safe topic to talk about. "Have you asked her about it?"

"Not really. I called her when I got back this afternoon, but it was just an 'Are you okay?' kind of call." He glanced at her, but kept his attention on his driving, too. "Tell me, did she win a lot of buncos?"

"Just three, but she won the booby prize. But she said it was an address book and everyone at the party signed it. I think she made some new friends," Rita told him. She reached across the seat and rested her hand on Brian's shoulder. "I remember when my father died, many of the friends my parents knew as a couple

seemed to drop out of sight. Do you think that's happened to Iris?"

"Of course not. She's always been surrounded by
friends. She was popular in high school, always at some
party or going on a date. She and Estevan gave dinner
parties or traveled with others on weekend trips. I've
always envied her ability to move so easily among people."

"But, Brian, have you noticed any of these friends
around lately?"

"I'm sure they're just respecting her privacy. She's
grieving and wants to be alone."

"But if she's used to being surrounded by people,
why would she want to be alone?"

"Is there a point to all these questions, Rita?" His
voice took on that defensive quality he used whenever
Rita tried to discuss Iris's problems. She was starting to
understand why Iris found talking to Brian so difficult.
He wouldn't admit that things had changed. His image
of Iris didn't exist except in Brian's own mind. And who
should tell him the truth?

Rita chose her words carefully. "I just think Iris
might feel lost. She's not anyone's wife anymore. And
her role as Stefanie's mother is changing as Stefanie
grows up."

"She's still my sister. Nothing's changed about
that."

"Yes, it has, Brian. Our relationship changed things
between you and Iris. Just like my relationship with you
affected Abuelita's decision to move away." Rita groaned,
regretting her words immediately.

Brian had stopped the car for a traffic light. He
turned his face towards her. "What do you mean? What
does our relationship have to do with Abuelita?"

Rita trembled, pulling her hand away from his
shoulder to clutch them together in her lap. "She wants
me to have my own life. She said I shouldn't be burdened with caring for an old woman. That's probably

why Tía Minerva's in town. So I can go out with you and not feel guilty that I'm leaving Abuelita alone in the house."

He didn't reply, just looked back at the traffic signal. It turned green and Brian drove on.

Rita looked out the window. This conversation had taken more curves than the road Brian took to the movie theater. She was grateful they could just drop the whole thing for a couple of hours while they watched a movie. However, once Brian stopped the car, he unbuckled his seat belt and turned himself directly towards her, resting his knee on the seat and his arm across the back. He seemed to be settling in for serious conversation.

"Do you blame me because Abuelita's leaving?" he said first.

"Of course not." Rita unbuckled her own belt so she could face him. "In many ways, I'm relieved. I did give up things because of her. I used to feel guilty when I left her alone so I could have a good time. It'll be someone else's day-to-day worry now." She sighed. "Didn't think you fell in love with such a selfish soul, did you?"

"I fell in love with a loving person who's carried a tremendous responsibility on her shoulders for a long time. It's time for someone else to take over. Your Abuelita is right about one thing, Rita. You do have your own life to lead."

"Everyone should have the freedom to lead her own life, Brian," she said, thinking again of Iris. She reached out to smooth a frown from his forehead. "Let's go see the movie. It's supposed to be one of those happily-ever-after romances."

Brian leaned across the seat and kissed her tenderly. His fingers brushed the hair from her face as he stared at her. "I love you, Rita. Our relationship is the best thing that ever happened in my life. But if I had to walk away tonight in order for you to be happy, I would."

"If you tried to walk away, Brian, I'd run after you," she said, then followed her words with a romantic kiss. She knew then they would probably skip the movie and concentrate on their own romance tonight.

Chapter Ten

"What's in these boxes?" Brian groaned, then suddenly sneezed.

Rita clutched the legs of the ladder tighter. She looked up to where he stood, balancing a cardboard box in his hands as he turned his face away to sneeze again.

"Are you okay?" she called.

"It's just the dust." He lowered the box down to her. "There must be four or five of these up on the top shelves."

"They're filled with patterns," Rita answered, and wondered how tissue and slim packages could weigh so much. She grappled with the box then finally let it drop on the other side of the ladder.

"What will you do with them all?" he asked, bringing another box down from the shelf in the closet.

"I'd like to go through them, but the last box I opened looked like it had been a cozy little home for mice." After she took the next box from him, she shook it slightly near her ear and felt a shiver go down her back. "I think something's moving around in this one." She dropped the box with a dull thud on the brown carpeting in Abuelita's bedroom.

"Patterns, no? Brian can carry them straight to the trash cans." Minerva Navarro appeared in the bedroom doorway, wiping her hands on the faded apron she wore over the shapeless blue sweater and black slacks. "If they've been up in the closet this long, no one needs them anymore."

Rita knew her aunt wasn't a sentimental person, and as children, she and her sisters always said that's why no one wanted to marry Tía Minerva: she didn't know what love meant. But this tall, crusty lady with spiky silver hair was just perfect to lead the rest of them through the household, separating useless trash from family treasures, many of which had already been tagged with pieces of white paper that designated which family member should get it. Even all the pictures in the back room had a piece of masking tape across the glass with a name inscribed on it.

Tía had volunteered to sleep on the single bed in the back room "for as long as it takes" until things Abuelita wanted to give away had been distributed among the family and her personal belongings packed in the sturdy corrugated boxes in the corner of her bedroom.

"When you finish here, clean up for lunch. The *caldo's* ready now," Rita's aunt said, then left the room.

All day Brian was very helpful, and didn't seem to mind Minerva's bossy ways. And as Rita thought back to the weekend's activities Monday morning as she sat alone in the shop, she appreciated what a special man she loved. His presence helped Rita cope with the sadness she felt at Abuelita's leaving.

That sadness stayed with her this morning, and the sight of rain clouds over the cemetery across the street didn't help her mood. She had just returned from checking the bucket was on the restroom toilet when she was surprised by Iris Bonilla coming through the door with a cream-colored dress in clear plastic draped over her arm.

"Good morning, Rita. I'm in need of your expert services."

Rita was surprised at the pleasant smile on Iris's face. "Good morning, Iris. What can I do for you?"

Iris held up the dress by its satin-covered hanger. "I bought this dress for the *quinceañera*, but I've lost weight. It just hangs everyplace. I need a good seamstress right now."

"Well, let's try it on and I'll see what I can do," Rita said, happy to help Brian's sister with this problem.

Rita could tell from the feel of shimmery fabric that Iris paid a lot for the dress. It draped the neckline in soft folds before it fell around Iris's body. The absence of seam line, though, was going to make alterations very tricky.

"Should I have brought the shoes I want to wear?" Iris said as she stood in front of the oval mirror in the side room.

"I won't need them unless you want me to adjust the hem," she answered, standing behind Iris and pinching the material together on both sides of Iris's small waist. "Hmmmmm. About an inch on both sides, I'd say." She lifted the dress lightly at both shoulders. "I can tuck it here. That'll make the bodice fit better."

"I bought it last summer and Estevan really liked it. I'd really be grateful if you can make me look better in it," Iris said, her voice shaking slightly.

"You look beautiful in this right now. More like Stefanie's sister than her mother," Rita replied with a genuine smile. "But I can do a few things to make it fit better, don't worry."

Just then, the telephone rang.

"I'll be right back," Rita said, and hurried off to answer the phone.

It took two frustrating minutes to explain in Spanish to the elderly caller that she had dialed the wrong number. Just as Rita put down the phone, a new customer walked into the store.

"A friend recommended your shop. Can you make ring-bearer pillows?" the woman asked. "My niece's getting married and my son's carrying the rings."

Rita didn't even get to answer because the phone rang again.

"I'll get the phone." Iris had walked into the main area of the store, calmly ignoring the way she was dressed.

"Rita's Dress Shop. May I help you?" she said as if she worked there.

Immediately, Rita turned to the customer who came in. "I have a few ring-bearer pillows in the back room. Please wait a moment." She looked at Iris, who was smiling.

"Yes, Cecilia. It's me. Rita's busy with a customer. Oh. Just a minute and I'll ask her." Iris placed her hand over the mouthpiece to speak to Rita. "Cecilia Díaz wants to know if her mother-in-law's dress is ready."

"No—uh, tell her it'll be ready by tomorrow morning."

During Rita's conversation about ring pillows and ways to attach the rings so they would be safe, Iris stepped in to sign the invoice when a delivery man with a dozen bolts of white muslin and pearl satin walked through the door, and she answered two more telephone calls. Rita had just rung up the sale of the pillows when one of her regular customers arrived for a dress fitting.

"Are things always this busy?" Iris asked later, when they were finally alone again.

"No two days are ever alike." Rita sighed and leaned against the small table behind the counter. "Friday and Saturday were so slow, I was seriously contemplating closing the shop and just referring all my customers back to my great-grandmother's house. I may still do it."

"You mean close the store for good?" Iris sat down at the chair by Rita's sewing machine. "But why?"

"You've seen why. It's too much work for one person. Just recently I agreed to make costumes for the *Folklórico del Verano*. It pays very well, but I can sew and fit costumes at home just as easily as I do here."

Iris gazed around the shop. "Well, I have to admit that this place isn't much of showcase, especially with the view outside the window. But, you and Stefanie did make some nice changes. I'm glad to see all the plants gone anyway."

She almost revealed who bought the plants, but changed the subject instead. "Gosh, Iris. You're still wearing that dress. Let me get it pinned and then you can be on your way. I feel guilty I've made you hang around this long."

"Actually, this morning has been fun. I've always wondered what it would be like to stand on the other side of the counter."

"Not always fun, let me tell you!" Rita answered then laughed.

However, once Rita had pinned Iris's dress and Iris had changed back into her green sweater and black skirt, she didn't seem in any hurry to leave. She helped Rita sort through and stack the new fabrics, make room for the ring-bearer pillows in the display case, and change the dress on the sewing figure.

"This sequined creation's got to go," Iris had said. "Put a dress on display that a normal person would buy." And then she selected a colorful Mexican dress, hot pink with yellow, orange, and white ribbons circling the bodice and hemline, and put it on the figure.

"Do you have extra ribbon around?" Iris asked, and within ten minutes she had woven a variety of ribbons together into a bouquet that she inserted in the neck of the sewing figure. "Have you ever thought about selling hats?"

Rita had been sitting at the sewing machine finishing up Mrs. Díaz's dress. "Hats? I have enough problems with wedding veils. And now that my veil maker is leaving town, I don't know what I'm going to do."

"Why is your veil maker leaving town?"

"It's my great-grandmother, Iris. She's decided to move to Brownsville and live with her daughter. We've lived together since I was sixteen years old."

Iris snapped her fingers. "I suddenly thought of something. When the family was trying to decide what to do about Mamá Josie years ago, I remember her telling us that Isabel's great-granddaughter came to live with her so she could stay in her house. She asked why none of her great-grandchildren loved her that much. She made us feel so guilty." Iris sighed. "Stefanie was just a toddler then and Brian was deep into work and graduate school. Neither of us wanted to be bothered. It was very unselfish of you to move in with your great-grandmother."

Rita shifted uneasily in her seat. Her motives had been anything but unselfish at the time. "I'm not a saint, Iris. I just didn't want to move to Oklahoma with my mother and her new husband. Abuelita said I could stay with her and I did." Pausing, she looked up at Iris. "My father died when I was thirteen. I was never close to my mother, and after Dad died, she became very unpredictable. If it hadn't been for Abuelita, I never would have made it through those awful days."

"It helps to have someone who understands you, doesn't it?" Iris crossed her arms along the back of the sewing figure and rested her chin upon her hands. "I had just about reached a breaking point when Linda mailed me a plane ticket and insisted that I come to New Mexico for one week. I felt guilty leaving Stefanie, but I knew that if I didn't put some distance between me and that house, I would explode into a million pieces."

"Then you did the right thing, Iris. My mother did explode and there are parts of her that we've lost forever."

"My mother is a lot like Brian. She doesn't want to admit that things have changed. She was hurt when I didn't want to move to Del Rio and live with them. 'Who'll take care of you?' she asked me. But I had Brian here and Stefanie's never liked Del Rio. No matter how much I was haunted by memories, I wasn't ready to move out of my home. And it is my home now. Estevan's mortgage insurance gave me that security at least."

"It's a beautiful place," Rita told her. "Brian says you used to have a lot of parties there."

"I just can't get myself into the spirit of parties any-more," Iris replied with a slight shrug of her shoulders. "I wouldn't have done the *quinceañera* if it weren't for Brian. Stefanie was totally against the idea. And I didn't really blame her. The *quinceañeras* we had been to were so extravagant, and she didn't want to force the expense of a *damas* dress on her friends. But Brian insisted we honor Estevan's wishes. He spent days reading every-thing he could find about the custom. He even asked people at work about it. It was his idea to forget about the extras and just let Stefanie celebrate in church and have a family party afterwards."

"And how do you and Stefanie feel about the *quinceañera* now?" Rita asked, curious about her influ-ence on the girl. Had Stefanie talked to her mother about anything Rita had said?

Iris straightened up and thumped her fingers on the sewing figure. "Stefanie seems agreeable now. She stopped complaining anyway."

Rita didn't respond. She merely stared at Iris, wait-ing for her to reveal her own feelings. Iris caught her look and sighed.

"As Stefanie's birthday gets closer, I'm wondering if I can do this. Am I ready to hear 'It's too bad Estevan couldn't be here' a hundred times in one day? Will Ste-fanie be able to take it? I want it to be a happy day for Stefanie, not a day to mourn Estevan. We did that already."

"Then you need to tell everyone that," Rita said with a reassuring tone. "You need to say it to your fam-ily, and you need to tell it to your friends. And most of all, you need to tell Stefanie. She needs to know that she'll be the focus of the *quinceañera*; that you're not just doing it because Estevan or Brian wanted it. Ste-fanie deserves a special day to celebrate with those who love her and want her to have a wonderful life."

"You have a positive spirit about this celebration. You must have had a *quinceañera* when you were fifteen."

"I did. And my *quince* wasn't perfect, but it was special. I think this custom is a good one, something that all families should do. Nowadays, teenagers need as much positive reinforcement as they can get. How many ceremonies do you know of that just celebrate being a teenager?" Rita's gaze took her far beyond Iris and the shop itself. "I think when we're young we think a lot of traditions are dumb or old-fashioned, but once we've gone through them and grown up, we realize how much stability they bring to our lives."

Iris nodded. "You're right about that. You draw some comfort when things go on like they've always done. Like Christmas. It was a tradition that we gathered at our house. Going to Del Rio was awful. I knew it would be like that, but I let others convince me it would be best."

"Don't be too hard on yourself, Iris. Sometimes doing things differently works out better, sometimes not. We all make good and bad choices. That's how we grow." Suddenly Rita laughed. "I sound like Abuelita."

Iris's response was a little grin. "You told me that this would be a new year for me. It'll be a new year for you too, Rita." Then she laughed. "Aren't we being philosophical today?"

She walked back to the counter to pick up the scraps of ribbons she left behind when she was creating her decorations. "I guess I better get out of here so you can get some sewing done."

Rita stood up and put aside the dress as Iris reached for her coat. "Where are you going now?" She hated to see Iris spend the afternoon in the cemetery now that she seemed in better spirits.

"I'm not sure." Iris swept her auburn hair out from her collar then straightened her coat around her.

"You don't have to leave. I could use another pair of hands if you'd like to stay. How's your talent with a needle?"

A definite sparkle filled Iris's eyes. "Actually, I'm pretty good. Estevan was very hard on his clothes. I was always fixing a hem on his slacks or replacing a button."

"Perfect. I have three bridesmaids' dresses and two blouses which need buttons." Rita gave Iris a little wink. "I used to do a lot of my handwork during the evenings, but lately your brother keeps me busy at night."

Iris had turned slightly towards the door as if she felt a slight obligation to be across the street. But she jerked her shoulder around and started to take off her coat. "I'm sure going out with Brian is more fun than sewing at home. I'd be glad to help."

"Great! Let's hang your coat up in the storeroom and I'll get you started."

She welcomed Iris's company and her assistance with the work. But most of all, she was glad to offer Brian's sister a better option than sitting in a cemetery or inside a lonely house. She wasn't sure how to broach the topic of payment or salary, but she'd figure that out, too, as Abuelita had taught her, one problem at a time.

❤ ❤ ❤ ❤ ❤

"Ask her if she'd like to learn bead-work," Tía Minerva said that night to Rita after she told Abuelita about Iris's work in the shop that day.

The three of them sat together eating more *caldo*. Rita suspected it was the only thing Tía knew how to cook.

"Minerva's right. I taught her to sew beads today. I could teach Brian's sister," Abuelita replied, then took a sip from her spoon.

"Well, I don't expect her to work for me," Rita said to both women. "It was just something to keep her out of the cemetery. She wouldn't even let me pay her."

"You need a helper, Rita." Abuelita's dark eyes met Rita's across the table. "You do big jobs. Weddings, the costumes. When others see *Folklórico* this summer, you'll get more."

"I can do my own sewing. It's the shop part that's hard," Rita replied. She reached for a corn tortilla in the basket in the middle of the table. "Maybe I just need to work from this house, like you did all those years."

"I was old. I had children I couldn't leave," Abuelita answered. "You need to be with people. Not hiding in this house."

"I wouldn't be hiding, I'd be sewing." Rita ripped her tortilla in half. "I wouldn't have to deal with greedy landlords or worry about someone robbing my cash register."

Abuelita made a grunting noise. "You think a councilman's family will come here for more clothes? Send their fancy friends to a little house on Ruiz street? Pay you any more than minimum wage for your work?"

She wasn't expecting this argument from Abuelita. She thought her great-grandmother would feel as if Rita was making a sensible decision.

"Ladies will pay good money for special dresses," Abuelita continued. "But only in a place of business, not in your spare bedroom. In a house, you're only the hired help. Like a maid. That's the way you'll be treated."

Abuelita's bitter tone was unexpected, shocking. It never occurred to Rita that Abuelita wasn't paid fairly for her skills as a dressmaker.

"You never told me this before." Rita gazed at her great-grandmother. A heavy sadness drove away her appetite. "You seemed to make a successful life as a dressmaker working out of this house."

"Making dresses was enough for me. You are a different person. Don't put yourself in my place. Find your own."

In a shop across the street from a cemetery? Rita didn't think so. She felt as if the soup had rocks that sunk to her stomach.

"Eat your *caldo*." Tía Minerva's gruff voice rumbled around the table. "If three of us work on the beads after supper, we can get the wedding dress done faster."

"What? You have another place to go tomorrow?" Abuelita clicked her tongue at her grandniece. "Brian's taking Rita out tonight. Why should she sit with the old hens when she can crow with a rooster?"

"Then let the rooster carry those old drawers onto the back porch before he leaves the chicken coop," Minerva answered, her wide forehead pinched into a frown.

"You can ask Frank or Joe to move the drawers. Brian might be dressed up," Rita told her aunt. "I don't want him to think that every time he comes here you'll put him to work."

"Didn't know men to be good for much else," Minerva grumbled before she scooped a spoonful of broth, onions, and celery into her mouth.

Rita rolled her eyes, just like she did when she was a child. She and her sisters used to call Tía Minerva "lemon puss." And while she was grateful her aunt was there to help Abuelita, Rita felt Tía was an intruder on their privacy. She still wanted to tell Abuelita about the money Bea took with her, but she didn't want anyone else in the family to know.

But Brian knew the truth and listened to Rita's concerns later when they sat inside Nena's Cantina, a small bar downtown among the restaurants and shops in Market Square.

"I had just about decided to close the shop and work from the house until Abuelita said what she did tonight. Now, I don't know what to do," Rita sighed.

Brian slid his finger through a wet ring left on the table. "You need a new place to conduct business, Rita. But you know that. Seems to me, it's time to start looking. Even if it means taking a day off to do it."

"Mr. Arredondo was so nasty last time he was in the shop. I know for certain I can't stay there."

"Then give him your notice next week. Tell him you'll be gone by February fifteenth," Brian answered. "Why pay that joker any more rent?" He reached across the table to take her hand. "If he has another tenant who wants the place, maybe he'd be willing to let you slip out of your lease now."

"But what will I do with all my merchandise?" Rita replied, contemplating the problems that could arise if she closed her shop in the next two weeks. "I can't bring all that stuff into Abuelita's house. Everything's such a mess there. It seems like the more we throw out or give away, the more we find in drawers and closets."

"Rita, you have to do something sooner or later. I know that by March fifteenth Abuelita will be gone and you can work out of the house temporarily, but that's two more rent checks that go into Mr. Arredondo's pockets."

She knew Brian made sense. How she wished she had a partner, someone to share the decisions with her. The man across the table loved her, but she couldn't lean on Brian. Or Abuelita. She had to just take this next step on her own and pray she'd find a suitable place soon.

They continued talking as they left Nena's and walked through the brick-paved Market Square. The night air was cold but not uncomfortable as they strolled under the copper street lamps with glowing yellow globes.

A shop on the corner caught Rita's attention and she moved towards it, taking Brian with her. One window display showed western-style shirts and denim skirts with shiny silver belts set with aquamarine stones. There were many pieces of jewelry, attractive clothes, and accessories to admire, but Rita paid attention to the spotlights used in certain places to bring attention to the merchandise. She noticed the wooden

room divider where belts were hung by their buckles
and the pink armed racks for scarfs and hats. She liked
the black styrofoam silhouettes which were set up
underneath a yellow lace dress and an embroidered
western jacket. They were more subtle than a mannequin or a sewing figure and took up less space.

"Your face is glowing," he whispered in her ear.

"I've just gotten some ideas for my shop that's all. I
never take the time to look at other shops and stores to
get ideas. I feel so inspired."

"I can tell." Brian put his arm around her shoulders
and pressed her close. "I think you work too hard. But
people who go into business for themselves usually do."

Rita looked at him. "Bea left me so abruptly, I felt
like I couldn't afford to breathe. I had to learn quickly,
and I was so frightened. I hired Stefanie on an impulse,
but it turned out to be a major turning point in my life."

"It was a major turning point in her life, too, Rita."

"I guess we both needed something the other could
provide. It was nice to have someone in the store to talk
to again. Stefanie did the little things that I didn't have
time for. I got a chance to catch my breath, to think
about what I wanted." She smiled at Brian. "I even got
the chance to fall in love with a wonderful man."

He leaned over to kiss her. "A major turning point
in my life, let me tell you."

Rita looked over her shoulder once more at the market area as they headed towards the spot where Brian
had parked her car. She was filled with new plans and
dreams for a store named Rita's Dress Shop, and felt a
wonderful confidence that she could make it all a reality. Brian's arm stayed around her, and she leaned into
him, feeling so lucky to have his love and support as she
took the next steps forward in her business.

Chapter Eleven

Rita was optimistic, excited, as she went through the morning. When Cecilia Díaz came in to pick up her mother-in-law's dress, Rita explained her plans to move the shop, and her customer replied, "Just give me the new address, and I'll be there. I don't trust any of my alterations to anyone but you."

Mrs. Díaz had just put away her checkbook and closed her purse when Iris arrived at the store.

"Iris! How good to see you." Cecilia Díaz went to Iris and gave her a quick hug. "You seem to be in this store on a regular basis these days."

Iris's face darkened with a definitive blush. "I— well, Rita's fixing a dress for me and I—have another in the car. I wanted to see if she had time to alter it, too."

"Well, you've come to the right place. Rita's work is wonderful. But you know that. Look at the dress she made for Stefanie." Cecilia's friendly smile encompassed both Rita and Iris. "Nicky's been asking me to have you and Stefanie come for supper soon. I think he likes your daughter."

"Stefanie hasn't said much to me." Iris shrugged, yet gave her friend a brief smile. "Perhaps the children want an excuse to see each other again."

"Well, I can live with that. Better they're together in our dens than hanging around the malls. I always encourage Nicky to invite friends to our house. At least I know he won't get into trouble there," Cecilia said, then glanced at her watch. "I've got to run. It was so good to see you, Iris. And we'll get together soon, okay?"

"That would be nice," Iris answered, and stepped away from the door.

"Bye, Rita. And I'll expect an invitation to your grand opening!" Mrs. Díaz called before she opened the door and left the shop.

"A grand opening?" Iris inquired of Rita as she unbuttoned her coat.

Rita shut the cash-register drawer and grinned at Iris. "Rita's Dress Shop is on the move. I'm going to start looking for a new location today."

Then she told Iris about her conversation with Abuelita and her decision to maintain a place of business rather than work out of her house. She also mentioned Brian's idea to start looking for a new place and to discuss breaking her lease with Mr. Arredondo immediately.

"This sounds very exciting," Iris told her. "Do you know what kind of place you want?"

"Not really. I keep hoping that one place will just feel right. Does that sound dumb?"

"No, of course not," Iris said. "Every store has a different feel to it. Even big chain stores are different in different parts of town. But I like shopping in smaller shops and boutiques better than the department stores. You get more personal service. And the merchandise is one-of-a-kind. That's important to me."

Iris had just removed her coat. Today she was dressed in a white cashmere sweater with a slim red skirt and black leather boots.

In admiring Iris's appearance, Rita wished for someone like Iris to give her new store a touch of simple elegance. Bea's concept of style bordered on gaudy, and at the time, Rita had felt too inexperienced to oppose her. Even now, Rita wasn't sure what she really wanted.

"Iris, would you come with me this afternoon?" she asked.

"Come with you?"

"Yes. To look at these other places for a new shop."

"But I don't know anything about commercial properties. Why would you want me?"

Rita shrugged. "Moral support? Someone to listen to my ideas and tell me if I'm crazy?"

"Perhaps Brian could—"

"No, Iris." Rita shook her head. "This is something I have to do alone. I mean—I don't want to involve Brian in this aspect of my business. Besides, my customers are primarily women. I'd need a woman's opinion about things."

"Well, Stefanie does have her piano lessons this afternoon. I don't have to pick her up until five." Iris spoke as if to herself. She stared at Rita for one uncomfortable moment, then sighed. "If you think I can help, sure. I'll come with you."

"Great! I have to finish one dress for tomorrow's fitting, then we can get started. I already circled some places in the newspaper." Rita's stomach churned with a nervous excitement. She handed Iris the newspaper. "Tell me what you think."

Not waiting for an answer, Rita moved from behind the counter and made her way to the sewing machine. She picked up the last pink bridesmaid's dress she had to make for the Guerra wedding and started pinning the side seams together. After eight of these dresses, she was sick of the color. She glanced up at Iris who was still reading the ads.

"See anything promising, Iris?"

"Have you called about the properties yet?" Iris asked, looking up from the newspaper.

"I wanted to look at them before I talked to any landlords."

"Your time is too valuable, Rita. There's no reason to even look at a place unless it's in your price range and it's big enough for your needs." Iris glanced around, then picked up a pencil and a notepad by the cash register. "You keep sewing. I'll make a few phone calls." She came closer to the machine where Rita sat working.

"I don't mean to be nosey, Rita, but I'll need some information from you before I get on the telephone."

"You're right, Iris. Let me tell you what I would really like."

❤ ❤ ❤ ❤ ❤

"Every shop was just—I don't know." Rita circled her hand near her face as she groped for words to describe her feelings. She looked across the front seat at Iris, hoping she could better explain things to Stefanie, who sat in the back seat of Rita's navy blue car.

The three of them were driving back from Incarnate Word College where Stefanie studied piano two afternoons a week. Iris and Rita had lost track of time as they met with landlords and examined their properties, so Rita drove straight to the college a little before five.

"One needed a major paint job," Iris explained. "Another place had so many burglar bars and security locks, it looked like a prison."

"But they all sounded so nice in the paper." Rita sighed, stopping her car for a traffic signal. "Maybe I need to drive around and look for places on my own. Just pick out some of the streets that Brian and I talked about and see if there are any empty storefronts."

"Like that one?" Stefanie said, tapping her finger on the window.

Rita glanced out her window, then turned her head completely. Two buildings down Blanco Road was a renovated house. The crooked neon sign hanging over the doorway indicated it had once been a flower ship.

The exterior was painted white with powder blue trim around the large picture window and overhang. Hanging inside the door was a large FOR LEASE sign.

"Rita, isn't that an interesting place?" Iris had leaned closer to Rita's side so she could see better. "Let's take a look."

After parking the car in the front lot that was wide enough for about six cars, the three ladies got out to inspect the shop further.

Rita stood beside Stefanie, staring through the window. "It looks like there's another room to the left there. The carpeting looks clean."

"Rita, look at this!" Iris called from the side of the building.

Stefanie followed Rita to a narrow sidewalk which Iris had walked down. Now Iris stood on one side of a wooden gate hooked to a white picket fence that circled the back yard of the house. Iris opened the gate and all three of them walked past a back door and a screened-in porch, then stopped at the cement patio to look around.

"I bet there's an apartment here—you know, connected to the shop?" Iris said to Rita. "You could even live here if you wanted."

"Rita living behind the shop? Won't that make life easy! After you lock the door, you can walk down the hall and eat supper." Stefanie's voice carried a youthful enthusiasm as she walked around the patio.

Rita like the idea of living behind her shop very much. It would be convenient, and she wouldn't have to live alone in Abuelita's house, missing the ways they had lived together there. A small apartment would require less housekeeping, too. She'd have time for more important things, like spending time with Brian. She imagined a cozy dinner by candlelight, a romantic picnic under the stars.

"What do you think?" Iris asked.

"I think I want the landlord's telephone number," Rita answered, then smiled at Iris. "This place could be just the answer for everything I need."

Rita got the phone number then drove Iris and Stefanie home. They all talked about different ideas for the new store. Rita felt happy that Iris and Stefanie could share enthusiasm in Rita's venture without the tension that usually accompanied a conversation between them.

She didn't feel like she had to play referee. Perhaps the mother-daughter relationship was finally starting to develop into something more friendly. But when Stefanie begged Rita to stay for supper and she saw the same lost-puppy look in Iris's eyes, she realized they needed Rita to help them maintain the good feelings the afternoon had provided.

"We can call Uncle Brian, too," Stefanie added, as if it might sway Rita. "Wouldn't a real family supper be good?"

"Brian's working late tonight," Rita said.

"You're welcome to stay, Rita. But it won't be fancy," Iris said with hesitation in her voice. "I can throw a salad together. And there's a small ham we can slice up."

To Rita, Iris's food was far more appetizing than another bowl of *caldo*. She smiled at Iris. "It sounds fine. Thank you. I'll just call Abuelita and let her know I'll be home later."

"Gee, I thought only teenagers had to call home," Stefanie said as they walked towards the house.

"I don't want her to worry about me," Rita replied. "When you share a house with someone, you ought to be considerate of their feelings."

"But if you move behind the shop, you won't have to worry about anyone but yourself. Won't you love that freedom to come and go as you please?" Stefanie said, with a frown aimed in her mother's direction.

"She'll also have to learn to live by herself," Iris said, turning to unlock the front door. "That'll be a big change. Won't it, Rita?"

"Yes, I'm afraid it will." Rita hoped she could keep her fears at arm's length. Not that she worried about living alone. She just hated the thought of living without Abuelita's daily companionship. To whom would Rita turn for guidance? Where would she find an extra dose of confidence? Through the years, Abuelita's love was like a million candles filling the darkness with light and warmth.

Suddenly, Rita felt a hand close around her own. She glanced down, then up into Stefanie's greenish-brown gaze.

"Don't forget what Uncle Brian said. There's a difference between living alone and feeling lonely," the girl said before she gently squeezed Rita's hand. "You can always invite a friend to supper."

"You're right." Rita smiled. "Living alone has some advantages. I can sew late at night without worrying that the sewing machine will keep someone else awake."

"You can listen to the stereo as loud as you want," Stefanie added.

"My neighbors might have something to say about that." Rita grinned at the image of herself dancing around the apartment to loud music.

"It'll be fun to decorate an apartment for yourself," Iris said, opening the door and entering the house. She switched on lights as they moved from the entrance way into the living room. "Of course, you won't know much until you get in touch with the landlord."

"After I call Abuelita, I'll try to call him. Maybe he can meet me early in the morning before I open the store."

On the phone, Abuelita told Rita that she and Tía were going out, taking pictures and other things to Uncle Mike for his family to keep. When Abuelita asked if she had found a new store, Rita just told her, "Not yet. But we found a place on the way home from Stefanie's piano lessons that looks nice." She wasn't ready to tell Abuelita that she might not live in her house, afraid Tía might give it to a relative before Rita could make definite plans.

When she called the landlord's number, she got an answering machine. She left her name and phone number, and hoped her call would be returned first thing in the morning.

Rita left the living room and wandered behind the stairway into the kitchen. Iris stood at an L-shaped island counter in the middle of the big kitchen, a room that could easily fit all three of Abuelita's bedrooms within it. One wall had built-in oak cabinets that met with the two door cream-colored refrigerator. A shiny counter stretched over the stove, dishwasher, and trash compactor to the stainless steel double sink. Windows with sheer curtains gave a liberal view of the backyard and wooden deck outside the back door.

Abuelita's kitchen window faced the alley trash cans and barely allowed two people to pass between the stove and the sink. And it seemed even more crowded now that Tía had temporarily moved in.

"If I ever buy a house, I want it to have a kitchen like this," Rita said, coming to stand on the other side of the island. "There's so much space."

Iris looked up from the lettuce she was tearing apart. "Estevan got carried away when he designed the kitchen. An army of cooks could work in here. Of course, it goes along with the army of people who could eat at our dining-room table. Brian thinks we should buy a small table and chairs for a breakfast area like he has. Put it over there by the window."

"That's a good idea. Especially when it's just the two of you eating together."

"Stefanie usually takes her plate into the den and watches TV. Maybe if we had a table and chairs in here, she'd eat with me." Iris sighed. "Or I'd feel like eating with her."

"Maybe there's a good side to Abuelita's small kitchen and the table where we eat together every night. That tiny space is perfect for personal conversations. Sharing thoughts and plans over a daily meal." Rita sighed, feeling a slight pinching of her insides. "I think I'll miss that most when Abuelita moves away."

"I know what you mean. I didn't realize how much I talked to Estevan until he was gone. In my mind, I often feel like I'm talking to him, only he doesn't answer. No one answers."

"But you have Stefanie. You should talk to her," Rita said. Without thinking she reached for a small knife beside the tomatoes and started slicing them upon a circular wooden cutting board.

"Stefanie's still a child. I don't want to burden her with my loneliness." Iris resumed her job on the lettuce, dropping the leaves into a crystal salad bowl.

"Remember, Iris, Stefanie's lonely, too. I know that when I'd talk to Abuelita about missing my father, it helped both of us. And she missed him, too. He came and had breakfast with her every Saturday morning at five a.m. for years. I never knew that, because he was always reading the paper and drinking coffee when I woke up. We were able to talk about our different memories of him. It meant a lot to me."

"It's not that I don't want to talk to Stefanie. I just don't know what to say. How to put my feelings into words. I just feel like I'm lost in a black tunnel. I don't want to pull her inside with me when I don't know where I'm going."

Rita stopped slicing to stare at Iris. "A few weeks ago, Brian told me he felt like he was stumbling in the darkness trying to find a light switch. Now, you talk about a dark tunnel. What a funny coincidence."

Iris wiped her hands on a yellow dishtowel. "It's not so funny. We both hate the darkness. Since we were kids. I don't know about Brian, but I always felt if I couldn't see, I couldn't be ready."

"Ready for what?

"I don't know exactly. I wanted to be ready just in case something happened. I have to see it coming or I can't cope with it. That's why everything with Estevan was so painful. I wasn't ready to say good-bye. And I sure wasn't prepared to live without him." Her eyes revealed a grief that gripped Rita's heart with icy fingers.

A shiver dropped down her back. Rita warmed herself with quick movements. She lifted the cutting board over the bowl to scrape the sliced tomatoes over the lettuce. Then she walked over to the silver sink to rinse off the cutting board and the knife.

"Ah! It's nice to be out of prison clothes," Stefanie announced with an exaggerated sigh as soon as she entered the kitchen. "I wish I could just wear this to school." She was dressed in faded jeans and a lavender sweatshirt that had the comfortable look of a favorite.

Rita quickly shut off the faucet. She was relieved that Stefanie arrived with a change of subject at hand. Tearing a paper towel from a rack to her left, she dried her hands as she turned around to face the teenager. "When I was in high school, sometimes I wished for uniforms. Then nobody knew who could afford the nicer clothes and who was wearing her big sister's handovers."

"It's not so great looking like two hundred other girls. And then to walk around a college dressed in a uniform. How embarrassing!" Stefanie moved to the refrigerator to open it and peer inside.

"You should feel proud that you're talented enough to study piano on a college campus," Iris replied, her voice sharpened by impatience.

Rita had the feeling this was an old argument, something as worn out as Stefanie's shirt. She redirected the conversation quickly. "I always wanted to finish my college degree, but right now I wouldn't know whether to learn more about business or study fashion design."

"Why would you want to study fashion design?" Stefanie shrugged and shut the refrigerator door. "You already know how to sew something from a picture."

"But it's someone else's picture," Rita said. "I'd like to learn how to take my idea and put it down on paper. There's a lot to know about color and lines and fabric."

"So you want to design dresses? I didn't think you were so ambitious," Iris said, pouring dressing from a thin bottle over the salad.

"I don't think it's ambition, just a desire to learn more. But it's something I won't do any time soon. I've got too much going on with the shop to think about going back to college. Iris, can I help with something else?"

"I think everything's ready, such as it is. Stefanie, set the table please, and I'll get the iced tea."

"I'll take the salad into the dining room," Rita said, and followed Stefanie into the adjoining room.

Unlike the other rooms Rita had seen, the dining room had a cold, formal look to it. The traditional pieces, a tall china cabinet with a silver tea service, a buffet table with thick carved legs, and a long table with a stiff white tablecloth and crystal candle holders, was all very grand and beautiful, but didn't bring to mind family dinners brightened by laughter and warmth. This was a place where only perfect manners and polite conversation were allowed.

She saw Stefanie going through the motions of setting three places, one at the end of the table, one midway down, and another across from the second.

"Couldn't we all sit at one end so we can talk easier?" Rita said, uncomfortable with the space dividing them during dinner.

Stefanie regarded Rita with wide eyes, as if she had never heard such a suggestion before.

Rita put the salad down then moved one sleek black chair closer to the first place setting. "I'd feel funny sitting so far away from you and your mother. I'd feel like I was shouting when I was trying to talk to you."

"We never talk much during dinner," Stefanie said, but moved the chair closest to her down the table.

They rearranged the place settings and Rita smiled at Stefanie. "I think this will be much nicer for us, don't you?"

Stefanie stared at her a long moment then said, "How did you get my mother to go with you this afternoon?"

"I needed another opinion," Rita replied.

"But Mom? Why her?"

She didn't know how to interpret Stefanie's frown, and decided just to be honest with the girl. "I'd like to get a touch of class into my new shop. Don't you think your mother has good taste?"

"Yes, I guess so. But how did you two get together? Did you call her or what?"

Rita realized how little Iris and Stefanie spoke to each other. No wonder both of them were so lonely. Had Estevan been the only one each talked to? Had they only confided in him, not each other? No wonder his sudden death had left both of them so lost and shaken.

"Your mother came into my shop yesterday. The dress she bought for the *quince* didn't fit right. She stayed around and helped with some sewing. She came back this morning and—" Rita paused. She knew there wasn't another dress that Iris needed fixing today. It was obvious why Iris came back. "—and I just asked her to come along."

"My mother worked with you in the shop yesterday?"

"Don't you think she's capable?"

"Oh, she can do the job. But Daddy would've had a cow to see his wife working. He set up things so she'd never have to work, even now that he's gone."

"Would you mind if she went to work? Not for the money, but because she needed to feel useful?"

"If she wants to work, I could live with that."

"Perhaps you need to tell her so, Stefanie."

"She wouldn't listen to me. The only person she listens to is Uncle Brian."

Just then, Iris arrived in the dining room with a platter of sliced ham. "Stefanie, would you bring the pitcher of iced tea in here?"

Once the girl was out of listening range, Rita said, "Stefanie was a bit surprised you helped me in the shop yesterday."

"She disapproves, doesn't she?"

"No, she's only surprised we were together at all. Iris, she worries about you spending your days at the cemetery. She's told me that often."

"Why did Stefanie set the plates so close together?" Iris looked down at the table, her eyebrows bunching together unattractively.

"This was my idea, Iris. How can we talk together with so much distance in between?"

No reply. Iris just put the platter down. Then Stefanie returned with the pitcher of tea.

There was an awkward silence after the three of them sat down. Impulsively, Rita reached her hands out, one to Stefanie across the table, and the other to Iris, who sat at the corner.

"Let's hold hands while we say the blessing," Rita said, making eye contact with each one. "Abuelita always says it makes the prayers rise to heaven faster."

Stefanie stifled a nervous giggle. Iris' face turned pink. Yet they held Rita's hands and even each other's while they prayed the traditional words of Grace Before Meals.

"You don't know how good this tastes," Rita said after she relished her first bites of lettuce and tomato flavored with tangy ranch dressing. "My Tía Minerva has moved in for a while and all she cooks is soup."

Stefanie nodded, but kept her eyes on her plate. Iris's expression was an artificial smile. Neither seemed to want to carry on conversation.

Rita continued to eat until she felt as if the silence would push her down to the floor. She though back to the day's events, something or someone they shared an interest in, and a sudden thought enlightened her. "Stefanie, Mrs. Díaz was in the shop today. Have you talked to Nicky since the New Year's party?"

"No." Stefanie spoke as if the word was a hot pepper on her tongue. A dark blush crept over her cheeks as she reached for her glass of tea.

Rita turned to Iris, hoping for a better response. "Mrs. Díaz was one of the first customers I didn't get from Abuelita's connections or Bea's friends. I guess that is why her continued business means so much. And her recommendation has brought me a few new customers. That's how Alyssa Guerra got my name."

"Have you finished Alyssa's dress?" Stefanie asked suddenly.

"For the most part. Abuelita's doing the beadwork now."

"And have you thought much about what you'll do about beadwork once your great-grandmother moves?" Iris reached for the glass salt shaker and used it sparingly over her ham.

Rita started to relax as the conversation kept going. "I might be able to decorate more with delicate laces and ribbons. That's why I'd like some design experience. Then I could draw out gowns I can do, and not have to copy some magazine gown with lots of beadwork."

"I saw the *Folklórico*'s costume sketches. If you get more jobs like that, you can give up the wedding gowns completely," Iris suggested.

"You could drop the *quinceañera* dresses, too," Stefanie said. "I bet they're a lot of trouble to make."

"I'd never stop making *quince* dresses." Rita's tone was firm. "Few places sell them anymore. And those that do, try and make them serve double duty as wedding dresses to save money. A quince gown should look like a special dress for a teenager." Realizing that her adamance might be mistaken for anger, she paused then stared down at her plate. "I just enjoy making the *quinceañera* dresses, that's all."

"I just don't understand you, Rita." Stefanie set down her fork to glare at Rita. "You make *quinces* sound like such an important thing. Angie's not having one.

Neither is Micole. Only one other girl in my class will have a *quince* this year. And she's having her reception at one of the hotels on the Riverwalk."

Iris placed her hand on her daughter's arm. "Stefanie, you agreed that a party at home would be okay."

"No, Mom. You and Uncle Brian said it would be okay. Then you told me what I was going to do. You never asked me what I wanted." Stefanie had turned to give her mother one of those icy glares that Iris had often given to others.

Iris sat still, her face composed into an emotionless mask. She slowly exhaled, then finally spoke. "All right, Stefanie, tell me what you want. I love you. I just want you to be happy."

Stefanie's glares had melted into thick hazel pools. The girl struggled to keep her cool despite the tears. "I miss Daddy. And he wanted all this. I never asked for a *quinceañera*."

"No, but you deserve one," Iris told her daughter. "You should have a day to celebrate your passing through girlhood. And the rest of us who love you need to take the time to mark the occasion. If not, you'll grow up and be gone before we know it. This custom is a nice one, Stefanie. I want to do this for you. So does Uncle Brian. But if there's something else you want so that you can really enjoy your fifteenth birthday, please tell me."

The teenager glanced at Rita then looked back at her mother. "I do have something I want. I want to ask Nicky Díaz to be my honor escort. Can't you ask his family to come to supper this week? I'm too nervous to call him, but I could ask him if he was here. I know I could."

Iris's eyes widened at the request. "I suppose I can ask them to supper soon." She looked at Rita. "If the Díazes come over, will you and Brian come for supper, too? I think a small dinner party might be nice."

Rita responded with a calm voice, although she wanted to yell for joy. "I'll be here. I know Brian would come, too. Just tell us when."

Iris smiled at Rita. Then she turned to her daughter. "Nicky Díaz, huh? I thought you might ask Linda's son Billy to be your escort."

Stefanie shook her head. "He's too young. He's only thirteen."

"Don't you like younger men?" Iris laughed then, and Stefanie laughed, too.

Rita joined in the laughter, feeling for the first time that a group of friends were sharing dinner together. She knew other obstacles still lay ahead for Iris and Stefanie's relationship, but tonight a glimmer of light had appeared in the darkness to show them the way home.

Chapter Twelve

Rita quietly closed the front door of Abuelita's house. She carefully locked it then turned around. She gasped, her heart hip-hopping against her chest.

Abuelita sat in the wooden rocking chair, her black eyes leveled at Rita. One long silver braid hung over her shoulder. She wore a new-looking red cotton robe tied around her long white night gown.

"Don't be scared. It's only Abuelita," the old woman said in the same soothing tones Rita heard many times late at night when Rita would hear something in the darkness and cry out, "Who's there?"

Rita pressed her hand against her heart as if to silence its pounding. "I wasn't expecting you to be sitting there, that's all."

Her great-grandmother shrugged. "I couldn't sleep."

Guilt made her stomach tighten. Abuelita had often said she couldn't sleep until she knew Rita was safe in her bed. Whenever she went out, she always tried to get home early, but tonight, her thoughts were on Iris and Stefanie.

"I'm sorry, Abuelita. I lost track of time. I didn't mean to make you worry, or stay up so late." She started unbuttoning her blue coat. "How's Uncle Mike and Aunt Hallie?"

"Aaah! I can't sleep because of them."

"Is something wrong at their house?"

"No. Just this house." Abuelita gestured as if she was talking about the living room. "I'm leaving you an empty building."

Rita's eyes followed Abuelita's arm, over the furniture she loved as well as the boxes stacked around the room. "These are all your things, Abuelita. If you want to give them away, it's okay. Really. Better you go through and give away than me. How would I know who should get what?"

"This is your home, what's outside, what's inside. I shouldn't give things away. They only want more."

Tossing her coat on the sofa, Rita went to kneel on the gold rug under the rocking chair. She looked up at her great-grandmother. "Nothing in this house matters. Just you, Abuelita. I wish you could just send your things to Brownsville and you remain here."

The old woman's fingers sifted through Rita's hair. Each one dwelled in silence and private thoughts.

Rita remembered her mother arguing with other family members over her father's things when he died. She never wanted any part of that bitter anger and hurt feelings. She'd rather live in an empty building than have a flock of vultures fighting over things after Abuelita died. Her greatest fear was that the family would know how much of Abuelita's money had been invested in Rita's business before she repaid the loan completely.

She wrapped her fingers around the spindle arm of the rocking chair. She should tell Abuelita about Bea and the money. But it wouldn't help Abuelita's sleeplessness. That's for sure.

Her lips trembled as she said, "I love you, Abuelita. I'm going to miss you, the way we talk like this. What will I do?"

Her great-grandmother tilted her head to stare directly into Rita's eyes. "You will whisper good night to Brian, no?"

Rita gave no reply to that statement. "It's late, Abuelita. Shall we go to sleep?"

"Yes." Abuelita attempted to rise from the chair, and Rita quickly got up to help her. "Tomorrow, I'll go visit Anna, then Debra. I have things for them to keep."

"I'm sure they'll be glad to see Tía Minerva, too," Rita said, then giggled, remembering how Anna and Debra complained about their aunt's last visits. She had cooked a broth for Anna's baby, who suffered from colic, and Anna said it took three days to clear the smell out of the house. As for Debra, Tía slipped on a toy and fell in the kitchen. The woman was Debra's house guest for five days while she "recovered." It nearly ended Debra's marriage.

"We should share Minerva's good intentions," Abuelita said, wrapping her arm firmly around Rita's. The old woman chuckled. "We can share all the *caldo* in the refrigerator, too."

"I'll do the cooking the next few days," Rita whispered as they neared the bedrooms.

"Teresa is a good cook. But I will miss your face across the table." Abuelita's voice was hoarse, as if it was coated with tears.

Rita kissed her great-grandmother's cheek. *"Yo te quiero, Abuelita".*

"Que el angel de la guardia siempre te proteja," she answered.

When Rita awoke, she was glad for her guardian angel's protection. Her sleep had been restless. Dreams of horned landlords, Abuelita sailing away on a sea of soup. Noises in the dark that couldn't be seen in candlelight. She was almost relieved when the alarm clock beeped loudly, ending the troublesome night and starting a new day.

She was tired and nervous as she anticipated a new landlord's telephone call and another afternoon of looking at empty storefront properties. No one was awake when she ate her breakfast and scanned the newspaper. Rita felt lonely. She even found herself wishing for Tía's grumbling to send her on her way this morning.

And despite her desire for company, Rita wasn't happy to see her landlord, César Arredondo, enter her store soon after she opened the shop. The man reeked of cheap cologne.

Today he was accompanied by a stringy man who wore his slick black hair pulled into a ponytail. Three gold chains circled his scrawny neck. He wore a vinyl black overcoat over his purple shirt and black slacks.

"This is my nephew Willie. He may run a store here for me," Mr. Arredondo said by way of introduction.

Rita gave both of them a polite smile. "Good morning, gentlemen." She sat at the sewing machine, indulging her own mood by working on a blouse for herself. She didn't even get up when they entered the store.

Willie extended his hand towards Rita, and she noticed a purple heart with a green rose in its center tattooed on his wrist. She shook his cold, clammy hand and it took great effort not to wipe the touch of him off on her blue jeans.

"You run this shop by yourself?" Willie asked. He smiled, revealing a silver cap on his side tooth. His face was dotted with blemish scars.

"It's a small place. Easy enough to manage alone," she told him, then turned away and resumed her stitching on the side seam of the silk print blouse she hoped to wear when she saw Brian on Friday.

The two men talked in buzzing tones as they moved around the shop. Rita felt Willie's eyes on her and tried to ignore him. She thought they spent a little too much time in the storeroom and hoped nothing would be missing when she checked it later. Finally, they came back and stood by the counter talking about types of video game machines that were most popular with the neighborhood kids.

"I see you're looking for a new shop," Mr. Arredondo said.

Rita's backbone stiffened. She looked up from her sewing to see her landlord holding the newspaper with yellow circles. It must have dropped out of her pocket when she hung up her coat in the back room.

She gave Mr. Arredondo a bold stare despite her rumbling heartbeat. "I'm looking, yes. I need a place that doesn't leak."

He rubbed his fingers down his moustache and around his thick lips, studying Rita with narrowed eyes.

"What about the *mercado*? They do stuff like this down there," Willie said. "You ought to sell *piñatas*, too."

"I appreciate the suggestion," Rita said through gritted teeth.

"So, you're breaking the lease, huh?"

She looked at Mr. Arredondo. "No. I'm going to find a new place for my shop. If you want to release me from the lease so you can put a new business in here, I'm sure we can agree on something that would benefit both of us." She almost smiled at the professional tone she took with the man. Brian's colleagues would be impressed.

Instead, she found herself staring at the gold diamond ring on the finger that Mr. Arredondo pointed at her. "It says in the contract that if you break the lease, you lose your property deposit."

"I know what my contract says. But if I drag things out until March fifteenth, you'll miss out on the extra rent money you want to charge a new tenant." She motioned towards Willie, her voice still calm and confident.

Mr. Arredondo responded with a smile like the wolf gave Little Red Riding Hood. "I always give rent discounts to relatives. But if you want to forget the property deposit, you can get out by the fifteenth of this month."

Rita frowned. She had no intention of moving out of the store in a few days or giving that man her property deposit. She had a gut feeling that he wouldn't give back that money without a fight anyway.

"I thought you might be more reasonable about this," Rita said, folding her arms across her chest. "But I'll just take my time in finding something more appropriate for my customers. I can still open a new place by Easter."

Mr. Arredondo grunted then said, "I'll be back on Saturday for the rent check. It's the fifteenth you know."

"Don't trouble yourself. I mailed your check out this morning," Rita said, not blinking an eye as she lied to him.

Although he stared at her a long time, she didn't flinch. Finally, he said, "You want out? I'll take the rent check in the mail. I'll give you 'til the fifth of next month. We'll discuss the deposit refund then."

Rita nodded, although she already intended to send him a check today for the next month's rent, less the property deposit. She didn't trust this man, never would. Two could play his self-serving games. And if he complained, she'd just say, "We'll discuss the deposit on the fifth."

The two men left, laughing about something Willie muttered in Spanish; no doubt, a few words about her. Once they closed the door behind them, Rita had a strong urge to spray the whole shop for cockroaches.

❤ ❤ ❤ ❤ ❤

Iris looked up unexpectedly when Rita hung up the phone.

"Well, what did he say?"

Rita reached out to the cash register to steady herself, still unable to believe the amount the landlord wanted for his place on Blanco Road.

"Two thousand dollars." Rita stared at Iris, who had been working at a small table near the side room pinning red ribbon along the hem of a white Mexican dance costume.

"Two thousand? For a deposit?"

"No, a month. He wants two months rent as deposit."

Iris whistled then said, "Is this place painted in gold?"

"No, but it sure sounds like an ideal place." Rita sighed. "There's a one-bedroom apartment behind the store and the shop itself has three interconnecting rooms. Even a full-size basement that's paneled and carpeted."

"Lots of space there. Shall we go look at it?"

"Be reasonable, Iris. Why look at something I can't ever afford?"

Iris put down the ribbon and stood up. "I think you should just get what you want and forget about what you can afford."

"You make it sound so easy. And where am I going to get four-thousand dollars right now?"

"Get a bank loan, Rita, just like other small business owners do. Or find someone to invest in the business. Maybe one of your relatives?"

Feeling as she got jabbed by scissors in her stomach, Rita groaned. "I have no relatives with money to invest in my business."

"Then you need a business partner like your last one."

"No, thank you!" Rita's fist thumped on the cash register. She walked back to her sewing machine. She sat down and lined up the neckline to sew the facing down. She was just ready to start the machine, when she sensed Iris' presence beside her.

"Do you mind if I ask what happened between you and your last partner?" Iris's quiet voice was touched by a genuine concern. Her arms were crossed as she stood patiently, waiting for an explanation.

"She eloped with her boyfriend," Rita stated as a matter of fact. "And took most of *my* money with her." But then she told Iris about Bea's grand ideas,

Abuelita's investment, and her own mistakes about the business just as she had told Brian, only this time there were no tears, just a biting anger at her own inexperience and ignorance.

Iris listened silently, offering a frown or sympathetic hum as Rita talked. Eventually, there was a long pause. Rita just sat at the machine staring at the swirling patterns of her blouse that she didn't feel like finishing anymore.

"Tell me, Rita. What would you do differently if you had another partner?"

Rita looked up. "Well, the first thing I'd do is get a partnership agreement of some kind. And something in our bank account that wouldn't allow one person to write a big check without the other's signature. I'd need someone who could set up the business in such a way that no partner got cheated. We'd share the profits as well as the bills in a fair way." Rita paused, feeling old hurts coming back to haunt her. "I'd like to have a partner who had faith in my judgment. Someone who thinks I'm not just a person in the back room making dresses, but a real partner in a successful dress shop."

She looked down to see that her hands had crumpled the material she had been holding. Her eyes stung, but she told herself she had to learn from those bad experiences and move forward into something better for herself. She had admitted to herself, to Brian, and now to Iris, that she needed a partner of some kind. She had to trust again, find someone who respected her work and needed a creative but profitable career as much as she did.

Carefully, she smoothed the wrinkles from the material and raised her eyes to see Iris offering her the supportive smile of a new friend. And in that moment, she saw Iris as if she was in a spotlight, or perhaps it was her pastel-yellow sweater dress that gave the impression of hope, a candle in the window after a weary journey. In the middle of the shop stood a woman who respected Rita's work, enjoyed her company, and needed to discover her own talents in a challenging area.

Iris had a friendly way with people, she had a sense of style that Rita admired, even envied. And Iris was willing to do things, even minor sewing jobs, to help Rita. Besides her stitching was neat and even; it would even pass Abuelita's high standards.

"What? You're staring at me." Iris laughed, a bit self-consciously.

"Iris, what would you say if I asked you to become the partner I need in my business?" Rita's smile was a visible sign of the enthusiasm shooting off inside her like bottle rockets.

"Me?" Iris's hazel eyes widened, her hand circled her throat which was starting to turn crimson like her cheeks. "You want me to be your business partner?"

"Yes. You. I think you'd make a great business partner. What do you think?"

Iris's complexion faded into a pale pink shade; her eyes slipped into liquid browns and greens. "I don't think anyone would pay good money for my sewing skills."

"There's more to this shop than sewing, Iris. We could sell more ready-made dresses and offer alterations. Find some unique accessories. You suggested that I should sell hats, too, remember?"

Iris turned and moved towards the front window. She stared out, seeming to look for answers. She started talking, but it seemed more for herself than for Rita. "What have I done in my life? Gone to parties, arranged dinners for my husband's friends, engaged in mindless shopping ventures. I spent money and wasted time. I lived the role of the perfect wife and mother, but it seems like I was just acting on a stage. None of it seems real anymore."

Rita stood up and walked to where Iris stood. "Iris, I think you and I could make a good team. There are a million possibilities with two creative minds working together instead of one. But know this. I'll be your friend no matter what you decide. I asked you to join me as a partner because I trust you. I admire you. I think you have the qualities to help me. Your sense of style could add so much to my business."

Iris turned to face Rita. Her eyes were clear now, as if she had left emotions behind her and was thinking more rationally. "But you need money, don't you? I mean, if you ask me to be your partner, you'd expect me to invest my money in this shop, too, wouldn't you?"

"Yes. I don't know how a legal partnership works, but we'll hire someone who does. Iris, just think about it. That's all I'm asking."

Iris released a sigh before she shook her head. "What you've suggested is wonderful and exciting and I'd love to do it."

"But?"

"But it's very complicated."

"Are you thinking about Stefanie? You might be surprised if you asked her opinion about you going to work."

Iris shook her head again. "It's about the money I'd want to invest—you know, my fair share? Brian would have to approve if I went into business with you."

Rita just laughed. She wasn't worried about Brian. "Iris, of course he'd approve. He's very happy that we've become friends. Just like I assume that you're happy about my relationship with Brian."

"There's more to it, Rita. Brian controls my money."

"He controls your money? I don't understand."

"Estevan's estate is made up of trust funds. There's one for Stefanie, for her college education. And another for both of us. There's a quarterly distribution of the earnings. That's what we live on."

Rita didn't understand exactly, but still she nodded.

"Brian is the trustee of both accounts." Iris' stare seemed to pass right through Rita. "Estevan set things up about three years ago. At the time, I liked the idea, because if anything happened to both of us, I wanted Brian to take care of Stefanie and protect her inheritance. I never expected Estevan would die suddenly and—and when he first died, I was relieved that I didn't have to worry about anything since Brian's executor of the will, too. And as long as I have a comfortable allowance, Stefanie and I could do fine."

Iris tossed her hands up and walked towards the sewing figure wearing the colorful Mexican dress. Her fingers slid over the ribboned neckline as she moved behind it. "I suddenly feel so angry. Angry that my husband didn't think I had the intelligence to take care of our money. And angry that he put my little brother in control of that money. And angry because I would love to go into business with you, but I have to ask Brian for the money to do it. It seems that my happiness has always been in someone else's hands." Iris stood straight as a brick wall, her hands clenching into white-knuckled fists by her side.

"You know what I realized after I went to see Linda in New Mexico? I've never had control of my own life. I went from Daddy's house straight into Estevan's. I've always lived with men with outdated ideas of protecting their women from the realities of life. And I just let Brian take up where they left off."

Rita said nothing. What could she say? A father's protectiveness was just a childhood memory of drying tears and a cozy lap. She had been raised by women who took care of themselves. At that moment she could even love and admire Tía Minerva, who bought her own house in Sabinal and always drove a nice car; usually the only reliable one in the family whenever Abuelita wanted to travel.

"Rita."

Her eyes met Iris's. "Yes?"

"I want to go into business with you." Iris' lips parted into a pleased smile. "I'm flattered that you'd trust me with your business."

Each woman walked to meet the other. Rita took Iris's cold hands into her own. "I'd be so proud to have a partner like you."

Suddenly, they both broke into happy laughter and hugged each other tightly.

"I really don't think you'll have problems with Brian," Rita told Iris moments later. "Brian once offered me his own money to open a new shop. He's been very supportive of my work. And he knows how much I need a second person in the shop with me. I'm sure he'll see our going into business together as a great thing."

"And you think Stefanie won't mind either?"

"Iris, she wants you to be happy." Rita felt very positive about both of their lives right now. "I think Stefanie will jump for joy to have you excited about something again."

"This Friday will be quite a night for new beginnings," Iris said. "We're going to tell my brother I'm going into business with you. I'm having my first dinner party as a single hostess. Even my daughter's going to ask a boy to be her first date. You think we can all survive so many 'firsts' in one night?"

"By the time Friday is over, we'll all have a lot to celebrate," Rita answered, giving her new business partner a confident smile.

❤ ❤ ❤ ❤ ❤

They had only gotten through two bites of the spicy *carne guisada*, beans, and steamed vegetables that Rita had cooked before Rita knew she had to share her news with Abuelita or just explode. She set down her fork and smiled at her great-grandmother. "Abuelita, today, I asked Brian's sister if she would become my new business partner, and she said yes."

Reaching over, Abuelita patted Rita's arm. "That makes me happy. *Comadre* Josie will be happy, too." Her shiny black eyes twinkled when she grinned. "I asked you to become friends with Josie's children. Look what it's brought you."

"Yes, I know. Iris and I are very excited. We have so many plans."

"Shouldn't you be more certain of Brian before you go into business with his sister?" Tía Minerva's words were like buckets of cold water drowning the warm feelings around Abuelita's supper table.

"Tía, I'm certain Brian will be pleased about what I'm doing. His sister's been through some very bad days since her husband died. Iris is very happy about going into business with me," Rita said, trying to keep her voice in polite tones despite her annoyance.

Pointing her fork in Rita's direction, her aunt made a grumpy noise. "And if things between you and your boyfriend don't work out? Can you still work with his sister knowing he may come into the shop to buy something for another woman?"

"That's not going to happen. Brian and I love each other."

"How many times have I heard words about love one day only to hear words of hate two days later? Especially from a young girl's mouth." Tía Minerva's bushy salt-and-pepper eyebrows rose above her hard brown stare. "You can't be certain of a man until a ring's on your finger, and even then, you better put a ring through his nose so you won't lose track of him like some grazing bull."

Rita's fingers clamped onto the side of the table. "You are very hard on men, Tía. You make it seem like they're all cut from the same pattern. But each man is different. You can't blame all of them because some man hurt your feelings a long time ago."

"What I'm trying to tell you is that if you go into business with this woman, do it because of the woman, not because she's the sister of a man you love right now. Then no matter what he does, it won't affect your business. You have a good business, no? Don't let any man take that away from you," her aunt said. And her brown stare had softened, despite the tough edge on her words.

Abuelita's calloused hands rubbed over Rita's wrist. "You might want to listen to your *tía*, Rita. She's thinking of you first."

Her emotions were twisted together like a tight braid that was beautiful to look at but caused a bad headache at the same time. She had to appreciate her aunt and great-grandmother's honesty, their good intentions to make Rita look at other aspects of her new partnership with Iris. But she also had to endure painful feelings of resentment, even anger, that they didn't trust her instincts about Iris and didn't have more faith in her relationship with Brian.

Could the partnership flourish without Brian? If something changed, if Brian discovered he didn't want to continue their relationship, could she still face him as the brother of her business partner without old romantic feelings getting in the way of sound business decisions? What if Rita's feelings changed or her ambitions and goals didn't include a permanent relationship like marriage? Would Iris want to dissolve the partnership, leaving Rita abandoned, perhaps even worse off than her situation with Bea?

"Don't rush into this with your heart only," her great-grandmother said. Abuelita's loving voice gently wove its way through Rita's thoughts.

Her words seemed a contradiction to Abuelita's well-worded advice to trust your heart when making a big decision, but Rita didn't mention it now. She liked to think she had learned something from her mistakes with Beatrice Zamora. And she'd use the experience to make sure her head and heart were working together to insure success with her business partner this time.

"I do appreciate what both of you have told me," Rita said, making eye contact with both Abuelita and Tía Minerva and offering each a gracious smile. "And I'll keep it in mind as Iris and I determine what will be best in our partnership. And as for Brian, our relationship is not even two months old, so we still have a lot to learn about each other. I'm sure I can handle whatever problems come up."

"They used to say in the old days that a girl could catch a man's heart just by filling his stomach," Minerva said, stabbing her fork at pieces of meat on her plate.

"Men were easier to catch in those days," Abuelita replied.

Rita wondered if her calm, confident words had fooled either of them, especially when her hand shook as she picked up her fork to continue eating. At least when she told Brian about her plans, Iris would be there, too. They would be like a sharp needle and sturdy thread, able to mend the pieces of Rita's dreams that Bea Zamora had ripped away.

Chapter Thirteen

"What's on the menu tonight?" Rita asked on Friday morning as she straightened the shoulders on Iris's cream-colored dress.

"Lasagna," Iris answered, and turned sideways to check the fit. "It's one of those dishes popular with everyone. Besides, a lasagna pretty much cooks itself."

Rita caught Iris's satisfied look when she turned around to the front.

"It looks beautiful. We ought to call our new shop, Miracles by Rita."

"Very funny. this was a tricky job. I'm glad it came out so well. Uh—can I show you something? I'd like your opinion."

Rita walked to the rack where she kept partially completed and finished dresses and pulled out two hangers. One was the blouse she made yesterday and the other was a rust-colored rayon blend skirt. The skirt had a narrow waistband and two thin pleats about six inches down each side. She laid the blouse against her chest and placed the skirt over it. "What do you think? I thought I'd wear this tonight."

"Rita," Iris said, visibly impressed. "I saw you working with that material yesterday. The blouse is gorgeous. You made the skirt, too?"

"Yes. I saw this style in a magazine. I made it last night."

"You work so fast. At this rate, you can come up with a variety of ensembles before we open the new place. Some for you and me to wear and others to sell. You need to wear this when Brian takes you to another company party." Iris took the blouse sleeve between her fingers, then raised her eyebrows as she regarded Rita. "We should find out how to order those embroidered dress labels with your name on them. Pretty soon, everyone in San Antonio will want a dress designed and made by Rita Navarro."

Iris gave Rita another smile, something magical that made her eyes a rich golden brown. Now that Rita saw more happy expressions on Iris's face, she understood why Brian and Stefanie missed the way Iris used to be. Iris was enchanting. When she smiled or laughed, she made you feel like celebrating with champagne.

"Have you told Stefanie anything about our plans?" Rita asked Iris after she had changed out of the dress and was getting ready to leave.

"I told her about it." Iris laid her dress over the counter and then slipped on her coat. "She only made a remark about the money. 'I guess Rita could use some extra financial backing.' When she said that, I got a chill down my back. She sounded exactly like her father."

Shoving her fists into the pockets of her red smock, Rita sighed. "Iris, this partnership isn't only money. It's about sharing the responsibilities. And the headaches. I want someone who has the same goals that I do. As I look back on my last partnership, I realize that the biggest mistake I made was going into business with someone who could only see dollar signs in front of her. I know there's a place for two creative ladies to show what they can do with a piece of material and make a comfortable profit at the same time."

Iris hugged her coat around herself. "I like the way you put it, Rita. You give that same speech to Brian and Stefanie tonight, okay?"

"No, Iris. We'll both make speeches. We're partners, remember?"

"That's right. You just keep reminding me to do my share."

Rita arrived at Iris's house near six-thirty. Brian had called after five from Austin and said he would drive straight to his sister's house because he was running so late. His car was already parked in the driveway when she drove up. She hadn't realized how much she had missed him until he answered the door and pulled her into his arms.

She enjoyed his lengthy kiss then pulled back to smile at him. "I've never dated a man whose work makes him travel. Actually, you're the first guy I've dated in the last year who has a steady job." Then she laughed. "My brother-in-law's friends leave a lot to be desired."

"Well, I hope you've told your family they don't have to set you up anymore," Brian said, bringing her into the house and closing the door behind her.

"I won't have to. Abuelita and Tía spent the afternoon visiting my sisters. I felt my ears burning all day. I'm sure Anna will invite us to supper soon so she can check you out." Rita unbuttoned her coat and Brian helped her remove it.

He responded to her new outfit with a low wolf whistle. "I do like what you're wearing, Rita."

She did a model's spin and grinned at him. "I made this while you were gone. I'm glad you like it."

He had laid her coat over his arm then studied her with a slight frown. "I know I made a thoughtless comment about what you wore in the store a few weeks ago. But as I see those legs of yours, I think I'd like you to keep wearing your jeans and red smock. One look at you in a skirt like that and you'll have every cloth salesman and pin peddler asking you out to lunch."

"Pin peddler?" Rita giggled and walked over to kiss him again. Her fingers massaged the thick weave of his navy blue sweater against his arms. "Iris says I should wear more things I make when I'm in the shop. She says it's good advertising for my business."

"I better talk to Iris about advertising something I want for myself." He winked at her and she responded with more laughter, pleased that he was learning not to take her teasing so seriously.

Rita entered the empty living room as Brian went to hang up her coat in a small closet under the staircase. He returned to the living room with Iris right behind.

This was all so different from the last time Rita came to Iris's house feeling so insecure about her place in Brian's life and his role in Iris's. She didn't feel that she and Iris were competitors for his affections. Now she and Iris were friends, and soon to be business partners.

"Well, is everything ready? Where's Stefanie?" Rita asked Iris.

"Upstairs. The last time I checked, she was telling her closet that she had nothing cool to wear. She'll come down sometime, I hope," Iris answered, then gave an artificial laugh.

Seeing Iris standing between herself and Brian made Rita suddenly apprehensive, when all day she had felt excitement about telling Brian about their plans. Was she putting too much confidence in his love for her when he took his responsibilities to Iris and Stefanie so seriously?

"Why don't we all sit down and talk a few minutes before the Díazes arrive?" Iris said, her voice sounding very calm.

Rita felt drum rolls inside her head as she went to sit down on the shorter of the two mint-green sofas. Brian sat beside her, resting his arm across the back. Iris sat in the armchair striped by royal colors to their right. She crossed her legs and rested her elbows on the armrests as she looked at Brian like he was the only one there.

"Brian, while you were out of town I made an important decision. I've decided to go into business with Rita. I've spent a lot of time thinking about this. And

I'm—we're—both very excited about forming a partnership."

Rita smiled at the confidence Iris presented to her
brother. There was nothing left of the jittery woman she
had seen at the anniversary party. Then she looked at
Brian and saw a tiny ball of a muscle tighten in his
cheek.

"You're going into business with Rita? Just like
that?" He lifted his arm away from the back of the sofa
and planted both hands on his thighs as he looked at his
sister. "I don't think you understand what owning your
own business means, Iris."

"I know what it means. It means that I'll be out
among people and doing something different every day,
not stuck in this house waiting for the hours to pass."
She leaned forward, her fingertips pressing against each
other. "It's time for me to do something like this."

"I'm glad you've finally come through this mourning
stage, Iris," Brian said, adjusting himself back against
the sofa. "This dinner part is a first step, and the
quinceañera's only weeks away. It's only natural that
you're ready to get on with your life. But there are
dozens of other things you can do with your time. What
about volunteer work? Taking up a new hobby? Going
into business is a major undertaking. I don't think
you're ready for that responsibility, Iris."

"Brian, I'm thirty-five years old. That should be old
enough to handle any kind of responsibility."

"Iris, you're not making a decision about which
dress to wear to a party, you know. We're talking about a
substantial financial investment and the day-to-day
operations of running your own business. Do you realize
what's involved in something like this?"

"Of course I do. I've spent time in Rita's shop. We've
talked a lot about her work, the store itself. If there's
one thing I know, it's clothes. We have a lot of exciting
plans for the new shop."

"Oh?" Brian turned to frown at Rita. "Did you find a new location while I was gone?"

"Not yet. But with the two of us looking—"

"Whose idea is this anyway? I mean, my sister knows very little about running a business. Why would you want her as a partner?" He turned back to Iris. "And if you want to go into business, why would you want a dress shop like Rita's?"

"Well done, Brian. You managed to insult both of us at the same time," Iris told him, rising from the chair to begin pacing the carpet in front of the coffee table.

Rita shifted on the sofa as if pins had suddenly broken through the material. Holding herself on the edge of the sofa, she glared directly at Brian. "Iris and I bring two different strengths to this partnership. She has the eye for style, and I have the talent with the needle. And, yes, Iris may not have a lot of business experience, but she has a lot of people experience and that's going to be an asset when I open my new shop."

"Too many of your business plans right now are dependent on ifs and whens," Brian answered.

"All of life is dependent on ifs and whens," Iris replied. She stopped suddenly to say, "If you wait until everything is perfect, you'll never get anything you want." Her pacing resumed.

Brian kept looking at Rita. "I just don't think Iris needs to get involved in your rebound off a bad partnership."

Rita's fury at his tone was getting harder to keep under control. Her fingers pinched the sofa cushions at her side. "That bad partnership taught me a lot about what I need in a good partner. I asked your sister to become my partner because I trust her. Can't you understand that?"

His unwavering eye contact made her face feel hot.

"Trust isn't the point right now," he said.

"Then what is the point?" She jumped on his words, just waiting for him to mention money. And she was primed and ready to argue about that topic with him. Her anger was fueled by hurt and disappointment; he didn't think her shop was good enough for his sister.

"The point is—" Iris' voice increased in volume, as if she wanted to take control of the conversation. "The point is that I want to go into business with Rita, and I'll do it with or without your approval, Brian."

Now he stood up, packing his hands onto his hips. "That's right. You do need my approval. And I don't think you're ready for the responsibility of a business partnership, Iris. Estevan put me in charge because he knew I would always have your welfare at heart. And Stefanie's, too."

"Don't sound so noble." Iris's words snapped like a whip. "He put you in charge of that trust fund because he didn't want some second husband to run off with my money. All of this paper signing happened right after Mrs. Lozano's second husband ran off with his secretary to Acapulco. And Estevan and I were leaving for that vacation in Spain. My thoughts were on Stefanie and her inheritance, not me and possible widowhood. If I had been smart, I never would have let him put my welfare into your hands."

Brian stepped around the coffee table, his arms out towards his sister. "Iris, just calm down. If you need to find some creative outlet, a way to get out of the house more often—well, we can figure something out that won't be such a risk for your money."

"I'm not asking for the whole estate, for heaven's sake! Rita can't possibly expect that much money." Iris motioned towards Rita as she spoke. "She even told me that you were willing to invest in her business. Why did you offer her money if you thought it was such a risk?"

"That's between Rita and myself. We're talking about what's best for you right now, " Brian said, taking his sister's hand between his own.

Rita rose to her feet, feeling even more troubled than that first time she came to Iris's house. It appeared

that Brian had sided against her. And Bea's theft and
desertion felt like eating a marshmallow compared to
the *jalapeños* burning Rita from the inside out.

"I don't think you know what's best for Iris," Rita
said in a strong voice that was meant to crash right
through Brian's brotherly moment. "The only person
who knows that is Iris herself. Iris needs to be her own
person, and you need to accept the choices she makes for
herself."

"She's right." Iris jerked her hand out of Brian's.
"And I don't really need your permission for this. You're
not my husband or my father. You're my little brother."

"No, I don't suppose you need my permission to go
into business with Rita." Brian's lips straightened into a
tight line across his face. With eyes that seemed almost
black and a dull reddish tint sweeping his complexion,
his face was like a billboard, advertising his true feelings about their plans.

"Just remember that you will need my authorization if you want to take money from the trust fund. And,
Iris, I will not give it to you. I'm sorry." He turned to
look at Rita, but she didn't even let him mouth a word
in her direction.

"Before you say anything to me, Brian Esparza, I
have something to say to you. I never asked for any of
Iris's money. All I wanted was her good taste and sense
of style for my new shop. If she wants to invest money,
it's her idea, not mine. And I told Iris, just like I told
you—I want a partner, not an investor. However, right
now, I want nothing from either of you." Rita's feelings
were so close to the surface, she had to get away from
Iris and Brian immediately or face more humiliation.
She made the sudden decision to leave Iris's house
before the Díazes arrived. She would just walk away
from all of them. The *quinceañera* dress was finished.
She had been paid well. It was time to move on.

"Iris, I can't stay for supper. I'm sorry." Rita turned and walked away, even though she heard both Iris and Brian call her name with alarm.

It was Stefanie's appearance that made Rita stop at the edge of the room. The teenager stepped from around the wall, and from the distressed look on her face it was obvious she had been eavesdropping.

"Don't leave, Rita. The Díazes are expecting you to be here. You just can't mess this up for me." The girl's words pushed through a tight smile.

Stefanie's selfishness was only another reason for Rita to get away.

"Tell them I'm sick to my stomach. They'll understand."

"How could you people do this to me?" Stefanie's voice raised as her fiery stare moved beyond Rita to scorch her mother and uncle. "Did you have to get into this discussion about Mom and Rita's business before Nicky's family got here? Now everyone's in a bad mood. This dinner's supposed to be fun. You look like a bunch of enemies! This *quince* stuff was all your idea, remember? The least you could do is make things pleasant tonight so I can finally get something I want out of this stupid birthday celebration."

Stefanie's words weakened Rita's desire to leave. She couldn't abandon her now, or Iris, as she took on her role as hostess for the first time in months. And Rita was not a person to leave loose threads hanging.

Meanwhile, Iris had walked over to her daughter and placed one hand on her shoulder and the other on Rita's.

"Don't worry, baby," Iris said. "Everything's going to be just fine. I won't let Rita leave. And there won't be another word about the business tonight. I promise. Just wait and see how charming Uncle Brian can be at one of my dinner parties."

The sudden chime of the doorbell made all of them look towards the front door.

"I'll greet our guests now. Brian, you can be bartender tonight. Rita, please sit down and make yourself at home. Stefanie, you can take Nicky, Jennifer, and Robert into the den if you wish," Iris said, completely taking charge of her home as a proper hostess should.

Friendly introductions were made. Rita used the excuse of getting acquainted to avoid Brian's constant looks in her direction.

She had always kept a respectful distance with her customers, but at the first mention of "Mrs. Díaz," the woman said, "Please call me Cecilia. I feel like you're my friend, not just my dressmaker."

Jesse Díaz was a fortyish, black-haired man who kept a watchful eye on his youngest son, a fidgety adolescent named Robert. Older daughter Jennifer was a brunette beauty who possessed her mother's easy smile. Nicholas looked very nervous. Stefanie took the young people into the den, while Iris invited the adults into the living room for a drink.

Rita purposefully placed herself in the chair that Iris had sat in earlier. Her feelings of anger slowly simmered away as Brian stayed attentive anyway. He made sure their fingers touched when he gave her a glass of wine, and stood beside her chair rather than sit down as he discussed computers with Jesse. He talked about his college work at Trinity University, where Jennifer Díaz had been offered a scholarship.

"Of course, with her grades I imagine she'll have a dozen scholarship offers," Cecilia said, her face shining with pride. She looked at Rita. "The last time I saw you, you were going to look at some new locations for your shop. Did you have any luck, Rita?"

"There was one place near Blanco and Hildebrand we liked a lot," Rita answered, then wanted to bite her tongue for using "we." She hoped her business affairs wouldn't make it into the conversation tonight. "I'm still looking. Did your mother-in-law like her dress?"

"Very much. I think she'd prefer some other things—you know, same style but different fabrics? There are so few store-bought dresses that are long enough for someone in a wheelchair. Would you have time to make her some other dresses if I bring in fabrics she likes?"

"Probably not 'til the first of March. I have a deadline for a dance troupe, and I'll be moving the store. But it won't take long to make her a few dresses in the same pattern once I get started."

"That'll give me time to buy some pretty spring fabrics," Cecilia replied. She then turned to Iris who sat on the sofa beside her. "And the *quinceañera*? How are the plans going?"

"I was waiting on the invitations, but I received a call from the printer and they're ready to be picked up." Iris's face looked calm, but Rita noticed her white hands and their stranglehold on her wine glass.

"I haven't looked at the guest list in months," Iris said. "There will need to be some changes since we're having the reception here and not in the country club as my husband had planned." Then she shrugged, "I think I'll ask Stefanie whom she wants to invite. It's her party, after all."

"Aren't we lucky to have daughters? I keep praying that Jennifer won't pick a college too far from home. We're just so close, she and I." Cecilia's hand rested on Iris's arm. "I guess you share that same kind of relationship with Stefanie. Of course, it's different between girls and their father, isn't it?"

"Yes, very different," Iris said, her voice low, her eyes sad.

"I'll say it's different," Brian said with a lighthearted sound to his words. "Iris used to get away with everything when we were kids. My father never got after Iris the way he did me. Iris even got a new car when she was sixteen. When I turned sixteen, my father bought a riding lawn mower for me to do the yard."

Everyone laughed, especially Iris, and Rita felt her love for Brian overcome her earlier resentment. He had managed to ease a difficult moment for Iris, and his sister's eyes shone with gratitude. Even Rita raised a glance up towards Brian to catch his uncertain smile in her direction.

As Iris stood up and suggested they move to the dining room, Rita rose from the chair to feel Brian standing close behind her, only he didn't touch her this time.

"Please don't run out of here after dessert," he whispered close to her ear. "I have to talk to you."

She turned slightly and fastened her eyes upon him before she whispered her reply. "I have a few things to say to you, too, Mr. Esparza."

He stepped back and motioned towards the dining room. With a slight bow, he said, "After you, Ms. Navarro," and followed her out.

Iris had shortened the dining room table to accommodate a smaller group, and used an embroidered eggshell tablecloth and woven place mats for this gathering of friends and family. Rita was surprised by the different look of the room, something more in keeping with the warm colors and personal touches that made the rest of the house so attractive. Two fresh flower arrangements replaced the stiff candlesticks. White china plates decorated with tiny roses and pale pink stemware gave the table a pretty presentation without making the dinner guests feel insecure about what fork to use.

The food was delicious and the conversation relaxed. Stefanie and Nicky sat across from each other, stealing glances, exchanging smiles. Robert was quiet unless asked a question, but Jennifer joined in the conversation confidently, asking Rita more about her shop and talking to Brian about using a modem with the computer she wanted for college.

Not long after dessert, Robert asked to watch a Superbowl Special Preview on television and was excused from the table. Stefanie asked Nicky if he wanted to look through her father's telescope from the upstairs balcony.

"It's such a clear night, we ought to be able to see a lot," Jennifer said. "I'd love to come upstairs and see the constellations with you."

Stefanie's eyes widened, obviously distressed by Jennifer's words.

"Jennifer, why don't you let me show you what I've done with Stefanie's personal computer in the library," Brian said suddenly. "There are some interesting things you can get through a telephone link-up like she has."

"Oh. Okay. That might be helpful. I can get an idea of what I want," Jennifer said, completely missing the look of relief on Stefanie's face.

And as Stefanie passed her uncle's chair, she patted his shoulder in thanks. Nicky followed her out of the room.

"Mind if I see the computer, too?" Jesse asked as Brian and Jennifer rose from the table.

"Brian to the rescue," Iris said with a grin aimed at Rita.

"As always," Rita answered, her wounds from that awful argument before dinner not as raw and painful in the wake of Brian's chivalry tonight. She started to feel that she wasn't completely crazy to love Brian, but she still wasn't ready to forgive and forget some of the things he had said.

"Jennifer's usually not one to intrude on Nicky and his friends. I'm sure she didn't think that the kids wanted some time alone," Cecilia said, then raised her china cup to sip her coffee.

"Cecilia?" Iris shifted in her chair at the end of the table and leaned closer to Nicky's mother. "There's a reason why Stefanie wanted a little time alone with your son. I wasn't sure whether to mention it before, but I think since Stefanie has her chance now, I'll tell you.

Stefanie would like Nicky to be her honor escort for the *quinceañera*. Would that be all right with you and Jesse?"

"How sweet!" Cecilia laughed and reached over to squeeze Iris's hand. "I was hoping I wouldn't have to invite myself to this party. I haven't been to a *quinceañera* in years. Actually, we haven't kept up with any of the customs from the old neighborhood. My *abuela* made the best brown sugar and raisin *tamales* every Christmas Eve. I often wish we could get together and have a *tamalada* during the holidays. Of course, I can't see my pristine Jennifer putting her hands in a mound of *masa*, can you?"

They all laughed together and began sharing family stories like a trio of *comadres* who had known each other all their lives. And that's how Stefanie and Nicky found them later, laughing over one of Rita's stories about peeling the meat off the cow head for *barbacoa* only to start screaming when she heard it moo; she discovered it was just her Uncle Gilbert hiding under the kitchen table.

"Are you all right?" Stefanie inquired, frowning at the hysterics around the dining room table.

Iris patted her eyes with the pink linen napkin from her lap. "Yes, we're fine. Just sharing stories about our childhood." She giggled but tried to control herself as she reached her hand to her daughter.

Stefanie took her hand, but looked back at Nicky.

He seemed to swallow something big in his throat before he stepped up to the table and leaned on the back of an empty chair. "Mom, Stefanie asked me to be her escort for her birthday party. Is that okay? She says I ought to wear a tux and stuff."

"A tuxedo. Well, now. I guess we'll have to get something really nice. After all, she'll be in a beautiful dress that day. Gosh! My little boy in a tuxedo. I just might cry at the sight of you," Cecilia replied, clasping her hands together at her heart.

"Aw, Mom, don't." Nicky's eyes rolled upwards as his freckles darkened against his face. "I'll be embarrassed enough as it is." Then he looked at Stefanie with a troubled frown. "I don't have to walk you down an aisle or anything, do I?"

Stefanie laughed and thumped Nicky on the arm with her fist. "Just dance with me at the party. That's all you do."

"I guess I can do that." He turned to face Stefanie. "My school's having a dance tomorrow night. If you meet me there, maybe we could practice a little, huh?"

Now it was Stefanie's turn to blush. "I—I don't know." She looked down at her mother. "Could I go, Mom? Please?"

"Well—perhaps we can discuss it later—"

"If it makes any difference, Iris, Jesse and I are chaperoning. Perhaps Stefanie could invite a few of her friends to come with her. The more girls the better, when a boys' school gives a dance." Cecilia winked at Stefanie and her mother, then chuckled.

Iris's fingers raked her hair. "Well, I suppose Stefanie could call her best friends. I can talk to their parents, offer to drive the girls to the dance. I guess it all goes with having a teenage daughter, huh?"

"Thanks, Mom! I'll call Angie and Micole later." Stefanie tossed her arms around her mother's shoulders and kissed her cheek.

The spontaneous act seemed so natural between a parent and child. Only Rita had to smile at Iris's astounded expression. Perhaps Stefanie and Iris would learn to grow closer with friends like the Díaz family to show them how.

Chapter Fourteen

No sooner had Iris closed the door on the Díaz family then Stefanie called out, "Good night!" and bounded up the stairs.

"That's new," Brian said. "Usually, she begs to stay up later."

"I better go talk to her. It's too late to start telephoning friends and inviting them to a dance tomorrow. Excuse me, please," Iris said, then made her journey up the stairs.

Rita turned and walked back into the living room, feeling a nervous quiver in her stomach now that she and Brian had a moment alone. She sat down in the striped chair and stared down at her hands.

"You don't seem quite as hostile as you were earlier," Brian said, his words coming out in a slow cautious pace.

She sat there; said nothing. She heard his sigh, and felt him approaching. He sat himself at the corner of the green sofa closest to her. She looked up to see him sitting there, elbows and forearms resting on his thighs, watching her.

"I thought you had some things to say to me," Brian said.

"I did. But I've had a nice time tonight, and I hate to lose those good feelings now by going through those awful things you said before dinner."

"What awful things? You and I both know that Iris doesn't have the experience you need in a business partner," Brian replied, his voice very matter-of-fact. "And you keep saying that you don't want Iris's money, but you and I both know that you could use an investor. And using the word 'partner' doesn't change things. There's money involved in a partnership, too. Am I right?"

That *jalapeño* burn started up again. She blinked away the watery sensation in her eyes.

He put out his hand and let it fall to her knee, rubbing it gently. "Rita, I love you. I love Iris. I'm glad you two are friends. I'm grateful for the confidence you helped my sister find again. But going into business together isn't a smart move. Especially for Iris. She doesn't belong behind the counter of your dress shop."

His words reopened that raw sore spot. Poured iodine all over it. She sat up stiffly in the chair and swept his hand off her leg.

"Why don't you just say it? You don't think my shop is good enough for your sister to work there."

"I don't think that shop is good enough for you to work there. It's a leaky hole-in-the-wall that's owned by a stingy loser. You deserve better than what you have now. Why do you think I offered to invest in your shop?"

"I can get out of that hole-in-the-wall—as you so tactfully put it—without your money, Brian. And I don't want our relationship weighed down by some loan agreement, or even worse, an investment that you can show as a loss on your next tax return."

Brian's eyebrows rose over widened brown eyes.

"What? You don't think I know the lingo of the business world?" she asked in a cool voice. "I read the business pages of the newspaper, too."

Suddenly, a frown crinkled, changing his expression completely. "Reading the business section isn't going to help you with your current problems, and going into a partnership with Iris won't either."

"Do you have a problem with your sister selling clothes? Or making a living like the rest of us? What do you want Iris to do? Just stay home and gather dust like the rest of the beautiful things in this house?"

"Iris doesn't need to work. Estevan worked hard, made wise investments, and had good insurance. Why does Iris need to be burdened by the headaches of running a business when she has a comfortable life right here?"

"Maybe she'd like to do something more with her life than be someone's widow," Rita answered, weary of the effort it took to be tactful. Now she just wanted to make him see things the way she and Iris did. "Estevan may have made it easy for Iris to live in a pretty house and keep her nice clothes, but he thought nothing of her personal happiness if he should die. She needs a life as Iris—something separate from her role as Stefanie's mother. She needs an identity just for herself."

Rita suddenly noticed the slow arrival of Iris into the room and clamped her lips together.

"I think I should be having this argument with Brian, Rita," Iris said as they made eye contact. "I don't want anyone fighting my battles for me. Not anymore." She stopped near the sofa, not far from where Brian sat.

Brian rubbed his forehead like he had a headache, then sighed, shaking his head slowly. And Rita understood what he was feeling. It seemed like they kept arguing but got no place further than before.

Finally, she stood up. "Well, Iris, if you're ready to talk to Brian, then I'm leaving. There's no reason for me to get into the middle of a family discussion."

"You can't just walk away, Rita." Iris bent her arms, resting her hands on her hips. "You're involved with us now. You can't act like you're nothing more than Brian's date tonight. I thought we were going to be partners. What about our plans?"

And suddenly, Rita recalled Tía Minerva's warning about Iris and Brian. If she had to choose between a new partner who could bring a quality and elegance to her shop and the man who brought a treasured, fulfilling relationship into her life, could she make the right decision?

Looking from Iris to Brian, she could only throw her hands into the air. "A couple of days ago my sweet *tía* asked me if I was going into business with Iris because I loved her brother or because of Iris herself. It feels like I have to make a choice between you, and the truth is, I can't. Not right now. Maybe not ever." She looked at Brian and kept her eyes on his face a long moment before she said, "Please. Just let me go home now. I feel like a piece of cloth getting torn in half."

Both seemed so stunned by her words that neither moved when she turned and walked quickly into the entrance hallway. She ignored the whispered voices over her shoulder. She went to the closet, and grabbed her coat and purse, only tossing them over one arm in her haste to leave. She heard heavy steps behind her as she reached the door.

"Rita, I want to follow you home. It's late. I won't even get out of my car, but I would feel a lot better if I knew you got home safely."

His thoughtful gesture didn't surprise her. She just nodded, then opened the front door. All the way home, she forced herself to concentrate on her driving, not the pair of headlights in her rear-view mirror. She didn't even look back at his car before she ran into Abuelita's house. She was just relieved this day was over.

❤ ❤ ❤ ❤ ❤

Rita added more sugar to her cinnamon tea and listened to the tinkle of the spoon as she stirred. She had run out of tears near two a.m., and her brain stopped zig-zagging about three-thirty. She was tired, heart-sick, and had no appetite for breakfast. But she had a busy day ahead and knew she needed to get a bowl of cereal down before she left for the store.

"*Canela* settles the stomach," Abuelita had often said about the cinnamon tea that she liked to drink instead of coffee every morning.

Suddenly, Rita remembered a carnival gypsy long ago who guessed a person's future by reading tea leaves. Staring into the *canela*, at the slivers of tea bark that had sunk to the bottom of the white mug, Rita wondered if there was some hidden message that she missed because of her ignorance.

"Did you lose something in your tea?" Abuelita asked as she came into the kitchen.

The question made Rita sit up self-consciously, but then she laughed. "No. I was trying to see my future in the pieces of *canela* on the bottom of the cup. Good morning, Abuelita."

"Rita, the gypsy, no? That *viejita* stole two dollars from a young girl who had better ways to spend her money. And did she tell you anything that has come true?" Her great-grandmother sat on the kitchen chair across from Rita.

"Well, let's see. She said that I'd win a doll from the booth next door." Rita grinned. "I spent all my money and didn't win a thing."

"So much for tea leaves and gypsies. You want to know the future? Look at your hands. They can get you whatever you want. Just work hard."

"I do, Abuelita, I do. But sometimes your heart wants more than your hands can give," Rita replied then sighed.

"Ah, yes, Rita *linda*, they do. So drink two cups of canela today. It'll help you feel better," Abuelita answered.

Rita's heart seemed to thud at a snail's pace. Everything was literally in her hands. She had no doubt that Iris would come to the shop today. They had already agreed that she could help behind the counter since all the *Folklórico* dancers were coming in for their measurements. What would she say to Iris this morning after all that had been said last night? And she also knew that Brian would appear at some point to try and resolve the difficulties between them. Then what?

Rita took a long drink from the tea and heard the clap of her aunt's slippers as she entered the kitchen.

"*Buenos días*, Minerva. Did you sleep well?" Abuelita said.

"Well enough. In my own bed I sleep better," she answered, shuffling towards the stove and setting the silver tea kettle back on the gas flame.

"Minerva and I leave for Sabinal this afternoon to see family there. We'll come home Monday. Finish the wedding dress and do the packing. Teresa can come get me in two weeks."

A gallon of *canela* wouldn't soothe the sour feeling Abuelita's words left curdled in Rita's stomach.

"You're ready to leave? So soon?" Rita felt like she was the only one getting left behind. Even when her mother and Imelda moved to Oklahoma she didn't feel like this. "But there's more to do, right?"

"Abuelita says everything left belongs to the house," Tía said as if she couldn't understand Rita's panicky voice. "The trash is gone and the other small things given away. We're leaving you a clean place, Rita."

"This house means nothing without Abuelita," she said without thinking.

"This house means a lot to your sister Debra," Tía Minerva said, pulling out the third chair and sitting down with a groaning sigh. "She'd take the place for her family in a second and put you out in the street for all she cares."

"Debra wouldn't treat me like that," Rita replied, wondering if she'd even miss the irritation Tía Minerva carried around like a suitcase whenever she came for a visit.

"It's good we went through everything and gave away what needed to be given away," Abuelita said in a tired voice. "I pray for their happiness now." Then she tapped her finger on the tabletop. "We must go to the bank, too. Rita and I will do that." She looked at her grand-niece. "Once you bring me back Monday, Minerva, you can go home. You helped so much. Thank you."

"I could drive you to Brownsville," she answered.

"No," Rita said, knowing that she needed to steal more hours with Abuelita before the old woman left permanently. "I want to take Abuelita to Brownsville. I'll close the shop an extra day, and maybe do some shopping in Mexico while I'm there."

"You won't need to close the shop if you have a partner."

Tía's comment made Rita feel very sad, but she tried to keep from revealing her troubles on her face as she said, "Well, I've got two weeks to make those arrangements. Tía, I, too, want to thank you for your help. We never would have done things so quickly. And thank you for your help on the wedding dress." Her voice thickened like greasy *caldo*, but she kept the words coming. "Tía, you've done your share for Abuelita's benefit. It's my turn now. I want to take you to Brownsville, Abuelita."

"It'll be an easier good-bye, no?" her great-grandmother said.

"Probably not. But it seems better to have a few last hours together in the car than for me to wave from the back porch." Rita managed a brave little smile for her great-grandmother's sake, but she knew there would be nothing but tears on that good-bye day.

❤ ❤ ❤ ❤ ❤

Rita didn't know what shocked her more. Seeing Brian's car parked outside her shop or the window-sized white sign with thick red letters proclaiming: Coming Soon! Willie's Video Games Pizza & Pool. It was attached to a thick white pole buried inside a pothole of the gravel parking lot directly in front of the main window of the shop.

She knew Brian would show up eventually, although she never expected him so early. But the sign made her just ignore the man getting out of his car. She just leaned against her fender and stared in open amazement.

"I gather from your expression that this sign wasn't up here yesterday," Brian said, slowly walking over to her.

"If I had an ax in my car, I'd use it on this thing," she said, feeling a surge of angry strength pulsing through her body as she read the sign over and over again. "What a jerk! This thing hides my window."

He stood beside her and studied the sign, hands on his hips. "Well, I don't have an ax in my car, but there's a chain saw in the trunk that could do the job quite nicely."

"You're joking, right?" Rita frowned a puzzled look at Brian.

"Yes, but I have one in my garage. I'll come back and cut it down for you if you want."

"Well, I'm tempted, but we'd better not. Mr. Arredondo was pretty mad that I took my five hundred dollars out of the last rent check. If I aggravate him any further, I might find pinball machines in my storeroom." Rita sighed, trying to put the irritating sign out of her mind long enough to think about Brian's unexpected presence. "Now, is there something I can do for you?"

"Rita, I'm very sorry for the way things ended last night."

It would have been simpler to turn towards him and find security in his arms, but she knew nothing was simple anymore. She stepped away from him and tried not to let the distressed look in his eyes weaken her resolve.

"Everyone was disappointed in the way things ended last night. Except for Stefanie. She got what she wanted, didn't she?" Rita said.

"Yes. At least one of you went to bed with a smile on her face," Brian replied.

Rita didn't comment. What could she say? Hadn't it all been said last night? And to what end?

The silence between them was like a wall of ice, and Rita just didn't have the energy to chip away at the layers to reach Brian.

Then Brian took a step forward and took her arms between his hands. "Rita, you said some things that kept me awake all night. When you said that you might have to make a choice between Iris and me and that you couldn't, I realized that I put you in a terrible position. And I meant it when I told you weeks ago that if I had to walk away in order for you to be happy, I would do it. Rita, I love you that much."

Because of his glasses, she saw shades of his love magnified in his dark eyes. "Rita, if this partnership with Iris means that much to you, then I'll give you my support and even authorize Iris to take funds from the trust. But, please. For everyone's sake. Be certain that this partnership is exactly what you really need right now."

She thought she'd be happy when he finally said that he'd give his approval of the partnership, but his words only left her feeling more insecure about her own judgment. Was there someone else who would be better suited to a partnership than Iris? Could she distance herself from her personal fears, her love for Brian, and affection for Iris long enough to make a solid business decision?

"I don't know," she whispered. "I'm so confused I can't even think straight."

Brian's hands slid around her shoulders and pressed her body against his. His leather jacket was cold against her cheek. Her fingers squeezed the leather as she clung to him like he was a rescue rope down a deep hole.

"I know that Iris is coming over here to help you today. With Stefanie going to the dance, the three of us can get together tonight and talk further. We'll get this all straightened out, Rita. And if you decide that this partnership won't be the best thing for your business, we'll help Iris find something else to do with her time."

Why did she have the feeling he expected to find a solution quickly and painlessly? He wasn't working with computers here, but with human beings who didn't live by pre-programmed responses.

She raised her head to look directly into his eyes. "I want you to meet with Iris tonight. Just the two of you. Just sit down and be honest about your concerns. I won't talk to either of you about what I want for my business until the two of you talk to each other privately. And when I see Iris later, I'm going to tell her the same thing."

If Brian didn't like her suggestion, he didn't show it. He just kissed her forehead and said, "I'll call you later, Rita."

She felt cold when he dropped his arms from around her body.

Brian turned then walked towards his car.

Knowing it was crazy to stand there shivering, Rita turned around and walked towards the front door of her dress shop, ignoring that tacky sign and trying not to wince at the sound of spinning gravel as Brian drove away.

❤ ❤ ❤ ❤ ❤

Rita was grateful for non-stop activity in the shop. Iris had just arrived when the first dancer did, and Rita gave brief instructions before she moved to the other room. The other two dancers arrived as did the show's producer, a fussy little man named Eduardo, who kept hawking on the authenticity he wanted in the costumes.

"I'm going to buy the trim in Mexico in a few weeks," Rita said, hoping that detail might satisfy him. "I've been sewing authentic costumes over ten years."

"You don't look that old," he replied.

"Today I feel a lot older than I look." She smiled at her own private joke then walked over to the table in the corner where she had left the *Folklórico's* pictures to discuss a few details that the artistic director had left for the producer's final approval.

By the time the dancers left, Iris was busy with two women who had been sent to the store by Cecilia Díaz. Their husbands worked with Jesse, and they too needed something festive for the company Fiesta party. Both women found dresses to buy. However, the shorter lady needed the hem raised, and Rita was busy with the alterations when another customer came in to pick up a dress Rita had finished.

After one p.m., things in the store quieted down long enough for Iris to ask Rita if she should consider a sale to reduce the inventory.

"There will be less to move that way. And the word 'sale' always attracts attention."

"Well, I could spend tomorrow going through the storeroom and decide what's worth moving. A sale might be a good idea. Perhaps next week." Rita rubbed her forehead with her fingertips. "There's so much to do. Maybe I need someone like my Tía Minerva in here. She did such a great job sifting through stuff at my great-grandmother's house."

"Isn't she the same lady who asked if you were going into business with me only because I'm the sister of the man you love?" Iris leaned against the counter, her hands behind her. She gave Rita a disappointed look. "So is that all there is to this partnership, really?"

"How can you ask me that? After what I told your brother last night? I asked you to be my partner because of who you are, not because of him. I stayed up half the night trying to decide which of you I needed more. What a choice! I'm so torn up, I even seriously considered moving with my great-grandmother to Brownsville and just leaving all of you behind me." Rita turned away and walked towards the sewing machine. She picked up Alyssa's satin and lace train, which she had finished this morning, and went to hang it in the other room until she had time to iron it.

Rita had just smoothed out a wrinkle and folded the train over a wide satin-covered clothes hanger when she heard Iris's voice behind her.

"You wouldn't really leave town over this, would you? Brian's never loved anyone the way he loves you. Don't you know that?"

Her fingers wrapped around the cold chrome bar of the dress rack. "Yes, I know that. He was here early this morning to tell me just how much he loves me. And he said that he'd even given his authorization for you to withdraw money from the fund—"

"Oh, Rita! Did he really say that? How wonderful!" Iris's voice quivered with excitement. "Now we can really make some plans."

Rita jerked around, her eyes burning up the distance between herself and Iris who looked like a child getting a gift from Santa Claus. Only Rita knew Santa wasn't real. "Your brother also told me that I needed to be absolutely sure that you would be the best choice as a business partner. You see, he has my welfare at heart, too."

The happiness melted from Iris's face. "Then we aren't any better off than we were last night, are we?"

"Now you know what I'm feeling." Rita hugged herself, her hands sliding up and down her arms. "Iris, I sprang my ideas on you so quickly, and I know we've talked a lot, but is this partnership something you really want to do? Do you have the right reasons? Do you truly understand the responsibilities?"

"Now you sound like Brian," she said, dismissing Rita's questions with a wave of her hand. "I'm not a child who wants a new toy because I'm bored with the old one. I want to do something different, something challenging. I'd like to use this business education my parents paid college tuition for. Did you know that I'm short about thirty hours for a business degree? I married Estevan before I could finish, and stupid me never thought I needed to."

Iris's revelation did surprise Rita, but it didn't do much to ease Rita's mind. "All right, Iris, tell me this. Does Brian know you studied business in college? Does he know you want to do more than be Stefanie's mother? Does he know that you are serious about the partnership? That's not a whim, or a toy to play with? Iris, talk to Brian about this—just the two of you—tonight would be the perfect opportunity. Stefanie will be at the dance."

"I would think Brian would want to spend his Saturday night with you, not with me," Iris replied.

"You're just using me as an excuse to put things off. I'm serious, Iris. If you two don't take this opportunity to talk, I'm going to just make my own plans without you."

"And without Brian?" she asked coolly with a raise of an eyebrow.

"I hope not," she answered truthfully. "But our relationship is shaky right now. Brian and I won't have a chance if we keep going like we are."

The door to the shop opened then, and Iris returned to the front room. Rita stayed in the back, getting things ready for an afternoon of final bridesmaid fittings for the Guerra wedding.

A little after five, Iris informed Rita, who decided to explore the storeroom a while, that she had locked the register and was getting ready to leave.

"Thanks for all your help today," Rita said as she opened a dusty cardboard box and looked inside. Then she laughed.

"What did you find?"

"A box of mylar balloons. One of Bea's great ideas, only she didn't know how much a bottle of helium was going to cost us. She used to buy a lot of stuff without thinking her ideas through."

"Maybe we could sell them to Angie's aunt. Her flower shop delivers balloons, too," Iris said as she tightened her coat belt around her. "I need to go over there next week and order the flowers for the *quinceañera* anyway. I can ask her."

"I may find a few other things back here that a flower shop can use," Rita replied. Then she looked up at Iris, wanting a leave her friend with a smile. "I hope Stefanie has a good time at the dance."

"Me, too." Iris smiled back. "Stefanie's been with Micole all day. When I called her mother after lunch, she told me the girls had tried on everything in her closet a dozen times. Then they walked back to our house and spent the afternoon trying on Stefanie's clothes." She glanced around the storeroom then looked back at Rita. "Rita, let Stefanie and I help you go through this mess. We'll get together tomorrow and spend the day here. I'm sure Brian would want to help, too."

Rita started to turn down the offer, but common sense took the steam out of her protest. She had to be out of the shop in three weeks and she couldn't do it without help. "Thanks for the offer. Meet me here by ten, okay?"

"We'll be here. I'll even pack a picnic lunch. Bye," she said, and turned to leave quickly before Rita could change her mind.

As she heard the door close, Rita looked around the storeroom and groaned. She started to think about leaving, too, but then wondered why. Abuelita and Tía Minerva were gone, and she had made it pretty clear to Brian where he should spend his evening. Why not do some work around here?

Rita pushed up the sleeves on her sweater then went back up to the front room to start going through all the junk under the counter.

Chapter Fifteen

"Thanks for coming to help me," Rita said to Stefanie the next morning when she and her mother arrived. "How was the dance?"

There was a moment of hesitation before she spoke because Brian and Iris had stopped talking about where to put the picnic basket and had turned to listen to her answer. "Well—uh—it was okay. Nicky acted a little stupid all night. I think it was because of his friends being around. I don't know."

Brian put his arm around his niece's shoulder. "Maybe he was just nervous. Sometimes a very nice guy can act really stupid around someone he really cares about." He looked at Rita, a plea for understanding in his eyes.

"You might give him another chance," Rita said, giving Brian an encouraging smile. "It takes time to develop a good relationship."

"Have you and Brian made up?" Iris inquired a bit later as she and Rita stood in the storeroom going through a pair of brown cardboard boxes that had been taped shut. The words PRIVATE PROPERTY were printed with a black felt marker. These two mysterious cartons were stuck in the corner behind a lot of smaller boxes which Brian and Stefanie had carried into the other room.

"Things are about the same as yesterday, Iris."

"We talked last night like you wanted. I told him what we were doing today, and he wanted to help," Iris answered. "After what you said to Stefanie a while ago, I think there's still hope for you and Brian."

"I'm worried, Iris. Our personal relationship's gotten so tangled up with you and me that I'm not sure I can separate my feelings anymore."

"Rita, since I spent yesterday with you and talked to Brian last night, I've been thinking a lot about all three of us. I wonder if it's wise to even involve Brian in what we're doing," Iris said, stripping off the last piece of tape from the box in front of her.

"I don't understand how we could uninvolve him," Rita replied. "He seems to be calling the shots with your money, you know?"

"I know, but I keep thinking about you and Brian. You don't need to be arguing about me or our business. I think we need a more neutral person to help us with this partnership." Iris had unfolded the top of the box just as Brian appeared.

"Rita, those boxes in the other room are filled with some very odd merchandise for a dress shop. One is filled with party hats and bags of confetti. Stefanie's going through another with baskets of small soaps and bottles of designer perfumes. What have you two found in here?"

"Stationery and hand-painted cups," Rita said, folding the flaps down on the brown carton so Brian could see what was inside.

His hand rubbed over her shoulder. "Well, I'll take it in the—"

Suddenly, an ear-splitting squeal came from the other room.

"Could Stefanie have found another dead mouse?" Iris asked, pushing her brother out of the way to get to her daughter.

Rita and Brian stumbled over the boxes behind her, and nearly knocked Iris down when she stopped suddenly just outside the storeroom door.

Stefanie was kneeling on the worn brown carpeting, pulling satin and lace women's lingerie from one box, holding up a pink camisole then a seductive short black gown against her body. With each discovery, she let out an excited shriek. There were a variety of pink panties and bras strewn around her, two red lace teddies, and a lavender garter belt.

"Now why couldn't I find a box like that?" Brian commented.

"Stefanie! What are you doing?" Iris asked, her voice squeaking.

"Aren't these beautiful? They're all brand new. Rita, where did they come from? Are they for sale? They should be. Mom, can I buy—"

"Stefanie, put those things away. You'll embarrass your Uncle Brian," Iris snapped before Rita could say anything.

The contents of her storeroom were growing more interesting with every box they opened. Only Rita kept wondering when and where Bea bought all these things. Why hadn't she told Rita about any of the purchases?

Moving Brian and Iris aside, she went to the box where Stefanie knelt and began rummaging through it.

"What are you doing?" Stefanie asked, sitting back on her heels, an almost-transparent yellow nightie in her hands.

"I'm looking for a receipt. Something to show that my old partner wasn't a thief in more ways than one," Rita answered, completely ignoring the silky softness teasing her fingertips before she reached the bottom. Patting around, she found no paper and sighed.

"I don't think this is stolen merchandise," Iris said in a calm voice, kneeling beside Rita and opening the box containing soap baskets and thin boxes of perfumes. "I bet she bought this stuff at a closeout. Perhaps these items were being discontinued, or a store was closing. A smart buyer can get some real bargains that way. I bet your ex-partner bought this stuff with her own money and planned to make a profit by selling it through the store."

"Without telling me?" Rita was feeling dumber by the minute. What must Brian and Iris think of her? Brian would definitely have his doubts about Rita's instincts about partners. Iris would probably question her own decision to go into business with such a gullible partner.

As if she knew Rita's thoughts, Iris rested her hand on Rita's arm. "Your old partner could only see the dollar signs. Didn't you tell me that? It doesn't surprise me that she would try to make extra money on the side if she could get away with it."

"Christmas," Stefanie said suddenly with a snap of her fingers. "All of the boxes we brought out from that corner of the storeroom had the word Christmas in tiny letters on one corner. I bet she planned to sell this stuff in the store before Christmas."

"Well, Bea must not have thought much of this stuff if she left if all behind when she eloped to Alaska," was all Rita answered. Then she shrugged. "All this junk can't replace the money she stole from me."

She felt as if someone left a knife in her back. She might have given into her depressed feelings, even started to cry, except that she was startled by another shriek from Stefanie.

"Why can't we do the same thing? Let's have a sale. We'll put all this stuff on tables, call all our friends. Put an ad in the paper. We could make tons of money!"

Rita had to smile. "I don't think we could make tons of money with this." She gestured weakly around her.

"But Stefanie's right, Rita. We should have a sale. Use the money for the new shop. That lingerie alone could bring in a couple of hundred dollars. And you might even sell some of your dresses, too, if we get the right people in here." Iris squeezed Rita's arm. "As your new partner, I think this would be a good idea. But what do you think?"

Iris's words renewed Rita's sagging spirits. She used to want Bea's approval for everything because she rarely felt qualified to make a decision. But only because Bea always told her, "Leave it to me. I have more experience than you do in these matters."

With Iris, it was "What do you think?"

Perhaps Iris didn't have the education and experience that others demanded in a business partner, but now Rita knew for sure she didn't want someone around who would make Rita feel inferior. If they were both still learning the ropes, so be it. The two of them would learn together and share the successes and mistakes together in a fair equal partnership. It's what Rita wanted from the very beginning.

She looked behind her to tell Brian exactly what she was thinking, but he wasn't in the doorway any more. She then returned to the storeroom where Brian was stacking a few smaller boxes together to move into the other room.

"Stefanie has a good idea about selling everything, you know?" he said, seeing her.

"Yes, I know." Rita stopped his movements by placing her hands on his arms. Her eyes raised to meet his. "I also know that Iris would never buy a thimble without consulting me first. Brian, I could run the business myself, but I asked Iris to be my partner. I know she respects me. Bea used to make me feel like my opinion was worthless. I don't want anyone around me who's going to make me feel that my judgment isn't worth much when I know that it is."

Brian stared at her a long moment before he said, "And I did that to you to, didn't I, Rita? I'm so very sorry."

She hadn't realized how much she wanted to hear those words until he said them. For all their talking, she felt that something had been missing. His sincere apology filled in the gap.

"I only want you to realize how much you hurt me," she told him as she took his hands in hers.

"I'm sorry, Rita. I love you so much," he said, then leaned down to place a soft kiss on her lips. "I only want the best for you."

"Then what could be better than Iris as my partner, tell me that?" she replied, feeling she could truly forgive him now. "Isn't she the best?"

"What can I say? She's my sister." Brian smiled.

"Can you two come back in here? You're not going to believe what we found in this box!" Iris called to them from the other room in a loud voice.

Hand in hand, Rita and Brian returned to the other room. She felt happy that her personal relationship with Brian seemed to be made of durable fabric. Could a partnership with Iris become as strong? She didn't want her work with Iris to be merely an accessory of her relationship with Brian, but rather a complete outfit that needed nothing else to enhance its appearance.

❤ ❤ ❤ ❤ ❤

"So tell me about this place at Blanco and Hildebrand," Brian said, reaching across the green flannel tablecloth spread upon the floor to get a couple of carrot sticks. "Maybe we should all go look at it later."

Rita and Iris exchanged a look of warning. The two of them had worked alone most of the morning. Rita had told Iris that she agreed that they should keep Brian out of their business plans as much as possible not just for the sake of her personal relationship, but also to keep their decisions between them...like a true partnership and not as Iris put it, "Two partners and a third person."

"Mom said the landlord wanted too much money to rent the building," Stefanie replied, looking at her uncle. "It's too bad. The place was bigger than this one, and it had an apartment behind it where Rita could live."

His eyebrows rose as he posed a silent question in Rita's direction.

Iris said, "Rita and I can find a better place. I'd like something less isolated anyway. Like a row of shops around us. We can share each other's customers and it would be safer at closing time."

"Would anyone like another sandwich?" Rita wanted to change the subject completely. She raised the styrofoam plate with three _bolios_ filled with deli-slices of turkey and cheese. But as she looked around, they all shook their heads. She smiled at Iris and put the plate down. "Iris, this picnic was such a nice idea. Thank you."

"I know you get too busy and don't eat. A person could starve working for you," Iris said, grinning at her new partner.

"Perhaps you need a small refrigerator in the storeroom," Brian suggested. "Like the kind students use in a dorm room."

"Good idea," Iris said, then turned to look around the shop. "We did a good morning's work here, Rita. What should we do next?"

Rita followed Iris's gaze. All the boxes in the storeroom had been examined and labeled with a marker briefly describing their contents. Then they were stacked neatly awaiting the individual pricing that Rita and Iris would have to do before they sold anything. Three boxes of trash stood near the door to be tossed in the dumpster.

"I don't know. Maybe we've done enough for today." Rita wiped her hands with a napkin then tossed it on her empty plate. "You still have invitations to addresses, and I'd like to finish some bookkeeping before I sit down and talk about this shop and a solid partnership agreement."

"You won't change my mind about this partnership, Rita. No matter what's in the books," Iris told her, reaching over to pat her arm. "We can make this little dress shop into something good for both of us."

Rita appreciated the vote of confidence and smiled at Iris.

"Does that mean we're through now?" Stefanie grabbed her mother's empty plate and stacked it on top of hers.

"What's the rush?" her mother asked with a bemused smile at her daughter's activities.

"Uh—I have some homework to do," she said, not looking at her mother but concentrating on her efforts to clean up the picnic area.

"I think she wants to get on the phone with her friends," Iris whispered to Rita, who just nodded. Stefanie's sullen moods seemed to have been replaced by typical behaviors for any teenage girl.

"Well, once I get these invitations out, I'll be able to concentrate on our new business venture," Iris told Rita after she sent Stefanie out to the car with the basket and the empty tea jug.

"Iris, the *quinceañera*'s only three weeks away. Don't you need to make it your first priority?" Brian asked his sister. He stood by the door, a box of trash in each hand.

"Brian, the *quince* has been in the planning stages for months. Years, even. The food's been ordered, Stefanie and I have been to see Father Emmanuel, and the invitations will be out by tomorrow morning. I've only the flowers left to order, and I told Angie's aunt I'd be in this week. I've got things under control." Iris's voice carried a hint of anger. Her eyes were very bright as she glared at her brother.

"I guess you do, Iris. Excuse me, please," he said in an ultra-polite voice. He turned and walked out the door, leaving Rita to shut it behind him.

"I wonder sometimes who's the older sibling around here," Iris said, more to herself than to Rita.

"Perhaps you need to give Brian extra time to adjust to the new Iris Bonilla," Rita said out of sympathy for the man she loved.

"He's so darn sensitive. He takes my right to make a decision as a negative reflection on the way he was doing things." She buttoned up her canvas jacket. "He just takes thing too personally, that's all."

"But he is personally involved with both of us. And because of certain decisions you and your husband made years ago, he's legally involved with your money. Whether you like it or not."

"Is this conversation leading somewhere?" Putting her hands on her waist, Iris stared at Rita.

Just then the shop door opened and Brian walked back inside. His frown was almost identical to his sister's. And Iris's defensive pose and impatient tone were very familiar, too.

Rita merely sighed, fearing if she spoke to either of them, she'd just say something one or the other would take too personally.

Luckily, Stefanie walked back into the shop.

"Mom, can we go now?"

Iris nodded, then spoke to Rita in her own version of an ultra-polite voice. "I'll need to buy stamps and mail the invitations early in the morning, but I should be here no later than nine-thirty, Rita."

Offering words of thanks and farewell to Stefanie, Rita followed them to the door of the shop, then closed it behind them, leaving only Brian inside with her. She almost wished he had left too. She had run out of all the energy it took to be sympathetic, or diplomatic, or even romantic with anyone.

"Are you leaving right away?" he asked.

Pushing herself away from the door, Rita walked past him and around the counter. "I almost said the same thing. But to answer your question, yes, I think I'm going home. I'd like to take a nap then I'll do some work on the books."

He looked as if he was going to say something, but instead turned away and went to get his jacket which had been thrown over the shoulders of the dress figure. "Can't you spare a little time just for you and me?"

Brian's hurt expression made her feel very guilty that she wasn't spending the afternoon with him. "Brian, it's nothing personal. I'm just tired. I didn't sleep much last night."

His entire body tensed before he turned to look at her. "This business with Iris built up a wall between us, and I'm not sure if things will ever be the same again. Doesn't that worry you at all?" He strangled his jacket between his hands.

Rita's hand rested on her box of invoices and receipts that she was ready to take home, but her work seemed very unimportant at this moment.

"I'm worried about stuff, yes. But not you and me. I love you."

Dropping his jacket, he walked towards her. She came around the counter. Within his tight embrace, she rested against his gray sweatshirt, feeling his kiss press against the top of her head.

"Brian, I love you," she whispered.

"And I love you. I just want some time alone with you. Am I being terribly selfish and inconsiderate?"

Rita's hands slid around Brian's neck. "No. Actually, I'm tempted to put off doing the book work, but—well, I don't want your sister to think she is dealing with a half-rate business woman."

"You will never be half-rate, Rita. Everything you do is your best," Brian said then smiled. "Anyone who looks at a dress you've made can tell that about you. But I know it on a more personal level. You found a way to reach Stefanie and become her friend. You pulled words and feelings out of me that I never thought I'd share with anyone. And now you've given Iris a positive outlook about herself that I never could."

"You're being too nice. I've made my share of mistakes with all of you." She laughed softly, trying to deal with all his compliments.

"Oh, Rita. I'm the one who's been making mistakes. I regret so many things I said to you the past few days.

When it came to showing my faith and trust in you, I let you down. Iris, too. I'm going to do everything in my power to make it up to you. I promise."

And as Brian sealed that promise with a kiss, Rita made her own silent promise to keep this relationship a priority. Like a sparkling diamond, it grew more valuable with each passing day.

❤ ❤ ❤ ❤ ❤

There's no harm in looking, Rita told herself as she hung up the telephone Monday morning. She had just made an appointment to see the storefront on Blanco road.

If her relationship with Brian had taught her nothing else, Rita had learned that she had to keep moving forwards, no matter what new fears or unexpected problems crept up. Looking at the shop would give Rita and Iris a means of comparison. That would be helpful, especially since Rita didn't spend a lot of time outside her own shop, a fact she planned to change once she had a permanent partner to help her. Luckily, Iris had spent a lot of time shopping. She would know ways to make their shop stand out among the competition.

As she had promised, Iris arrived at the shop at nine-thirty. Rita had just finished the last alteration before the move out. Rita had already called her regular customers and told them she wouldn't be taking any more work until March first, and made certain each client had Rita's home telephone number and address just in case she had to temporarily work from there. She also promised each a postcard announcing the opening of the new store.

Iris came near the sewing machine, extending two envelopes in her hand. "I hope you will forgive this hand delivery, but I wanted you to be the second person to get this. I gave Brian the first one on Saturday."

Rita set the dress aside, and took the invitations, one addressed to Rita and the other to her great-grandmother. "Thank you, Iris. It was nice of you to invite my great-grandmother."

"You looked so sad when you told me that she planned to leave in two weeks. I thought she might stay another week for the *quinceañera*, and it would give you a little more time with her. Besides, Mamá Josie would be so disappointed if the *comadres* didn't get together once more before your great-grandmother moved even farther away." Iris put her hand gently on Rita's shoulder. "Now that we've made new connections from their old friendship, maybe we can figure out ways to get them together more often."

"Abuelita would like that," Rita said, then turned the envelope over to open it.

She pulled out a pink invitation with delicate scalloped edges. An embossed heart filled the center, and within it were the words *Mis Quince Años*, and below them *Stefanie Suzanne*, all printed in maroon ink. Inside the invitation was a pretty maroon script declaring: "Mrs. Estevan Bonilla requests the honor of your presence at a Mass of Thanksgiving celebrating the fifteenth birthday of her daughter, Stefanie Suzanne." It gave the date, time, name of the church, and mentioned the reception immediately following at Iris's house.

"The invitations are beautiful," Rita said, looking up to smile at Iris. "I feel privileged to be invited."

"In some ways, I think we have you and Brian to thank for this whole celebration," Iris said, removing her coat to fold it over her arms.

"I think you would have done right by your husband's wishes without me or Brian, Iris. I just made the dress," Rita answered.

"You and I both know you did more than that." She gave Rita a pretty smile. "Stefanie and I actually spent some pleasant hours together yesterday talking about the guest list. I didn't know my daughter felt like I did about so many of Estevan's old friends. We decided to include more of Stefanie's school friends and their parents, and of course, family. I hope I made the right choice here. Some of those awful wives of Estevan's friends might spend a lot of money in our new shop."

"Yeah, but who wants awful customers?" Rita laughed. She stood up and turned towards Iris. "We can still send them all cards about the new shop, and if they ask about the *quinceañera,* just tell them Stefanie wanted a party for her friends instead. It's the truth."

"You're right. I've got to learn not to let someone else's opinion control my actions. If I want to invite only certain people to my daughter's *quinceañera,* then it's my right to do so. They'd probably sniff their noses at the whole affair because Stefanie didn't want fourteen girls to honor her, and the reception isn't at Oak Hills."

"Big *quince* parties always bring big headaches," Rita told Iris, not wanting her friend to doubt her choices. "Only a few months ago I saw one mother of *quinceañera* almost have a nervous breakdown over the arrangements. Mrs. Menchaca came to me two weeks before the *quince* in a panic because three girls dropped out and she needed someone to make the last three dresses for some out-of-town relatives. I thought it was a crazy thing to sew for girls with mail-order measurements, but she tripled my usual fee, so I did it." Rita laughed. "The dresses came out okay, but I think Mrs. Menchaca is still taking tranquilizers. Trust me. You and Brian have the right idea to keep things simple."

"I bet you have a book full of stories about *quince* and wedding dresses that make mothers and daughters crazy." Iris grinned at Rita. "How do you keep from getting in the cross fire?"

"By demanding a big deposit before I start," she said, drawing out the word "big" and then laughing again. "Put your coat back on and I'll tell you a few good stories on our way."

"On our way? Where are we going?"

"To see the shop on Blanco Road."

"What did you do, win a jackpot last night?"

Rita allowed herself a satisfied smile. "I'm feeling very optimistic, that's all." She moved past Iris and went to get her coat. "And I think we ought to look at the place and get some ideas of what we want, Iris."

"We need to get something we can afford," Iris replied.

"That's true. But let's go look anyway." Rita slipped on her coat and went behind the counter to get her keys.

On the way, they discussed plans to advertise the sale. They decided on prices for some of the goods that Bea left in the storeroom. By the time they arrived at the shop on Blanco Road, they were both in optimistic spirits.

Neither woman was surprised that the shop was an impressive showplace, with new paint and carpeting and lots of display space. The apartment behind it was intimate and cozy. The landlord was a courteous businessman who didn't seem upset that the two women were "still looking."

"I'm sure we'll find a place just perfect for us," Rita said once they were back in the car. She tried to sound cheerful, although it hurt to think about all the wonderful possibilities for such a good spot to open a store with that comfortable place to live just behind it.

"Mamá Josie always said that a strong faith is rewarded by a gift from the heavens," Iris answered, as if she, too, was trying to keep her disappointment at arm's length.

Rita looked at Iris with a genuine smile. "Abuelita used to tell me that, too. Let's just keep the faith going, partner."

Chapter Sixteen

When Rita arrived home that night, Abuelita was the only one there. She took extra pleasure in the long hug and kiss, gestures that were becoming more precious to Rita every moment.

Abuelita slowly moved towards the stove. She lifted the lid on a boiling pot and the strong scent of *comino* filled the kitchen. "Your cousin Dalia sent *albóndigas*. I'm cooking them for our supper."

"They smell wonderful. Did you enjoy your trip to Sabinal? What's the family gossip from there?" Rita quickly washed her hands at the sink so she could start heating *tortillas* to go with the thick meatball soup. "And where's Tía Minerva? She must have been in a rush to go home."

"It was best Minerva left, no? Did we need any more *caldo*?"

Her great-grandmother teased Rita with a smile.

They shared a pleasant supper together discussing the family and Rita's plans for the upcoming sale. When Rita told her great-grandmother about the invitation to the *quince*, Abuelita needed no convincing to stay another week.

"It may be my last visit with *comadre* Josie," she told Rita.

"No, it won't, Abuelita. Iris said we'll find ways to get you two together more often. We'll have you both come here for Christmas or something."

"It's sad that I go. But I leave you with Josie's family." Abuelita's tone was bittersweet. "They will watch over you."

Rita managed a smile, but quickly rose from the table to start washing dishes. Just keep busy, she told herself. Three weeks left with Abuelita, and she shouldn't waste them crying.

❤ ❤ ❤ ❤ ❤

"Do you feel better now?" Brian said, his gentle voice close to her ear. His lips pressed against her hair as his arms tightened around her shoulders.

"It was just the TV show," Rita said, sniffing back the tears that had spilled without warning. Suddenly she had just turned to Brian and sobbed uncontrollably against his chest as they sat on a sofa in the back room watching television after Abuelita went to bed.

"Mr. Spock didn't really die. He comes back to life in the sequel. You know that, right?"

Rita started laughing then, feeling foolish for trying to lie about her tears. "Abuelita hasn't left yet, and I miss her already. What will I be like when she's really gone?" She straightened up and looked at Brian, self-consciously wiping her hands across her wet cheeks.

His fingers slid under her chin. Then he leaned over to kiss her. "You will be very sad, and I will be here to hold you when you cry."

"Abuelita told me today that she was sad to leave, but she was glad that Josie's family would watch over me. I'm lucky to have you and Iris and Stefanie for my friends." Her hands caressed his cheek. "I don't know what I'd do without you."

Brian turned his face slightly to kiss her palm. "And where would we be if you hadn't given Stefanie a job? And pulled me under some mistletoe decorations so I'd have to kiss you on that first date?"

"Pulled you under the mistletoe?" Rita enjoyed the teasing Brian used to cheer her up. "It was a coincidence, that's all."

"I don't know about that." He slipped his arms around her again, smiling. "You just couldn't wait to get your lips on mine. I could tell."

Laughing softly, Rita massaged Brian's shoulders. "I didn't hear you screaming when it was over."

"When it was over, I wanted to scream, 'Again. Again.'"

"So why didn't you?"

"If anyone heard me, they might have wanted to kiss you, too."

"So you were protecting my virtue, huh?"

"Just saving the best for me," he said before he kissed her.

For that brief time, she felt relief from the sadness she kept pushing away. She tried to concentrate on Brian, on their love, on other positive things happening in her life.

"Iris and I went to see the place on Blanco Road," she said suddenly. "It was absolutely spectacular. Iris and I both thought so. The apartment was nice, too. It would be so convenient to live behind my new dress shop. And well—I've never really lived by myself, in my own place. That would be exciting, too."

His eyebrows raised and his smile was a little crooked as he said, "Rita, I thought this shop with the apartment was out of your price range. Did you win the lottery or what?"

Laughter came easy now. "No, of course not. But I still think it would be a good idea to move. Living here without Abuelita would be hard for me. I thought maybe my sister Debra could pay me to use the house, and I'll use the money to rent a new place."

Brian nodded. "You seem to have it all figured out."

"Not quite. But I'm trying. Debra watches the landlord's children in exchange for half-rent. I may not be able to find an apartment for what she pays. On the other hand, there's no rush to move out of here until I get the new shop going. Deal with one problem at a time. That's what Abuelita always says," Rita told him then leaned over to kiss his lips. "It's late. Perhaps we need to say good-night."

He kissed her again as they stood beside the front door. Brian held her hands and said, "I have a feeling we could work together to solve each of your problems."

Rita gave him a little smile. "I'd like that, Brian." And her heart beat with tiny flutterings of hope.

❤ ❤ ❤ ❤ ❤

"You're very quiet this morning," Iris said as they sat in the store the following morning pricing items for sale.

Rita shrugged. "I have a lot on my mind, I guess. Actually, I feel weird that I'm not sewing right now." She wrote numbers on a white sticker, then pressed it on top of a box of perfume.

Suddenly, Iris laughed. She reached into a box with lingerie and pulled out a black satin body suit decorated with fuchsia ribbons. "I think this lingerie is a good excuse to drive out to the mall this afternoon. I wouldn't know what to price this interesting little outfit, would you?"

Rita shook her head, then changed the subject. "What about the balloons? Did you talk to your friend, the florist, yet?"

"Yes. I promised I'd take them over tomorrow." Iris dropped the body suit back into the box and stood up. "If you don't mind, I'm going to call her right now and order something I forgot."

"That's fine. I'm almost finished with this box. Then I'm going to take my machine down. We can use the top of the desk for the sale items."

"I have four card tables in my garage. I could go get them after I call Angie's aunt. I bet we could borrow a few more from the Díazes." Iris had moved behind the counter and put the phone book on top. "No one will buy anything if they can't see it."

Iris's words gave Rita an idea. Leaving Iris to her telephone call, Rita went into the side room and looked around.

"If I take all the bolts off the shelves, we could use those, too," she said, talking to herself. "And if I take home Alyssa's train and veil and those dance costumes, I could use that rack to hang the nightgowns. And we could set up a few card tables over there for the stationery and perfumes."

She headed back to the storeroom to get some large bags to protect the fabrics and garments. Iris was still discussing flowers and ribbon colors on the telephone. By the time Iris came to join Rita in the side room, Rita had packaged all the bolts of fabric and was getting ready to carry them to her car.

"Are you moving out now?" Iris asked, eyebrows raised.

"Well, I'm not going to sell my materials, and we could use the shelf space for our special sale," Rita answered, lifting the awkward bundle into her arms.

"Where are you going to store these things?"

"In the trunk of my car for now. Once I get home, I'll figure something out."

Together they loaded Rita's car with fabrics and garments carefully bagged in white plastic to keep them clean. Rita's sewing machines were next, then trays of buttons and thread and a variety of other boxes that had been stored under the counter with business papers, fabric swatches, and pattern books.

They had just finished with what Rita called "the first load" and were standing beside the car discussing a drive over to the mall, including a detour by Iris's house to get the tables, when they heard a car horn and saw Brian's maroon car pull into the lot in front of the store. He smiled and waved at both of them.

"Have you had a chance to talk to Brian about our business?" Iris turned to look at Rita, her forehead pressed together in a frown.

"I thought we wanted to keep him out of our business," Rita said, feeling a crinkle across her own forehead.

They heard the car door slam and Iris lowered her voice.

"That's what I mean. Have you told him?"

"Me? What about you?" Their whispered voices made Rita feel like a pair of spies exchanging important information before the enemy closed in. "You need to tell Brian that you need his signature to release your money, but that's the only way he's going to be involved."

Then she turned quickly with a smile as Brian approached them, carrying some white papers under his arm.

"Hi, ladies. What are you two doing out here? Aren't you cold without your coats?"

Rita shrugged. She had been working hard; organizing everything into her car had kept her body warm. She started to say something, but Brian leaned down for a kiss, so she did that instead.

"What are you doing in this neighborhood?" Iris asked her brother.

"I have a twelve o'clock appointment close by. But I brought over something I hope you both can use. I did them myself." His eyes shone brightly as he flipped over one sheet and showed it to them.

It was a sign, boldly printed in firm black letters, advertising a moving sale for Rita's Dress Shop. In the corner of the sign was a simple map showing the location of the shop.

"Brian, these are great," Rita said, pleased by the professional quality of the flier. She smiled at Brian, feeling her heart swell with love. "They'll be perfect. Thank you." She handed the flier to Iris. "Wasn't it sweet for Brian to do this for us?"

"No one ever said my brother wasn't sweet," Iris replied. She then pursed her lips together as she looked at the paper.

"I took the idea from a newspaper ad. This morning I experimented with my graphics program. We probably need to put some dates on it. This is just a sample, really."

"This sign is a good start, but we need something better," Iris said.

Iris sounded almost ungrateful, and Rita didn't want Brian's feelings hurt. She appreciated his efforts, his time on the computer. "Maybe if we made more signs like these, I wouldn't have to advertise in the newspaper. It's very expensive."

Slowly Brian lowered his gaze to meet Rita's. "I also thought I could give notices of your sale to some of the women I work with."

"That would be great, Brian."

Iris waved the paper like a fan. "Well, little brother, you seemed to have done a good deed today. Thanks for your help."

Although Iris smiled, Rita didn't miss the troubled look in her eyes. It wasn't going to be easy telling Brian that it would be best if they handled the business on their own. Especially when he brought good ideas with him.

It was then they heard the faint ringing of the telephone.

"The phone! It may be the florist. She wasn't sure if she could get the gladiolas I wanted. Good-bye, Brian," Iris said before turning to run back into the shop.

Brian glanced at his watch. "I'd better go, too, Rita. I'm going to Del Rio tomorrow and won't be back until Friday. Can I see you tonight?"

Rita stepped around to face Brian, slipping her fingers up his printed silk tie. "Abuelita's spending the evening with friends. I can come to your place later."

He kissed her lips softly. "How soon can you get to my house?"

Rita giggled at the seductive gleam in his brown eyes.

"Iris usually leaves about five. Then I'll be on my way."

After a healthy until-we-meet-again kiss, Brian left and Rita walked back inside the shop, trying to keep her thoughts on the business at hand, not on her plans for a romantic meeting in a few hours.

Iris had just hung up the telephone. "Maxie got the flowers I wanted. That takes care of everything for the *quince* for now." She picked up the papers Rita left on the counter. "I wonder why we didn't think of this."

"Maybe we had too much else to think of." Rita glanced around her at the various boxes with so many different items inside. "We really need customers who enjoy bargains. Except for the lingerie, we've got a lot of junk for sale."

Iris came around the counter and stood by Rita among the boxes. "I'm starting to see why working with your last partner was so frustrating. You wanted a nice place to show clothes you made and sell a few other dresses for special occasions, and she wanted a flea market."

Rita laughed, and put her arm around Iris's shoulder. "That's true in many ways." Suddenly, she felt an imaginary light bulb blink on. "You've given me a great idea! We'll put an ad in the classified section where it lists yard sales and flea markets. It doesn't cost much, and there are lots of people who love shopping that way."

"But that might mean they'll want to haggle over our prices," Iris replied.

"But it might also mean that someone would make us a good deal on whatever we have left over," Rita said, not wanting one piece of Bea's junk to be moved into her new shop. She and Iris would create a classy clothes shop some place else and leave memories of this shop far behind.

They left the shop soon after.

First, a stop at Abuelita's house to unload Rita's car and stack everything in Rita's bedroom. They took time to have sandwiches with Abuelita, who was eager to listen to their excited plans.

They stopped by Iris's for her card tables, then took a hurried walk through the lingerie departments of three different mall stores, making notes of prices. But Iris slowed them down when she stopped outside a small women's boutique near the food court.

"Wouldn't it be nice to have something like this?" Iris said.

"Do you have any idea what it would cost to rent a shop in the mall?" Rita replied, almost shuddering at the thought of asking how much.

"I don't mean to have a shop inside the mall, but to have this kind of merchandise. Look at the window displays, and those glass shelves back there. This place has dresses, nice purses, even shoes. Let's go in and get some ideas. Just a few minutes, Rita. Come on."

They browsed among the attractive dresses and accessories, past green-curtained dressing rooms, and commented on the western blouses and denim skirts mounted on the walls with a bandana-red banner and the message "Go Rodeo." The saleslady was pleasant, but didn't hang over them. She easily moved among the half-dozen women who were in the shop.

Rita and Iris stood near the glass shelves where colorful beaded necklaces and eye-catching earrings were displayed. Suddenly, an older woman in a smart navy-blue dress came out of a back room with a young woman, who looked like a college student. The girl who was writing down something in a spiral notebook.

"It's the start-up costs that surprise people. A place like this needs maybe fifty to a hundred thousand just to open its doors. And it's not just the merchandise, but fixtures, too. Money to pay electricians, and plumbers, and carpenters. Even a nice space needs renovation."

The woman gave Iris and Rita a brief smile before she turned again to the red-haired young woman beside her.

"Don't you worry about the competition from the big department stores?" the redhead asked her, poising her pencil to write down whatever the shop owner said.

"It's tough competition, let me tell you. But I have my regular customers. I know what they like. When I get something new, I'll call them and invite them into the store."

"But developing that rapport with customers—regular customers—takes a lot of time, doesn't it?"

"That's why you need so much capital in the beginning. There's a lot of money going out that first year. It may be two or three before you see a profit, at least in this business anyway." It was then that the shop owner saw someone she recognized and moved to the other side of the store, with the young woman and notebook following close behind her.

Iris turned and stared at Rita. "Did you hear all that?"

"Of course I did. It sounds depressing, doesn't it?"

"Can you imagine what Brian would say if I asked for fifty-thousand dollars out of the trust fund?" Iris' hazel eyes rounded.

Rita said nothing, unaccustomed to thinking about so much money. Abuelita's small loan wasn't anywhere near fifty-thousand dollars. Of course, if she paid two- or three-thousand dollars in rent, she understood how the money would be used up quickly. She looked at Iris, wondering if she was having second thoughts. "Did you and Brian discuss an amount at all?"

"We were thinking maybe eight or ten thousand. Gosh, Rita. Are we crazy?"

"No, just naive, I guess." Rita turned to look around the store. "Of course this place is bigger than my shop. And a bigger place needs more merchandise to fill it up. And we are standing in an exclusive mall boutique. We can't afford something like this. We'll just have to start smaller, that's all." Thinking positive was difficult, but she didn't want to give in to her fears that she couldn't have the nice shop she and Iris had dreamed about these past weeks.

"But I want something bigger than a closet, you know? I want a pretty place with pretty things for sale," Iris answered. She shoved her purse under her arm. "Let's go, Rita. It was a mistake to even stop here and think that we could have something like this."

Silently, they left the store and returned to Rita's car. As they walked, Rita couldn't help but wonder if Iris thought going into business with her was a mistake, too. Once they sat together in the front seat, Rita turned to her friend to ask her, "Have you changed your mind about the partnership?"

"I don't know. I don't think I'm ready to turn over fifty-thousand dollars to you," Iris replied, turning to put her seat belt on rather than looking at Rita.

"I never asked for fifty-thousand dollars." Rita snapped out the words impatiently. A headache began pulsing at her temples. "I don't need that kind of money for the kind of shop I want."

"What about the shop that I want? Do you think I want to be stuck in a leaky place near a cemetery?"

"You think that's what I want? I want a small dress shop in a nice location. I've always said that. Maybe you have this impression that we're going to have an exclusive ladies' boutique that will cater to snobs." She bit off the words "like you," stopping herself before she insulted her friend. Despite their different upbringings, Iris had never been condescending in any way. Rita was just frustrated. So was Iris.

"I don't know what I want, Rita. Right now, I feel very confused," Iris answered, her voice as sad as the pathetic look she gave Rita.

It was a quiet drive back to the shop. All the earlier excitement and enthusiasm for the upcoming sale seemed to have shriveled up like a balloon with a slow leak. They spoke only of where to display items, or discussed prices for the lingerie before Rita hung them on the rack. They did have three different customers who bought some merchandise, but the sales didn't cheer up the two women working in the store. Iris left about four, and Rita left soon after.

As she locked the shop door behind her, Rita noticed the storm clouds brewing in the distance. She sighed loudly then got into her car.

Chapter Seventeen

"You seem preoccupied, Rita. Do you want to talk?"

Brian handed Rita a glass of white wine in a fluted goblet before he eased himself on the den sofa.

How elegant it looks, Rita thought, holding the glass up so the lights sparkled through it. She sighed, wondering if bad wine in a beautiful glass would still be unfit to drink.

She took a long drink of wine, almost choked into awareness by the sweet cold liquid sparkling down her throat. Then she set her glass down on the lamp table beside her.

Brian also took a drink then set his glass down. Sitting back in the den sofa, Brian rested his arm across the back, eventually to circle her shoulders. "What are you thinking about, my love?"

"I'm with the man I love, and that's the only thing I want to think about right now, okay?"

She curled her legs under her to lean against Brian.

"Don't take this wrong, Rita, but I feel like you've got more on your mind than me," Brian said slowly. "A lot more."

There was a clap of thunder then and the sound of a steady rain outside. Rita naturally looked to the windows. Brian's pretty view of the city skyline had blurred and faded to a misty gray.

The dreary outlook suited Rita's thoughts about her working with Iris. Had she given up on the partnership? Were their goals too far apart? No room for compromise? Not even a chance to talk about it further?

Brian's hand rubbed Rita's shoulder. "Did anything happen between you and Iris? She seemed to be moody when I saw her at your shop."

Rita stared at him, wondering what to say. Didn't she and Iris want to keep Brian out of their business affairs? But who else could she talk to? He loved her; she trusted him. Friendship had been the cornerstone in this relationship.

"Everything seems to be getting complicated, Brian."

Complicated. Iris had used the same word weeks ago, and it turned out to be a prophecy for their partnership plans.

"Nothing is ever simple," he said gently, moving back on the sofa as if he wanted to give her room to think. "If something's wrong, please tell me. I want to help."

Rita pulled her legs to her chest, glad she could tuck the long beige skirt around her ankles. She wrapped her arms around her knees, staring at stocking feet since she left her wet shoes by Brian's front door.

"Brian, Iris and I think it would be best if we didn't involve you in our business plans. If I start talking to you now, it'll just make things worse."

"Why don't you want me to be involved in your business plans?"

She sensed his hurt feelings and groaned, her fingers scratching through her black hair. "It's nothing personal, Brian. We just want to do things on our own. Can't you understand that?"

"I guess so," he replied, but he didn't sound as if he did.

Here was a chance to settle things with Brian. She had to speak her mind. She felt Iris had deserted her. If the partnership was doomed, then she would be going on alone anyway. Alone?

A nervous shiver wiggled down Rita's back. She hugged herself tighter. Finally, she looked into Brian's serious face. The loving concern in his eyes helped guide her through this maze of crumbling dreams.

She sighed then looked away. "I just don't know how to talk about everything. Iris suggested that we get a neutral person to help us work out the partnership. She felt if you got involved it would put a lot of stress on our relationship. I agree with her, Brian."

He placed his hand on her knees. "Rita, don't shut me out. I can be neutral about you and Iris even if I do love both of you. First and foremost we're friends, right? Obviously there's a problem with Iris. I can see that you need a friend to talk to. Please, trust me. Did something happen today?"

Rita shrugged. "I don't know if anything 'happened'— but I think Iris is having second thoughts about going into business with me."

"Did you two have an argument?"

"I'm still not sure what has happened between us," Rita said before she gave him a detailed replay of the afternoon. He listened without comment until she mentioned the fifty-thousand dollars.

Brian whistled his amazement, and she thought he might say something negative about the money and Iris's trust fund, but he just shook his head slightly and said, "Go on. I'm listening."

"Brian, you know that for me this partnership has never been about money. I like Iris. I like working with her. And I think she needs a chance to do something successful for herself. Iris said that you two had discussed an eight to ten-thousand dollar investment and honestly—that is far more than I ever expected."

She noticed him chew on his lip a moment, thinking about something.

"What is it, Brian?"

"I'm trying to be neutral here. Why don't you tell me what kind of store you have in mind," he told Rita.

"Well, I don't want a boutique in the mall that caters to the rich and snobby. Actually, what I have now wouldn't be so bad if it didn't face a cemetery. And the roof leaks and the landlord's a jerk. But I like my customers and I enjoy sewing for them."

"I think if Iris wants to run a store like you described, then she needs to get a job in one. You seem very certain about what you want, Rita. You shouldn't have to compromise your plans for anyone."

Rita smiled, glad to hear him say what she had been thinking all afternoon.

"Besides," he said, as if it was an afterthought. "I know you can't afford to open an exclusive boutique in the mall."

"I wouldn't be comfortable there. It's not my world. But stores like that are part of Iris's world." Rita expressed a sigh. "If only we could find a middle road. Some place that would suit us both. If any of this is even possible anymore. Could I have been so totally wrong about Iris?"

She braced herself, expecting Brian to say "I told you so" or put on his protective armor and defend any criticism of Iris like he usually did. But he surprised her with a thoughtful look and a slight shrug of his shoulders.

"It seems to me that you and Iris need to make some serious decisions now. Even if it means that you don't go into business together. You two have to be more than positive that this partnership will work for both of you. It's a big commitment financially—and emotionally, too. It's like being absolutely certain you know a person well before you marry them. Breaking an engagement is painful, but it's less complicated than a divorce."

"Do you think you'll ever get married?" Rita knew that she had changed the entire course of the conversation. But his comparison had made her curious.

His eyebrows had raised at her blunt question, but he seemed quite relaxed as he said, "I see myself being married someday." His fingers stroke her jaw. "I think I've found the woman I want to marry. Only she's very involved with her work right now, and I'd like her to have her business plans more settled before we discuss wedding plans."

His honesty only strengthened her trust in their relationship, and in Brian himself. She felt as if she could tell him anything and he would understand.

"When I get married, I want it to be for the right reasons," she told him.

"The right reasons?"

"My sisters rushed into marriage because they were pregnant. I think my mother married my stepfather because she believed it would be better than living without a man the rest of her life." Rita heard the bitter sounds in her words and tried to hold back the old pangs of anger and sadness. But they pushed even harder for release. "They all ran off to find their own personal happiness and just left me behind. My *quinceañera* was the last time my family ever wished me some happiness."

Brian's hand slid over her arms, rubbing them gently. "You managed to make your own happiness, Rita. I admire you for that. And as I get to know you, love you, I realize how very special you are. Given the circumstances, somebody else would have become very bitter."

Her voice was very quiet. "I have my moments."

"We all do, Rita." He kissed her cheek. "I love you very much. And I'm sorry that all this happened with Iris. Maybe later I'll drive over to her house and talk to her."

Rita shook her head, winding her arms through Brian's. "Please don't do that, Brian. You can't solve our problems for us. If Iris and I can't work this out, I don't want you caught between us. It really will be for the best if Iris and I talk to someone else about our partnership."

"Then I guess all you two want from me is a signature, right?" He didn't sound upset, but she saw something different in his eyes.

"Brian, we both want your love and support. Iris does need your signature, true. But I just want you for yourself. I need you to love me no matter what happens between me and Iris." Then she kissed him.

When Rita left Brian's house near eight, she felt more relaxed then when she had arrived. She was still worried about Iris; her plans and feelings about the partnership. Rita faced the possibility that she and Iris wouldn't work together as planned. On the other hand, Iris would have to respect what Rita wanted for her business if this was to be a true partnership. No matter what they decided, Rita wanted to keep her relationship with Iris intact. A good friend was worth more than money; even fifty-thousand dollars.

On an impulse, Rita decided to drive to Iris's house. She wanted Iris to know that there would be no hard feelings if Iris had changed her mind.

Both front rooms of Iris's house were still lighted, and the porch light was on, too, as if visitors were expected. Rita wondered if Iris wanted Brian to appear sometime tonight. Her suspicions were confirmed when the door was answered after the first ring, and Iris's anxious, pale face revealed shock, the disappointment that Rita stood on the porch.

"Rita? Are you alone?" Iris peeked around the doorway into the dark, damp night.

"Hello, Iris. I thought the two of us should talk. Would you mind?"

"Well—I have a headache—I'm not feeling well—"

"I'm sorry you're not well—but—can we talk? I won't stay long."

Iris stepped back and gestured for Rita to come inside. "Okay. I just wasn't expecting to see you tonight."

Rita walked into the entranceway, unbuttoning but not removing her navy-blue raincoat. "I'm sorry we didn't talk more this afternoon. I guess both of us wanted more time to think about the partnership." She walked into the living room and sat on the striped chair.

Iris took a place on the sofa. She was dressed in a purple satin hostess robe, but didn't look comfortable. Her back was straight against the sofa, her hands clasped tight in her lap.

"Did I hear the doorbell? Is Uncle Brian here?" Stefanie thumped down the stairs and slid into the living room on her thick pink socks. She wore an oversized pink sweatshirt that hung past her knees. "Rita! Hello. Where's Uncle Brian?"

"Hello, Stefanie. I just came by to talk some business with your mother."

"Gosh, I really need him right now. Daddy's printer isn't working right. And my English essay is due tomorrow."

"Why don't you call him at home?" Rita suggested. "I just left him. He was packing for his trip to Del Rio."

"I will. Thanks." And with that, Stefanie turned and went back upstairs.

"Brian and I printed up a few new fliers tonight. I have them in the car if you want to see them," Rita said, trying to start the conversation with positive messages that their working together was something Rita still wanted.

"This is your sale, Rita." Iris shrugged. "It's your shop. I've been thinking that I might go with Brian to Del Rio tomorrow and visit with Mom while he's working the next few days. Stefanie can stay with her great-grandparents."

Rita didn't know what to say. Had she taken Iris's help for granted? She never dreamed that she'd have to sell all of Bea's junk by herself.

"I'm a little surprised, Iris. You gave me the impression that you wanted to help me sell everything and move out."

"I just need some time to myself, that's all," Iris said, moving around as if she was sitting on a giant pin cushion.

"Iris, I'm going to be very honest here. I can't have a partner who's going to get headaches or leave town when things don't go her way. I need somebody who's going to tell me what's on her mind. Someone who can handle the setbacks and problems and not give up. If you're not going to be in town to help with the sale, that's fine. But I'd like your permission to offer Stefanie a job for the next few afternoons and on Saturday. I need someone dependable to help me in my store." The calm yet strong tone in her words satisfied Rita. She just didn't have the luxury of standing still until Iris made a definite commitment to the partnership.

"Stefanie's very busy lately. But you can ask her if you want." Her gaze was icy, her words topped with frost. She rose from the sofa and walked out of the room to call her daughter's name loudly.

"Mom, Uncle Brian's coming over to help me. He said he'd bring his printer along just in case he can't get Daddy's working."

Rita stood up at Stefanie's announcement. She had a hunch Brian was glad for this excuse to come to Iris's house.

"Rita wants to talk to you," Iris told her daughter, and both of them came into the living room.

Smiling at Stefanie, Rita said, "I wondered if you'd like to work for me after school and on Saturday."

"As in a paid job? Or am I helping you and Mom out for free like I did last weekend," Stefanie replied, crossing her arms.

"It will be just like we worked together at Christmas. A paying job. Are you interested?"

"Aren't you working with us?" Stefanie gave her mother a curious look.

"Your mother may go out of town this week, and I need some help," Rita said before Iris could answer.

"You're going out of town? Again? Where?"

"Your Uncle Brian's going on a business trip to Del Rio. I thought I'd go with him and visit your grandparents. You could stay with Grandma Carmen and Grandpa Charlie while I am gone," Iris answered, her voice shaking slightly as she spoke.

"You can't leave. What about the sale? You've been talking about it for days. And we were invited to the Díaz's house for supper Thursday night. Mom, what's going on? How can you leave town with Uncle Brian when both Rita and I need you here?" Stefanie looked at Rita a moment, then back at her mother. "Mom, what's going on?"

Iris glanced down at the floor then back at her daughter. "I'm not certain I'll be working with Rita after all. It'll be better if you help her."

"Better for who? Mom, since you started hanging around Rita, you're almost like your old self again. Tonight you were crying; you said you have a bad headache. What's going on?" Stefanie frowned at Rita. "Did you two have a fight or what?"

"There wasn't any fight." Iris's voice was sharp. "But I realized today that Rita might want a different type of shop than I do. It seems pointless for the two of us to make serious plans about working together when we hope to serve different types of people."

"Rita sews for nice people like Mrs. Díaz. I can't believe that you wouldn't want customers like her," Stefanie said. "Would you prefer snobby witches like Mrs. Cavazos or Mrs. Guerrero? Just last week you told me you realized how phony all those ladies were. Do you really want to sell clothes to women like them?"

"It's not about the customers, but the image I want to project." Iris looked back at Rita. "I want a classy place that I can be proud of."

"I don't think a classy place is determined by location, Iris. It's about unique merchandise and the quality of the service you provide." Lowering her voice, Rita gave her friend a patient look. "Iris, I have an established list of customers just like that shop owner said she has. I have money saved for a deposit on a new lease and some extra to buy new merchandise for a new shop. But our shop will not be an exclusive boutique like we saw today. I can't afford it. Frankly, it's not what I want.

"I guess I don't know what I want." Iris looked from Rita to her daughter. "It was such a pretty store, though. You should have seen the lovely dresses and jewelry, Stefanie."

"Iris, maybe I've misled you, but I don't want to just make ladies' clothes. I like to make things for brides, and babies, and western shirts for Tejano singers. Dresses for *quinces* and suits for *charros*. I enjoy making Mexican dance costumes and working with special clients through the Fiesta Commission. I want my shop to project an image that we can do anything."

"You do?" Iris asked, her eyebrows raised. "I had no idea. It would be more challenging to serve a variety of customers like you do. Much better than the snobby witches, anyway."

"Are you certain about that?" Rita tried not be harsh, but she needed Iris to be sure about her motives for working together. "I know what I want out of this business, but I'm not certain that you do, Iris."

"Rita, I appreciate your willingness to come here and talk to me tonight. It looks like I need to break the old habits and not hide out waiting for someone else to solve my problems. I'd like to learn to see things as a challenge as you do. Perhaps we shouldn't call this a partnership. Let me be your apprentice instead." Iris gave her an apologetic looks. "I'm sorry I didn't talk to you about what I was feeling. I should have."

"You're right." Rita put her hand on Iris's arm. "But we're talking now, and we just have to keep talking, Iris. But if you really feel that you need to go to Del Rio and think about our partnership more, then go."

"No. That would be a terrible mistake. My mother reacted the way Brian did when I told her I was going into business with you. If I see her now, she'll only make me feel like I can't handle my own life."

Her face had regained some of its color. "No, Rita. I plan to be in that shop early tomorrow morning and the rest of the week. And if Stefanie wants to earn a little money, she can help, too." Iris put her arm around her daughter's waist and smiled at her. "I should have talked to you tonight about my worries instead of working myself into a headache. You made a good point about Rita's customers. They are nice people, the ones I've met so far."

"And the fact that one of them has a good-looking son named Nicholas helps a lot, doesn't it?" Rita laughed and gave Stefanie a wink.

"Since Brian's on his way over, will you stay for a while, Rita?" Iris asked her. "I can make coffee and there's still some cinnamon coffee cake in the freezer."

"Thanks, but I can't. My great-grandmother should be home by now, and I don't like leaving her alone at night," Rita answered.

"I understand," Iris said.

Stefanie offered a quick good-bye and went back to her essay and computer problems.

As Rita stood by the door, she told Iris, "I had a long talk with Brian tonight. I told him we wanted a neutral person to help us through the partnership. But I have to admit, he was very neutral as I poured out my troubles to him tonight."

"So he knows his sister's crazy, huh?"

"Iris. You aren't crazy. I only wish you had more faith in our relationship. I can't see that we'll be good partners if we aren't better friends."

She took Rita's hands between her own. "I promise to trust you and our friendship from now on. I've never known anyone to like me unconditionally, Rita. Except for Brian."

Rita smiled, suddenly understanding the heart of Brian and Iris's relationship. She though relationships were different between a brother and sister, but now she knew it was the unconditional love between them that made them so close. She knew that same kind of love with Abuelita, and felt herself anxious to get back to the old woman and make the most of these last days together.

They were still at the door discussing a few details about the sale when the doorbell rang and Brian arrived.

"Stefanie didn't tell me you were here," he said to Rita.

She grinned. "I brought Iris an aspirin for her headache."

"And I hope you brought a printer with you," Iris said just as Stefanie called out, "It's printing! I got it to work all by myself!"

The next day Rita made phone calls to her regular customers inviting them into the store to shop before the advertised sale, while Iris went out to put notices about the sale on community bulletin boards and the college campuses in the area. Customers trickled in steadily all day, and on Friday, once the ad had come out in the morning paper, a variety of people stopped in to see what was for sale. Rita had left the rack up with the last of the evening dresses and colorful cotton dresses from Mexico. She didn't think anyone was going to buy them, but they sold, too.

Abuelita came by after lunch with her friend Jovita and four other ladies from the neighborhood. Rita and Iris were amused at the six old women who inspected every piece of merchandise, even the lingerie.

When her great-grandmother came up to the counter with a black negligee, a short satin gown with v-strips of revealing black lace, Rita couldn't contain her giggles.

"Abuelita, why are you buying that nightgown?"

She put it on the counter and started digging in her gray purse for her wallet. "It's for a lady I know. She might get married soon, and I want her to have something special for the honeymoon." She pulled out her wallet and looked up at Rita. "I know the man she loves. He'll like this one."

"I bet he will, too," Iris said, slipping her hands over Rita's shoulders as she passed behind her to ring up the sale.

Rita's eyes rolled up to the ceiling. She walked away, knowing embarrassment had blushed streaks of red across her face.

The older ladies left as a group of college students arrived, and they bought out most of the perfumes, underwear, and stationery. A kindergarten teacher bought a lot of the paper hats and party supplies, and a man who said he ran a flea market told Rita to call him with her leftovers and he'd make her a fair offer.

"At the rate we're going, I can close up this place by early next week," Rita told Iris as she locked the door and turned the sign around to read CLOSED. "I can hardly wait to turn over the keys to Mr. Arredondo."

"I can't believe how much stuff you already sold," Stefanie said, coming out of the side room. She had been dropped off at the shop after school by her friend, Micole Balboa, and her mother. Mrs. Balboa bought one of the evening dresses and six packages of white streamers to decorate for her high school reunion in two weeks.

"I was tempted to tell that flea market man to take it all now, but we did advertise the sale was Friday and Saturday," Rita told Iris, who had opened the cash register and was taking the money out.

Rita watched her quickly put it in the leather bag, then stuff that into Rita's canvas bag. Iris then turned the small silver key on top of the register so they could get a total for the day's sales.

"Hey, it's Uncle Brian," Stefanie said just before they heard a knock on the shop door.

Rita returned to open it and welcomed Brian with a kiss. "Hello. I missed you."

"I missed you, too." He closed the door behind him and smiled at his sister. "How's the sale been going?"

"Very well. One man even gave Rita a few dollars for her bag of scraps that we had hidden under a table." Iris laughed. "It's been fun, but my feet are killing me."

"Well, I came to take you tired businesswomen to supper," Brian said, then noticed Stefanie. "Hello! So what grade did you get on the essay?"

"A, of course."

"Then I'll buy you a big sundae after dinner," Brian told her.

"Are you crazy? Do you know how fat I'll get? And my *quinceañera's* next week and everything!"

"I'll take the sundae then," Rita said, feeling like she deserved a treat after the tiring day selling off Bea's junk. She preferred sewing to selling any day. But Iris was a born saleswoman, and their individual talents promised a fruitful partnership.

With Brian's arm around her waist and Iris reading off the day's total sales, Rita felt as if all the pieces of a complicated outfit were finally coming together. And she couldn't wait to see the finished product.

♥ ♥ ♥ ♥ ♥

"I suppose I shouldn't take the keys until I inspect the building," Mr. Arredondo said, his bushy eyebrows pointing downwards. His fat fingers closed over the sticky keys Rita had placed in his hand. "There was a property deposit in your lease, you know."

"I scrubbed the walls and steam cleaned the carpets. It's cleaner now than when Bea and I moved in." Her stare never wavered.

"So what's left behind besides the wall and carpets?"

"Well, the counter, that wobbly table behind it. Just what you gave us. That's what I left."

"What about my cash register?" he asked, snapping off the words.

Rita crossed her arms over her. "Your register broke down a month after we opened the shop, Mr. Arredondo. You never had it fixed, so we bought our own. Yours is in the storeroom."

Suddenly, a clap of thunder sounded above the roof of Mr. Arredondo's small real estate office. A glance out the front window revealed the steady rain beating on Rita's car.

She couldn't help but smile. She had removed everything she had bought out of the shop, including the mop bucket that had rested on the bathroom toilet. She thought about warning Mr. Arredondo about the leak and the mess he might find, but dismissed it as quickly as it came.

"I have another appointment, Mr. Arredondo. I've given you the keys, and I'll be going now. Good-bye."

The man put out his hand for a shake. Rita decided to ignore the gesture, turning quickly and heading out the door. She stood for a moment to open her umbrella on the cement step beneath a striped awning.

It was a dreary, cold afternoon, but to Rita, it felt like the rain washed away the last traces of her business relationship with that greedy man. She would never have to drive across town to this office, or listen to the man's excuses, or feel his clammy hands touch hers again.

Rita had cut the final tie to her former partnership and looked forward to a new beginning with Iris.

As she drove out on the interstate, Rita looked back on the last few days with a sense of satisfaction. By Saturday noon, the last of the good merchandise had been sold, and when Rita had called the man from the flea market with a price, he came and picked up the rest of the stuff an hour later. It took them the rest of the afternoon to toss out the trash and load up Rita's, Iris's, and Brian's cars with the dress racks, the small appliances, the cash register, and boxed accessories that hadn't been sold and take them to Abuelita's house for temporary storage.

Brian had helped Rita do the heavy cleaning on Sunday, since both of them were anxious to be rid of the old shop and its landlord as soon as possible. Two days later, Rita was able to turn over the keys.

Now, she drove towards the patch of blue skies slowly appearing in the horizon.

Chapter Eighteen

Rita walked into the back bedroom and stopped near the dress figure wearing the exquisite wedding gown. A blue emotion draped her heart. This was the last garment that she and Abuelita would work on together. It was finished, every pearl bead now in place over the bodice and cuffs. Even now, Abuelita was on the telephone telling her daughter that Rita was driving her to Brownsville a week from Sunday.

Rita felt grateful for the past few days of working alone with her great-grandmother on Alyssa's wedding dress. Even though she found the bead work tedious and boring, she treasured the chance to listen to Abuelita tell old family stories, especially any that included the Esparza family.

Now, as she stared at the beautiful gown, Rita couldn't help but imagine herself in the dress, floating down the aisle to meet Brian and become his wife. His eyes would sparkle and she would smile, as if they shared a private secret. Yet everyone watching would know how much they loved each other.

"Are you dreaming of a wedding? That isn't the dress for you, Rita." Her great-grandmother had suddenly come into the room and caught Rita with her love for Brian shining on her face.

Rita walked around the gown, inspecting it for flaws before she delivered the dress at noon. "You don't think I'd look pretty in something like this, Abuelita?"

"You'd be *linda* in any dress. I want you to wear the one I made for your mother," Abuelita said, tugging on one of the satin sleeves.

"I did pull the box with Mom's dress out of your chest. I always thought it was so pretty. Do you think it would fit? It didn't fit any of my sisters."

The old woman harumped. "Your sisters wanted new store-bought dresses, that's all."

"But each of them looked so beautiful. There's something magical about a wedding dress, isn't there?" Rita's hands skimmed over the shoulder of the gown in front of her.

"The magic comes from love. A dress is a dress."

"Oh? I thought that only applied to store-bought dresses." Rita cocked an eyebrow at her great-grandmother.

Now Abuelita smiled. "You have learned well, Rita *linda*. You have learned well."

The telephone rang then. Rita kissed her great-grandmother's cheek before she left the room.

"Who's crazy idea was it to have a *quinceañera* anyway?" Iris's breathless voice rushed past Rita's "Hello?"

"The catering company decided to declare bankruptcy this morning! So now I have no food for the reception. And my daughter informs me at breakfast that *mariachis* would be embarrassing, and she wants a disc jockey to play dance music instead. Where am I going to find a disc jockey in a week's time? Then Cecilia calls and asks if she could invite both sets of Nicky's grandparents and his godparents because she thinks he'll be so cute in a tux and they shouldn't miss it. Do you think I should have told her that they could come if they bring their own food?"

Rita laughed, even though she knew Iris probably wasn't in the mood to see the humorous side to what she said. "If it will help, I'll bring a sack lunch to eat."

Then Iris sighed, and finally chucked. "I should have know things were going too smoothly."

"Well, no one expected your caterer to declare bankruptcy. What an awful thing to happen."

"The worst of it is that Brian had already paid him for the reception food. That money's gone now. I started to call Brian and tell him the news, but then I decided that I needed to find another caterer and pay him myself. I just can't go running to Brian anymore."

Rita was glad to hear the determination in Iris's voice. "Well, can I do something to help?"

"You have. I just needed a friend to listen."

"I'm free to listen further. Abuelita's going to have lunch with a neighbor, and I have to deliver a wedding gown. Want to meet for lunch?"

"Yes! And I know just the place, too. I promised the florist I'd pay her today. Next door to the flower shop is a cute tea room. Shall we meet about twelve-thirty?" Iris gave Rita directions to the place, then hung up the phone.

Rita had only taken one step down the hall when the telephone rang again.

"Hello, Rita. Are you free for dinner tonight?" Brian's tender voice was a pleasant surprise.

"Hi, Brian. Actually, I planned to fix dinner for Abuelita and myself. Will you join us here?" she replied.

"Well, I need to talk to both you and Iris. I have a special surprise for the two of you."

She started to tell him about lunch, but then decided against it. He might decide to take over Iris's problems and solve them himself. Iris deserved a chance to handle the situation herself.

"Brian, why don't you come to supper, then we can go to Iris's later?" Rita suggested.

"Hang on a second, please," Brian said suddenly. She heard muffled voices and finally his loud sigh. "Well, supper's out. I think I'm on my way to Austin in the next ten minutes. But I'll meet you at Iris's later. About seven?"

"Fine. I'm meeting Iris for lunch. I'll tell her to expect us."

"Great. I love you, Rita. I'll see you tonight."

❤ ❤ ❤ ❤ ❤

Rita had passed the new strip of shops on Fredricksburg Road half-a-dozen times in the last few months, but had never really paid attention to them before today.

The long building had a beige brick exterior, and each individual shop had high windows and glass doors trimmed in brown siding. The two corner shops had windows on the side. One was the tea room that Iris spoke of, and the other was a dance studio with a white FOR LEASE sign in its window. In between were four other shops, a hair stylist, a photographer, a children's book store, and a florist. Near the street was a towering sign. Strips of white plastic stretched across silver poles, each strip advertising an individual business name in bold black letters.

Rita stood on the sidewalk admiring the retail center as Iris's sleek white car pulled up beside her.

"Hi," she told Iris as they met in front of the tea room. "I was just looking around. It's a nice shopping center."

"Isn't it? You know, when Stefanie insisted that I order flowers from Angie's aunt's flower shop, I wasn't very enthusiastic. I have a florist I've used for years. But I decided to trust my daughter's judgment. I've been very pleased. Come on."

Iris led the way into the shop called Flowers by Maxie, a narrow but deep store brightly decorated with red heart balloons, red cardboard cutouts of Cupid and Valentines, and lots of red, white, and pink ribbons, stuffed animals, and boxes of candy lining the shelves.

The shop smelled of flowers and healthy green plants. Rita could almost taste the jelly beans, chocolate, and peppermint. Delicate wind chimes tinkled as a ceiling fan created a slight breeze in the room. The place was filled with merchandise and a large refrigerator with glass doors, but there was plenty of room to walk around, admire the lovely plants, and look at everything else Maxie had for sale.

A thin man in a business suit stood at the counter holding his hand around the ribbons of a balloon bouquet. Rita noticed one of the birthday balloons was one that Bea had ordered. Obviously, Maxie had wasted no time selling the balloons she had bought from Iris.

Maxie was a short, square woman with dark hair piled up in a fat top knot on her head. She gave the customer his receipt, thanked him for his business, then showed a toothy new smile to Iris and Rita.

"Iris! Glad to see you. You know, just this morning I got in that peach colored ribbon you wanted for the altar flowers. When I'm finished at the church, it will look elegant enough for a pope's visit."

Iris laughed and gestured towards Rita. "Maxie, this is Rita Navarro. Rita, this is Maxie García."

Maxie took Rita's hand for a friendly shake. "You're the dressmaker. Thanks so much for selling me those balloons for such a good price."

"It was Iris's idea. I'm glad you were able to use them."

"Oh, yes. Lucky for me, birthdays happen every day."

Rita stepped back and looked around the shop. "I can see you're ready for Valentine's Day. It must be a busy time for you."

"Uh, you don't know! I've got Angie coming in every day after school and on Saturday and Sunday. My sister helps out, too. Even my lazy son has a job during February delivering all the orders." Maxie winked at Iris. "Now, you know that Angie told me she could only work until noon next Saturday because of the _quince_."

"As a matter of fact, I want to order two extra corsages for Angie and Micole. So many of the other girls stopped talking to Stefanie after my husband died. But Angie and Micole didn't let Stefanie down. If we had gone the traditional route, those two girls would have been *damas*."

"The three of them are good girls," Maxie said just as the phone on the wall rang loudly. "Excuse me, please."

Rita moved to the display of Valentine cards on a nearby iron rack. How long had it been since she had bought a romantic card for someone on Valentines Day? She smiled to herself, daydreaming about a passionate Valentines celebration. She lingered on those intimate thoughts, hoping her happiness with Brian would ease the lonely ache she anticipated after her great-grandmother left town.

"If I bought this for Stefanie, do you think she'd feel like I was treating her like a child?" Iris asked from another spot in the shop.

Rita turned to see Iris holding a lifelike stuffed cat with large golden brown eyes shining out of a calico furry face. Pinned across its calico body was a red ribbon decorated with pink letters that read "You're purrty special, Valentine."

"I think it's cute. It looks so real." Rita had to walk over and stroke its silky fur. "Maybe I'll buy that gray and white one over there and give it to Abuelita. She loves cats, but the past few years, her sinus problems wouldn't allow us to keep any in the house."

"Thank goodness, it was only an order for a hospital." Maxie came around the counter, wiping the perspiration from her upper lip with her bright yellow shirt sleeve. "I was afraid it might be another person wanting to look at the dance studio. I'd have to close the shop to show it today. My helper had to take her mother to the doctor. I tell you, when I agreed to manage this center, I never thought it would be such a pain in the neck. The rest of us have been in here a couple of years and we're happy. We just can't keep that corner place filled."

Rita had to ask, "Is something wrong with it?"

"No, it's a nice place. I even thought about moving there myself, but what would I do with four dressing rooms and a wall of mirrors?" Maxie shrugged her shoulder. "I told the landlord that we don't need any more dancing on the corner. We need to rent the shop out to someone stable with a good head on her shoulders."

Rita and Iris exchanged a surprised look, as if Rita's thoughts had met Iris's in midair.

"We're looking for a place to re-open my dress shop," Rita said, with a cautious smile in Maxie's direction. "Would it be okay if Iris and I looked inside the dance studio? You don't have to close your shop, if you'll trust us with the keys."

"A dress shop, huh?" Maxie's shiny brown forehead wrinkled with skinny lines. "That would be different." She turned around and grabbed something off the desk under the counter. "Here's the key. Look around."

The telephone rang again as Rita took a brass key ring with two keys on it from Maxie.

"Do you think this could be a place for our shop?" Iris asked in a quiet, uncertain voice as they left the flower shop.

"Well, you yourself said that it would be good to have a shop around other businesses so we could share customers." Rita held open the door for Iris to pass, then followed her down the sidewalk. "This building is relatively new, and we're facing a busy street."

They walked next door to the empty studio.

Rita's fingers trembled as she fit the key into the door lock.

She figured the room was not quite double the space of the flower shop. The floor was in bad need of a wax job, and some spots on the wood floor looked very worn.

Maxie was right about the mirrors. They covered one entire wall. The back and side walls, with pretty flowered wallpaper, looked clean. They circled around to the other side of the room and stopped at the trio of

wide windows that led around to the front of the building.

"Makes me think that Fred Astaire should come
waltzing in," Iris said as she stood in the middle of the
room looking around.

"It's not a big place," Rita said. "I'd guess about as
much square footage as my old shop." She walked
through the main room towards the opening in the back.

Iris followed her to the rear of the building and both
were surprised by the two roomy restrooms on one side
and four double-sized dressing rooms across from them.
Beyond, they discovered a wide storeroom, still filled
with a dozen empty boxes, three headless mannequins,
and a variety of chrome clothes racks dismantled in the
corner.

"I wonder if anyone's going to claim those mannequins and racks," Rita said, knowing that she could
easily put them to good use.

"This isn't as spacious as that place on Blanco Road,
is it?" Iris said in a hesitant voice.

"No, it's very simple. Basically, one square room."
Rita turned and walked past Iris back into the old dance
studio.

"But if I had a whole wedding party in here trying
on their dresses, there's plenty of mirrors and dressing
rooms. This place even has a men's room. The *charros*
will appreciate that." Rita glanced up, pleased to see so
many panels of light among the squares of the sus-
pended white ceiling. "I think there'll be good lighting in
here, especially with so many windows."

"You like this place, don't you?" Iris said. When Rita
caught her eyes in the mirror, she saw her partner's
doubtful expression.

"I can see good possibilities. We need to talk to
Maxie about rent, security, things like that. I'd like carpeting in the store, and the owner might not be willing
to pay for it." Rita saw her own dark brown eyes
brighten as she smiled at her own reflection. "But I

think we could really dress up this place with your good taste and my ideas."

She saw Iris slowly turning around, her eyes narrowed as if she looked at the place with her own plans. "This place could work for us, Rita. And mirrors always make a place look bigger than it is. Let's go talk to Maxie."

They returned to the shop and began asking Maxie questions. The rent was about one-hundred dollars more than Rita had planned for, but she knew it was very reasonable for a corner shop.

They learned that the landlord was a Dallas businesswoman, Barbara Coleman, and that all the tenants in the center were women.

"Do you ever share customers among the various shops here?" Iris asked.

"You bet! People order wedding flowers from me and hire Suzanne to take pictures. People stop by the book store after lunch in Gabriela's tea room. You'd like Suzanne and Gabriela. Chris runs the book store, and Marilu gives the best haircuts for miles."

The fact that Rita would share the building with other women was definitely a plus. She wouldn't have to worry about condescending male landlords. And perhaps another woman would understand the need for nice carpeting in a classy dress shop and not argue with Rita's request.

The telephone rang again, and Maxie moved away to answer it.

Rita turned towards her business partner. "Iris, I think I want to take the studio. Make it into my new shop—our new shop. It's just about halfway between our houses, and I can afford the rent. Most of the regular customers could get here without any inconvenience, and if Maxie's right, we'd have a lot of new customers just waiting for us to open our door."

"I agree with everything you said, Rita. I could enjoy the challenge of making that old dance studio into our shop. I don't think it would hurt to find out how to get in touch with the owner. And we'll need a lawyer to draw up the partnership papers."

"My great-grandmother's lawyer is a woman I trust. I think you'd like her, too. That is, if you're ready to truly commit to our partnership, Iris." Rita smiled at Iris, hoping they were both ready for the next step.

"You can count on me, partner," Iris replied immediately. "Let's get this partnership going and get started on opening a new place." Her hands spread out from her body, pantomiming words on an imaginary sign. "We could call it 'Navarro and Bonilla Unlimited.' Because there are no limitations on what we can do."

"Navarro and Bonilla Unlimited, huh? I think I like it," Rita said.

There was a confidence in Iris that gave Rita good reason to smile. An optimistic excitement swelled inside her. She found herself almost impatient to get started, so they could begin creating a successful place of business out of their dreams, ideas, and plans.

Maxie looked relieved that she had a sensible tenant for the corner shop, and willingly gave Rita the telephone number of Ms. Coleman in Dallas. She said that she would take the sign out of the shop that afternoon.

Rita protested since they hadn't signed a lease agreement or anything, but Maxie said her helper had called and would be out a couple of days. "I won't have time to show the place this week anyway. And if you change your mind, just call me and I'll put it back in the window."

All the way back to Abuelita's house, Rita's mind worked overtime, planning and arranging everything that had to be done. She figured it might take up to six weeks for the shop to be opened. There would be shopping trips into Mexico and up to Dallas, making new clothes to sell, and countless other details in between. She could only take preliminary steps until the *quinceañera* was behind them, but she knew the time could be spent going through magazines and pattern books and sewing a variety of spring clothes. She had to restock the layette items she made, as well as baptismal gowns, and first communion dresses. She also wanted to sew a wedding dress to display in the new store. Maybe she could use her mother's gown as a model, but create a different look. So many plans, and it seemed like such a short time to get everything done.

"Did you enjoy lunch?" Abuelita asked Rita when she came in.

Rita sat at the kitchen table making lists of things to do the next two weeks. "We went to a nice place, Abuelita. I'll have to take you there. The food was very good; so good, in fact, that Iris hired the restaurant owner to cater the *quince* party." She tapped the pencil on the paper. "And how was your lunch with Mrs. Alonso?"

Abuelita pulled out a chair and sat down. "I'll miss her *calabacita*. No one cooks it like she does. And what are you writing here?"

"Things to do before we open the shop. I think we found a place today. I'm very excited, Abuelita. It's in a strip of shops, each owned by a woman, no less. I'll fit right in." Rita beamed her delight.

"And Iris likes this place?"

"Yes. As a matter of fact, I called Janice today and set up an appointment on Friday for Iris and me to discuss our partnership with her."

Her great-grandmother nodded with satisfaction. "Janice is a smart lady. I was foolish not to tell you to talk to her last time. This business with Beatrice was not a good thing. Janice would have known better than we did."

Abuelita's words yanked Rita out of the clouds, reminding Rita of something she still hadn't explained, but should, especially since they planned to go to the bank tomorrow morning.

"I made a big mistake going into business with Bea, Abuelita. The only thing good that came of it was that I realized I could run a business by myself after she ran off." Rita took a deep breath then talked slowly, as if she was afraid she might stop breathing completely. "When Bea eloped, she cleaned out the checking account. She took your money, Abuelita. I have the money now to make last month's and this month's payments, but it's only because I sold all the junk of hers."

"It doesn't matter about the payments, Rita." Abuelita wrapped her fingers around Rita's arm. "Keep the money for your new shop."

"I promised to repay you, Abuelita. And I will, every single penny," Rita answered, not breaking eye contact with the old woman. "I feel so ashamed that I didn't watch Bea more carefully. She bought things I knew nothing about and then wrote a big check for herself. I was very stupid."

"We all do stupid things. You learn. You go on. Don't wish for things to be different in the past. Look to the future. Iris is a good woman. She respects what you say. That's important."

"Yes, it is. And I respect her, too. And not just because she's Brian's sister," she added, as if the spirit of Tía Minerva still haunted the table.

Abuelita coughed as her expression grew serious. "Rita, we must talk about what happens after I go."

"After you go?" Rita felt as if ice water rushed down her body.

"Today, Mrs. Alonso asked about the house. Her husband wants to buy it for Socorro and her children. I think you should sell to them."

"Sell to them? But I—"

"I want you to move. This is not a safe place for a woman alone."

Her great-grandmother had never said that before. She had always talked about their good neighbors and the Alonso's big shepherd being a great watchdog for both houses.

"I was thinking of getting an apartment, Abuelita. But I thought you might want to offer the house to Debra."

"Your sister would expect you to give her the house. You need to sell it and make a little money. You'll need it for your business, no?"

Rita stared hard at her great-grandmother. "Wait a minute. You want me to sell the house? But it's your house, Abuelita."

Her head shook from side to side. "This is your house, Rita. It's been in your name for the last four years. I'm old. I never know when God will call me home. This is your house, Rita."

Rita's eyes lifted to the narrow shelves above them, to the white cabinets, sink, and stove, as if she was seeing them for the first time. But the knowledge that she owned the house didn't change her real feelings. This place would mean nothing without Abuelita. Hot tears stung her eyes as she looked again at her great-grandmother.

"I love you very much, Abuelita. Thank you for the house. And I'll sell it to Mr. Alonso like you want."

"Did you know that your father bought this house for me?" Abuelita said suddenly in her storytelling voice.

Rita had to smile. "I didn't know that."

"Made your mother mad, I know. I rented a long time from Señor Barrientos. Right after Debra was born, your father asked the old man to sell the house to him. But he put my name on the papers. Your mother said he'd kill himself working two jobs for two house payments. I guess she was right." The old woman's crooked shoulders raised and lowered. "I had the money all the time to make the payments. But he wouldn't take it. So I gave it to his baby girl instead. He called you his *mariposa*."

She had forgotten the nickname. *Mariposa*. Butterfly.

Not until a salty tear touched her lip, did Rita realize her tears had slipped out. "You gave Mom the money for my *quinceañera*, didn't you?"

Abuelita's black eyes grew watery. "Every girl deserves a *quinceañera*. Your mother forgot. I helped her remember."

Rita nodded. She didn't need a more specific answer. The money wasn't as valuable as her great-grandmother's willingness to make Rita feel loved. And that one special day being the center of attention gave Rita the inner confidence she needed to make decisions about her future. A rebirth of that spiritual strength filled Rita's heart now as she sat with Abuelita and contemplated her plans for the future again.

Her mind's eye carried her to a place where the *mariposa* had broken free of its cocoon, smoothed out its beautiful wings, and prepared to take flight.

Chapter Nineteen

Rita arrived at Iris's house before Brian did and used the time to bring Iris up to date on Rita's telephone calls to her lawyer and the Dallas building owner, who was willing to carpet the shop as long as they chose a neutral color and supervised the job themselves. Ms. Coleman would mail them contracts for the lease within the next few days.

"You aren't wasting any time, are you?" Iris asked as they sat on the living room sofa talking.

"We're not making any money until we open the shop," Rita replied.

"Don't tell me my partner's got dollar signs in her eyes." Iris's lips curved into a playful grin.

"Just trying to be a smart businesswoman." Rita spoke with conviction then settled back into the green sofa cushions.

Iris's hazel eyes were shiny with enthusiasm. "I'm glad my partner has so much initiative. We do have to get our business going. I can be of more help to you once this *quince* is over. But we can settle things with a lawyer and sign the lease next week."

"We'll need to discuss when we can travel to Dallas, Iris. I plan to go into Mexico after I leave Abuelita in Brownsville. But we ought to go back again and shop together."

"I've been thinking about trips since you mentioned Dallas last week. Stefanie can stay with my grandparents. Grandpa Charlie took her to school many times during the first months after Estevan died. A trip into Mexico sounds interesting. Stefanie told me just this week that she has a four-day weekend coming up because of Presidents' Day. Would you mind if she came with us?"

"Not at all." Rita smiled, pleased that Iris would include her daughter in their work. With Stefanie's involvement and input in the business, the mother-daughter relationship could only grow stronger.

The front doorbell chimed then, and Iris rose to let Brian in.

He was still dressed in his black business suit, although his silk tie was loosened around his neck. His face looked tired as he sat next to Rita on the sofa. But she noticed a gleam of excitement in his brown eyes as he leaned close for a kiss.

"Hello, Rita." His lips were cold and moist upon her own.

"So you have a surprise for us, little brother?" Iris said in a teasing voice as she sat down on the striped chair.

"Yes, sister dear, I do." Brian smiled, looking from his sister to Rita. "I know that the two of you want a neutral person to help you iron out the details of a partnership. I admit, I was hurt that you didn't want my help, but then I thought about it and realized that Iris was right. Rita's relationship with me could be affected if I get too involved in the details of your partnership."

"It's for the best that way, Brian," Iris said. "But you won't be left out completely. I know that you and Rita are best friends and you talk about everything together. I know she'll talk to you about her worries. I suppose I will, too."

"I appreciate that, Iris. And I can assure both of you that I can stay neutral if you two get into a problem and want some advice. I love you both and only want you to be successful in your business together."

Rita's hand rested on Brian's thigh. "Thanks for your support."

"And that brings me to the surprise I have for the two of you." Brian reached into the pocket of his suit coat and pulled out a thin packet of white papers. "I know that in the beginning I wasn't very supportive when you told me you planned to go into business together."

He rolled the papers in his hands nervously as he talked. "Actually, I insulted both of you by my reaction, and I'm deeply sorry about that."

"We have your support now," Rita said in a tender voice. "That's the most important thing."

He nodded, then looked at Iris and back again at Rita. "I wanted to make it up to you for my first reaction; all those insensitive comments that almost ruined our relationship." He returned his gaze to his sister. "I was wrong not to respect your decision, Iris. And if you want a partner, I can't think of anyone more trustworthy than Rita. Now I just want to show both of you how much I respect and trust what you're doing together. I wanted to do more than sign a slip of paper so Iris could invest in the partnership."

It was then that he unrolled the papers and opened them. "So today, I signed a lease for that shop on Blanco Road. I paid the deposit and promised to give Mr. Kelly a cashier's check for the first six-months rent tomorrow morning."

Rita's heart jolted upwards. Through some automatic response, she took the papers from Brian's hand, but she felt like the words on the paper were printed in Chinese.

"You did what?" Iris found her voice before Rita did. "You signed a lease on the shop without even telling us?"

"But you wanted that shop. Both of you told me that it was a nice place. I saw it myself. It's great. And Rita could live there. She told me she liked the idea of living behind the shop," Brian told his sister.

"Brian, the rent money is more than we can afford," Iris replied, her voice rising in both volume and pitch. "How will we pay it?"

"I told you. I took care of the first six months."

Rita finally found her voice. "You expect us to make an extra two thousand every month to pay the rent after being in business for six months? We'll be lucky to show a few hundred dollars profit on the books after a year. We're opening a small dress shop, not a big clothing store."

Turning his attention to Rita, Brian frowned at her. "You don't seem to have much confidence in your business prospects, Rita."

"When I make a profit, it gets reinvested almost immediately in new fabrics or merchandise. I've already budgeted how much I can afford in rent every month. Now you're asking me to hold out an extra twelve-hundred dollars? That money can be better spent in my store, not making a new car payment for a greedy landlord."

"Mr. Kelly is nothing like Mr. Arredondo," Brian said. "I had him checked out carefully. He owns some very nice properties all over San Antonio. That shop on Blanco Road will be perfect for the two of you."

"And how do you propose that we fill the three rooms in that shop with merchandise?" Sarcasm sharpened Iris's words with pointed edges. "You want me to take fifty-thousand dollars out of the trust fund? You want Rita to start sewing twenty-four hours a day? That should do miracles for your relationship with Rita, Brian!"

Suddenly, Iris shot out of the striped chair as if fire burned her seat. "You had no right to do this, Brian. You had no right to take the choice of where we opened our shop out of our hands. Estevan used to do this to me all the time. I'd choose a menu to cook, then he'd call and say he booked a caterer. I'd talk about a vacation we might take, and he'd choose a trip for us and pay a travel agent. He made the decision to put all our money into trust funds when he died, without discussing it with me. And I put up with that controlling behavior because I loved him. Well, he's dead, and I don't plan to let you run my life in his place."

Brian stood up. His hands shoved his coat back and tightened as fists on his hips. "I'm not trying to run your life, Iris. I signed that lease because I wanted to show my support for your business. I'm willing to invest my money in it. Doesn't that prove how much I hope the two of you have a successful partnership together?"

"I thought you understood that Rita and I didn't want you involved in our business plans," Iris said, then turned her tense form in Rita's direction. "I thought you explained all that to Brian."

Despite the fireworks shooting off between the brother and sister, Rita managed to stay seated and speak calmly. "In a way, I think Brian misunderstood what I said to him."

"I didn't misunderstand anything." Brian's voice coiled with impatience. "You said you didn't want to live in Abuelita's house after she left. You said you wanted a place that both you and Iris liked. This place is the perfect solution to all your worries."

"But, Brian, it leaves us with an even bigger worry. How are we going to pay such a rent after the first six months?" Rita replied, disappointed that Brian's good intentions had been misguided once again.

He merely hissed out a sigh and shook his head, his eyes lowering to the floor.

"Listen, Brian. Rita and I have already found our new shop. We made a verbal agreement to take a place just today. It costs less and will be a much better location than Blanco Road." Iris announced her news with a superior tone. "And we won't need you to pay our deposit or rent."

It was at that moment that Stefanie came thumping down the stairs and raced into the living room waving a slip of paper between her right hand.

"Mom! Mom! I have the name and phone number of a disc jockey we can use. Micole got it from her cousin. I just called the guy and he can do the music for the party. But he says you have to call him and mail him a check for half the money. Hi, Uncle Brian. Hi, Rita. Mom, can you call him back right now?"

Stefanie's rush of words and untamed excitement was like a cool breeze in the stiff, airless room. Her face glowed, and she wore a smile that sent a sparkle into her eyes. Rita was probably the only one who noticed. Iris had folded her arms across herself; Brian's face carried a stormy expression as he regarded his niece.

"Why do you need a disc jockey for the party?" Brian asked Stefanie. "I hired one of the best *mariachi* groups in San Antonio to play after your *quinceañera*."

Stefanie's hazel eyes rolled up to the ceiling. "You want my friends to dance to *mariachis*? Get real, Uncle Brian."

Her typical teenage response put fire into Brian's eyes. They blazed with a sudden anger that had been smoldering deep inside him the past few minutes.

"Stefanie, do you know how much I paid for those *mariachis*? Do you expect me to just cancel the group and kiss my money good-bye?"

"Excuse me, Uncle Brian. But you never asked me if I wanted *mariachis*. You and mom just made the decision. Why didn't you ask me what I wanted?" Stefanie's voice was surprisingly calm considering the explosive tone her uncle used.

Folding her arms across her chest, Stefanie looked at Brian as if she was the adult and he was the child. "The disc jockey only costs a hundred dollars, and he'll play music my friends can dance to. Only old people like *mariachi* music, Uncle Brian. But don't worry. I'm not going to ask you to pay for the disc jockey. I still have my money from working for Rita. I'll pay for the disc jockey myself."

"Well, I guess all three of you have everything under control." Brian tossed his hands into the air, his furious glare sweeping all three females. "Obviously, you don't need me around. So I'll just take my deposits and leave." In a wink, he had tugged the paper out of Rita's fingertips and turned around.

"Brian, wait." Rita stood up.

In quick, determined strides, Brian walked out of the room. She heard paper ripping as he tore up the lease agreement he had been so proud to show them earlier.

Iris caught Rita's arm. "Let him go, Rita. Just let him go."

"Are you crazy? He's so upset. We have to talk to him." Her voice trembled with alarm. "Don't you even care that we've hurt his feelings?" She jerked her arm out of Iris's fingers and ran towards the front door.

Brian was already through the wrought-iron gate by the time Rita got outside. The night was ioo oold, and she had left her coat on Iris's hall tree. Her gasps came out in smoky puffs. Her legs felt stiff, her arms heavy.

"Brian, please. Wait. Let me talk to you."

He stopped just beside his car and turned around. Even in the darkness, she could read the raw pain in his eyes.

"What's there to talk about? Go back inside. Just make all your plans with Iris. You don't need me around here." He was a wounded animal, ready to lash out at anyone who tried to come to his aid.

Rita wrapped her arms around her, rubbing herself to fight off the cold. "Brian, please don't act like this. I love you. Iris and Stefanie love you, too."

"Spare me the sentiment, Rita. It just gets in the way of good judgment. Go back inside the house. You'll catch cold." He ground his heel into the driveway as he turned and walked around his car. He didn't even look at her before he got inside the car, started the ignition, and drove away.

She was stunned by his rejection. Her only sensations came from the cold black night around her. Shivering, she turned around and walked slowly back into the house.

Iris opened the door just as Rita reached for the knob.

"I tried to tell you. When Brian gets his feelings hurt like that, he won't listen to anyone. Just give him some time alone, Rita. He likes it better when he can go off by himself and sulk."

Rita listened to Iris's complacent voice and felt her anger rise. "What if you're wrong? Maybe he'd like to talk to someone about his feelings."

"If that was true, you'd be in his car talking, not standing here with me," Iris answered. "I know my brother. He prefers to work through stuff by himself. You'll need to get used to that."

The hard shiver down Rita's back wasn't caused just by the cold night. She hated the thought of Brian shutting her out when she knew he needed her most.

Iris closed the front door then led Rita back into the living room.

Stefanie sat in the striped chair, her hands twisting in her lap, her expression downcast. "I'm sorry if I made Uncle Brian mad, Rita. I knew he had paid for the *mariachis*. I wouldn't have asked him to pay for the disc jockey, too."

"I told Stefanie that her timing was wrong, that's all," Iris said.

"So was yours, Iris. You made it sound as if the place we found was much better than the shop he rented. It's not really true. We just found a place we could afford. That's the truth." Rita sighed. "I think we handled this whole mess very badly, Iris."

"I suppose we did." Iris sighed and gently rubbed her temples. "It's just that Brian's actions brought back such awful feelings. Here we were making decisions that made me feel like I knew what I was doing. Then Brian comes along and tells us that he's signed a lease on a shop he picked out for us. I used to just hate it when Estevan did that to me."

"Brian wasn't trying to control us. He was trying to help us. He thought it was the shop we both wanted." Rita shook her head sadly. "I never expected this—he was going to give us sixteen-thousand dollars. It makes my head swim just thinking about all that money."

Stefanie stood up and walked to her mother. "He spent a lot of money on the *quinceañera,* too. I'm sorry, Mom. I'll tell Uncle Brian the *mariachis* will be okay."

Iris placed her arm around the girl's shoulders. "We'll talk to Uncle Brian tomorrow. The *mariachis* are only supposed to play for two hours. The disc jockey can show up after that. I really want you to have the fifteenth birthday party you want. I know how it feels to have someone else force their decisions on you. I must apologize, Stefanie. We were wrong to make you go through with the *quinceañera* when you didn't really want to."

"But I want it now. I think it'll be fun the way we've planned it. I'm glad you wouldn't let me get out of this. And I acted like such a brat about it, too. I'm sorry about that." Stefanie leaned her head against her mother's.

Rita noticed for the first time that Stefanie was now slightly taller than her mother. She was happy to see the other apparent changes between Iris and Stefanie, too.

She felt that Brian should be here to share this, but he had cut himself off from them. His solitary pain made Rita very sad.

All the way home, Rita went over tonight's conversation, knowing they were all to blame for the misunderstandings and hurt feelings. From the first time they all started to become friends, Rita wanted Brian to fol-

low his heart. She wanted Stefanie to deal with problems maturely, and for Iris to make decisions for herself.
Everyone did that, and the results were a disaster.

Rita felt drained of energy as she walked inside
Abuelita's house. She found her great-grandmother
watching her *novelas* in the back room.

"Rita, you're home."

"By any chance, did Brian call?"

"He didn't go to his sister's?"

Rita sighed and plopped herself down on the sofa
beside Abuelita. "No, he was there. But there was a big
misunderstanding and he was pretty mad when he left.
I just hoped he might call. I want to talk to him."

She was surprised when the television suddenly
went out, then noticed the remote control in Abuelita's
hand.

"So why don't you call him?" she asked Rita.

"Iris said that when Brian gets really upset, he
prefers to be alone. I tried to talk to him before he left,
but he just sent me away. I guess Iris knows Brian better than I do." She felt such an ache inside her, it almost
hurt to breathe.

"Some men can't share their troubles, Rita. No matter how much they love the woman."

"But I didn't think Brian was like that. He's always
talked to me before this. Why would he shut me out
now?"

"Too much hurting. He can't find the words. Maybe
you know the words he can use."

Rita frowned at her great-grandmother. The old
woman merely raised her gray eyebrows, wispy little
stripes on her wrinkled brown face.

Maybe you know the words he can use. Abuelita's
words came back into Rita's thoughts as she stood up
and went to the hall telephone. She stretched the cord
on the phone into her bedroom, flipped on the light
switch, then closed the door. She set the telephone on

her bed, then lay on her stomach beside it and began dialing.

Her heart raced as she heard it ringing, only to feel a disappointed thud-thud as she listened to Brian's recorded message on his answering machine. After the high-pitched beeping, Rita started talking.

"Brian? It's Rita. I love you. When you get this message, please call me. The phone's by my bed. And I doubt if I'll get any sleep tonight if I don't talk to you."

She sighed. "Brian, it was a very sweet thing you did for me and Iris. I love you for it. And I understand why you felt like you had to solve my problems. It's what you do for a living, isn't it? But just because we don't want that shop on Blanco Road doesn't mean I don't need you. I need someone to listen to me. Someone to let me talk so I can see my way clear to solving my own problems. I rely so much on being able to talk to you. And with Abuelita leaving soon, I'm going to depend on our friendship even more. Iris said I should just leave you alone tonight. But I can't do that. I'll never be able to do that. So you'd better decide now if you want me to be a definite part of your life, or if you like it better being left all alone."

She heard a strange click in her ear and thought her machine time was over, but in the moment it took to frown, Brian's voice came over the line.

"No, Rita. I don't want to be left alone. I want you to be a part of my life."

She whispered a sigh of relief. "You were there all the time. Why didn't you pick up the phone?"

"I didn't know what to say. I still don't." There was a long pause, then he said, "I did a very stupid thing, didn't I?"

"It was a sweet thing, Brian. I had no idea you would do something like that to make me happy. Why would you spend so much money on my shop? You know I didn't want you to invest in my business."

"It wasn't an investment. It was a gift. No strings attached. I had to show both of you that I believed in what you were doing." Brian groaned. "I never expected this to backfire in my face. Iris was so angry. If I had known Estevan used to undermine Iris's plans, I never would have done this. Well, that's not true. I still might have rented the shop, but I would have asked her first. And you, too."

"Do you think you can get your money back?" Rita asked.

"I don't know. At least Mr. Kelly doesn't have the cashier's check I have on my dresser right now. I'm just lucky they sent me to Austin all afternoon." The sound of his voice grew stronger. "But I don't want you to worry about Mr. Kelly, Rita. It was my mistake, and I'll deal with it. Now. Tell me more about the shop you and Iris found."

And they stayed talking on the telephone for almost an hour. Rita shared her excitement about the new shop and the women who shared the building. She told him of Abuelita's generosity with the house and of her new financial security. They moved back to discussing what had happened at Iris's house that night and together tried to understand Iris's reaction and Stefanie's request. Brian admitted he had an unrealistic perception of Iris's marriage to Estevan and knew he had to become a better friend to his sister.

"It's pretty obvious that Iris doesn't know me too well either," Brian said just before they hung up. "I know that I usually walked off and told everyone 'Leave me alone.' But I always wished one person could come after me and say something to make me feel better. Today someone actually did. Thank you, Rita. I love you very much."

❤ ❤ ❤ ❤ ❤

Abuelita caught Rita and Brian wrapped in each other's arms, locked in a passionate kiss, when she came into the kitchen the following morning. It took a few seconds for Rita to sense the presence of the old woman, and she reluctantly broke away. She still held tight to Brian as she turned her face towards her great-grandmother.

"Good morning, Abuelita. I invited Brian for breakfast."

"He came for more than *papas con huevo*, no? *Buenos días*, Brian."

"*Buenos días, Señora Navarro,*" Brian replied, slowly relaxing his hold around Rita's waist.

Raising her hand in a little wave, the old woman said, "You must call me Abuelita. Soon you'll marry my Rita, no?"

"Abuelita!" Rita's eyes widened at her great-grandmother's words.

"I want to marry Rita someday, Abuelita," Brian said, smiling.

"Rita already has a wedding dress," Abuelita said then chuckled like she knew a big secret but didn't plan to tell it.

Brian kept his arm around Rita's waist as he turned to her great-grandmother. "When we get married, Abuelita, you can come live with us if you want to."

Rita's hand slid up and down Brian's back. His generosity wasn't surprising; it only made her love him more. "It would be great to have you with us."

Abuelita gave Brian a nod. "Thank you. But I want to live with my daughter now. I will come for a visit. At Christmas. When my *comadre* will be here, too."

Rita let go of Brian and went to give her great-grandmother a tight hug. As she pressed her cheek against the soft gray hair on the top of Abuelita's head, she felt a burst of gratitude and overwhelming love for this tiny lady with the giant heart. Her voice was choked by tears, and she dreaded the thought of those final good-byes next week.

Abuelita must have sensed those dark, apprehensive emotions taking hold of Rita because she gently stepped back and stroke Rita's cheek. She raised her round face to look over Rita's shoulder to Brian.

"Would you take us to Brownsville, Brian? Rita's car's not so good for long drives."

Brian's hands slid over Rita's shoulders. He squeezed them gently. "I can do that, Abuelita. And there will be no rush to get back. I have a week's vacation coming up following the *quinceañera*."

"That's very good," she answered with a twinkle in her black eyes. "Rita wants to shop in Mexico. You can carry her shopping bags."

Her great-grandmother laughed then, and so did Rita, just as tears spilled down her cheeks. She would miss her great-grandmother terribly. But now she had Brian's love to help her when the pain was too burdensome to carry alone.

❤ ❤ ❤ ❤ ❤

"Do you think I should have come here by myself?" Brian asked Rita as they stood on Iris's front porch later that night. He had been ready to ring the doorbell, but stopped and turned to her.

"You promised that I wouldn't have to play referee," she replied.

Brian kissed the tip of her nose. "I promised you a romantic evening while your great-grandmother and her friends gossiped and watched *novelas* together."

Rita pressed her body close to his. "There will be more romantic evenings, won't there?"

"If we talk fast, there will be a romantic evening happening very soon." He chuckled slyly then reached out to ring the doorbell.

"Hi. Thanks for coming over. Can I take your coats?" Iris said, leading them into the living room.

"No, we're fine," Brian said, and winked when Rita gave him a surprised look.

"You two were probably going out when I called," Iris said, slipping her hands into the pockets of her white jumpsuit. "I'm sorry, but I really wanted to talk to Brian about what happened last night."

"Would you like me to wait in the other room?" Rita offered.

"No, of course not. Please. Won't both of you sit down?"

They found a place on the sofa. Brian took Rita's hand, holding it tightly.

"I want to begin by apologizing, Iris," Brian said. "I never should have signed on a lease without yours and Rita's consent. I talked to Mr. Kelly today, and he was very nice about returning my check." He looked at Rita. "I hope your new landlord has as much integrity."

"She will," Rita replied with confidence.

Iris shifted in the striped chair, sighed, then leaned forward to stare at her brother. "Brian, I want you to know that I appreciate everything you've done for me and Stefanie. I fell apart after Estevan died, and you were there to make decisions, watch over me and Stefanie. I couldn't have asked for a better man to take care of things for me. But now, I want to take care of things for myself. Can you understand that?"

Brian nodded. "Sure, Iris. I understand. And I'm happy that you're ready to do things for yourself. Really, I am." He relaxed his hold on Rita's hand. "Lately, I've been torn apart by my obligations to you and Stefanie and my feelings and obligations towards Rita. Last night I realized that there's a limit on what I can do for any of you. Some things you'll have to do on your own."

"I'll have to learn not to be dependent on you, too," Iris said, her eyes reflecting something sad, even lonely, in her words, "You and Rita must make each other your priority, especially if you get married. And Rita and I will learn to make decisions together for the good of our business. It's best for all of us this way."

"I won't interfere in your business plans again," Brian said, first looking at his sister, then Rita. "But I want you both to know that I would still like a chance to invest in the business if you ever want to expand or open another store."

"Doesn't my brother have confidence in us?" Iris said with an amused gleam in her hazel eyes.

Rita smiled, hoping Brian's optimism would be a lucky charm for the new shop.

"Now, what about Stefanie's party? Do I cancel the *mariachis*? Brian asked his sister, not wasting any time in dealing with the matters he came to discuss.

"Don't cancel the *mariachis*, Brian. We'll let them play for the two hours like we planned. I told Stefanie her disc jockey could come at seven and spin music until 9:30. She wanted her party to last until midnight, but I don't think I'd survive that."

"We can stay and help you chaperone," Rita said, knowing many of the older family members wouldn't stay once the kids dance music began.

"Would you do that? That would be great! When I told Daddy that the tempo of the party was changing at seven, he said he was going to make reservations at a hotel for the night."

"I'll talk to Dad," Brian said. "They can take Mamá Josie and stay at my house where things will be much quieter."

Iris's smile slowly faded away. "There is one last thing that you can do for me, Brian, if you don't mind."

Brian glanced at Rita, then looked at his sister. "Yes?"

"Will you give the father's speech?" Iris asked, her hands rubbing together in a nervous gesture. "At every *quince* we've ever been to, the father stands up during the reception and makes a speech about his daughter. As Stefanie's godfather, would you do it?"

Rita held her breath, trying to read the emotions on Brian's face. She saw his eyes change and his lips open slightly, but then something else appeared in his expression that she wasn't certain about.

Suddenly, Brian let Rita's hand go, stood up, and walked to where his sister sat. He knelt on one knee and took her hands between his.

"Iris, you have to give that speech for Stefanie. I'm her *padrino*, yes. But you're her mother. You need to show the rest of the family that you're ready to take full responsibility for yourself and your daughter. I can't do this for you, but I'll be nearby, celebrating the moment, too."

Rita's eyes stung with tears as she listened to Brian. He had put aside his protector's shield and had given his sister his emotional support for something she must do on her own.

Iris gave Rita a watery gaze then looked back at Brian. "You're right, of course. Here I am telling you that I want to do things for myself, and then I ask you to do this for me. Brian, I'll give the speech. And I know just what I will say. Thank you."

"Who gave this fatherly speech when you had your *quinceañera*?" Brian asked as they walked towards his car about fifteen minutes later.

"My Uncle Gilbert. He gave a nice speech, but it wasn't the same as having my father talk about me." Rita stopped Brian as they reached the gate and turned to face him. "What you told Iris tonight was very important. Everyone needs to know that Iris and Stefanie can go on without Estevan. I wish someone had encouraged my mother to speak for her family. Iris is very lucky to have a brother like you."

Brian put his arms around Rita and held her very close. They shared a spiritual intimacy in that moment that took them inside each other. She had never known such a bonding of mind and heart, and she raised her lips to Brian's. A special kiss only reaffirmed their pact of love.

Chapter Twenty

The afternoon sunshine filtered through the narrow stained glass windows of the church. Rita stood just inside the swinging wooden door leading into the main part of the church, listening to the chatterbox whispers of Abuelita and Mamá Josie as if they were trying to catch up on a year's worth of gossip in five minutes.

Brian appeared behind the old women. He gave Rita a secretive smile, then leaned down to his great-grandmother.

"Can I take you down the aisle, Mamá Josie?"

"Yes. Then come back for my *comadre*. And don't forget Rita," Mamá Josie said, wagging a finger at Brian.

Rita watched Brian slowly walk down the center maroon-carpeted aisle with his great-grandmother on his arm. The small woman raised her head high as if she wanted everyone to notice both of them.

"Brian walks down an aisle good, no?" Abuelita said. It wasn't much of a whisper.

Rita stepped away, pretending she didn't hear the comment. She hoped no one else did either.

She looked around the church, at the rows of dark wooden pews, most of those near the altar filled with adults, teenagers, and a few younger children anxiously awaiting the start of Mass and Stefanie's presentation. She recognized a few faces; some of Brian's relatives, and the Díazes. Their son Nicky sat with his parents, brother, and sister in the second row on the left. The tuxedo on the husky youth gave him a very grown-up appearance today. Just as Stefanie's gown would remind everyone that she was claiming her hold on the adult world, too.

As Brian returned up the side aisle, Rita noticed Brian's parents and grandparents coming into the doorway where she and Abuelita stood.

"Isabel, we want you and Rita to sit with our family," Brian's grandmother told them. "Where's Mamá Josie?"

"Brian just took her down the aisle," Rita said. She smiled shyly at Brian's parents, wondering if their son had said anything about her to them.

Brian's mother, a thin brown-haired woman, gave Rita a friendly smile when their eyes met. Brian's father, a very tall man who carried an air of authority about him, just nodded at Rita without much change in his expression.

"I thought I'd put Rita's great-grandmother near Mamá Josie," Brian said as he walked up behind Rita.

"I'll take her," Brian's grandfather said, and offered his arm to Abuelita. "I've always wanted to take my favorite *madrina* into the church."

"Favorite *madrina*, eh? Charlie, you're still a little goat," Abuelita said, but took her godson's arm nonetheless.

As Brian's parents, grandparents, and great-grandmother started down the aisle, Rita turned back to Brian.

"Would you mind if I just walked alone down the side aisle? I feel like everyone's watching us. Wondering, you know?"

"Yes, I know. We can just wait for all that aisle walking when it's our day," Brian answered. He moved closer and slipped his arm around her waist. "Have I told you how gorgeous you look this afternoon?"

"Thank you." She whispered to Brian. "I've noticed how handsome you look, too." She wished she could kiss him, but knew it wasn't appropriate now. Instead she placed her hand on his arm and squeezed it. "I'll see you after Mass, Brian. Give Stefanie my love. Bye."

Rita made her way to the second pew where Brian's parents, Mamá Josie, and Abuelita sat. She genuflected then moved in beside her great-grandmother. From their spot in the second row, she could admire the beautiful altar flowers, two stands with multi-colored blooms and trails of white and apricot-colored ribbons. Sitting beside Abuelita, surrounded by Stefanie's family and friends, Rita felt her own growing anticipation of the events to come.

She was thinking that a *quinceañera* was more of a social and cultural celebration than a religious one. It wasn't tied to a sacrament, like Baptism or Matrimony. Sometimes Rita wondered if it was just another excuse to have a *fiesta* in the family. But having gone through the experience herself, Rita knew that Stefanie would remember this day forever. She was old enough to appreciate the tradition and say her own prayers, and she didn't have to share the limelight with a bishop, like in Confirmation, or worry about the duties and obligations to a new husband. It was a celebration just for the girl herself, accepting her role as a young woman, and asking for the spiritual strength and moral guidance she would need to make adult decisions.

Rita then realized that Stefanie's *quinceañera* actually symbolized a rite of passage for all of them. This ceremony marked a momentous change in everyone's lives. Even Abuelita was moving into a new phase of her life. Rita prayed for her great-grandmother's happiness with Teresa and her family in Brownsville, and for more long, healthy years in her life.

Rita thought of herself and Brian, hoping to spend their lives together as man and wife. She prayed for their love to continue to deepen; that their faithfulness to each other become strong enough to battle life's challenges that still lay ahead of them.

And she thought of Iris, still moving through passages of grief and loneliness as a widow. Rita prayed for her friend, for their partnership; for Iris to find spiritual guidance in her role as a single parent. She hoped that she and Iris could strengthen their relationship as friends, and some day as sisters-in-law.

A few seconds later, the sounds of guitar music filled the church as the group in the choir loft began singing a poignant hymn in Spanish. Male and female voices harmonized in a song calling for blessings of a young pilgrim on a journey through life.

During the second verse, a bell rang in the rear of the church and everyone stood up. Most people turned halfway to watch the procession down the aisle.

First came Stefanie, who looked like a princess and walked like a queen. Slowly, she came down the aisle, her chin raised and smiling happily at the faces around her. Her long brown hair was pulled up into a twist, and a small tiara was placed on her head. She wore simple white pearl earrings and a pearl necklace. She held a small bouquet of pink and white roses and peach-colored carnations with streamers of red and pink ribbons.

The *quinceañera* dress that Rita had made shimmered under the church lights. The silk and lace skirt gave the impression that Stefanie was gliding towards the altar. As Stefanie got closer to her family, Rita heard the complimentary whispers about the dress. She felt proud that she played a role in Stefanie's beautiful appearance today.

Stefanie walked up the two wide carpeted steps to the altar and stood beside a single wooden kneeler that had been draped in satin and had two pillows for her to kneel upon. She waited there, her head bowed as if she was praying.

Down the aisle came Brian and a pretty blonde-haired woman whom Rita assumed was Linda, Stefanie's godmother. Brian carried a small white leather book, and Linda carried clear rosary beads between her fingers. Behind them walked Iris, looking regal in her ivory dress.

Iris carried a thin crystal vase with three long-stem red roses, and a small white box. Behind her walked two altar boys and the priest.

Iris, Brian, and Linda took their place in the first row, and once the tall priest, with the trimmed gray beard, and his altar boys took their places, the Mass was ready to start.

The musicians finished their song, and the priest smiled directly at Stefanie. Then he raised his gaze to the rest of the congregation.

"Good afternoon. I'm Father Emmanuel, the pastor of this church. I've known the Esparza family a long time, and I am honored they invited me to celebrate the *quinceañera* of Stefanie Bonilla. The last time I saw many of you, the occasion was a sad one. Stefanie, dear, we all know that your father is looking down upon you right now, celebrating your birthday with all of us who know you and love you."

The girl nodded her head as if she agreed with him.

Father Emmanuel clasped his hands together then continued. "Although I'm not of the Mexican culture, I admire this celebration of the fifteenth birthday. It allows teenagers to celebrate their youth and vitality, and it reminds the rest of us that teenagers are good. Nowadays we hear too many negatives about young people. But today we celebrate the positive and the beautiful. The young lady before us will be our symbol of God's goodness and never-ending love."

And then, with the sign of the cross, Father Emmanuel began the celebration of the Mass.

Although Stefanie did not want the traditional court of honor to share her *quinceañera*, she still managed to have her close friends involved in her special day. Her best friends, Angie García and Micole Balboa, did a reading from the Bible. Then they joined two other girls to sing a lovely "Alleluia" response before the Gospel reading.

After reading about the Annunciation and Mary's willingness to accept the will of God to become the mother of Jesus, the priest then came around the altar and stood in front of Stefanie. He was flanked by his altar boys, one carrying a candle and the other a silver container of holy water.

He invited Stefanie's mother and her godparents to the altar and asked them to witness Stefanie's renewal of her Baptismal vows.

In a quiet but steady voice, Stefanie repeated the vows that Brian and Linda had spoken on her behalf fifteen years ago. Then the priest invited the three adults to lay their hands upon Stefanie while he prayed for her. When it was completed, he invited Stefanie to read her own prayer of dedication, a simple verse asking for guidance and validating her own commitment to God and His commandments.

When the prayers were over, the priest blessed the Bible, rosary, and the item in the white box. After he shook holy water over them, Iris took a gold chain with a cross on it from the box and placed it around her daughter's neck.

As Brian escorted Iris and Linda back to their pew, Rita noticed all three of them were tight-lipped and rapidly blinking back tears.

The priest told everyone that the Mass would continue, and the musicians began to sing another song in Spanish, a special hymn about Mary. During the song, Stefanie left her kneeling position to walk back to where her mother sat and accept the vase of roses from her.

Slowly, Stefanie walked to the side altar and deposited the vase at the foot of a tall wooden statue of Mary, the mother of Jesus. Once she returned to her place, Nicky Díaz, Micole, and Angie came down the aisle carrying a glass container with water, the wine, and the gold chalice with the bread. They looked so solemn during these duties that Rita had to smile. She knew that hours from now Stefanie and her friends would be laughing over the nervous feelings they were probably experiencing at this time.

The bilingual Mass continued with extra prayers for Stefanie inserted throughout the liturgy. After a rendition of the Lord's Prayer sung in Spanish, Father Emmanuel called for the *Saludo de Paz*.

"Stefanie will give the *abrazo* and kiss of peace to her family," Father Emmanuel said. "We share in her joy by exchanging a sign of peace with one another."

There was a long pause in the Mass as Stefanie went to each of the relatives in the first two rows and wished them God's peace with hugs and kisses.

Rita was glad to have an excuse to hug and kiss Abuelita and Brian in Church, and offered a handshake to others in Brian's family. When she embraced Stefanie, the girl whispered, "Thank you for everything, Rita. I love you so much." Then it was Rita's turn to chew her lip and blink back tears.

Everyone watched Stefanie receive communion under both species, the bread and the wine, then the rest of the people in church made their way up the aisle to receive communion, too. Music continued throughout these reflective moments.

Just before Father Emmanuel gave the final blessing to end the Mass, he offered a few last words to Stefanie.

"A mature person is one who will make a commitment and decision, and stay faithful to them even when it's very difficult to carry them out. This Mass of Thanksgiving has celebrated your gift of life, but it's also an opportunity for you to accept the duties and responsibilities that life brings with it. Go in peace, Stefanie, and know that when you live according to love and follow the commandments of God, you will be renewing all of the promises you made in this church today."

The priest then gave a blessing, and to the strains of *Las Mañanitas*, Stefanie turned around to face her friends and family. Suddenly a loud burst of applause filled the church. She laughed, shrugged, then finally waved at everyone.

With a radiant smile and glistening eyes, Stefanie started to walk from the altar. She stopped by the first wooden pew, turned towards her mother, and pulled one of the roses from her bouquet. She handed it to Iris, and Rita saw her mouth the words "I love you, Mom." They embraced; then Stefanie finished her walk down the aisle.

Iris and Linda took Brian's arms and followed Stefanie out. Then came the altar boys and Father Emmanuel, who paused to shake hands with Iris's parents and grandparents.

Abuelita's hand searched out Rita's. She gave it a strong squeeze. "It was beautiful, no?"

Rita smiled down at her great-grandmother. "Absolutely beautiful." Her heart was filled with so many emotions she couldn't name them all. It was as if she had stood with Stefanie, reaffirming her commitment to love, the source of all life, and taking from this special celebration the spiritual presence that would guide her choices in the years to come.

Suddenly, Rita felt a great sense of peace and satisfaction. Only months ago, Abuelita had asked Rita to befriend Josie's relatives. Who would have thought that those old threads of friendship and new family ties could come together in such a beautiful canopy of love?

❤ ❤ ❤ ❤ ❤

The Bonilla household welcomed everyone to celebrate Stefanie's birthday with garlands of fresh flowers intertwined in the staircase, colorful bouquets on tables, and wreaths of flowers on the wall. Bouquets of birthday balloons floated in the four corners of the living room, which had been transformed into a festive wonderland.

The large piano was gone, and all the living room furniture, too. The room was filled with a dozen small tables with white linen table cloths and black enamel chairs.

A rectangular table had been set in front of the fireplace, decorated with a pink table cloth and a cascade of white carnations. There Stefanie sat with Nicky Díaz. Iris was with them in the beginning, but eventually moved around the room greeting family and friends.

The dining room table became a buffet of hot and cold foods that Gabriela's Tea Room had provided. In the middle of the table was a three layer cake, frosted in pale pink and decorated by tiny red rosettes. On the top layer stood a small crystal heart, trimmed in gold with the number fifteen etched in the center.

Brian and Rita sat with his parents, grandparents, and their great-grandmothers. Most of the talk was about Stefanie, stories they all remembered about her childhood.

Eventually, the conversation came around to Iris and Rita going into business together, and Rita was pleased that Iris's family supported the venture. Even Brian's mother seemed to have finally accepted her daughter's decision and gave Rita a few ideas about the type of nice dresses she should make for older women like herself who didn't see much variety in the stores lately.

Rita was getting a cup of coffee for her great-grandmother when she was approached by Stefanie's godmother, Linda Allison. They had only been introduced briefly when Rita arrived, but Rita had hoped for a chance to talk to her.

"I owe you a debt of gratitude," Linda told Rita as she served herself coffee from a silver pot.

"Why is that?"

"You've saved my best friend." Linda turned to face Rita. "I've been so worried about Iris. She was so despondent at Christmas I thought she might do something crazy. That's why I sent her the plane ticket to visit me. When she told me about your idea to become business partners, I knew she was going to survive this ugly spell and move on with her life."

Rita smiled at the slim woman in the blue-print dress. "Iris told me that you saved her life when you sent her that airplane ticket."

"We had a chance to talk a lot. She needed someone to listen to her and not pass judgment. I love her parents and Brian, too, but I think they just wanted to keep her safe in an ivory tower. I told her that she just had to make some grown-up decisions." Linda shrugged. "I've been a single parent for seven years now. It's not easy, but I learned to cope with problems as they come up. I knew that Iris had the strength to deal with the grief and find her own niche in the world, but no one in the family wanted her to take the chance. You gave her that chance, Rita."

"Iris is going to be an asset to my business. We have a lot of exciting plans. I hope you'll come back when we open the store."

"I promised Iris that I'd come back for a vacation in June. I have a thirteen-year old son who's never been to Texas."

At that point Brian came up to the table where they stood talking.

"I understand that you've got a thing going with Iris's new business partner." Linda grinned at Brian. "Is it serious? Do I hear wedding bells?"

He merely laughed. "I don't have a thing going with Iris's new business partner. Iris decided to go into business with the woman I hope to marry." Placing his arm around Rita's shoulders, he gave Rita a fond look. "Linda's always been like a second big sister to me, Rita."

"Tell her the truth now," Linda replied. She looked directly at Rita. "Brian once asked me to marry him."

Rita looked uncertainly from Linda to Brian. She remembered what Iris had said weeks ago; that her brother and best friend would make a great couple. But she always thought Iris was only testing Rita's feelings about Brian.

"You wanted to marry Linda?" Rita's voice was a little shaky.

"When I was five years old." Brian gave Rita a reassuring smile, pressing her closer to him.

She expressed a slight sigh of relief and realized it was she who was taking things too seriously and that Brian was the teasing one. She could only laugh at herself and grin at the man she loved.

Their attention was drawn to the six *mariachi* musicians bustling into the house at that moment. They stood near the door, plunking and tuning, waiting for a sign to make a formal entrance into the party area.

"Excuse me," Brian whispered and left the women abruptly.

Then everyone heard several sharp clinking sounds, and those milling around the food table started towards the living room where Iris was hitting a crystal goblet with a fork, trying to get everyone's attention. She stood near the table where Stefanie and Nicky sat. Angie and Micole had pulled their chairs up to one corner of the table, and so had another boy Rita didn't know. Rita quickly made her way back to her table and set the coffee cup down in front of Abuelita.

Iris stood midway between her daughter's table and that of her immediate family. Once she felt that everyone had come back into the area, she extended a wide smile around the room.

"I want to thank all of you for coming to Stefanie's *quinceañera*. We've been through some very lonely days the past few months. But as I look around at the faces of my family and so many new friends, I can't help but feel fortunate. I know Stefanie feels the same way."

Iris then stepped to the side and moved around so she was facing her daughter's table. She gave her an affectionate smile then spoke in a distinct voice. "Stefanie, today you begin a new phase in your life. You are no longer a little girl to us, but a young woman taking her first steps into the adult world. I am very proud of you, Stefanie. You have stood beside me through the difficult months after your father died. I couldn't have asked for a more sympathetic, more understanding daughter. Sometimes, you even had to show me a better way of dealing with problems, which only proved to me that you are well on your way to becoming a responsible young woman. No woman could ever boast of a more talented, more beautiful daughter than the one I have sitting before me right now. I don't need to tell you that as you grow older, more things will change, and some of those changes will seem to turn you upside down. But there is one thing that will never change. And that is my love for you. Happy Birthday, Stefanie. *Feliz cumpleaños.*"

The entire room broke out in applause as Iris went to her daughter and embraced her. Both were laughing and crying, wiping a tear from each other's cheek. Rita's own happiness for Stefanie and Iris left tears stinging her own eyes. She looked for Brian and saw him standing at the edge of the room. He smiled at his sister, applauding the loudest of all.

Iris turned around to face the family and friends seated and standing around the room, and raised her hands for silence.

She took a deep breath as if she was trying to compose herself to speak again. She dabbed her eyes then said, "I know that it's customary that the girl celebrating her *quinceañera* take the first dance of the party. And while I can give a speech to honor my daughter, I don't think I'll dance with her. I'd like to give that honor to her godfather, my brother Brian. From the very beginning, Brian knew how much this celebration meant to Stefanie's father, and I know that Estevan would wholeheartedly approve if Brian took his place to dance with Stefanie tonight."

At that moment the *mariachis*, dressed in the traditional black pants and short jackets, began playing and slowly made their way into the room, dividing among the tables. There were two guitarists, a violinist, a tall man carrying the fat *guitarrón*, and two trumpeters. After a short instrumental opening, one of the trumpeters lowered his horn and began to sing about the love between parents and children.

As the musicians continued the touching ballad, Brian took his niece to the center of the room where a small space had been left, no doubt for this special moment. As Stefanie and Brian danced, Rita felt happy for them.

Iris stood by the table watching them, tears flowing unchecked down her face. If they were tears of happiness for Stefanie or regrets for Estevan, only Iris knew. Soon Brian's grandfather Charlie walked over to Iris. He took her arms, leading her out to dance near Brian and Stefanie.

Charlie Esparza said something that made Iris laugh then handed her a handkerchief out of his jacket pocket. He said something to Brian that made him and Stefanie grin, too.

The song ended soon after and everyone applauded again.

❤ ❤ ❤ ❤ ❤

"Well, for a girl who said that *mariachis* would be terribly embarrassing, Stefanie seems to be enjoying the music a lot," Brian said, laying his arm across the back of Rita's chair.

It was almost an hour later, and there was no shortage of dance partners for anyone who felt like dancing.

Even Nicky and Stefanie had danced twice to the Spanish tunes, although many of the Esparza male relatives monopolized most of the dancing with the birthday girl.

Just as one song ended, Stefanie appeared at the table and sat down in the empty chair by Brian. Aside from the two great-grandmothers, Brian and Rita were the only ones left at the table. The others were visiting with other relatives.

"Are you having a good time?" Rita asked Stefanie, pushing her glass of punch in the girl's direction.

"Thanks. Yes." She took a few sips from the glass and pushed it back to Rita. "Thanks for the drink." She smiled at Rita, her hazel eyes looking like shiny jewels. "It's just what you said. Everyone wishing me good luck and telling me how beautiful I look. All that good stuff makes me feel so special."

"You are special," Brian told his niece.

"You're biased, Uncle Brian." Stefanie gave him a kiss on the cheek. Then she laughed. "And guess what? Angie and Micole want to have a *quinceañera* just like mine. They convinced their moms that something like my *quince* party wouldn't be too expensive or get really crazy because of all those extra girls and escorts. And of course I told my friends that Rita could make their dresses."

Brian's eyebrows raised. "You're better than a TV commercial. Perhaps Rita and your mother ought to hire you for marketing *quinceañera* dresses."

Playfully, she socked him in the arm, then had to leave the table when Nicky invited her to get some punch.

"Everyone seems to be having a great time." The cheerful statement came from Iris, who seemed to appear out of nowhere. She took the chair her daughter vacated only seconds before. "Even Aunt Bertha has nothing to complain about."

"The best thing is that you and Stefanie are having a good time," Brian said to his sister. He reached over and set his hand upon hers. "I'm glad we did this, Iris. Estevan would have been pleased."

"I'm not so sure about that." Iris looked at her brother as if she had something on her mind. "Estevan always loved a big show. Stefanie would have gone through the motions of a fancy *quinceañera* just to please her father. But I know she wouldn't have been happy parading around like a circus horse in front of Estevan's friends. No, Brian. I think we chose a better way than Estevan wanted. This wouldn't have been enough for him. But Stefanie is very happy, and that's the most important thing."

Brian nodded, a satisfied smile upon his lips.

Iris leaned closer and shared a grin with both of them. "Now that we have the *quince* behind us, what about you two? When can we start planning the wedding?"

Brian moved his hand from Iris's to rest upon Rita's. His fingers intertwined through hers, but he didn't answer his sister.

Rita gave Brian a little smile. She had been thinking about having a reception like this for their wedding. A cozy gathering of friends and family after she married Brian; not an expensive event like Councilman Guerra planned for his daughter.

"My *comadre* says it'll be a Christmas wedding."

This news flash came from Mamá Josie, who sat on the other side of Abuelita.

"Rita's going to wear the dress Isabel made for Rita's mother," Mamá Josie told Iris.

A mischievous gleam appeared in Iris's eyes before she said, "Rita's great-grandmother bought something very sexy for Rita to wear on her honeymoon, Mamá Josie. Did she tell you that, too?"

"Can we change the subject here?" Rita stopped the flow of conversation about weddings and honeymoons before her face got redder than the birthday balloons floating in the corner. "Long before any wedding, Iris and I are opening a new dress shop. We have a lot of planning to do for that first."

"Rita's right. The two of you must come to San Antonio for the grand opening of our store," Iris told the old women.

"And do you have a name for this new store?" Mamá Josie asked.

The new partners exchanged a smile before Rita said, "We're thinking about the name Navarro and Bonilla Unlimited."

"Too long," Mamá Josie said, shaking her head and looking at her _comadre_. "And what does it all mean? Unlimited? And when Rita marries Brian, she'll have to change the sign. That's not good."

"You should call the store, Stefanie's." Abuelita spoke in a quiet voice then looked at Rita. "The girl brought you all together, made you friends."

"Stefanie's, huh?" Rita liked the idea, but still gave her partner a questioning look. "What do you think, Iris?"

"Stefanie would be so flattered." Iris sat back into her chair, and rubbed her chin as she thought more about the idea. "'Stefanie's.' It sounds like a pretty boutique for ladies to shop at. But Rita makes costumes for men, too. Wouldn't they mind coming into a place called Stefanie's?"

"They came into a place called 'Rita's Dress Shop,' didn't they?" Brian told his sister. "Rita's customers will go wherever she is. Her business cards could easily read 'Stefanie's,' and right below the shop name would be printed 'Rita Navarro, seamstress.'"

"But what would my business cards say?" Iris inquired, a slight frown appearing across her forehead.

It took only a moment for Brian's eyes to brighten from a sudden inspiration. He smiled at his sister. "Your business cards would say, 'Iris Bonilla, manager.'"

"I could live with that!" Iris's face brightened with a wide grin and shades of gold shining in her eyes.

The *mariachis* began playing again, an old Mexican love song familiar to most of the people in the room, because they started applauding almost immediately.

"That was Estevan's favorite song." Iris' earlier sparkle faded, but her voice wasn't filled with sadness, just a statement of the memory. Then she turned to her brother. "You should dance with Rita, Brian. The words of the song are so romantic."

Iris leaned over and kissed her brother's cheek before she stood up and stepped back into her role of hostess for her daughter's party.

"Shall we dance?" Brian said, and led Rita out to the center of the room where only four other couples danced, including Stefanie, who was dancing with Brian's father.

Rita rested her head against Brian's shoulder. His arms tightened around her waist as they moved slowly to the music. The lyrics spoke of love that outlasted time. It was a song for lovers, both young and old. Yet it seemed appropriate for Stefanie, too, who probably dreamed of finding that special love between a man and a woman sometime in her future.

Celebrating this *quinceañera* together had left everyone touched by love. It was a day of faith and hope, a day that held the promise of an exciting journey through life for all of them.